Dead Mourning

Stay scared!

OTHER BOOKS BY ANTHONY GIANGREGORIO

THE DEAD WATER SERIES

DEADWATER
DEADRAIN
DEADCITY
DEADWAVE
DEAD HARVEST

ALSO BY THE AUTHOR

THE MONSTER UNDER THE BED
DEADEND: A ZOMBIE NOVEL
DEAD TALES: SHORT STORIES TO DIE FOR
SOUL-EATER
DEADFREEZE
DEADFALL
DEADRAGE

Dead Mourning

A Zombie Horror Story

∞

ANTHONY GIANGREGORIO

Copyright © 2008 by Anthony Giangregorio.

ISBN: Softcover   978-1-4363-0752-9

All rights reserved. No part of this book may be reproduced or transmitted in any form or by any means, electronic or mechanical, including photocopying, recording, or by any information storage and retrieval system, without permission in writing from the copyright owner.

This is a work of fiction. Names, characters, places and incidents either are the product of the author's imagination or are used fictitiously, and any resemblance to any actual persons, living or dead, events, or locales is entirely coincidental.

This book was printed in the United States of America.

To order additional copies of this book, contact:
Xlibris Corporation
1-888-795-4274
www.Xlibris.com
Orders@Xlibris.com

ACKNOWLEDGEMENTS

Thanks to my wife, Jody, for putting up with me and helping me finish this book in a timely manner. Also, to my son, Joseph, for helping with the editing.

Until you try to make a book yourself, there's just no way to realize just how complicated it can be, what with all the commas, correct spelling, and other small things that go into making a work of literature worth reading and hopefully, enjoyed by others.

AUTHOR'S NOTE

While the city of Boston, Dorchester, Roxbury and the Franklin Park Zoo are all real locations, I have taken certain fictional liberties with them.

If you happen to live near there, don't go looking for your favorite bar or hang-out spot because the sun is rising on a new morning and you might not like what it brings.

Foreword

CAN YOU IMAGINE what the world would be really like if the dead walked? I mean, the simple logistics of it would be mind-numbing. Imagine looking out your living room window and seeing decaying corpses shambling about.

Recently, I pondered once more my fascination with zombies and the undead in general and I came to an epiphany.

To me, it is not the actual zombies that are the fascination as much as what they would represent to the world, and myself, if they came to be.

If the dead walked, then civilization as we know it would crumble. Social and protective services would collapse like a house of cards and each of us would find ourselves responsible for ourselves and our families.

You see, in a world where the dead walked, the rules of existence would change. No more would money and how big your home or motor vehicle is would define who you are as a success in the world. Instead, if you were alive and had food in your belly and a safe place to live, then you would be defined as a success.

What would happen to those movie stars and politicians that are looked up to or flat out idolized in today's culture? Would they survive or just become more fodder for the undead?

In a world where the American dream has become harder and harder to attain, a collapse of civilization would in fact make things much simpler.

In 2007, an average two family home in a decent location on the East coast costs about half a million dollars, while fifty years ago the same home would have went for maybe sixty thousand dollars or so.

How about all those Mom and Pop stores that the adults of our world grew up with? They're all gone now, replaced by Home Depot's and Wal-Mart's, not to mention the internet. Someday in the future even the supermarkets will be gone, replaced by faceless warehouses.

When my father was young, he worked three jobs at the same time. Nowadays, one job ends at four and the other job begins at three. If you tell the second job there's a conflict, they tell you to choose which job you want or quit. Years ago, jobs would make allowances for other jobs so people were able to work harder and earn more and thereby slowly begin to save.

I laugh when I see commercials about whether I'll have enough money to retire on. For me and my family that's not a concern because there are no funds to retire with. With taxes and the cost of simple living becoming higher everyday it's a simple enough task to make it to the end of the year in one piece, let alone worry about twenty years from now.

So, if I just arrived in the United States with a few dollars in my pocket, then what are the odds that I would become a success like my father or grandfather?

Sure it could happen, but not the same way it once did back in the 50's and 60's. In today's world, with the internet now a prevalent subject in all our lives, a warehouse full of DVDs halfway across the country can now take the place of every video store in your neighborhood. I don't know about the rest of America, but here in the Boston area there's another store closing every day.

But I digress. What I'm getting at is that I believe that I am, as well as many of my friends, smart, intelligent people, but despite this, the same culture that makes some people stars and rich beyond their dreams keeps many, many more of us down.

In a world where the dead walk, only the quickness to solve problems and intelligence and common sense would rule the day. Now, I of course don't want the end of the world to come anytime soon. After all, if the world fell into darkness what would happen to my family and everyone I care about? But is it so wrong to long for a time where a man or woman with the will and determination to succeed actually had a chance?

Take writing for example.

I wonder if some of the great artists like Stephen King and Dean Koontz, to name but two, would be so successful in today's world where every person who wants to can have their own blog and there are more books on the internet then one person could read in a lifetime. If Stephen King submitted Carrie to some of the publishers out there today would he even be acknowledged? Or would they refuse him because they didn't believe his book had enough punch in it to grab readers. I wonder how many of the successful in the world today would still be where they are if they had started in the world of the 2000's, instead of in the previous century.

Nowadays, is it possible to even find an original idea?

That's why Shakespeare, Hemingway and others are so amazing, because when they thought of their stories and plots they were *actually* one of the first ones to do so.

In 2007 can you even imagine that? To be the first to think up an idea that hasn't been put into a book or made into a movie.

So while the dead walking is a work of fiction and will one be as long as the laws of nature apply, I still can't help looking back to a time when life was simpler and the world wasn't as large. When all a man needed was the will to succeed and the drive to get his hands dirty.

But then again, with the constant threat of biological warfare, bird flu and terrorists around every corner nowadays, maybe the world I long for isn't that far away, after all.

Let's just all pray I'm wrong.

Anthony Giangregorio
October 2007

Inat genesis semen mortis est.

    That which created us holds
    the seeds to our destruction

Prologue

IT WAS WELL past midnight in the Forest Glenn nursing home in Dorchester, Mass. and Emma Andrews was fast asleep.

She tossed and turned in her sleep, the sheets under her becoming damp with sweat, her limbs writhing in fear; the heart shaped necklace she wore sticking to her damp chest. Her chocolate colored skin was covered with a sheen of perspiration as she fought the demons in her nightmares.

She called out once, but no one heard her, the nurse's aids and orderlies all in the front of the building, watching television in the break room.

No one would come to check on Emma for at least another hour, unless she pressed the nurses call button, but in her fitful sleep that wouldn't be happening.

Behind her eyelids, her eyes darted back and forth, seeing nothing, yet at the same time everything.

Ever since Emma was a little girl, she was gifted (or cursed) with the gift of foresight.

These visions would only come to her in her dreams and she had tried to live with them her entire life. Only her late husband and her mother, long dead, had known she possessed the gift and both had taken the secret to their graves.

Emma was lost in a vision now, one that made her heart beat frantically. She saw a world that was nothing but a husk, covered with death. Desiccated limbs and rotten bodies flashed past her eyes.

The walking dead.

In the world she glimpsed, the dead had risen and had devoured the living, consuming the entire planet like locusts. Only a few stragglers of humanity fought to survive and somehow, though she couldn't see that far ahead, she believed even they were doomed.

There was something else, as well, though it stayed at the outskirts of her vision.

Evil.

Evil that would attack from within and destroy all that was left of the good and righteous.

Though her legs were riddled with arthritis, she found she could walk easily through the valley of death. Her foot came down on a small skull; the sole of her foot pulverizing it into dust, the bone was so old and brittle.

A newspaper blew in the wind and she reached out and plucked it from the air, like she was picking an apple.

The byline read in bold type: **THE DEAD WALK, SCIENTISTS BAFFLED!**

She released it to flutter away in the wind and she continued walking. There was a city on the horizon, and though she wasn't sure, she believed it to be Boston, Massachusetts. The glass of the John Hancock building glistened in the setting sun, though more then half of the glass was either missing or shattered.

To her right was One Financial, one of the tallest buildings on the Boston skyline. Where there had once been forty-two floors, now there was only twenty, the top half of the building gone, like a giant warrior had sliced the building in half with a sword.

Next to the building was rubble, filled with stone and metal three-stories high. A few arms and legs could be seen scattered throughout the wreckage and she turned to look in another direction, not wanting to see the carnage anymore.

There was a flash and her perspective changed. She looked down and realized she was standing on soft, green grass. Off to her left were the Swan boats, floating quietly, patiently waiting for their next customers in the heart of the Boston Common.

The small pedestrian bridge that protruded over the water was gone now, shattered, the wreckage filling the pond. When she moved closer, she saw the distinctive outline of bodies floating in the water, some no more then children.

She looked away, toward Back Bay, hoping at least there the destruction would be less.

She was wrong.

Where the Hilton Hotel and the Prudential Center once stood there was nothing but flames. The latter building crumbled to the street even as she watched.

Turning away horrified, she closed her eyes, trying to will herself to wake up, but it was no use. She'd had hundreds of visions in her long life and she knew she would have to see it through to the end, only then would she be able to return to the waking world.

A moaning floated to her on the wind, the trees and statues making it hard to discern where exactly the noise had come from. She looked left and right, and behind her, but nothing could be seen.

Another moan, this one more high pitched, came to her ears, and her head snapped to the right, searching for the origin of the sound.

Her eyes focused on the shadows in the trees, trying to pierce the gloom within and then she saw it. A rotted, ghastly form stumbled out of the tree line, arms out-stretched, its mouth hanging open.

And the creature wasn't alone.

Behind it hundreds upon hundreds of dead people stumbled out of the gloom and into the sun, moaning and groaning with their pain.

Maggots filled eye sockets and night crawlers squirmed underneath pale-gray skin. Arms fell to the grass, as limbs became detached from rotting bodies.

She could only stare as this army of the dead slowly shuffled forward.

Their treacle-like movements gave her time to come to her senses and she started to back away, only to turn suddenly at the sound of more footsteps crunching in the grass and leaves behind her.

Spinning in place, she saw thousands of bodies coming for her, mouths open wide, swollen tongues hanging, and blackened teeth gnashing as they prepared to devour her alive.

She was trapped. There was nowhere to run. Knowing it was hopeless; she dropped onto the grass and sat perfectly still. She knew this was a dream, a vision, and she'd be damned if she would run around screaming like a five-year-old.

The ghouls moved closer and she waited, staring up at them defiantly.

"This won't happen," she said to the undead crowd. "I don't know how, but some one will stop this from coming to pass."

If they heard her, they gave no sign, but continued shuffling forward; their torpid movements resembling underwater divers slowly moving across the ocean floor.

She closed her eyes and waited for the inevitable.

But instead of feeling cold, dead teeth on her aging flesh, she felt a gentle shake on her shoulder. She opened her eyes to see the night nurse smiling down at her.

"I'm so sorry to wake you, Emma, but its time for your medication."

Emma blinked the sleep from her eyes and slowly came back to reality.

"Oh. No, dear, don't apologize, I was having a doozy of a dream and I'm glad to be rid of it." She took the small paper cup with two pills inside it and the small cup of water, washing the pills down in a matter of seconds.

The night nurse smiled and took the cups from her hands. "Oh really, what was your dream about, anything scary?"

Emma pursed her lips and shook her head.

"Oh, dear, I don't really think you want to know my dream, now do you?"

The night nurse nodded and smiled. "Yes I do, I've heard you've had some doozys, too. So come on, spill it, what was it about?" She sat on the edge of the bed, waiting patiently. She was running early for rounds and had always enjoyed talking with Emma.

Emma's face grew hard and she leaned close to the night nurse's face.

"I saw death for everyone and everything. Death and destruction for as far as the eye could see . . . and it's coming . . . soon."

The night nurse leaned back and then stood up. "Oh, Emma, you're such a kidder. Fine, if you don't want to tell me, that's okay. You get some rest, now. I'll be back in the morning to check on you."

Emma watched the nurse leave, the cart in the hall squeaking with a bad wheel as she made her way to the next room.

Emma lay there quietly, the wisps of her dream still prevalent in her mind.

She knew she wasn't wrong, she never was. Whatever was coming, was coming soon.

And God help them all.

Chapter 1

"I'M TELLING YOU, this is your last chance, Carl. If you screw this up, then I guarantee I'll personally see that you're back in prison by the end of the week. Part of your parole agreement is that you maintain a job. You hear me?"

Carl Jenkins nodded while he slumped further in the wooden chair he was now occupying. Across from him, sitting behind a metal desk, was his parole officer.

At the moment James Rubin wasn't a happy man. Carl was just one of over fifty parolees that he had to baby sit and unfortunately for Carl, things hadn't gone so well since he'd been released from jail a little over a month ago.

Carl had managed to get fired from every job he'd taken and now he was about to get his last assignment.

Rubin handed him a slip of paper with an address scrawled across it.

"Here, take this. Be at this address by nine o' clock tomorrow. This is your last chance, Carl. I'm warning you, don't screw it up."

Carl sat up straight in his chair and reached for the piece of paper.

"Not to worry, Ruby, I'll be there, I promise, and thanks for another chance," Carl said, as he rose from his chair.

Rubin waved him away. "Well, it goes against by better judgment, but no one else wants this job. Now get out of here and send in the next guy on your way out. And don't call me Ruby!"

"Yes sir," Carl said and quickly vacated the small cubicle surrounded by a dozen other cubicles that made up the second floor of the Suffolk courthouse.

On his way out, he slapped the next guy in the waiting room on the shoulder and pointed back the way he'd come. The man grunted and then headed off to meet with Rubin.

Carl headed for the elevator, and once he had made it to the ground floor, he strode out into the lobby and out into the cool spring day. With a skip to his step, he strode off down the street. He had already decided he would cut through the Commons and then grab the "T" at Park St. It was a beautiful spring day in Boston and after being locked up for almost a year and a half, he relished any time he could spend outside, not wanting to be cooped up in the train system for any length of time.

Carl wasn't a bad man; he had simply been in the wrong place at the wrong time and hadn't had enough money for a real lawyer. The public defender, already hopelessly overloaded, had pleaded him down to two years, with a chance at parole after a year and a half. At least that had gone smoothly. Now, as he walked down the street, he silently swore to himself for the hundredth time that he would never touch pot again.

He never should have gotten in trouble in the first place. He'd been having a fight with his downstairs neighbor at the apartment he'd been living in. After blasting his radio to get even with his neighbor for vacuuming at three o' clock in the morning, he'd been more then a little surprised when he'd received a knock on his door. Innocently he'd opened it, forgetting he had his stash sitting on his kitchen table. Two cops were at his door and one was easily able to see over his shoulder at the one pound bag sitting out in the open on the table.

Fast forward a year and a half later.

Carl cut through the Commons as planned and then realized he hadn't looked at the address on the slip of paper. Reaching into his pocket, he felt a flutter of fear deep in his stomach when his grasping fingers couldn't find it. Then he remembered it was in his other pocket.

With a look of embarrassment on his face that the people walking by him had no idea was for; he reached in and pulled it out.

On the wrinkled paper, in clear script, was the address to a funeral home.

"Rossi Funeral Home, 1969 Market St. Boston, Mass," he read out loud. "Oh man, a funeral home? Damn, those places freak me out."

Sighing, he shoved the paper back into his pocket. "Oh well, a job's a job," he mumbled to himself. Besides, beggars couldn't be choosers.

Reaching into his back pocket, he pulled out his wallet and opened it. A wrinkled and dirty twenty dollar bill stared back at him.

He smiled. It wasn't much, but maybe it would be enough to get him buzzed at the bar down the street from the flop house he was now presently staying in.

Mumbling to himself, he cursed his luck and wondered what he had ever done in this world to have so much bad fortune. Maybe this job would be the one to turn his life around.

Putting the job out of his mind for the moment, he continued down the street, already tasting the first beer when he finally got to the bar.

* * *

The bar was a dingy dive on the outskirts of Chinatown. He had been coming here almost every day since he had gotten out of jail and the bartender, Bobby Spencer, who was also the owner, frowned when he walked in. The only reason the man put up with Carl was because he had been friends with Carl's father back in the war and had promised to look out for the kid when Carl's father had died of a heart attack a few years ago.

"Not you again, Carl. Listen to me carefully, no more credit, you've already run a tab the size of the NASA space shuttle fund. Unless you got money, you're out of here."

Carl moseyed up to the counter and slid onto a chair. "Relax, Bobby my man, I've got you covered," he said slyly, pulling the twenty from his pocket and sliding it across the counter.

Bobby looked down at it like it was a pile of dog crap. "What's this?" He asked, brusquely.

"It's money. You use it to purchase food and services instead of using the barter system like in the old days."

Bobby made a face that said he wasn't pleased with Carl's remark. "I know what it is, smartass, but what's it for?"

"It's for some of my tab, so I can drink tonight," Carl said innocently.

Bobby picked up the twenty and waved it in front of Carl's face. "This," he said angrily, "wouldn't cover one percent of your tab," he finished, tucking the twenty into the register.

"Hey, wait a second!" Carl yelled. "If that won't cover anything then why did you take it?"

Bobby leaned over the counter and placed his face no more than an inch from Carl's. "Because it's probably all I'm ever gonna get from you and its better then nothing."

Carl frowned, not feeling very happy at this present moment in time. "Well then, what can I drink?" He asked.

Bobby tinkered around behind the counter and then handed Carl a tall glass of a clear liquid. Carl's eyes went wide.

"Cool, what is it? Is it Vodka . . . or maybe Tequila?"

Bobby shook his head from side to side. "Nope, its water, now shut up and drink it before I throw you out of here on your ass, despite what I told your Pops before he died."

Mumbling unhappily to himself, Carl drank the water, the cool liquid tasting like nothing but failure.

An hour later Carl decided to call it a night, despite the fact there was still hours of sunlight left in the day.

"You win, Bobby, I'm leaving. Besides, I got a new job, starts tomorrow, and I swear I'll get you all your money, you'll see."

Bobby took his empty water glass and grunted. "I'll see it when it happens, now you stay out of trouble," Bobby said, his temperament softening slightly. "You've already wasted more then a year out of your twenty-two years on this earth in jail, that's enough, now. No more trouble, you see trouble, you walk away."

Carl waved as he slipped through the door. "Hey, I always do; its trouble that won't stay away from me." Then he was gone.

Bobby wiped the counter and shook his head. Another barfly waved for another beer and Bobby got back to work, for the time putting Carl from his mind.

Outside on the sidewalk, Carl blinked a few times, letting his eyes adjust to the sunlight. When he was sure he wasn't going to blindly walk into someone, he started down the sidewalk, his destination, the small one room apartment the state had helped him get when he had left the penal system.

In less than ten minutes he was on the east side of Tremont St, stepping over the bum lying across the doorway and stepping into the dingy hallway that led to the stairwell and eventually to his apartment on the second floor. The building was six floors of rubble. Paint was peeling from the walls and the carpet looked as if it should have been tossed into the trash ten years ago.

The sounds of people yelling and too loud televisions carried into the hallway and he walked through it and up the stairs. The distinctive odor of marijuana floated in the air.

After spending his time in jail, the sounds drifting from the other apartments was almost music to his ears and he slowed to savor the ambiance for a moment.

Opening his apartment door, he slipped through and walked across the small room, pushing the door closed with his leg. To say the room was sparsely furnished would have been a compliment.

There was no kitchen, but instead was a counter with a microwave and a sink. To the left was a dingy pullout couch that he had inherited with the room and off to the right was a closet of a bathroom, barely big enough for one person, let alone two.

Tossing his keys on the small kitchen table that sat next to the couch, he grabbed a beer from the small, dorm-sized refrigerator.

With the exception of the six beers inside it, there was an old package of salami, a jar of mustard and a bottle of orange juice, well past its *sell by* date.

Flipping the cap of the beer into the sink, he dropped down on the couch and turned on the small twelve-inch black and white television.

Flipping the few channels he was allowed without cable, he settled on a news show.

Taking a long pull from his beer, he sighed. "Ah, this is the life," he said sarcastically to the room, waving his hands outward as if he was the happiest man in the world.

"My ass," he mumbled. In jail he had gotten three meals a day and had a color television with cable. Sure, he was locked in his cell like an animal most of the time, but even a free man with a home, a mortgage, a job and a family was in some ways as much a prisoner as he had been.

Finishing his beer, he tossed it at the waste can in the corner, frowning when he missed and it bounced on the dirty carpet.

He'd get it later, when he got up again. For now he closed his eyes and drifted off to sleep. This was his last day off for quite a while and he wanted to enjoy it.

He wondered to himself, as he slipped off to sleep, if he would actually get to see any dead bodies at the funeral home tomorrow. Then, deciding he didn't really want to know the answer, he dropped off, dreaming about Florida beaches and gorgeous women in small bikinis who couldn't keep their hands off of him.

Chapter 2

CARL STOOD ON the sidewalk in front of the Rossi Funeral Home.

From the outside, the building looked like an ordinary home, clapboard for shingles and shutters on all the windows. The lawn was immaculate. Either someone who lived there really loved their lawn or they had a landscaper come every week.

There was a long horse-shoe driveway that led to the front of the house, a green awning over the front door and a flag pole with an American flag blowing in the light breeze at the top of the driveway. Another driveway led to the back of the building and as he walked up the driveway, he wondered if the rear one was where they brought all the stiffs.

Reaching the front door, he checked his watch. It was five before nine. He was actually early for a change. He grinned to himself as he pressed the doorbell. Maybe this job would be good for him and in fact, maybe his luck had finally changed.

The door opened and a tall man with a gaunt face looked down on him. The man had to be at least six-three and with his skinny frame, seemed like some kind of scarecrow.

"Yes, can I help you?" The man asked, his face creasing into a rictus grin.

Carl swallowed and held up the small paper with the address on it.

"Ah yeah, hi, my name's Carl Jenkins and I'm supposed to be working here. I'm supposed to be starting today."

The man's eyes turned to slits and Carl felt like a specimen on a lab table, but then the man's face seemed to lighten and he stepped back so Carl could enter the house.

"Of course you are, Carl, it's nice to meet you. You're parole officer called me yesterday and told me all about you. I'm Jasper Wagner. I run this place, come in, come in," he said waving Carl deeper into the house, patting Carl's shoulder like a grandfather might.

Carl stepped through the doorway and felt like he had been transported to the 1970's. Paneling covered all the walls and a red shag carpet adorned the floors, with the exception of a room off to the right. That one had hardwood floors and wallpaper, though the decor was still in much need of an update.

Jasper was standing quietly, waiting while Carl looked around. When Carl's curiosity was satiated, he looked up at Jasper.

Jasper stood perfectly still, his face making him look like a statue.

"So, uhm, what exactly am I gonna be doing here?" Carl asked.

Jasper seemed to snap out of it and he started to move deeper into the home.

Carl followed, assuming that was what Jasper wanted him to do.

"Oh, a little of this and a little of that." He turned and stopped in the hallway so abruptly, Carl almost walked into his back. "You're not squeamish are you? Not afraid of a little blood, perhaps?"

Carl shook his head. "Well, not really, but what are we talking about? I don't want to be cutting people up and stuff."

Jasper chuckled, his laughter sounding like sandpaper. "No, of course not, don't worry, I'm just teasing you; I can't help myself. Just a little mortician humor. But seriously, have you ever seen a dead body before?" He started walking again and after a second, Carl followed.

"Only when I was younger and one of my aunts or uncles died, and then there were my grandparents and a friend of the family that died just a few years ago." He seemed to hesitate then, his voice dropping lower. "And there was my father. I lost him a few years ago."

Jasper stopped and turned around, his best face forward. "I'm so sorry for your loss, Carl, but hopefully he's in a better place now. Come and follow me and I'll show you where we make people look their best. You see, when you view them in the caskets they are a far cry from how they arrived at my doorstep. It's my job to make them look as beautiful as the day they died. If I do my job right, you'd expect them to just get up out of the casket and shake your hand."

Jasper talked all the way to the rear of the home, where a small door stood off a modest kitchen. Jasper waved him to follow and Carl did, walking down a steep flight of stairs. At the bottom, he found himself in the basement of the home. The walls were tiled a creamy beige and stainless steel gurneys sat silently in the middle of the room. Tall vats with some yellow liquid inside them stood by the tables and hoses hung from hooks attached to the sides of the vats.

Following Jasper into the center of the room, Carl noticed how the floor seemed to slant downward to the middle of the room, where a shiny steel drain marred the otherwise flawless surface of the floor.

Behind Jasper was a large stainless steel door that reminded him of a giant walk-in freezer. Jasper saw him looking there and he walked over to the door and opened it. Cold air escaped and Jasper's breath puffed out in front of him as he talked.

"This is where we keep the recently deceased," he said calmly.

Carl swallowed heavily and backed up a step. "Is there anybody in there now?"

Jasper smiled again, the smile worse then if he had kept his face neutral. "I wish, but no, at the moment we're dry. But one can always hope for a pileup on the interstate or an accident in the city, right?"

Carl just stared back, not really having an answer. But though macabre, he saw where Jasper was coming from. If your job was to bury people then you needed a steady supply or you'd be out of business in a month. To Jasper, death was his business. The only question was whether business was good or bad?

"So, what will I be doing here?"

Jasper closed the walk-in and moved next to Carl, tidying things as he went. "Can you drive a stick shift?"

Carl nodded. "Hell, yeah, my first car was an old Trans Am. It was a stick. Why?"

"Because that'll be one of your duties for me. I'll need you to make pick ups from different locations across the city and the suburbs. Sometimes I might need your help around here, but I have an apprentice that helps me with the preparation of the deceased. You'll meet him later, I'm sure. His name is Tyler."

"So where will I be driving to exactly?" Carl asked, curious despite himself.

"Oh, there are many places." He started ticking them off using his fingers. "There are nursing homes and the coroner's office. Sometimes you'll go to hospitals after someone has passed on. The police morgue after the body has been released after an autopsy. There's a few more but for the moment I don't think it matters. I'll always supply you with directions." Jasper looked down his nose at Carl. "Do you have any problem with anything I've told you?"

Carl shook his head. "No, man, its cool, I think I can handle it. Is that all?"

Jasper tapped his chin, thinking. "Pretty much. The other thing I'll have you doing is supply runs, which is what you'll be doing later in the day. But for now, how about you grab that mop and bucket and give the place a quick once over. Once you're done, it'll probably be time for you to go. I need you to pick up a shipment of formaldehyde for me. Without it I can't embalm my customers."

Carl grabbed the bucket, and spotting the small janitor's closet off in the corner, got to work.

"Not a problem, Mr. Wagner, just tell me when you need me to leave," Carl said while filling the bucket with warm water and a squeeze of soap from the bottle on the shelf in the closet.

Jasper grinned again and nodded. "Please, call me Jasper; we're all informal around here. If you need me, I'll be upstairs. I have a few clients coming in to see me in about an hour."

Carl waved to him and Jasper disappeared up the stairs. Carl got to work, whistling to himself and trying to shake the tickling feeling crawling up his back.

What was he so nervous about? The place was empty, no stiffs on the premises.

Clearing his mind, he concentrated on the menial job of washing the floor.

Chapter 3

JASPER GAVE HIM an hour for lunch and he spent it at a nearby Burger King. Low on funds, he had to settle for one of the hamburger kid meals. He stared at the toy action figure sitting on the table in front of him the entire time he ate, finally deciding to give it to a small blonde-headed kid who had come into the restaurant with his mother. The mom smiled at him and told him thanks, saying what a nice young man he was.

Carl smiled back, bashfully, not used to the attention. Then he left and walked the three blocks back to the funeral home.

When he walked through the back door, Jasper was waiting for him.

"There you are. I've been waiting for almost ten minutes. I think if you're going to work here you'll have to get a cell phone so I can find you when I need you."

Carl grinned, almost wanting to laugh. "Sure, I'll see what I can do about that," he said with only enough sarcasm to make him feel better. Jasper never picked up on it and walked toward him with a set of keys in his hand.

Tossing the keys to Carl, he said: "Here, these are for the small truck out back."

Carl nodded. He had seen the truck, similar to a small moving van, but hadn't given it much thought.

"What are these for?" He asked, jingling the keys in his hand.

"I need you to go to Waltham and pick up a shipment of chemicals for the home."

"Chemicals? What kind?" Carl asked, suspicious.

Jasper waved his concern away. "Nothing dangerous, unless you drink it," he chuckled. "Just some of the formaldehyde and a few other choice chemicals used in the embalming process. I need you to pick them up and then drive back here with them. Once you get back, you'll need to bring them through the side door. There's a dolly there you can use to move the barrels."

"Barrels? Exactly how much am I getting?" Carl asked.

Jasper handed him an invoice. "It's all in there. Ten barrels all together, enough to last me about six months or so. Now, no screwing around, Carl. Once you pick up the shipment, you come right back here, okay."

Carl nodded and prepared to leave. "Hey, before I go, there's something that's been bugging me."

Jasper's eyebrows went up in expectation of Carl's question.

"What's the deal with the name of this place? It's called the Rossi Funeral Home, right? That ain't your name."

"That was the previous owner; I purchased the business from him. I decided to keep the name the same, as most people in the city know it by the name Rossi. Now, I need you to get going before rush hour starts. If you get stuck on I-93 it could be hours before you get back here."

Carl nodded and with a wave to his new employer was out the door and climbing into the truck. The engine surged to life and Carl pulled out of the long driveway and into traffic. The truck had a radio and he turned it to a rock station, and with the Eagles singing about *Hotel California*, he headed to the interstate and his designated pickup.

* * *

He had found the warehouse with almost no trouble, the directions given to him by Jasper almost perfect.

He had quickly loaded the truck and had then started back to Boston.

The traffic was light, most of the cars leaving the city. Carl decided he had more then enough time to stop for a beer, so he drove over to his favorite bar, parking the truck in a small parking lot in the rear of the building.

The parking lot actually belonged to an empty office building on the street behind the bar, but seems it was deserted, the bar patrons usually used it when parking was tight on the street, which was every day.

Strolling into the bar, keys in his hand, Carl's eyes lit up with happiness when he saw his best buddy, Clarence, who was sitting at the counter nursing a draft beer.

Clarence turned when the door opened and he swung around to smile at Carl. "Well, well, look at who's here. I swear, Bobby will let anybody drink in here."

Carl walked up to Clarence and sat down on the barstool next to him.

Clarence was a tall, black man in his early twenties. He had a naturally smiling face that put people at ease the second they met him. His clothes were casual, part rapper, part yuppie. Clarence had repeatedly told Carl in the past he was making a fashion statement with his attire and give it another year and everyone would be mimicking him.

Carl thought he was nuts.

"Hey, I just got a new job, how about buying your buddy a beer?" Carl asked with a sly smile.

Clarence frowned. "A job huh? Doing what?"

Sitting taller on his stool, Carl told him. "I'm working for a funeral home; maybe you've even heard about it, it's been there forever."

"So give, what's the name?" Clarence prodded him.

"It the Rossi Funeral Home over on Market Street, ever heard of it?"

Clarence nodded and took a sip of his beer, leaving a beer mustache on his upper lip. "Oh sure, yeah, I know of it, so you're working there now, huh? Seen any dead guys yet?"

Carl shook his head. "No, thank God, but the guy I work for said it's just a matter of time. So, how 'bout that beer?" He asked again.

"Seems if you're the one with the job, it should be you buying me a beer," Clarence joked but he still waved Bobby over and ordered another two beers. Bobby frowned when he saw Carl, but when Clarence pulled out a twenty, Bobby poured them and slid them to the two men.

Carl picked up his mug and toasted Bobby with it. "Here's to a great guy," he said and drank half the beer in one gulp.

Bobby gave him the finger and then moved to the other end of the counter.

Clarence nudged Carl with his arm. "What's that all about?"

Carl shrugged, finishing off his beer. "Its nothing, Bobby wants me to pay my tab, so if it wasn't for you, I would already be out on the sidewalk. Listen, once I get paid, the next times on me, okay?"

Clarence frowned. "I'll believe it when I see it."

Carl turned slightly so he could talk to his friend without turning his head. "So, how's your job at the factory? And when are you gonna get me in there?"

Clarence pursed his lips and sighed. "Look, Carl, we've been over this before. If you've got a record, they won't hire you."

Carl sagged on his stool. "That sucks, man; it sounds like a sweet gig. So tell me, have any of the guys working there turned into three eyed mutants or grown an extra arm yet?"

Clarence started on his second beer and after taking a sip, turned to stare at Carl. "Listen, you dumb bastard, I told you the stuff we process isn't radioactive, but it is toxic. As long as you don't drink it, you're fine."

"Uh-huh, so you can still father some children someday if you ever find a woman stupid enough to sleep with you?"

Clarence punched him in the arm, annoyed. "Cut that shit out, Carl. I'll find someone, sooner or later. I just don't want to fall for the first woman that comes my way. When I find that one person, I know she'll be special."

Carl started laughing. "Special? Let me tell you something, man, any woman that lets you stick your dick in her *is* special. The sooner you figure that out the better off you'll be; so, how 'bout another beer? I figure I've got at least an hour before I need to get back to the Funeral Home."

Clarence's eyebrows went up in mock surprise. "So you're supposed to be working, but instead your getting drunk with me, way to keep a hold of your job, man. Aren't you white boys supposed to be more responsible than that?"

"Ha, ha, forget about me, look, what about you? Shouldn't you be working, too?"

Clarence shrugged. "Nah, I got the day off."

"So you're a janitor there?" Carl asked, snidely.

Clarence flashed him an annoyed look. "No, I've told you before, I'm a custodial engineer."

Carl made a satisfied grunt and took another sip of his beer. "Exactly, you're a janitor."

"Hey, lay off, man, it's a steady job, and you've got a lot of nerve criticizing me when you're playing hooky right now?"

Carl waved his worrying away. "Oh relax, Clarence, the old guy I work for thinks I'm stuck in traffic on 93 and without a cell phone he can't contact me, I'm golden."

Clarence got Bobby's attention and ordered two more beers. Bobby frowned, but once again slid the mugs across the counter. Carl grinned at him, and Bobby growled, the noise carrying to Carl even over the jukebox.

Carl decided he'd antagonized Bobby enough and concentrated on his beer.

Clarence noticed the only pool table in the back of the bar was empty.

"Hey, Carl, you up for a game of pool?"

Carl picked up his beer and started over to the table before Clarence had realized he'd left. "Hell, yes, loser buys another round."

Clarence frowned, picking up his beer and leaving the counter. "What the hell does that mean? I'm the one buying the beer anyway; you've got no money."

Carl flashed him a smile and racked the balls. "Exactly, you break."

Clarence sighed. He knew how Carl was and despite his utter lack of responsibility and his knack for never paying for anything, he was still his friend. Clarence set his beer on the edge of the pool table and prepared to play, somehow knowing whether he won or lost, he'd still be buying the next round.

Chapter 4

CARL AND CLARENCE stepped outside into the fading light of the day. Carl looked at his watch and mumbled a few choice curses.

"Shit, I didn't realize what time it was, I need to get back to the funeral home. Want a lift?"

Clarence shrugged. "Sure, just drop me off at the nearest T stop and I'll be good."

"Cool, follow me, my trucks in the back lot."

The two men walked through the small alley until they had reached the rear lot. The moment Carl saw his truck; he let out a howl of panic and started running towards it. "Hey you kids', get the hell away from my truck!"

Four teenagers looked up from inside the truck and jumped down, running away. In seconds they were gone from sight.

Clarence watched him go, not understanding what his friend was yelling about, but when he got a little closer to the truck, he quickly realized what the problem was.

The pull-up door on the rear of the truck was wide open and on the ground were seven or eight barrels, their contents spilling out to stain the parking lot a sickly yellow color. Clarence reached his friend and shook his head.

"Jesus, what a mess. Was this the stuff you were supposed to bring back to the home?"

Carl looked at Clarence, his face filled with worry. "Of course it was; what the fuck am I supposed to do now? My parole officer already told me if I can't keep a job, he's going to revoke my parole. This was my last chance." He started walking around in circles, his feet splashing in the formaldehyde.

Clarence inspected the rear of the truck and stopped Carl from walking with his hand.

"Let me get this straight. There was no lock on the truck's door and you still parked it in an abandoned lot so you could get a beer instead of bringing it back to the funeral home? And now a bunch of juvenile delinquents trashed everything?"

"So I screwed up, fine, I admit it, but I shouldn't have to go to jail again for it. Oh God, I don't want to go back there, I don't."

Clarence could feel the angst coming off his friend and despite himself, he felt sorry for him.

Despite his better judgment, he spoke up.

"I might have a way for you to get out of this mess, though for the life of me I can't imagine why I'm even suggesting it."

Carl turned to Clarence and stepped so close, Clarence could smell his breath. "What, Clarence, what's your idea, tell me, for the love of God, tell me!" He screamed, grabbing Clarence's shirt in his panic.

"Get off me, you crazy bastard!" Clarence said, extricating himself from Carl. "All right, listen, I know this sounds crazy, but what if you and me drive over to my job and fill up these empty barrels with some of the stuff they got sitting in the storage tanks at the rear of the factory."

Carl looked at the truck and barrels and then at his watch again. "Shit, are you serious? How long will it take? And even if we did, won't the guy at the funeral home know it's not the right shit?"

"What the fuck do I look like, a mortician? I don't know, but either we give it a try or you can just go back there and explain how you let all his shit get destroyed."

Carl seemed to think on it for all of three seconds; then he nodded and pulled out his keys.

"Fine, Clarence, you win, but first we need to get all these barrels back into the truck. Will you help me, please?"

Clarence sighed. "Shit, Carl, of course I'll help you, but remember this, when you get back on your feet you owe me big time."

"Ain't it the truth brother, ain't it the truth."

The two men got to work and quickly loaded the barrels back onto the truck. Thankfully, the truck had a hydraulic lift on the back to load and unload supplies. Within fifteen minutes they were both inside the cab and driving out of the lot, the tires splashing in the large pool of chemicals.

"Wow, I wouldn't want to be the poor bastard who has to clean up that mess back there," Carl said as he forced his way into traffic. Rush hour was now in full swing and he had to push and shove to get out of the parking lot. Boston drivers were notoriously rude and selfish, on par with New York commuters, but Carl had lived in Boston his entire life and was used to dealing with assholes.

A few horns beeped their displeasure at him and he stuck his finger out the window and gave them the one finger salute, then he pulled into the left lane without signaling and headed for Kneeland Street.

One of the rules of city driving was never to signal. If you signaled, all you would do is warn the driver behind you that you were going to pull in front of him, thereby pushing him back another car length. No, the key to city driving in Boston was to swing in quick, before the other driver knows what you were going to do, thereby beating him before he pulls up to block you.

Carl worked his way through traffic until he'd reached the Boston Herald Building. Clarence directed Carl to drive in a small driveway next to the red brick building and to follow it. Carl did as he was told, driving down the narrow drive.

A few minutes later, Carl slowed, spotting the large warehouse that housed Clarence's workplace.

"Is that it? That's where you work?" Carl asked.

Clarence nodded. "Yeah, I know it ain't much to look at. Look, it's a paycheck, alright? Go to the left and follow the driveway to the rear of the building." He checked his watch. It was a little past five. "Only the security guard should be back there by now. Most of the workers leave at four and the bosses leave at around three, nice job if you can get it."

Carl said nothing, but continued driving. When a gate came into view, he slowed. Pulling up to the rolling gate, a man in a security uniform stepped out of a small guardhouse. Carl swallowed deeply when he saw the gun strapped to the man's waist.

"Now just be cool and let me do the talking. I know this guy, he's pretty cool."

Carl nodded, his heart hammering in his chest. If this didn't work out, by tomorrow he'd know where he'd be and he didn't want to think about it.

Clarence leaned out the window and flashed his best smile. "Hey, Larry, how's the wife and kids doing?"

Larry shrugged. "About the same, Clarence. The wife wants to go to Canobe Lake Park this Sunday. Do you have any idea how much it costs to bring a family of four to an amusement park these days?"

Clarence shook his head. "No, not really. You should go, though, it'll be fun, all that family bonding and shit."

Larry chuckled at that. "Yeah, I know, and I'm sure we're going, but if I don't argue a little, the wife will win, you know? Got to make it hard for them; make them think they earned it when you give in."

"I hear that, listen, Larry, my buddy here wants to see the tanks and shit, so I thought I'd bring him by. Is it okay if we go inside and drive around for a little while?"

Larry rubbed his chin. "I don't know, Clarence, if you got caught, it'd be my ass."

Clarence nodded. That's why I came after everybody went home." Clarence held out his hand, a fifty dollar bill sticking out of it. "I sure would appreciate it. Besides, what the hell could we do in there? Nothing, that's what. We should be back in a few minutes."

Larry stared at the fifty and then up at Clarence. "Only a few minutes? Then your gone?"

Clarence smiled widely, knowing he had him where he wanted him. "Absolutely, just one trip around the yard and then we're out of here."

Larry thought for another second and then he snapped the fifty from Clarence's hand like a cobra attacking prey.

"This'll help on Sunday, thanks Clarence. All right, go ahead, but don't touch anything and if you get caught you slipped inside while I was on the shitter, got it?"

Clarence beamed at him. "Sure man, it's cool. Deniability, I get it."

Larry swung the gate wide and Carl drove through. Looking in his rear-view mirror, Carl let out the breath he'd been holding.

"Wow, I can't believe that worked. I thought for sure he was going to tell you to fuck off," Carl breathed.

Clarence leaned back in his seat. "Nah, man, Larry has three kids, he's strapped for cash. I knew he'd go for it, besides, there's nothing in here anyone would ever want to take. Even if we were terrorists or something this place would be a waste of time."

Carl nodded, driving through some of the three-story tanks. "So what's in these things exactly?"

Clarence shifted position in his seat. "We get stuff like medical waste from hospitals, you know, like when someone gets liposuction and all that fat is left over, we get that."

"Oh shit, that is so nasty, what else?"

Clarence gave it some thought. "Well there's all the shit they pump out of the sewers when they clean them. Those trucks with the big vacuum hoses, you've seen them right?"

Carl nodded.

"Well, all the shit they suck out of the sewers gets brought here, too. They put all kinds of bacteria and shit into the tanks and it eats the bad stuff like its dinnertime. Then when everything is nice and healthy they transform it into fertilizer. Look, I don't know how they do it exactly; I'm a custodial engineer for Christ's sake."

"You mean a janitor," Carl smiled at him.

"Fuck you, man," Clarence said. "There, stop by that tank with the green stripe on it," he told Carl.

Carl did as he was told and a minute later both men were standing outside the truck, the engine ticking in the cool air.

Clarence went to the tank and pulled a long hose from a side hook mounted to the tank. "Carl, man, get to work, get the truck open and get those barrels ready. We've only got a few minutes before we need to leave. Larry may be a greedy bastard, but he wouldn't let us do what we're doing, so move, dammit!"

Carl snapped into action, quickly opening the truck and unsealing each barrel. The smell was horrible and he wondered if breathing all the fumes would make him sick. A second later, Clarence was handing him up the hose and turning on the spigot at the other end.

"Okay, man, start filling them up, and a word of warning, don't get any of it on your skin."

Carl shoved the nozzle into the first barrel and started filling it up.

"Why, what would happen to me?"

Clarence smiled. "Maybe you'll grow an extra arm or become sterile; your guess is as good as mine."

Carl frowned. "You're fucking with me, aren't you?"

"Yeah, man, I'm just messing with ya, but seriously, don't get that shit on you, I really don't know what they put in it. When the lab guys test it, they're always wearing these chemical suits that cover their bodies from top to bottom."

Carl took his advice and one at a time filled the barrels up until he was finished.

Clarence took the hose and hung it back up and then jumped back into the cab.

"Okay, man, get going and just act natural when we get back to the gate."

Carl nodded and drove the truck away from the tanks. Three minutes later, the truck slowed when it approached the gate. Larry came out of the guardhouse again and his face looked serious. "I was just about to go look for you guys, what took so long?"

Clarence shrugged, checking his nails on his right hand, casually. "Sorry, man, we lost track of time, Carl here was pretty interested in how they make the fertilizer."

"Really, no kidding? I think it's the most boring shit in the world. Well, your back, so I guess it doesn't matter. Now get out of here before we're all caught."

Clarence nodded and nudged Carl to go. Larry opened the gate and Carl pulled through, flashing Larry a wan smile as he passed by him.

Larry waved and then walked back into his guardhouse. Carl drove down the driveway and once he'd reached the Boston Herald building again, he let out a loud gasp.

"Holy shit, I can't believe that worked. You saved my ass big time, Clarence. How can I ever repay you?"

"Well, for starters I want that fifty back as soon as possible, you hear me?"

Carl nodded, enthusiastically. "Not a problem, man, when I get my first paycheck, the money's yours, plus a night on the town, on me."

Clarence grunted. "I'll see it when it happens, now drop me off at the next T stop, I want to go home."

Carl did as he was told and five minutes later Clarence was walking away from the truck, toward the street opening for the train.

Carl beeped once and then pulled back into traffic. Checking his watch, he saw he was hours late for when he should have returned to the funeral home.

Racking his head for an excuse, he pulled into the next lane and pointed the truck's nose for the funeral home, wondering how he was going to explain his long absence to Jasper.

Chapter 5

CARL PULLED INTO the driveway for the funeral home. Pulling around back, he turned off the engine and jumped out of the cab.

The back of the home was wreathed in darkness, dusk falling over Boston more quickly then he would have preferred.

Walking towards the rear door, he almost jumped out of his skin when Jasper opened the door, his face a mask of concern.

"Jesus, man, you almost scared me half to death," Carl said, holding his chest.

"I'm sorry about that, but when I heard the truck, I had to come out here, it's so good to see you. I feared the worst."

"The worst? Why? I mean, I know I'm late, but I'm fine?" Carl said.

Jasper nodded. "Yes, my boy, when I saw the pile-up on the news I just assumed you were involved in it, after all, why else would you be so late?"

"Pile-up?" Carl asked, dumbfounded.

"Yes, the pile-up. Ten cars out on 93 North. I just assumed you were caught in it. They only started to clear the highway of the wreckage a little while ago."

Carl smiled inwardly. He had been so worried about what he was going to tell Jasper, he hadn't realized an excuse had been fabricated for him. He cursed himself for not listening to the radio on the way back after dropping off Clarence, but he had been so preoccupied and worried, he just hadn't been in the mood for music.

"Oh, yeah, the accident, that's right. Happened right in front of me. I've been stuck on that damn highway for hours. Thank God they finally opened it up again."

Jasper patted his shoulder in a fatherly way. "Well, I'm just glad to see you're all right. Now, I need you to unload those barrels and put them down in the basement. There's a storeroom just off the main room, Tyler is down there with a client and will show you where to place them. Thanks to that accident, we're going to be pretty busy in a day or so, once the coroner is finished with the bodies, that is."

Carl nodded, not understanding what he was talking about and did as he was told, unloading one barrel at a time. The work took a while and when he finally had all the barrels on the ground, he was hot and sweaty.

Deciding he'd go inside for something to drink, he stepped down the small ramp and into the main room. All the lights were on and he stopped dead in his tracks when he saw the dead body of an old woman lying on one of the steel gurneys; a tube sticking out of each side of her neck, one end connected to an embalming machine—though Carl didn't know this yet—and the other to a drain in the floor.

The body was of a woman, well past her prime, wrinkles stood out in stark contrast in the harsh fluorescent lights, but then he had remembered how Jasper had looked in those lights and realized dead or alive, the lights did nothing to help a person's appearance.

The corpse had a large V-shaped scar on its chest and abdomen and Carl assumed it was from the autopsy she must have had. Her skin was covered in liver spots and the dead eyes gazed up at the ceiling, the vacuous stare unsettling. The wilted breasts sagged to each side of her chest and the grey and white pubic hair covering her nether regions said she hadn't believed in scissors. She reminded him of his own dead grandmother and he wished someone would cover her up and give her a little respect.

The corpse farted, causing him to jump where he stood. A second later a man walked out of one of the small supply closets just off the main room, and Carl jumped yet again.

"Jesus Christ, why the hell is that body farting?" He asked Tyler as the man moved over to the corpse.

Tyler smiled, his brown teeth—from far too many cigarettes—showing through his thin lips. He was a man in his late thirties, with dark brown hair and a few more pimples than a man of his age should have.

His white skin seemed even paler under the lights and his brown eyes seemed to be looking everywhere at once, instead of looking at Carl, as the rest of his face was pointed.

"Relax, Carl, its just gas. Even when you're dead your body keeps building up gas, mostly due to decomposition. Aunt Mildred here is just rotting away as we talk. She's got a 3:00 pm viewing tomorrow, so I need to work on her all night to get her ready. Luckily, she died of natural causes so there's no reconstruction to do, just the standard cosmetic stuff."

He held out his hand for Carl. "Tyler Wimberley, at your service," he said politely.

Carl moved closer, wary of the corpse nearby and shook his hand. "Carl Jenkins, but I guess you already know that."

Tyler nodded. "Yes I do, Jasper filled me in. Did you get the supplies we needed from Waltham?"

Carl nodded. "Yup, the stuffs out in the driveway. I was about to bring it in, but I wanted to get a drink first."

Tyler nodded to a small refrigerator in the corner, similar to what would be found in a college dorm room. "There's bottled water in the fridge if you want."

Carl nodded and walked across the room, grateful to be away from the corpse.

Upon opening the fridge, he was once again startled. On the top shelf was a few bottles of water, but on the second and bottom shelf were pans full of what looked like internal organs. With a start, he jumped back, letting out a small scream.

"Holy shit, there are pieces of people in there," Carl said, slamming the door closed.

"Hmm? Oh yeah, sorry about that, we use the fridge for double duty. Just ignore them, they don't bite."

Carl frowned, but opened the fridge again, this time prepared for the gruesome sight. There were a half dozen stainless steel bowls filled with what looked like kidneys and livers, and one looked like it had something that resembled a spleen. Trying not to focus on the slimy body parts, he reached up and grabbed a bottle of water, then quickly slammed the door closed.

While he drank from his bottle, he watched Tyler repositioning the large tubes in poor Aunt Mildred's neck. Some kind of pump was hooked up to her and after all the tubes were connected, Tyler gestured for Carl to come over to him.

Hesitantly, Carl did as was requested.

"Listen, Carl, once you get those barrels put away, you can take off for the day. But do me a favor and bring me one of the barrels of formaldehyde, will you? I need to top off my tanks so I can embalm Millie here."

Carl nodded, now having a little motivation for finishing up. The first thing he did was bring in a barrel for Tyler, who quickly connected a small pump to the top of the barrel and started to fill the tank of some kind of vat with the tubes coming off it.

Tyler saw him watching and pointed at the contraption. "This is what we use to embalm our clients, Carl. See these tubes going into her neck?"

Carl nodded slightly. He did, though he wished he didn't.

"Well, they suck out all her blood while the machine pumps the formaldehyde into her system, thus allowing Mildred here to stay fresh for a few more days before we plant her in the ground."

Carl watched the vat fill up with the yellowish fluid that was supposed to be formaldehyde, but was instead something from one of the tanks from Clarence's processing factory.

All he could do was cross his fingers and hope Tyler didn't notice the difference.

"Look, I want to finish up and get out of here; it's been a long day," Carl said, walking away.

"I can imagine, been a rough first day, huh?"

Carl shook his head. "Brother, you have no idea," he said under his breath as he went back outside to retrieve the last few barrels.

Thirty-five minutes later he was finished placing all the supplies from the truck into the funeral home storage room. Wiping his forehead of sweat, he couldn't wait to get back to his dingy dive of an apartment and take a shower.

Jasper came up to him, and patted him on the back. "Well done, my boy. Thank you for all your help. I just got off the phone with the city coroner and I was right. When you come in tomorrow it should be pretty busy around here. We're expecting at least four more clients; all from the accident on Route 93 today. Tragic I know, but hey, I've got to make a living, right?" He smiled then, a wide smile that made him look like the corpse lying on the table behind him.

Carl nodded slightly. "Okay, then, I'm gonna go now. I'll see you tomorrow."

Jasper waved slightly. "Okay, Carl, see you tomorrow at eight o' clock, bright and early. I'm sure we'll need your help with all the extra clients."

Carl kept walking, not looking forward to tomorrow. He glanced over his shoulder once before leaving the preparation room and saw Aunt Millie being pumped full of chemicals. He could only hope neither Jasper nor Tyler noticed the difference, after all, the old bag was dead, it's not like she could complain.

Carl left the funeral home and walked down to the nearest T stop. He had just enough for a token and when he was finally on the platform; he let out a long sigh.

What a day, he thought, and he had a feeling tomorrow wouldn't be any better. And now he had to be in at eight in the morning. He didn't even know there was an eight in the morning, always sleeping in since he'd lost his last job.

The train pulled up and Carl climbed aboard, his first day could have gone better, but then again, it could have gone worse, at least he hadn't gotten fired. While the train shot down the tunnel, Carl leaned back and put his head against the glass, closing his eyes and trying to put the images of dead, naked old ladies out of his mind.

Chapter 6

THERE WAS A serial killer in Boston.

The papers had dubbed this person the Three-Bladed Killer because all the killings were done with three blades.

The police had another name for this killer. They called the suspect, the *Unsub,* short for Unspecified Subject.

No one had yet identified the Unsub as either a man or woman, as all the killings had been done quick and clean, leaving no trace of the killer's identity.

The police were doing their best to keep things quiet, not wanting to frighten the populace or deter tourism. Boston was a popular city in the spring, summer and fall. To the south there was Cape Cod and Plymouth Rock and to the north there was New Hampshire, which was a big draw when the leaves started changing.

So when bodies started turning up across the city, the first in Boston Harbor, the second across town near the city limits bordering on Cambridge, the police knew they had a serious problem on their hands.

Decoys had been sent out, walking the streets, hoping to catch the killer when he hunted again, but so far he hadn't bitten.

If it was a he.

Almost all serial killers in the history of the United States were male and there were some in the department that believed a male suspect was once again on the prowl.

But there were others with more open minds that knew with the right circumstances, a woman could be just as deranged as a man.

Around eleven o' clock at night, about the same time Carl Jenkins was relaxing with his last beer from his fridge, a lone woman exited the T onto Mass. Ave.

The symphony wasn't playing tonight, so the street was relatively quiet. A few college kids were hanging out, some of them cutting through the Christian Science Center reflecting pool.

Kelli Williams was doing just that. After reaching street level, she crossed the street and walked parallel with the reflecting pool. The pool was twelve inches deep and was half the size of a small football field. Water flowed over the edges of the pool to be recycled into a canal that surrounded the edges. A pump constantly kept the water flowing and the lights set in the trees reflected off the water, looking like a thousand stars had fallen to earth.

Kelli walked quickly, though not afraid, she was still a cautious woman. Her apartment was in a large twenty-story building on the other side of the pool, near the Hilton Convention Center and Lord and Taylor.

As she walked, her shoes clicked softly on the red bricks, the pool only adding to the echo. There was a slight chill in the air and she wrapped her arms around herself just a little more, picking up her pace.

She paused at the end of the pool, realizing some of the streetlamps were out, shadows dancing across the bricks at her feet. She scanned the darkness, looking for any movement that didn't belong. She saw nothing unusual. A dog barked in the distance and an airplane flew by overhead, on its way to Logan Airport, no doubt.

Only two dozen feet away a car drove by, honking at a cab that was making a U-turn on Boylston Street and on the far street a young couple laughed as they walked hand in hand. All this movement put her at ease, despite the fact that by standing near the reflecting pool, she was hidden from view, the broken lights wreathing her in a blackness that couldn't be pierced by the bright lights from the street.

She paused for only a second, realizing she was just being foolish. Boston was one of the safest cities in America, as long as you weren't stupid and decided to take a walk into Dorchester or Roxbury in the middle of the night.

Making herself continue onward, she started walking again, her eyes trying to peer into the shadows around her.

When she had made it through the darkness and was once again back under the warm glow of a street lamp, she involuntarily let out a sigh of relief.

She was just about to turn right and head down the small side street that led to her apartment building when a figure dressed in black lunged from the nearby shadows and pulled her to the red brick sidewalk.

She was about to scream an alarm, the street with cars driving past her so close she felt she could reach out and touch the people there, when she felt something penetrate her throat.

At first there was no pain, but then a sharp, throbbing came from her throat and she started to go numb. Her mouth opened and closed, her mind telling her mouth to form words, but nothing came out but a few hushed, gargled whispers.

She looked up into the eyes of her killer and she saw no mercy there. Her hand reached up to the face above her, but then she felt another piercing stab to her chest. She exhaled her last breath, still not understanding what was happening to her, when yet another pain filled her stomach, a third knife plunging to the hilt. Blood flowed freely from the wounds and spilled out onto the sidewalk beneath her.

It didn't matter though. By then her brain was shutting down, her heart beating its last.

All the hopes and dreams of Kelli Williams were being snuffed out, like a candle in the wind, and there was no one to witness it but the Unsub. Kelli's eyes took on a vacant stare and her pupils stopped moving, her blood slowing until it was only seeping out of the ragged gashes in her flesh beneath her jacket.

The Unsub stood up, breathing hard and looking down at the slaughtered woman. The Unsub's heart was beating a mile a minute, the thrill of the kill so powerful the Unsub thought he/she would die from the excitement.

Then the Unsub came back to his/her senses and realized he/she had overstayed his/her welcome.

Disappearing back into the shadows, the Unsub started running, but quickly slowed to a walk when he/she had made it back to Mass. Ave. The Unsub knew better then to draw attention by running.

A few minutes after leaving the body, a scream sounded across the reflecting pool. The body had been found.

Smiling to his/herself, the Unsub moved deeper into the city. Another night, another kill.

But there would be more killings, many, many more. People would continue dying until either the Unsub was caught or the Unsub was able to exorcize the demons within him/herself.

The Unsub turned a corner leading to his/her condominium in the Back Bay and stopped dead in his/her tracks.

Police cars filled the street and men in police uniforms were running back and forth through the opening to the Unsub's building.

They had found him/her. Somehow he/she had slipped up and had left something behind for the police to track him/her down with.

Stepping back around the corner, the Unsub moved across the street and deeper into the city. The Boston Commons were close and on the other side were a half-dozen hotels, some affordable.

Realizing everything at the Unsub's apartment was lost, the silent figure moved off towards the safety of the city.

He/she had escaped the police dragnet and that was just luck. Unless some kind of miracle happened he/she knew it would just be a matter of time before he/she was finally caught.

But until then the hunt would continue, for however long that was.

Chapter 7

THE NEXT MORNING Carl arrived for work at the funeral home with five minutes to spare.

Walking around to the rear door, he stepped inside the large, basement preparation room. He was greeted by both Tyler and Jasper, both men wearing aprons.

Carl thought both men looked like they were about to go to a barbecue. The only thing missing was some writing on the front of Jasper's apron that read: **KISS THE COOK**.

"Carl, it's so good to see you, right on time," Jasper said with a smile that gave Carl the chills.

"Hey Jasper, Tyler, what's up?" Carl said.

"A lot actually. The city coroner called me late last night and informed me they have a few pickups for you," Jasper said.

"For me?"

Jasper nodded and reached into his pocket for a set of keys.

"Here you go, my boy. These are for the van in the rear lot, perhaps you passed it on your way in here? Well, it has shelves to place the deceased on, so make sure to strap them in thoroughly. We don't want anyone falling out of their roost, so to speak." He walked

Carl back to the rear door. "I need you to go there now, please. Do you know where to go?"

Carl shook his head no. He had absolutely no idea where he was expected to go.

"Do you know where Boston City Hospital is? It's over on Harrison Street."

Carl nodded. "Oh yeah, sure. It's by the Goodwill store. Sometimes I'd go there and get a jacket for cheap money."

"Exactly. Go on the Alpine Road side of the hospital; that's where the bodies are. Just ask someone where the morgue is. I'm sure you'll have no trouble."

Carl nodded, looked at the keys in his hand and then started to leave.

"Oh and Carl?" Jasper called to him.

Carl turned back around. "Yeah?"

"Just make sure you watch where you park. The meter maids are ruthless over there."

"Okay, sure." Then he was out the door and walking to the van. While he walked, he looked around some more at the grounds of the funeral home. There was a wide lawn that went back into a small tree line and flowers surrounded the house. The sounds of traffic could be heard, the city encroaching on the home and the few other dwellings nearby.

Carl hopped into the van and frowned when he saw the radio was only AM. The old van should have been mothballed more then a decade ago, but when he started it, it surged to life, belaying its age.

Swinging the van around, he pulled out of the driveway and started to fight his way to the hospital. Morning rush hour was in full swing, angry commuters frustrated as they fought their way through the maze of streets. The BIG DIG was still in full gear, making things twice as bad for Carl and the other commuters around him. Maybe in twenty years the roads would be better, but until then it was even more of a clusterfuck then normal. Anyone who didn't believe it just needed to go for a drive around eight in the morning to see for themselves.

But Carl was a Boston driver his entire life and he knew how to push and jockey for position like the best of them.

Thirty-five minutes later he was pulling into the driveway of Boston City Hospital. After asking a few people walking along the sidewalk, he finally got the answers he was looking for and parked in a small lot for deliveries and visitors.

After asking yet more questions, he finally found out exactly where he needed to go and he hopped back into the van and drove around to the side of the hospital and drove into an underground garage. Following the directions he'd been given, he drove to the bottom level and drove to the far end of the garage. Sure enough there was a sign that read: **CITY MORGUE.**

Carl found a parking spot near the door for pickups and walked to the set of double doors, whistling happily while swinging the van's keys in his hand. The doors were unlocked and he entered the building.

White cement walls and a polished white tile floor greeted him. With his footsteps echoing with every step taken, he moved further into the building.

Another set of double doors greeted him and he pushed them open, sliding through. There was a chest-high desk on the far wall of the hallway and a woman in a lab coat was seated behind it. Carl thought she looked like a woman who didn't get laid much, the look accentuated by the way she had her mouth clenched tight.

"Uh, hi, I'm here to pick up a few stiffs for the Rossi Funeral Home," he said quietly.

The woman looked up at him curtly and frowned at his choice of description for the deceased, then pointed to a sign-in book on the counter in front of him.

"Sign in," she said, brusquely.

Carl did as he was asked and when he was finished, she pointed to another set of doors behind her and handed him a security badge.

"Down there," was all she said.

Carl nodded and said thank you, but the woman had already forgotten him.

Walking down the hallway, his nose began to smell the distinct odor of antiseptic. And something else, something he couldn't quite pinpoint.

Pushing through the set of double doors, he stopped in his tracks. His jaw dropped and his tongue seemed to slide out of his mouth. Before he realized it, he had turned to the side, spotted a small trash can, and was hurling last night's beer and Fritos into the container.

When he thought he was done vomiting, he wiped his mouth and looked up, a masked man now looking at him with more than a little bit of curiosity.

"Are you okay?" The man asked.

Carl didn't say anything.

"Sir, I said, are you okay?"

This time Carl snapped out of it and nodded, slightly. "Yeah, I'll be fine, it's just . . . I didn't expect to see," he pointed at the table below the man. "That."

The man looked down to what Carl was gesturing to. Below the man, on a steel table was the body of a woman. Her chest was sliced in a triangle incision and a rib spreader was lodged into the wound. Next to the man was an assortment of internal organs, all catalogued and inventoried. As for the man, he was covered in scarlet from head to toe. The plastic gloves on his hands and arms were covered in red, looking like the man had jumped into a pool of blood and swum around for a while. The picture was finished by the goggles the man wore over his eyes and the surgical mask on his lower face and the top of his head, also covered in vermilion.

"I take it you've never seen an autopsy being performed," the man said.

Carl shook his head from side to side, his eyes never leaving the visceral scene of death before him.

The man waved him closer. "Who are you exactly, what are you doing here?" The man asked, looking at the visitor's pass on Carl's chest.

"I'm here to pick up some bodies for the Rossi Funeral Home," Carl said quietly.

"Oh, of course, you must be Jasper's new kid." The man held out his hand for Carl to shake and Carl just stared at the bloody appendage.

"Oh sorry, look, I'm just about finished here. This one's for you, too. The last one actually." He pointed at the corpse's head, a deep gash in the woman's forehead apparent. "This autopsy was a waste of time, anyway. It's pretty damn apparent it was blunt force trauma to the head caused by lack of a seatbelt."

"How do you know that?" Carl asked, curious despite the gruesome scene in front of him.

The man pointed to the woman's shoulders and neck. "See here? No bruising. If she had been wearing a seatbelt there would be bruising. Even after death your body tells a tale, my friend."

"Wow, that's pretty cool," Carl said, actually interested. "Can I ask who you are?"

The man seemed to blink for a moment, realizing Carl was right, he hadn't introduced himself.

"I'm sorry, I'm Dr. Edwards. Jasper and me are actually old friends, you make sure to tell that old fart I said hi."

"Sure, I'll do that." Carl looked down at the corpse again. "So what do I do until you're finished?"

Dr. Edwards gestured with his chin to a wall lined with small stainless-steel doors—each measuring two feet by two feet—on his left. The doors were four high and five across. Each door had either a name or a number on its shining surface.

"Your other passengers are in there. They're in the bottom row on the left. There all dressed and ready for their trip, I'm sorry to say."

Carl walked over and checked the tags. **William Berman** was on the first one he saw and next to it was another name that had to go with the first. **Terri Berman, it** read. Next to Terri was another that read: **Charles Berman.**

Carl turned back to Dr. Edwards. "These say the Berman's, is that the ones?"

Dr. Edwards nodded his head, his hands once again inside the corpse's body, pulling out something that looked like raw liver. Carl looked away, not wanting to throw up again.

"Those are them. Poor bastards got hit head on by an eighteen wheeler. They never had a chance."

"How do I get them to the van?"

Dr. Edwards used his elbow to point to a rolling gurney across the room. "You can use that; just bring it back when you're through with it."

Carl nodded and grabbed the gurney, rolling it across the tile floor.

When he was ready, he opened the door for William Berman and slid the metal plank out. The plank slid out easily, the underside on rollers. The body inside was in a body bag and Carl decided that was just fine with him.

It took only a few tugs to get the corpse onto the rolling gurney and when he was finished, he wheeled the body to his van.

Returning a few minutes later, he did the same for Terri Berman. He was getting better now, and he quickly rolled the corpse to the van and then returned once again.

This time, when he opened the last door and pulled out the body, he let out a small gasp. Though hidden in a black body bag, the outline and small form of a child was evident. Carl stood perfectly still, looking down on the small shape inside the bag.

Dr. Edwards walked up behind him, now with clean hands and minus his bloody apron.

"It's a crying shame, it is. That little boy was only six years old and now he's dead. He'll never have a first kiss with a pretty girl or go to the prom, now he's nothing but an empty husk. I ask you, what God would let that happen?"

Carl didn't know and so stayed quiet.

Five full minutes went by and then Dr. Edwards nudged him. "I know its hard son, but he needs to go to the home so he can be put to rest with his family," he said softly.

Carl looked up, and blinked away a tear. "Huh, what? Oh yeah, right, no problem, it's just, he's so small . . ."

Dr. Edwards patted his shoulder. "I know, but if you're going to do this kind of work for any amount of time, you need to harden yourself to stuff like this. It's not your fault he's here, you didn't put him here. You need to detach yourself emotionally or you'll go crazy."

"Is that what you do?" Carl asked, his voice cracking.

Carl turned to look at Dr. Edwards. Now that he had his mask and goggles off, Carl could see he had one large eyebrow and a scalp that was almost void of hair, only a few tufts around the ears still hanging on. He had to be at least sixty-five, but his eyes seemed to belong to a man half his age.

"Not at first. When I started this job years ago, I took all their faces home with me. I can't tell you how many nights I woke up in tears, covered in sweat. But slowly, I learned to remove myself from the equation. The job I do, and you also, is a necessary one. Someone needs to take care of the dead and it might as well be me . . . and you too, maybe."

Carl let out a sigh and then pulled the small body bag onto the gurney.

"I'll be okay. I'm gonna bring little Charlie here to his family, they're waiting in the van."

Dr. Edwards smiled. "Okay, son, you do that, and by the time you get back I'll have the other one ready for you."

Carl wheeled the gurney out to the van, sliding the small body onto the top shelf, making sure to secure the tiny corpse with the straps attached to the shelf.

When he was finished, he returned to Dr. Edwards, and true to his word, the last body was now in a body bag. Carl had to wonder how the doctor had managed to slide the body in by himself, but then he had been doing his job for a long time and must have become very adept at his work.

Carl slid the last bag onto the gurney and Dr. Edwards patted the top of the bag. "You take good care of Lisa, here, Carl. Make sure she gets to the home safe."

"Her name was Lisa?" Carl asked, looking down at the black bag.

Dr. Edwards nodded. "That's right. Her name was Lisa Giovanni and she was thirty-five. According to the information given to me by the police, she was single, with one living relative, a brother. He's out in California, I don't know if he's been notified yet."

Carl nodded, not knowing if he was supposed to say anything, so decided to just stay quiet again.

An awkward silence passed between the two men and it was Carl who broke it.

"Well, Doc, I guess I'll be going, now," Carl said, getting behind the gurney to push it out of the room.

"Okay, Carl, it was nice meeting you, perhaps we'll meet again."

"Not if I can help it," Carl muttered to himself as he pushed the gurney out the door. This job was too much for him. All this death. What a downer, no, as soon as he could, he was going to go see his parole officer and get the hell out of this creepy job.

"Did you say something, Carl?" Dr. Edwards asked, catching some of Carl's mutterings.

Carl shook his head, no. "No, Doc, just talking to myself."

Dr. Edwards nodded and waved to, Carl. "When you're finished with that gurney, just leave it by the rear door, one of my helpers will retrieve it."

"Okay, thanks, see ya," Carl said and disappeared through the doors. He was thankful for small favors, anyway. Now he wouldn't have to walk all the way back into the morgue. He could just load up his last passenger and go.

And that was exactly what he did, slamming the van's doors tightly and pushing the gurney into the side hall. Then he jumped into the driver's seat and got out of there, pulling back into traffic and fighting his way back to the funeral home.

His mouth ached for a beer, but he knew he would be pushing it to stop at his favorite bar on the way back to the funeral home.

Checking his watch, he saw it was going on eleven in the morning. He sighed, realizing he still had more than half a day to get through before he could go home.

Weaving through the city streets, he was soon pulling into the front drive of the funeral home again. He noticed a few more cars lining the front driveway then when he'd left, but didn't give it much thought.

Parking in the rear, he climbed out of the van and went inside to tell Jasper he was back.

As he stepped into the basement, he slowed to a stop. Tyler and Jasper were placing Aunt Mildred into a mahogany casket with gold plating on the sides. The corpse was now dressed in a flower print dress that looked like it had come off a rack from the Salvation Army.

Her hair was done up, looking like the woman had stepped out of a beauty salon.

Just before they set her down, her body hovering in the air, Carl could have sworn he saw the corpse's fingers twitch. But then the body was inside the casket and Jasper fussed for a few seconds over the body, then closed the casket with a muffled slam.

Shaking his head, he brushed away what he thought he'd just seen. It must have been a trick of the light. The woman was dead, pumped with enough chemicals to classify her as a toxic landfill. He had seen the autopsy scar himself. Her internal organs were missing, probably sitting in a barrel at the morgue somewhere in a container labeled **Hazardous Waste**.

Jasper finally noticed him standing there and called him over. Carl did as requested and stopped at the foot of the casket. His eyes noticed how the wood reflected the bright lights in the room, like it was polished glass. He idly wondered how much the casket must have cost and who'd paid for it, then Jasper was talking to him and he needed to focus.

"So once you get those bodies inside, I need you to help out upstairs," Jasper finished.

"Upstairs? You mean where the people will be?"

Jasper nodded, smiling like he was talking to a five-year-old. "Exactly, where the people will be. You see, Tyler needs to help me prepare the bodies you brought back with you for their viewings tomorrow. We need to get the entire Berman family done at the same time and then we need to attend to the Italian woman."

"Her names Lisa Giovanni, not the Italian woman," Carl said defensively.

Jasper patted his shoulder until Carl glared at the hand. Jasper pulled it away and tried to keep a half-smile on his face.

"There's a back room upstairs that has a few spare suits in it. You should be able to find one that fits you, or at least that's close."

"Do I have to go change now?" Carl asked, not looking forward to putting on a monkey suit.

Jasper shook his head, no. "Not at all. The viewing isn't until three, though there are already family members here, preparing for the event. You can stay down here until two or so, then I'll need you upstairs to help the guests. Show them where to park and what room the viewing is in, that's all, nothing complicated."

Carl grunted and stepped away from Jasper. "Well, I better go get the bodies, it's kind of warm outside and there's no a/c in the van."

Jasper waved him onward and he turned and went back to the casket with Tyler. The entire time Jasper had been talking to Carl, Tyler had been fussing with the casket and then with his embalming machine.

In short order, Carl brought in the four bodies. Jasper had a gurney similar to the one at the morgue and Carl made short work of the grizzly task. The transfer had gone smooth except for one time when he was bringing in the corpse of Lisa. While he was rolling the gurney down the ramp, he hadn't realized he hadn't secured the body to the gurney as well as he'd hoped. When the ramp slanted at its worst, the corpse started to slide off the gurney, the body bag slipping. Carl had reached out and caught the body, wrapping his arms around the corpse.

His stomach had rolled inside him and he almost thought he was going to throw-up. He managed to keep it down and thrust the body back onto the gurney. Pushing the corpse into the basement, and totally freaked out, he still couldn't help but think about how soft the body had felt inside the body bag, like the person inside could just sit up and climb out of the bag at any second.

Pushing such ridiculous thoughts away, he brought the body to the nearest open table. Thinking things like that would only give him nightmares. He made himself a promise, though. As long as he worked at the funeral home, he was going to give up horror movies, especially vampire and zombie films.

Now that he was handling dead bodies for a living, it just hit too close to home for his tastes.

When he was finished with the last corpse, he decided he needed a break and so using the old, *I need to go to the bathroom excuse*, he slipped away to take a breather, while Jasper and Tyler began to work on their new clients.

It was times like this that he wished he was still smoking; in fact, he might just start again for the hell of it.

Chapter 8

IT WAS A little before two o' clock in the afternoon when Jasper asked him to put on one of the extra suits from the back room.

Carl found a grey one with light pinstripes, and after checking himself out in the small bathroom mirror, he found he was pretty impressed with himself.

Walking back down to the basement, he saw Tyler closing the walk-in refrigerator. All four cadavers that had been brought back with him from the morgue had been embalmed and dressed. All that was needed now was to put each one in their prospective caskets.

Jasper had said the viewings for the Berman family wouldn't be until tomorrow, so there would be plenty of time.

Jasper turned and smiled from the preparation table. He had a red stained cloth in his hands as he cleaned up any residual blood left over after draining the corpses.

Carl casually glanced at the embalming machine, seeing almost all the fluid was gone from the vat.

He let out a silent sigh of relief. Neither Jasper nor Tyler had realized that the liquid they were pumping the bodies full of wasn't formaldehyde.

Clarence's plan had worked without a hitch. It looked like his job was safe.

"Not bad, Carl, in fact, if you do a good job today, I just might let you stay up top, instead of down here in the basement with Tyler."

Tyler made a face and flipped Jasper off, though Jasper couldn't see the gesture with his back to his apprentice. Carl saw it though and grinned. He guessed Tyler might not have been as happy as he'd first appeared.

"Thanks, Jasper, so what do I do exactly?" Carl asked

Jasper pointed to the casket which contained Aunt Mildred. "First you need to take the casket up to the first floor and place it in the second room from the elevator. That's where Mildred will be accepting family and friends. Put the casket at the front of the room, in-between the flower arrangements. I'll be up in a few minutes to check on you, make sure everything is in its proper place."

"Okay, not a problem," Carl said and did as he was told.

The elevator opened at the push of the button, already on the basement floor. Carl pushed the casket inside and then hit the button for the first floor. As the elevator started moving with a slight jerk, he could have sworn he heard a dull thump coming from inside the casket, but quickly dismissed it as ridiculous.

The elevator stopped with a slight jolt, the doors opening and he pushed the casket out into a red carpeted hallway.

The funeral home's décor was from the eighties, the wallpaper needing an update desperately. Oil paintings covered the walls of the hallway and statuary was spread out every few feet. Carl glanced at these while he pushed the casket into the second room from the elevator.

Fancy flower arrangements in everything from wreaths to hearts covered the front of the room and Carl wheeled the casket in-between them like he'd been instructed to.

Just as he positioned the casket into place, he could have sworn it thumped again, but he just assumed it was one of the wheels going over a bump in the carpet. There was a long white skirt off to the side and he quickly draped it around the legs and wheels of the casket, hiding them from view.

Finishing, he walked out of the room and turned off the lights. A few early family members nodded at him and he reciprocated, trying to mimic their dour expressions. Checking his watch, he saw he had almost forty-five minutes before the actual quests would be arriving.

Picking one of the numerous chairs lining the hall, he plopped down and stretched out, waiting for Jasper to come upstairs and check on his work.

Stretching out and relaxing, he closed his eyes, wondering if he could squeeze in a few minutes of sleep before Jasper arrived.

* * *

A gentle shaking of his shoulder woke him up. He didn't remember dozing off, but obviously he must have if he was being shaken awake.

Looking up into Jasper's face, he blinked the sleep from his eyes.

"Hey, guess I nodded off."

Jasper waved it away. "That's all right, my boy. Just make sure you never do it around the guests, please. One of the early arriving family members asked me about you and I told them a story of how you were up all night preparing Mildred. It seemed to have worked. So, let's see if everything's ready, shall we?"

Carl stood up and followed Jasper into the room. He had to admit the old guy was pretty cool for a boss. Jasper turned the light switch dimmer to full on and the room was bathed in a pale-yellow glow, the fluorescent light bulbs humming like there were insects trapped inside the ceiling fixtures.

Jasper walked around the room, nodding as he inspected this and that. Upon reaching the casket, he opened it, propping the lid up with a wooden pole. Carl was just able to see the cadaver over Jasper's shoulder and he took another step backward. Even with her clothes on, Aunt Mildred looked wrong. She didn't look like she was just sleeping, like so many people would often say at a viewing. To Carl, she just looked dead.

When Jasper was finished with the inspection, he walked back to Carl.

"Looks good. Now, when the guests come in, you'll hand them a pamphlet. It contains the history of the deceased as well as her surviving relatives." He smiled that creepy smile Carl hated. "It's an idea of mine, that way the guests know who all the players are, so to speak." He leaned over and picked up a pile of pamphlets from a small end table just inside the door. "Here you go, Carl, these were printed up last night."

Carl took them and glanced at the cover. It was a picture of Heaven, complete with fluffy clouds and a ray of light coming down from the middle of the cover.

"If you need me, I'll be downstairs, but I'll be up here with you at three o' clock sharp."

"It's cool, Jasper, I think I can handle it," Carl told him while shifting the pamphlets in his hands so as not to drop them.

Jasper patted his shoulder and then walked away. Carl watched him go, reminded of the Tall Man in the Phantasm movie, Jasper was just that creepy. But like a lot of people in the world, underneath his gruff or creepy exterior was a genuinely nice person, if only Carl wanted to take the time to get to know him better.

The truth was; he didn't. He wanted to get rid of this job as soon as possible. It was just too unsettling for him.

He sat back down and counted the minutes until the first car engine sounded from out front. He walked to the front door and opened it wide, using a piece of wood on the floor for just that purpose. Behind the first car another one pulled up, and soon the driveway was filled with cars, all the mourners of Aunt Mildred arriving and entering the funeral home.

Carl did his duty, handing out the pamphlets and looking mournful. His eyes gazed at a few of the women, perhaps nieces or great nieces. Even in their black dresses, their figures were easy to discern. Not for the first time since getting out of jail, Carl longed for a woman. When he had gone to jail, he had been single, no *girlfriend* to say goodbye to, and thankfully, he had remained single while he was in jail and when he had left jail, there was no *boyfriend* to say goodbye to, either. There were some people that the old timers in jail just knew not to mess with, whether because they thought he was crazy or just because he wasn't their type, no one had tried to get with him.

In that category, at least, he was still a virgin.

But looking at all the attractive women, now, made him so horny he thought he was going to explode. Walking into the room, he took one glance at Aunt Mildred and all ideas of sex were gone, vanished, like a set of brand new hubcaps on a new car in the middle of Dorchester.

With his perspective back, he glanced at the corpse. For just a moment he could have sworn he saw the head twitch. He looked around him, wanting to say something to anyone next to him who might have noticed it, as well, but he was all alone, the attendees all talking amongst themselves in the chairs and at the back of the room, near the doorway.

Deciding his eyes were playing tricks on him, he moved back to the doorway, nodding politely at the people who looked at him.

A large man who had to weigh three hundred pounds, at least, waddled into the room. His suit jacket was open, and Carl idly wondered if it was because the man's girth was so large to even attempt to button the jacket would have been impossible. The man was leaking sweat, an already soaking handkerchief in his hand mopping his brow. The small eyes were almost hidden in the folds of flesh on his face and he gasped as he took the pamphlet from Carl's hands.

Like feeding a hungry dog, Carl pulled his hand back quickly, feeling the man might attempt to eat it if he didn't remove it fast enough.

"Thank you, I'm sorry I'm late, 93 was a bitch," he said, in a winded voice.

"You're not late, you're fine, can I get you a glass of water or something, you don't look too good," Carl said politely. Actually he looked as if he was about to have a coronary right there in front of Carl.

Tubby nodded; the gesture barely noticeable with his two chins. "Yes, thanks, that would be great. I'm in the right place, right? I'm here for my Aunt Mildred."

Carl gestured to the casket. "There she is."

Tubby's face swiveled, barely, and his eyes went wide when he saw the casket. Carl was a little surprised. This man was the first person to actually show any emotion for the deceased. Up until now, the people had just shuffled in, like it was a job that had to be done and when it was over their lives would resume as if nothing had happened.

"I'll go get you that water," Carl said. Tubby barely heard him, the man pushing his way through people to reach the casket.

A man in a tweed suit walked up to Carl and nodded in Tubby's direction.

"That large man there was Mildred's favorite nephew. I hear they were fairly close. Truth is; he almost never leaves his house. I guess it had to be something truly big, like the death of his Aunt, to actually get him to leave."

Carl looked in the large man's direction and then nodded. "Oh, I see, well, thanks for the information." *Even though I didn't ask you*, he thought. Then he shuffled his way through the small crowd. All together there were about twenty people who seemed to be staying the entire three hours of the viewing with a few others coming and going.

Not a bad turnout, if Carl's opinion mattered. It helped that the weather was nice out. No one wanted to go to a wake when the weather was crappy, just made a distasteful chore even worse.

Carl walked out into the hallway to get the water for Tubby. There was a water cooler at the end of the hallway and he moved toward it, his eyes roving over the few attractive women he came across.

God he needed to get laid, and as soon as possible.

Just when he was filling up the cup with water, Jasper appeared.

"How are things going up here?" He asked.

"Fine, I guess, weren't you supposed to be up here a while ago?" Carl asked, turning with the cup of water to return to the room.

"Yes, I'm sorry about that, but Tyler needed some help with the last client. He's doing some cosmetic work on her head and he needed my assistance."

"Are you talking about Lisa?" Carl asked.

"Why yes, I am. Mrs. Giovanni needs a lot of work. She's having an open casket. Luckily we have until the day after tomorrow to get it done. The Berman family is all closed casket so there's very little to do there."

"Uh-huh, look I need to give this water to one of the guests before the guy collapses."

"Of course, my boy, go, and I want you to know you're doing a splendid job. You could have a real future here if you wanted one."

Carl smiled slightly, forcing it not to become a scowl. Then he headed back down the hallway. Jasper was already talking to one of the guests, doing what funeral directors did best.

Carl walked the few feet to the doorway of the room and when he was about to enter and give Tubby his water, he stopped cold.

At the front of the room, Tubby's head was hidden from view. The man was bent over the casket at an odd angle, and to Carl's utter shock, Aunt Mildred was hugging him, her mouth buried in the folds of his neck. For one brief instant the entire room was absolutely quiet. If someone had snapped a finger or clapped their hands together, the sound would have been deafening.

Then the silence was shattered as women screamed and people fought to escape the room, and a few brave heroes ran toward the casket to try and help Tubby.

With chaos erupting around him, Carl stood motionless, the cup of water sliding through his frozen fingers to splash onto the carpet at his feet, while only a few feet away from him, an embalmed woman attacked her nephew.

Chapter 9

TWO MINUTES AND thirty seconds earlier.

Tubby walked down the center aisle toward the casket. He was so hot in his suit he thought he would just die. He wished someone would turn up the air conditioning about twenty degrees.

He barely acknowledged the other mourners around him, but instead concentrated on reaching the casket.

His Aunt Mildred had been a good woman and he had loved her dearly. She had never judged him because of his weight, but had loved him as he was. She had always supported him in whatever he did, or didn't do, as the case may be. Tubby's real name was Markus Newton and he had been overweight his entire life. Luckily, he had become very adapt with computers and so was able to work from home, helping other people who weren't as smart as him when it came to the developing technologies of the twentieth century. He would spend six hours a day at a desk in his small office, telling people how to turn on their computer or load software into their hard drives.

True, it wasn't glamorous, but it paid the bills and allowed him free time to explore his hobbies, such as collecting comic books and action figures. Spawn was his favorite, though Star Wars was a close second.

So he was a geek, so what. He was happy and he didn't bother anybody, what else could anyone expect from him? His mother expected much more from him and so did his father, at least until he died from a heart attack at fifty-two.

His mother had never stopped nagging, telling him if he didn't lose weight, he would end up in the ground the same as his father.

Markus didn't listen. Not because he didn't agree. Hell, he knew he was too fat, but it was his will power. He sorely lacked it. He loved food and it was literally *everywhere;* all tasting so delicious.

But at least he didn't smoke, that was good, right?

So now he looked down at the face of his Aunt Mildred, the only person to love him for himself, not what he might be some day.

"Oh, Auntie, I'm so sorry. I'm gonna miss you," he said, a few tears falling down his cheeks. He leaned over to give her a goodbye kiss on the forehead when something happened that most definitely shouldn't.

With his chubby lips pressing down on her forehead, Aunt Mildred's eyes snapped open. But it wasn't as simple as that. Her eyes and mouth had been glued shut as part of the preparation for her viewing that day.

When her eyes snapped open, the upper part of her eyelids ripped off, the decayed skin becoming brittle.

Her eyelids hung down over her makeup coated cheeks; her eyes making her look like she was surprised at something. Markus's mouth hung slack as he stared at the ripped eyelids of his Aunt. Her eyes darted back and forth, seeming to be disoriented, then both eyeballs locked onto her nephew.

Markus was transfixed, too shocked to do anything other then stare at the old woman in the casket that was supposed to be dead. Mildred's mouth started moving as she tried to open it, but the glue kept them sealed.

Her brow creased with exertion and with a ripping sound, her upper and lower lips separated, only the bottom half of her lip remained glued to the top, the skin ripping completely off. She looked like she had two mouths, the upper one was closed, the lips stuck together and the other—the lower one—filled with teeth; the woman taking her dentures with her to the grave.

With her mouth now usable, Mildred let out a howl and leaned forward, wrapping brittle arms around her nephew, pulling him close to her in a death's embrace. Her teeth dove into his neck, trying to find his jugular, but the folds of soft flesh made it nigh impossible.

Markus tried to jump backward, letting out a yell of fear and panic, but only managed to pull the casket and Aunt Mildred down on top of him.

Both of them fell to the carpet with a crash, and Markus could hear the faint sound of people screaming in the background of the chaos he now found himself in. Aunt Mildred swiveled her head around in an impossible angle, her teeth flaring, ready to bite down on whatever was closest. Unfortunately for Markus, this was his nose. Aunt Mildred dove in like she was bobbing for apples and sank her teeth onto his nose, her head moving back and forth as she worried the nose free from his face.

With blood pouring down his throat, Markus let out a gargled yell for help. That was when two male mourners ran up to him and pulled Aunt Mildred off of him. No sooner had the first man done so, then Aunt Mildred swiveled her head around and sank her teeth into the man's cheek, the rest of Markus' nose falling from her mouth in her rush to attack the new prey.

The man let out a scream that nearly shattered the windows, and he threw Aunt Mildred away from him, the old woman rolling across the carpet to come up against a wall.

Shaking her head to clear it, she looked around at the legs of people as they tried to escape the room. Lashing out, she cupped the ankle of a woman and pulled her to the floor, and then immediately crawled on top of her and ripped out the woman's throat. The woman had time for one squeak of pain and then she was breathing her last, her eyes already glazing over in death.

Carl still stood by the doorway, watching the carnage taking place in front of him. People pushed by him, but for some reason all avoided him, like he was a stone pillar to be avoided instead of going through or over.

Jasper ran up behind him and let out a large intake of breath at the sight in front of him.

"Oh my Lord, what is going on here?" He gasped.

Carl shook his head. "The body in the coffin just got up and attacked the fat guy." He turned to Jasper, his face still in shock. "How the fuck can that happen, Jasper? The old bitch was dead, right?"

Jasper made a face. "Of course she was dead, you saw her on the damn table downstairs yesterday. She has no internal organs for God's sake!"

Carl nodded, slightly. "Okay, then how do you explain this shit?"

Jasper and Carl watched as the fat man rolled on the ground, both his hands over his bloody nose cavity, scarlet shooting out between his fingers like a broken water pipe.

As for Aunt Mildred, she was having a merry time, munching on the woman she had pulled to the floor. She had already ripped all the soft flesh from the dead woman's face and was now working on an arm. As for the man she had attacked and bit off his cheek, he was also rolling around on the ground, screaming for help.

"I'm going to call the police and an ambulance, Carl. You stay here and see what you can do," Jasper said and ran off down the hall.

By now all the mourners had disappeared with a screeching of tires and the revving of engines. A few horns blared as the frightened people drove onto the street, to the dismay of other motorists.

Carl didn't know exactly what he should do. Should he go help the fat man or the other guy? Or should he do something about the old woman who was supposed to be dead?

Then his decision was taken away from him when Aunt Mildred's head snapped up, her eyes staring directly at him. Her mouth and chin was slathered with scarlet, her dress stained a deep red.

She let out a hiss that almost made Carl pee himself, the animalistic sound seeming like it should be coming from some kind of wild animal instead of an old woman.

Aunt Mildred crawled off the mutilated body she had been feeding on and, still on all fours, started towards Carl.

"Now listen, you crazy bitch, just stay where you are, I don't want to hurt you. The cops are already on the way," he said, with an added *I hope* to himself.

If Aunt Mildred heard him, she didn't seem to care, but only kept moving towards him. Carl ignored the screaming, wounded men and women rolling around on the carpet, and started to back out of the room, deciding it was his own ass that came first.

Aunt Mildred slowly raised herself to a standing position, her back cracking as she did so. She leaned her head to the left and then the right, as if she was fixing her neck, then she leaned forward and ran at Carl.

Carl let out a soft squeal and turned to run, but before his first foot came down, he knew she would catch him. Reaching out with his hands, he grabbed the first thing that he could find, a bust of some philosopher he couldn't name if his life depended on it.

Picking the bust up and raising it over his head, he turned and slammed it down onto Aunt Mildred's head. But instead of feeling the solid thump of stone on bone, the statue shattered in his hand, the pieces falling over Mildred and coating her head and shoulders in white dust. The damn thing was just plaster. It was a phony.

But the plaster bust slowed Mildred enough so he could turn and run back down the hallway. The closest door led to the basement and he threw it open and ran down the stairs, in his haste not even bothering to make sure the door was locked behind him.

His feet pounded on the stairs and he fell down the last few steps, his legs finally giving out from under him in his terror. From up above, he heard Jasper scream and then thumping as of a struggle. Then Jasper let out a final shriek and all was silent.

Lying on his back, staring up at the door, he noticed something dripping from under the door and onto the top step.

Climbing to his feet, he crawled up the stairs, making sure to stay as quiet as possible. When he reached the top stair, he touched the liquid with his finger. Though the stairwell was shrouded in darkness, the unmistakable smell of copper filled his nose. Another sound floated from under the door, as well, the sound of an animal feeding, the ripping of flesh and tendons carrying easily in the quiet of the funeral home.

Slowly, he crawled back down the stairs, not wanting whatever was out there to hear him. When he reached the last step, he jumped when a hand landed on his shoulder. Holding the scream in his chest inside, he looked up at the face of Tyler. The man's face was one of confusion. He had been downstairs the entire time and with the exception of a few muffled screams, had no idea as to what was happening only one floor above his head.

"Carl, what the hell are you doing? What's going on? Why did I just hear screaming?"

Carl said nothing, just trying to catch his breath. After a few seconds passed, he felt he could talk, and he quickly tried to explain what had just happened upstairs. Tyler listened closely, his countenance becoming more unbelieving with each word Carl spoke. When Carl was finished talking, now sitting down on the stairs, his legs weak from terror, he said nothing more, just sat there staring at his shoes on the cold floor.

"That has got to be the most ridiculous story I've ever heard," Tyler said. "Where's Jasper, he'll get to the bottom of this."

"Jasper's dead, Tyler, and if you go upstairs, you will be, too."

Tyler scoffed and was about to climb up the stairs when a thumping came from the walk-in. Tyler's head swiveled around, surprised to hear anything. "Now what the hell is that?"

Carl climbed to his feet, Tyler helping him with a hand. Carl pointed to the walk-in. "Tyler, what's in there?"

Tyler made a face, as if the answer was obvious. "Just the Berman's and the other woman, Giovanni. But they're all dead."

"Uh-huh and so was the old bat upstairs, but that didn't seem to have slowed her down one bit," Carl said while inching away from the stairs to the middle of the room.

"Like I just said, that's ridiculous. All four bodies have been embalmed. They are absolutely dead," Tyler said and started towards the walk-in to investigate the noise.

"No wait, don't open that door!" Carl screamed, holding out his hand for Tyler to heed his warning, but Tyler ignored him, strolling over to the walk-in and pulling the door open.

Carl could only watch as four sets of hands, one set at about knee height, shot out of the darkness and wrapped themselves around Tyler. The hapless man let out a yelp of surprise that quickly turned into screams of pain as teeth and nails tore him apart.

Carl stood transfixed for exactly three seconds and snapped back to reality. That was it, he'd had enough.

Running towards the basement door, he charged outside into the daylight.

He still had the van keys in his pocket and he ran towards the vehicle, jumping inside and starting the engine.

Flooring the gas pedal, he drove down the driveway, almost clipping Aunt Mildred who was running down the middle of the drive, her face and chest dripping blood from her recent kills.

Carl swerved around her, instinct taking over, and with the sounds of sirens growing ever closer; he turned the van onto the street, making sure to go in the opposite direction of the sirens.

Just as he turned out of sight of the funeral home, other shambling forms appeared. Tubby and the woman with no face all stumbled out into the light of the day and seeing the street with automobiles on it, turned and headed into the city. As for Carl, he was on parole, after all, and wasn't looking forward to having to explain what had just happened in the funeral home.

Swerving onto the main road and cutting off a bread truck, he floored the gas pedal of the old van, planning on going to Bobby's and begin drinking until he was so drunk he wouldn't be able to remember his name, let alone the shit he had just witnessed.

While behind him, Aunt Mildred and the other blood-covered men and women ran off into the city, looking for more prey.

Chapter 10

CARL OPENED THE door to the bar and ran, more than walked, inside. When he'd reached the counter, he waved Bobby over to him. Before the bartender could say anything, Carl held up his hand to stop the man.

"Not now, Bobby, please, for the love of God, just give me a drink."

Bobby saw the look on Carl's face, the sheer terror behind his eyes, the pale white face, and nodded.

While he poured Carl a shot of Jack Daniels, he asked him a few questions.

"What's wrong with you, Carl? You look like you've just seen a ghost. And what's with the get up? You goin' to a funeral?"

Carl drank the shot and with a cringing of his face pushed the glass towards Bobby for another. Bobby didn't argue, but filled the glass up again. Carl drank the second shot and then slammed the glass onto the countertop. Breathing deeply and closing his eyes, he slowly regained some of his composure. The ride from the funeral home had been a blur of visions, of yelling pedestrians and beeping horns as he made his way to Chinatown and Bobby's bar.

"Believe me, Bobby, you wouldn't believe me if I told you." This time he reached out for the bottle of Jack and poured himself a shot.

Bobby normally would have scolded him, but Carl wasn't acting like himself, so he let it go.

"I'm putting that on your tab, Carl," was all he said and then he walked away to help another customer at the end of the bar.

Carl finished off the third shot and quickly poured himself a fourth. His body was already starting to feel the effects of the alcohol and he found himself calming down. His mind started to replay what had happened at the funeral home like a movie, and for the life of him, he still couldn't figure out what the hell had happened.

It was like some one's bad idea of a practical joke.

Yeah, he thought, that's what it was, a joke. Someone was playing a gag on him. In fact, if he went back to the funeral home, he'd bet that everyone would be hanging around, laughing, talking about what a sucker Carl had been and how he had fallen for the joke, hook, line and sinker. They'd probably be wiping the fake blood off their faces and having a beer together, all at Carl's sake.

As he continued consuming the Jack Daniels, the more he continued telling himself it was all just a sick joke, someone's bad dream come to life. By the time he was good and drunk, he barely remembered his name, let alone what he'd done earlier in the day.

Bobby called him a cab and when the taxi was out front, Bobby helped Carl to the cab.

While Carl was being carried out to the cab, the television was on, where it was mounted behind the bar on the wall.

With everyone in the bar talking and the music from the jukebox playing, no one paid any attention to the special news bulletin that had popped up on the screen.

An anchorman for Channel Five news was talking about the strange rash of attacks happening in the city. He went on to tell the viewers about an old woman who was running around attacking people and how the ones she killed appeared to be getting back up and then following her. How the victims would then attack any pedestrians near them. Downtown Boston was chaos, people covered in blood running around like lunatics, attacking and eating as many victims as they could find. The police had been called in and at the time of the announcement, no word had been given as to the status of the disturbance. The anchorman finished by saying his station would continue following the story and would give bulletins when needed.

The screen went black and then Jerry Springer came back on, a fight between an overweight Asian man and a midget filled the screen, daytime television at its finest.

But Carl didn't hear any of this, nor did any of the other patrons in the bar. Bobby told the cab driver where to take Carl and tossed the man a twenty. Then the cab took off into traffic, while Carl laid half-conscious in the back seat.

Bobby watched the cab pull out into traffic, shaking his head slightly. Carl was a good kid; he'd just made a few bad choices in his life.

Bobby looked up and down the street where there seemed to be a problem. A crowd had gathered and he could hear the distinctive sound of yelling, some rather high-pitched.

Deciding it was none of his business, he turned and walked back into his bar, leaving whatever was happening on the street to the cops.

* * *

The next morning, Carl was pulled from his drunken slumber by a loud banging coming from the front door of his apartment. With drool covering his chin, he rolled off the couch and stumbled to the door, his stomach already telling him he needed to get to the bathroom quick.

The banging continued, seemingly amplified with the pounding in his head. Opening the door, he was greeted by Clarence, his hand raised, prepared to knock yet again.

"What the hell do you want? Do you have any idea what time it is?" Carl asked, walking away from the open door and moving quickly to the bathroom. He had never been a very good drinker and knew he was going to pay for his night of drinking this morning and probably the rest of the day.

Clarence followed him inside the apartment and closed the door, then walked over to the window and peeked out through the tattered curtains. "It's two o' clock in the afternoon, if you didn't know it. Jesus Christ, man, I've been trying to get you all day. Don't you answer your phone?" He looked at Carl's outfit. "And what's with the monkey suit, you getting' married or goin' to a funeral?"

Carl shook his head, washing his mouth out with water. "No, my phone's been off. Can't afford the bill, why, what do you need that's so damn important that you need to beat my door in for? And forget about my damn clothes."

Clarence plopped down on the couch, his face covered in astonishment. "Holy shit, you really don't know, do you?"

Carl relieved his bladder and then washed his face. His stomach heaved inside him, but he was relatively sure he wasn't going to puke. At least that was something.

"Know what, dude? What the hell are you going on about?" Carl asked, falling onto the couch next to Clarence. He hoped he didn't need to get up again, because he really didn't know if he'd have the strength.

Clarence leaned over and put the television on. Scenes of chaos filled the small screen; looking like downtown Bosnia was being filmed. Police were shooting at attackers, other victims lying prone in the street. It was absolute bedlam. With the volume turned off, nothing could be heard, but the violent scenes said that wherever this was being filmed, it was total carnage. Carl watched for a few minutes, not getting what was so important, then he turned to Clarence.

"What exactly is this? Why do I care about what's happening in some other country?"

Clarence's black face seemed to turn a shade paler. "Jesus, man, you can't be that stupid. Take a look at what it says on the sides of the cop cars."

Carl leaned closer to the set and tried to see what Clarence was talking about. Slowly, his eyes grew wider. In neat black script on the sides of the police cruisers were the words: **Boston Police.**

Carl turned to look at Clarence, his friend nodding. "That's right man; that shit is happening across town. The whole damn city's gone crazy. People are just attacking people. But it gets better."

Carl waited for Clarence to spill it, but the man just sat there. "Yeah, so talk, what gets better?"

"People are saying that even though some of the attackers have wounds on them that should be fatal, they're still walking around. And get this, they're attacking and *eating* their victims."

"What, that's ridiculous," Carl said, but even as he said it, memories of the night before came back to haunt him. After all, how the hell did Aunt Mildred get out of her casket and start running around wild? The woman had clearly been dead. Carl placed his head in his hands and closed his eyes.

Christ, he thought, it's like a bad Italian horror movie, where the dead come back to life and start chomping on the living.

He opened his eyes to see Clarence sitting there waiting for him to speak. Should he say something? Should he tell his friend what had happened the day before at the funeral home?

Deciding against it, he stood up on shaky legs and walked over to his small kitchen. Opening the fridge, he pulled an old bottle of orange juice off the top shelf. Opening the cap, he winced at the smell, but still took a drink. When he was satisfied his stomach was going to keep it down, he drank a little more. Turning to Clarence, he held out the bottle. "You want some?"

Clarence wrinkled his nose. "No way, man, I'm cool." Then his face grew serious. "Look, what are we going to do about this shit? My parents have already got out of town. They're going to visit my sister in Springfield, at least until everything blows over. How 'bout you?"

Carl shrugged. "Don't know, frankly, I think this is all a big nothing. Maybe it's like those riots after the Red Sox won the championship. It'll probably blow over by then. You're welcome to stay here with me if you want. I'm not going to work today, how 'bout you, you working today?"

Clarence shook his head. "Nah, man, they closed the plant today, all this shit means no one can get in anyway. Far as I know, there's just a skeleton crew there." Then he grew curious. "So why aren't you going to the funeral home today? Shit, with everything that's happened I would think business would be real good there."

Carl tried to hide his uneasiness and instead took another swig of orange juice. "No reason; just had a rough day yesterday, that's all. Besides, I doubt anyone will be looking for me."

"Oh yeah, why's that?" Clarence asked, still pushing.

Carl sighed, and placed the bottle back in the fridge. "Let's just say that after yesterday, they're all dead tired over there and leave it at that, okay?"

Clarence gave in. "Fine, man, whatever. So what are we supposed to do here?"

Carl walked over to a small table and picked up a deck of cards and then walked back to the couch. A small coffee table was in front of the couch and he set the cards down on it.

Smiling down at his friend, he asked slyly: "So how much money you got?"

Clarence smiled back and pulled out a few dollars and some change.

"Oh it's on, white boy, it's on."

The two friends sat down and played some cards, Carl not worried about what was happening in downtown Boston. That was more than a half mile from where he lived. He was sure whatever was happening would be taken care of long before it ever got close to his apartment building.

Picking up the cards, Clarence had dealt him, he frowned. Already off to a bad hand right out of the gate.

Ignoring the scenes of chaos on the television, he concentrated on his hand. If he won, he could use the money badly, and if he didn't, well, he would just add it to what he already owed Clarence from past games of chance.

Chapter 11

THE DAY PASSED rather slowly and as night started to fall, Clarence stopped playing solitaire and looked out the one window that faced the street inside Carl's apartment. He could see a few parts of the city glowing, fires that were slowly burning out of control. The sounds of sirens had filled the air the entire day, never ceasing, but instead continued growing in volume as more police cars and fire engines entered the city from the suburbs and surrounding states.

Clarence glanced at the small television again. Carl was watching it now. In fact, he couldn't stop watching.

On the grainy black and white set, a man holding a microphone screamed at the top of his lungs, trying to talk over the sounds of chaos surrounding him. Behind him, people were running everywhere and the distinctive report of gunshots could be heard.

A man shuffled in front of the camera, his throat and face horribly disfigured. He slowed and stopped, turning toward the camera, then all of a sudden, without warning, he lunged at the camera and the cameraman holding it. The camera fell to the sidewalk and everything went sideways.

After that, nothing seemed to happen, until a small pool of blood slowly crept along the sidewalk, the corner of the lens catching it.

On the black and white set, the grey liquid didn't look that imposing, but both Carl and Clarence knew what it meant.

Gunshots echoed outside in the street and Clarence ducked lower, glancing out the window again to see if he could find the owner of the gunshots, but the street was empty. Only a few cars drove by infrequently. Evidently, most people were taking the warnings of the police seriously and staying indoors.

Clarence left the window and sat back down on the couch.

"Shit Carl, its really starting to get bad out there. What the fuck are we going to do?"

Carl shrugged, his eyes never leaving the television. "Shit if I know, man, I think we should just stay put until everything blows over."

Clarence frowned. "Christ, I should have stayed at my place. At least I have food in the refrigerator. I mean, look at this place, you've got nothing. If we have to stay here for a few days, we'll starve."

Carl looked around the apartment, nodding. "Shit, you're right. There's a Chinese supermarket at the end of the street. You want to go stock up on supplies?"

"You think they're open?" Clarence asked.

Carl smiled. "Open? Are you serious? They're Chinese. It could be friggin' Armageddon and they'd be open. That place never closes." He stood up and wiped a few crumbs from the stale bag of pretzels he'd been eating.

"You think its safe outside?" Clarence asked, moving towards the door.

"Hell if I know, but we've got to eat, so what choice do we have?"

Clarence nodded, said: "Good point," and opened the door.

Carl gestured for Clarence to go first and once he was through, Carl followed. Carl closed the door, but didn't lock it. Clarence noticed this and asked: "Aren't you going to lock your door?"

"Why?" Carl asked while the two men walked down the stairs that led to ground level.

"Why? So someone doesn't rob you," Clarence told him.

Carl chuckled. "That's a good one, Clarence. So what exactly are they going to take? My black and white television or my ten year old couch."

Clarence thought about that for a moment and then nodded. "Yeah, I see what you mean."

Carl only grunted a reply and stepped out onto the sidewalk. Dusk was just falling and the sky was a few different hues of orange with a mixture of red. Though looking over the buildings, he wondered if the reds he was seeing were the sun setting or the fires he'd been hearing about on the television.

"Come on, man, lets go. The sooner we're back inside the better," Clarence stated, walking down the street, his eyes trying to see into every alleyway and behind every car they passed.

Carl was more relaxed. After what he'd seen at the funeral home, he doubted anything could even come close to what he'd witnessed the day before.

As they moved down the block, crossing the street to the next one, what Carl didn't realize was that his assumption was very wrong.

* * *

The streets were eerily deserted, despite the fact it was going on seven in the evening. Crossing the first intersection, it was Clarence who spotted a dark figure moving towards them.

Both men stopped, too petrified to move, until the shape clarified into the clothes and face of a homeless man. When the man was closer, Carl could see it was old Abe, a local resident of the street. The man could often be seen begging for spare change on street corners and near the entrances of the T. The man would often ramble about God and the coming rapture. Of course, no one listened.

Carl patted Clarence on the shoulder, starting down the sidewalk once again.

"Relax, I know this dude, he's just some crazy old guy that hangs out around here." Carl said.

Clarence hesitated for another second and then followed Carl, trusting his friend. Carl knew how he felt. With things deteriorating in the city, it would have been nice to have some weapons to defend themselves with. But with Carl's record, a gun would be impossible to obtain. As for Clarence, well, Carl had never asked.

Old Abe started rambling as soon as Carl and Clarence were within earshot.

"Beware the walking dead! Beelzebub himself has sent his minions to punish the living. Now all the decadence humankind loves so much will be destroyed in a sea of death! You're all going to die!" Abe screamed, his eyes wide with paranoia. "What God creates, so too, can he destroy!"

Then he was past Carl and Clarence, continuing down the street, arms waving in the air like he thought he could fly if he just tried a little harder.

Clarence looked to Carl, a sly grin on his face. "Man, Carl, why are all you white people so damn crazy?"

Carl shrugged. "I think Abe is a special case, Clarence. He lost his nut in the Vietnam War. He saw some bad shit. Believe me, if you'd seen what he did, you'd be crazy, too."

"Yeah, well, he's still whacked," Clarence said and kept moving.

Carl chuckled. "Not going to get an argument from me."

The two men crossed the next intersection, only a few cars passing through to destinations unknown. A few of the cars were piled high with trunks and suitcases, the driver's faces wide with fear. Carl noticed this and pointed it out to Clarence.

"Looks like a bunch of people are leaving the city."

"That doesn't sound like such a bad idea to me Carl," Clarence replied.

"Look, I'm sure by tomorrow, or the next day, definitely, the police and shit will have everything under control. It's not like this is the first riot the cities ever seen."

Clarence had his hands in his pocket and he shrugged his shoulders slightly. "Whatever man, whatever."

Two blocks later, they had reached the market. The store was nothing but a square box, one-story high, entirely painted in white. There was one door, glass, at the corner of the building and above this in neat print were the words: **MARKET** and below that was the same thing spelled in Chinese, though Carl couldn't tell for sure, he just assumed it was spelling the words *market*.

There was a small parking lot on the side of the building, large enough to hold ten or twelve cars. At the moment there was only one car in the lot, a beat-up blue Volvo with more rust than paint covering it.

Both men stepped into the market, a tiny bell announcing their presence. Bright fluorescent lights bathed the store in a clean white glow, except for a few near the back which flickered constantly, as if they were secretly deciding if they were going to fail or try to stay lit for one more hour.

Behind the small counter was a small, Chinese man in a white coat and small wire-rimmed glasses. His black hair was parted to the side and his eyes were tiny. If the man stood an inch over five feet it was because of the shoes he wore.

Carl looked around the store, surprised. The shelves were almost completely empty, only a few ripped open boxes and dented cans were left, and some lay discarded on the floor.

"Holy shit, what the hell happened to this place?" Clarence asked, stepping into the market, his feet crunching on cornflakes covering the floor like a carpet.

"Many people come here today. All panicked. They buy everything I own. Now I don't know when new truck come with more supplies." His eyes actually managed to squint even more and he looked at Carl and Clarence suspiciously. "What you two want, I have no more food, there's nothing left."

"Whoa, there, fella, just calm down. We just want to grab a few things. We'll take whatever's left, okay?" Carl said calmly.

"You got money? No money, you go now. Some people steal food, I can't leave, so they rob me. I call the police, but they no come. It's crazy!" He pulled out a small wooden baseball bat and slammed it on the counter.

"Jesus, this guy's crazier than the bum!" Clarence yelled.

"Clarence man, show him you got money before he goes apeshit!" Carl said to Clarence, pushing his shoulder to make him move faster.

Clarence dug into his pants and pulled out a few twenties and a couple of one dollar bills, waving them in front of the clerk. "Look, man, its cool, I got money, so just chill, will ya?"

The clerk seemed to calm down slightly and he stopped banging the bat. Using it as a pointing tool, he directed it at the two men. "Fine, you go get what you want, then get back here. I'm closing soon, nothing left means why the hell stay here? Plus, my wife keeps calling me and telling me she scared."

Carl and Clarence did as they were told and quickly ran around the store picking up whatever was salvageable. Carl found a half box of crackers, a dented can of creamed corn and one of beets; man he hated beets. Two cans of tuna fish that had fallen under one of the shelves, probably kicked by some rushing customer and three bottles of water that had been missed in the back of the see-thru walk-in. Clarence had about the same, only he had a few cans of canned pasta and a box of bran flakes.

With both men carrying their purchases up to the counter, Carl looked at his friend. "You really think this is necessary, Clarence. I mean, Christ, look at what we've got to buy here."

Clarence shook his head. "Look, Carl, if all the food in the store is gone then that says something right there. Other people were thinking the same thing, except they got here a lot quicker then us. So let's just buy this crap and get back to your place before something else happens."

Getting to the counter, the clerk looked at the items and then at Clarence.

"What's wrong, man, ring this shit up." Clarence told him.

The clerk shook his head. "No need, how much you got in your hand there?"

Clarence looked down at the twenties and ones and quickly counted them. "I got sixty-four dollars, why?"

The clerk held out his hand. "That's the price, then."

"What? What kind of shit you pulling here, man? There's no way that stuff is worth sixty-four dollars!" Carl snapped at him.

The clerk shrugged. "Tough, you want it, that how much. Don't like it, then leave."

Carl's face grew dark with anger. He wondered if he'd be as mad if the man in front of him had been white or even black. It was just that with the broken English the clerk was spouting, it just seemed to piss him off even more.

"Well, what you do? Buy or leave, I don't care!" The clerk said angrily, waving his hand in front of him.

Carl looked down at the small clerk and seriously considered just decking the guy and taking whatever they could carry. From the looks on Clarence's face, he was pretty sure his friend was thinking the same thing.

Then rationality came to Carl and he let his anger go. Whether he liked it or not, the clerk was right, he didn't have to buy the food, despite the obvious price gouging.

"Man, just give the little chink his money and let's go," Carl told Clarence.

Clarence turned to look at Carl. "What, are you serious? Let this little fucker shake us down! No way, man."

"Look, we need the stuff and it's only money. I'll pay for half, I promise," Carl said.

Clarence stared at Carl for another three seconds and then with a muffled curse, tossed the money at the clerk. "Here ya go, you fucker, I hope you choke on it."

The clerk barely heard him, only picking up the cash from the counter and the floor where some had fallen by his feet.

The two men gathered their supplies and after packing them in a few plastic bags, left the store.

"Thank you, come again," the clerk called.

"Screw you, Apu!" Clarence called after him as they left the market. Once back on the street, the darkness had fallen completely, only the lights in the buildings and the street lights keeping the area illuminated.

"Just forget about him, man, it's not worth it. Let's just get back to my place and chill out," Carl said, walking across the street. It felt weird without the usual traffic on the streets. Crossing was too easy, without the challenge of dodging commuters.

"I can't, Carl, that little chink was a jerk. I should have beaten the shit out of him and just taken what we wanted. I mean, it's not like there are any cops around to stop us," Clarence said angrily.

Carl only nodded, knowing exactly what he meant. Instead, he tried to lighten the mood a little. "Hey, what's the idea of calling that guy Apu? Apu is an Indian or something, he's not Chinese," Carl said lightly.

"Yeah, so what, you got what I meant, excuse me if I don't know everything about the Simpsons like you do."

Carl winced. "It's not my fault. It was one of the main things I watched while I was in the can. Sorry if I said the wrong thing."

That made Clarence feel bad and he nudged his friend. "No, man, I'm sorry, too. I stepped over the line with that one. You know how I feel about you going to jail."

Carl smiled. "Thanks, its cool, I know what you meant."

The two friends walked silently for the next two blocks. There was only one more to go and as Carl passed by a dark alleyway on his right, he never saw the shapes shambling toward him.

Clarence did though, and he dropped his bag of groceries and shoved Carl past the alley and down onto the sidewalk. Carl rolled onto his side, groceries falling out of the bags in his arms. He was about to yell at Clarence for being so clumsy when he saw what had spurred his friend to shove him.

Coming out of the alley were four human shaped forms. But that's where the similarity ended. Carl could only lay there in shock as the four—what would you call them . . . *zombies*?—came to his mind in a flash.

He could only stare in shock as the four zombies charged out of the alleyway and swarmed over Clarence. With a muffled yell, Clarence was buried under the bloody bodies, his yells growing in pitch as he was ripped apart, his arms twitching from around his attackers until his limbs went slack.

Carl could see Clarence's left leg twitching heavily and then that, too, stopped and went still. Carl let out a muffled yell, holding his hand to his mouth to prevent it from escaping his lips.

One of the four ghouls turned to look at him. What was once a man in a three-piece business suit was missing one eye and had more then half his face ripped off, the red muscles and white of bone glistening under the streetlights. Carl started to crawl backwards like a crab and when he was no more then five feet away; he rolled over and pulled himself to his feet, running as fast as he could away from the carnage and his friend, who was surely dead by now.

Guilt flooded through him for abandoning Clarence, but self preservation overrode it. With arms pumping in front of him, he ran the last few blocks to his apartment building and ran through the doors to the lobby, taking the stairs two and three at a time. He fumbled with his keys, then remembering he'd left the door unlocked, he opened the door and charged inside, slamming the door shut behind him.

Leaning against the door, he slumped to the floor and placed his head between his knees, his hands covering the top of his head.

Despite his ears being muffled and the fact he had left Clarence three blocks away, he could have sworn he could still hear his friend screaming.

Chapter 12

THE NEXT FIVE days went by in a blur for Carl. He stayed inside his apartment, too afraid to leave its crumbling walls. Outside in the streets, things continued to become worse. Sitting on his couch, curled up in a ball, he watched his small television, keeping up to date with what was happening in the city by the news stations.

Martial law had been passed in Boston, the curfew at seven o' clock at night. Anyone found out on the streets after curfew was subject to arrest or worse, meaning they could be shot on sight. Carl had sat in the corner of his apartment, listening to the sounds of gunfire outside on the streets. The military was being true to their word and was shooting any citizens found out after curfew. There had been only one problem with that. Some of the citizens wouldn't go down even after being shot. In fact, after being shot they became even more aggressive, overwhelming the patrols and killing them in very gruesome ways.

One news report said that the victims of the attacks had gotten back up and had attacked their fellow soldiers, killing them horribly, but the newsman had made sure to comment that it was all speculation and rumor and highly doubted it was true.

On the fourth day, Carl had been sitting by the window, watching the street outside. Cars had stopped driving by days ago and the street looked like a war zone, crashed cars and a few stray bodies littering the pavement with small fires burning here and there.

Carl had been looking down the street when he saw a familiar face stumbling down the sidewalk. He didn't know how Clarence had survived his attack, but there he was, plain as day, walking down the sidewalk.

Carl was about to call out to him, when something told him to stop and wait.

Doing just that, he let Clarence stumble closer to his apartment building. The sun was high in the sky and it was easy to see Clarence's face. Only the right side of his face could be seen from Carl's vantage point and it was only when Clarence tripped over some debris on the sidewalk that Carl got a real good look at his friend.

His breath lodged in his chest and for a minute he couldn't breathe as he watched what was left of Clarence walk down the sidewalk. The left side of Clarence's face was almost nonexistent, only the white of his skull peering through. The left eye was missing and so was more then half his neck, ragged tear marks showing where teeth had sunk in and pulled the flesh from his body. As his friend turned to the side, Carl could see his right arm was hanging by a few tenuous strands of gristle, the arm swinging back and forth like a macabre pendulum.

Carl could only watch his friend stumble under his window and then move past the building, continuing down the street. Carl watched him for as long as he could see him and then fell to the floor, crying. His friend was definitely dead, but yet he was still walking around just like Aunt Mildred from the funeral home.

Though the reality of the situation was beyond unbelievable, the proof had just walked by his window.

Clarence was dead. And yet somehow, he was still alive.

If that wasn't the definition of a zombie, then he hadn't watched enough horror movies.

The realization that the dead were actually walking was somewhat refreshing to Carl. It explained everything that had happened to him, right from when Aunt Mildred had jumped out of her casket to go on a killing rampage. He wondered if the government had figured the obvious out yet. He highly doubted it, though he wasn't a scholar, he knew how bureaucracies worked. It would take the government another month at least to actually decide there was a real problem in Boston and by then it would be far too late to stop it.

Then he thought of something else. What if whatever was happening in Boston had somehow spread across New England. And worse yet, what if it continued spreading until the entire United States was infected.

Shaking his head, he decided thinking on such a large scale was irrelevant to his continuing existence. It was only when the power went out on the fifth day that he knew shit was really getting bad.

A massive explosion rocked his building and the rest of Boston and when he looked out his window, he could see a large smoke cloud rising from the direction of the Edison Power plant in South Boston. The Edison supplied all of Boston and more then a dozen of the surrounding suburbs. If something had happened there to cause it to explode, then the city was in real trouble. Without power, there would be no lights and no way to keep food from spoiling. Thank God it was spring and the heating systems in homes and buildings wasn't needed; the nights being relatively mild.

Carl watched the rising smoke cloud and then turned to look back at his raggedy apartment. He was down to his last box of saltines, all the food he and Clarence had salvaged from the market left on the sidewalk when he had run away. He sure as hell wasn't going to go get it, not with man-eating Bostonians running around.

Deciding he would need more food and have to leave the safety of the apartment or starve, he figured he'd see if any of his other neighbors were inside their rooms like him. He had thought he'd heard noise from the floor above him and below every now and then over the past few days.

Grabbing an old broom and taking off the brushes, he held the broomstick in his hands, waggling it back and forth for a second to see if it would work well as a weapon. Then deciding he was as ready as he was going to get, he opened his front door to go pay his neighbors a visit.

* * *

This was the first time he'd left his apartment since the attack on Clarence and himself on their way back from the Chinese market. Walking down the small hallway, he was surprised to see nothing looked any different. Outside in the street an explosion could be heard, sounding muffled by the walls of the apartment building and the faint sound of a car alarm drifted into the corridor, sounding more like an annoying alarm clock then an actual deterrent to crime.

He stopped a few feet down from his own front door and stood in front of his neighbor's door. He had heard nothing coming from the walls of his apartment and figured there was no one home, but a soft thump on the other side of the door told him differently.

With a shaking hand, he reached out to try the doorknob, surprised when it turned easily, the door opening an inch. He didn't really know if he was pleased or not about that. With the door open he would now have to go inside and investigate. Even if no one was home, maybe he could find some food in his neighbor's cabinets. He didn't know much about the woman who lived next to him. All he knew was she was overweight and wore nothing but hair curlers in her hair and pink muumuus; those overly large housecoats that fat men and women were so fond of.

Oh yeah, and she had a cat; a black one with a few stray white patches across its fur. Sometimes he would hear it howling at night, but it usually didn't last very long.

Opening the door wide enough to enter, he stuck his head inside the room.

There was no one inside. He debated calling out, but decided against it. Stepping into the apartment, he moved across the ugly green carpeting, slowing when he reached an area with a couch and coffee table of what was supposed to be the living room, but seemed more like a dumping ground for old food containers, celebrity magazines and TV guides.

So far so good, he thought.

Moving around the couch on his way to the kitchen, he slowed when his eyes spotted something on the carpeting, near the leg of the couch. He bent over to pick it up, having no idea what it could be until he held it in his hand.

Then he knew. It was the leg of a cat, ripped off at the joint. The limb drooped at the knee and he dropped it to the floor, totally creeped out.

"Oh, Jesus Christ," he mumbled to himself, now seeing the blood on the carpet near where the leg had been.

If the cat was missing a leg then what did that tell him about the animal itself? And if the cat did have a limb torn off then who exactly would do such a terrible thing to an innocent animal? Certainly not its owner, she loved that cat, he knew that much about her, anyway.

The bedroom door was closed. The layout of the apartment the same as his own and he decided the door could stay that way. Moving to the small kitchen, he stopped at the edge of the dirty linoleum. There, on the floor, was the rest of the black and white cat. The body was ripped open, its insides spread across the floor. Flies buzzed around the small corpse, feeding and laying eggs. The second he was over the small body, his nose picked up the smell. The animal hadn't been dead for very long, so the odor wasn't as bad as he thought it could be, but he could still smell the bile and blood. Turning away, he closed his eyes and tried to think of better things. He thought of pretty girls in bathing suits and beaches where the surf was pristine; not like Revere Beach, with its layers of seaweed covering everything.

When he thought he had control of himself and didn't think he was going to throw-up, he stepped over the small corpse and started rifling through the cabinets. He stayed away from the fridge, knowing with the power out nothing would be edible inside it.

He found a few canned goods and a stack of canned cat food. Deciding it was better then nothing, he loaded the canned food and the cat food into a couple of plastic bags he found in one of the drawers and then quickly finished searching through the rest of the cupboards for anything else that was edible.

Ten minutes later he was finished and quite pleased with himself.

With the two bags in his hand, plus the broomstick, he started to leave. He was halfway across the living room when he heard a thump coming from the bedroom, the door helping to muffle the noise.

"Hello? Is anyone in there? Do you need help?" He called to the door, not really wanting someone to answer. After all, what would he do if the woman had fallen down and hurt herself and needed help? He had enough to worry about with just himself; he didn't need some wounded woman to have to take care of, too.

The thump sounded again, louder this time.

"Hello? Can you here me in there? Look, I'm sorry I came in here uninvited, but I've got no food in my place and you know how bad it is outside. You understand right? I didn't even think you were in here. If you want, I'll leave this stuff on the couch and just leave!" He called to the door. "Oh and I'm sorry about your cat," he added after a moment.

Carl stood there in the middle of the living room, waiting for a reply from the bedroom.

He did get one, but it wasn't what he expected.

Without warning, the bedroom door burst outward, spraying jagged shards of wood across the room. Carl was far enough away not to be struck by any of the exploding debris, but it still made him yelp in surprise and turn away to shield his eyes. When he turned back around, his neighbor was pushing herself through the shattered door, bits of her skin catching on the jagged splinters. Blood dripped onto the floor and across the carpet as the woman forced her bulk through the opening.

Carl could only stare, too shocked to move while his neighbor squeezed through the frame and then started towards him. Carl's eyes first went to the jagged wound on her left arm, just about the size of a set of teeth. Carl had no way of knowing that she had gone outside a few days ago to get some groceries and had been attacked by a roving ghoul. The bite had quickly festered, killing her. But she had come back from the dead hungry, and the only thing in the apartment had been her beloved cat. So she had fed on it, until wandering into the bedroom and accidentally locking herself inside. She was content in there until hearing Carl's voice, then the hunger took over once again to the point that she knocked down the wafer thin door to reach him.

With a guttural growl, she leaned over like a dog and ran towards Carl. She was more then halfway across the room when Carl snapped out of his stupor. He screamed in fright and dropped the bags in his hands, desperately trying to bring the broomstick up in front of himself for protection. Like a charging bull, the woman came at him, Carl stuck the broomstick straight out, and turned his head away, too frightened to watch.

The woman literally ran into the broomstick, the dull point piercing her right eye and plunging into her brain. Carl felt the stick pulled from his hands and he screamed again, looking back to see what had happened.

His neighbor was lying on the carpet, twitching, the broomstick poking out of her head like a macabre flagpole. Carl didn't move, but just stared. Her skin was a pale white and he could see her veins easily, as if her skin had become translucent. Moving closer, he nudged the body with his foot, prepared to jump away when she moved, but she remained still, only a few farts escaping the bloated corpse.

He decided she could have his broomstick and he quickly picked up the plastic bags of food and got the hell out of there, taking an extra second to lock the door behind him. If she wasn't dead then at least there would be a locked door between her and the hallway.

Deciding he'd had enough for one day, he carried his food back to his apartment and after locking the door and taking an extra moment to push the couch in front of it; he let himself sigh with relief. He was safe, or as safe as he could be in a city gone mad.

Once he knew the door was as secure as it was going to get, he decided to unpack his scavenged food.

For the next three days, while the city fell apart around him, he survived on the food he had salvaged from his neighbor and water from the toilet. The smell of his neighbor's decaying corpse began to seep through the walls and he wondered how long he would be able to take it before the smell would be overwhelming. That was when he started to wonder if he should just leave. He didn't know where to go, but anywhere had to be better then in the city. As if to punctuate his thought, another explosion rocked the neighborhood, a gas main rupturing into a large fireball three streets over. The fires weren't close, at least not yet, so he tried to ignore them, instead concentrating on playing solitaire with his deck of cards. That made him think of Clarence and a pang of guilt and loss flooded through him. Clarence had pushed him out of the way of the attacking ghouls. His friend had saved his life while sacrificing his own. And now there was no way he could ever repay him for his bravery.

Sighing, and placing the Jack over the Queen, he wiped the one tear that rolled down his cheek, trying to force the bad memories away.

Chapter 13

O N THE MORNING of the fourth day after the incident with his neighbor, with the sun barely touching the sky, the decision to stay in his apartment or try to escape the city was taken from him.

The smell of smoke, oily and caustic, was coming in through the front window, threatening to suffocate him. Running to the window, he looked outside at the blackness covering the street. Though the sun had been up for almost an hour, it appeared to be dusk, the smoke so thick it blotted out the sky.

Flames licked the side of his apartment building, more then half the neighborhood already burning.

Coughing and struggling to breathe, Carl half-ran, half-crawled, towards his front door and stumbled out into the hallway. The air was slightly better in the hallway, the lack of windows helping to keep the smoke from infiltrating the building's interior, but it would only be a matter of time before the entire building was on fire and filled with smoke.

He paused when he saw a body on the stairs leading to the floor above him. Whoever it had been was a mystery; nearly the entire portion of their head had been blown off, the wall behind the corpse painted a black-maroon color, the face indistinguishable from that of a human being. He'd remembered hearing the loud report of a gun a day or so ago, but he had been sleeping at the time and had just assumed it had happened out on the street.

Stumbling to the stairs, his eyes watering from the smoke, he kept his gaze away from the gruesome corpse and climbed to the ground floor. He was so preoccupied with escaping the building, he didn't even think about who or what could be waiting outside for him.

He found out soon enough when the first thing he saw upon exiting his apartment building was a walking, burning corpse. So much of the flesh and clothes were scorched it was hard to define the actual gender of the figure and frankly, Carl didn't really give a damn.

The figure stumbled towards him, arms outstretched as if the figure wanted to give him a hug. Carl could see a little through the flames and the figure's eyes stared directly at him, though they appeared to be cooking in their sockets like hard-boiled eggs.

Carl jumped away from the stumbling corpse, the flaming ghoul tripping over its own two feet and falling to the sidewalk in a heap of ash and glowing embers. Carl didn't hang around to see what would happen next, but instead ran off down the street. He knew to go deeper into the city would be suicide, so he ran south, hoping he could get to Dorchester or Roxbury and maybe then, either find someplace to hide or grab a car and drive further south to Rhode Island or Connecticut. At the moment, anywhere was better then where he was.

While he ran through the streets, other people surrounded him, some with bags or small suitcases in their hands. Evidently he wasn't the only one trying to leave Boston. All wore masks of exhaustion and worry on their faces as they shuffled down the middle of Washington Ave, resembling the ghouls they were running from. All had vacant stares and slack jaws. Children were pulled along behind parents, screaming they were tired and hungry.

A helicopter flew by overhead, military by the look of it, the machine gun hanging out the side door a dead giveaway.

It hovered slowly over the streets, fanning the smoke into billowing clouds until it continued on to God knew where. A few seconds later, Carl heard gunshots, the staccato of a machine gun firing at something. Then an explosion ripped through the nearby streets, and Carl felt the ground rumble with its passing. The helicopter was shooting at something, that was for sure.

Carl watched it fly away, wishing he was sitting in the passenger seat right now, but he knew that was just wishful thinking. If he was going to get out of the city alive, he would have to count on himself, and only himself.

Turning around, he checked behind him, making sure no one was sneaking up on him. In the rolling clouds of smoke covering the street, he saw shambling figures moving about. They couldn't have been regular people because they moved about easily, ignoring the smoke that would have suffocated anyone that would have to breathe to live. And if that was true, then that could only mean one thing. That the figures in the smoke were already dead.

Deciding he should move a little faster, he started jogging, leaving the other refugees behind. After the first ten minutes, he was alone once again, the few people he had seen far behind him. He guessed it paid to travel light, though when he became hungry he was in real trouble. Two Army trucks full of personnel rolled by him, and he quickly got out of the street. Soldiers wearing gas masks and holding rifles at the ready watched him while the trucks rolled by. Not knowing what to do, he smiled and waved at them, holding his thumb out like a hitchhiker, hoping he wouldn't get shot if he appeared friendly. That would be all he'd need, to get shot by some hick in a uniform who thought he was one of the walking dead. One of the soldiers shook his head no and flipped him off, then the truck passed by him and rumbled out of sight, swallowed by the rolling smoke.

When the truck was fifty feet away, he started running again, hoping to be well on his way before another convoy came by.

When he reached the Dorchester city limits, he slowed his movements to a walk. He had never been comfortable with visiting Dorchester or Roxbury, fearing being either mugged or assaulted. The news stations would always be reporting on another drive-by shooting or murder in one of the urban cities, not to mention what would happen at night when the black gangs came out to play. If one of the gangs found him now, he'd probably end up wishing he'd been caught by one of the roving ghouls running around Boston. But it was still daylight, barely past noon, and in the daytime, when the gangs slept, it was usually safe, only hard working folk up and about on their way to work or bringing their children to school, though with the ongoing crisis, that piece of normalcy was probably shot to hell; the streets now resembling a war-torn, third-world country. Dorchester was more then sixty-percent black, the same as Roxbury, though in recent years other races had been slowly moving into the area and nearby communities to live and raise families, which was similar to what had happened in East Boston. East Boston had once been almost entirely Italian, now only a very small percent was left, the other ninety-five percent a mix of Spanish, Chinese, and Vietnamese descent. But Carl figured with the dead walking, people should have more important concerns than the color of someone's skin or race affiliation.

The streets were deserted here, also, but with the large conflagration behind him, he could see more easily, the smoke not as bad now, though the fires were slowly encroaching on the nearest cities next to Boston. A few small fires burned in some of the buildings and an old Ford minivan burned in the middle of the street. First floor windows were broken and shattered; at first glance looking like the damage was from rioters or looters. No matter where you lived in the world, there would always be people that would want to take advantage of any situation whether good or bad. Shots rang out a few streets over and he ducked instinctually, not wanting to be struck by a stray bullet.

A few dark, yet pale, vacant faces watched him from second and third floor windows, but when he looked their way, the faces seemed to dissolve back into the darkness of each framed window. He wondered if they were alive or dead. And if they were the latter, was it because they were too stupid to figure out how to get out of the building? Or perhaps they had plenty of food in there with them. Had they eaten their friends and neighbors and other family members?

Deciding he should just keep moving because he really didn't want an answer, he crossed the street and continued on. There was a soda machine in front of a ravaged convenience store, the machine busted open and cans of Coke and Pepsi spread out on the sidewalk like fallen change from an old man's pocket. Snatching a loose plastic bag blowing around in the wind, he picked up a few less dented cans, cracking open two of them immediately and downing each one in seconds. Feeling better with a partially full stomach—even if it was only soda—he let out a loud burp, then decided to move on.

A few minutes later, he found a bicycle lying on the sidewalk; no one around to claim it. Checking over his shoulder to make sure no one would shoot his ass if he took it, he picked up the bike and a second later was pumping hard, riding through the street and around a few stalled and abandoned cars like a bicycle messenger late to pickup a package in the city; the plastic bag full of cans bumping his knee while he pedaled.

He rode for the next ten minutes and slowed when he saw a church at an intersection. Though he wasn't overtly religious, he did believe in God, his parents raising him Catholic. As he stood there in the middle of the empty street, he felt the church calling to him. Deciding he could use a moment's respite, he pedaled to the front of the church and leaned the bike against one of the stone columns at the bottom of the carved, marble steps. Slowly walking up the steps, he paused at the grand double doors.

Pulling on the left one, it opened easily. Not much of a surprise, really. Churches usually kept their doors unlocked, welcoming worshipers at all hours.

Stepping into the shadows and gloom, he waited while his eyes adjusted to the lack of light. The main floor of the church was on the second floor and he walked up a set of wide, circling stairs. He stopped for a second when he saw large words spray-painted on the wall of the stairwell. **REPENT, THE END IS HERE**, was sprawled across the wall, defacing the church. Carl gulped, wondering if maybe he should just turn around and leave. But if there was a chance of finding help, a church would be the place to find it. He started to hear a weird sound, a whining sound that he couldn't put his finger on. And as he moved closer to the main floor, the sweet smell of decaying meat came to his nose. A small voice in his head told him to turn around and leave, but now his curiosity was peaked, and though he knew he was being foolish, he continued to the top of the stairs.

Reaching the main floor, he slowed as he looked out on the rows of pews and the front podium at the opposite end of the church. He let out a gasp of shock at the sight before him. The pews were filled with dead bodies, all in different stages of decay. Some appeared as if they could have been there for weeks, while others looked like the people were just sleeping. It was then that he realized what that whining sound had been. The light in the church was dim, but he could make out something he thought he'd never see in his lifetime. Thousands of flies filled the church, permeating the air like a massive, moving cloud as they fed on the rotting flesh of the corpses. Some of the closest bodies were covered in maggots, their flesh nothing but a rolling landscape of insectoid life.

Appalled at the grotesque scene below him, he backed away, kicking an errant piece of wood lying on the floor. The wood clattered across the tile, the noise rebounding off the acoustic ceiling. Carl stopped moving, expecting the bodies to jump up and see him, and then come for him, but none did.

No wait!

There were a few moving about, but they were at the other end of the church and not a threat. He could be down the stairs and gone before they had crossed half the hall.

As he stood there at the top of the stairs, he looked to his left and right, where a set of double doors were on each side of him. Opposite these doors on both sides of the church were more stairwells. That way the parishioners could leave easily and not be crowded by using only the one set of stairs, not to mention fire codes. Even God couldn't overcome the city bureaucracy and had to be up to code.

Then he heard a pounding coming from the other end of the main hall to his left where the other set of stairs were.

It was only the footsteps of one person and he stopped and waited. Maybe someone else was alive? It had to be. He couldn't be the only one left; that would be ridiculous.

The pounding grew louder and a second later the double doors were thrown open. Light cascaded into the room, the hallway lined with stained-glass windows. The figure moved closer to Carl, but with the light behind him, he couldn't tell who it was.

"Hello, who's there? Can you help me?" Carl asked hesitantly.

Stepping closer still, the figure moved deeper into the hall, now close enough for Carl to see the white collar on the man's neck.

Carl outwardly relaxed. "Oh thank God, Father, can you help me? What happened here? There are so many bodies. Why doesn't someone come and help you?"

The priest kept coming, never slowing and Carl took a step backward, realizing something wasn't right.

"Father?" He asked one more time. Then the priest was far enough inside the hall that Carl could see his face clearly. The man's face was ash white and his hair was an uncombed mess. But it was the eyes that freaked Carl out the most. He'd seen those eyes before, on the dead people walking around outside.

"Oh shit, Father? Tell me your not one of them," he said softly. The priest never slowed, but opened his mouth and let out a scream that filled the church and bounced off the walls. Carl looked to his right and saw more bodies standing up now, the flies filling the church and blotting out what light there was.

Carl decided it was time to leave and as he backed away, the priest came at him. Panicking, Carl swung the bag of soda at the priest's face, knocking the man to the floor. One of the cans burst in the bag and the bag started to drip soda onto the floor. The priest rolled onto his side and hissed at Carl, then started to crawl at him on all fours. Carl shrieked and slammed the bag of cans onto the top of the ghoul's head, the priest dropping to the floor, dazed. Carl could already see the priest was starting to move again, but Carl didn't wait around to see it happen. Waving away the thousands of flies now filling the air around him, he ran down the stairs two at a time, having to keep his mouth closed or risk swallowing flies.

The buzzing of a thousand tiny wings filled his ears, blocking out all sound. But then a moaning pierced through the whining and he looked over his shoulder to see dozens of bodies now heading towards him. Now he ran down the stairs, almost tripping and falling head first, reaching the double doors at the front and throwing them open.

A ghoul was waiting for him, but Carl was moving so fast he knocked the dead woman over, the body tumbling down the stairs like a sack of laundry. Carl followed her, and when he landed on the sidewalk, he heard the unmistakable sound of a neck cracking.

Picking up his bicycle, he glanced at the dead woman to see her twitching on the ground, her head hanging on her back like a jacket thrown over a shoulder to carry on a warm spring night.

After that he didn't care, but started to pedal again, just as the doors of the church opened and scores of the undead poured out. He glanced back once and thought he saw smoke, but then he realized it was all the flies, finally free of their holy prison.

Then he concentrated on pedaling and leaving the cursed church behind him.

* * *

He had covered three blocks when he finally slowed the bike down and stopped, planting his feet on either side of him. Though the street was deserted here, as well, it still felt slightly different, though he couldn't put his finger on it.

A screen door flapped in the slight breeze and a dog howled from somewhere. And something else, too.

The sound was distant, caught on the wind and slowly being blown his way.

It was an eerie sound, like a thousand dead souls were crying for release from their bodies. Carl stood motionless, his eyes trying to see every which way at the same time. He spotted a dead body lying in-between a couple of parked cars only a few feet away from him. He glided over to it to investigate and wished he hadn't. The corpse had been decapitated; the stomach and chest ripped open to expose the insides to the sun. Dried blood covered the pavement and continued under the nearest car. Carl had to look away or risk vomiting again. He had never been good with the sight of blood and lately, he'd seen enough to last him a lifetime.

The sounds of wailing increased and he turned to look behind him, at the nearest intersection. There was an Exxon gas station on the left and a small convenience store on the right. Numerous small stores selling clothes and trinkets filled in the rest of the corner.

Carl watched the corner, almost as if he could feel something was going to appear. And then it happened.

The first body shambled around the intersection and came into view, more then a thousand behind it. Carl's jaw dropped as he watched the unimaginable sight. Body after body stumbled around the corner and onto the street, like some form of bizarre migration.

The sounds the crowd made caused a chill to crawl up his back. A second later the unimaginable smell of death and decay assaulted him, causing him to cover his nose and try to breathe through his mouth. The slowly rotting bodies were covered with flies and crows and seagulls darted around them, diving in to rip a particularly juicy morsel from a face or neck.

In the light of the day, with eyes watering from the smell, he was able to see their faces clearly. Black, White, Chinese, Spanish, Indian, and Lebanese; all the different cultures and races of Boston's population, all marching together.

Though Carl wasn't necessarily an insightful man, he couldn't help but notice the irony of the approaching crowd. In life, these people had clashed constantly from everything to religion to how each race dressed. But in death, they were one and the same, all working toward the same purpose. No more prejudices between them, only the same goal.

To eat him.

Wouldn't it have been nice if these same people could have gotten along when they were alive?

And there was no question in Carl's mind that the entire crowd pouring into the street was dead. From where he stood, watching, he could see the gaping wounds on necks and chests. Stomachs were ripped open, trailing intestines behind them. Others were missing limbs and walked lopsided, not used to the missing appendages. Others still had faces that were nothing but tendons and small bits of flesh still hanging, eyes gone. The ones with missing eyes kept one hand on the creature in front of it, leading it to wherever the crowd marched.

The moaning, howling sound filled Carl's ears, almost making him want to drop to the street and cover his ears with his hands. He felt his testicles curl up inside him, the fear was so strong. He knew he should get moving, but his legs wouldn't move, the sight of the ghastly march of the dead overwhelming his sense of reason and what was supposed to be normal in the world.

A metal trash can rattled behind him and he swung his head around to see more walking corpses coming out of alleyways and from inside first floor doorways.

If he didn't move soon, it wouldn't matter. He would be surrounded and soon he would be caught, ripped to pieces; and then what? If he was lucky there would be enough of him left to join their ranks . . . or would it be better to be consumed so that there was nothing left to return?

Shaking his head, he slowly snapped out of his fright,

"No way, man. I ain't going out like that," he mumbled to himself, hoping to psych himself up.

A ghoul shuffled at him from the right, the meter maid uniform still easily discernable in places, despite the gallons of blood covering it, and Carl used his foot to kick the walking corpse away from him. The massive parade of the undead was only twenty feet from him when he turned his back on them and started pedaling the bicycle. More filled the street, seeming to appear from nowhere. He weaved in and around the slow moving corpses as they tried to reach out and grab him.

One ghoul, an old black woman wearing a bloody housecoat, managed to grab his shirt and Carl let out a frightened yell as he shrugged out of her grasp and left her his shirtsleeve for her trouble. Then he was through the worst of them, the other ghouls that had appeared joining the massive crowd and all continuing down the street, filling it so full of bodies some had to wait while others shuffled by.

He rode for the next two hours, leaving Dorchester behind and pedaling into Roxbury. Roxbury was the same, if a little more destroyed. Fires burned everywhere and cars littered the streets, abandoned and broken. Graffiti covered the sides of buildings, unnamed artists declaring their love for this and their hatred of that.

He was glad he was on a bicycle. If he had tried to steal a car, he wouldn't have made it more then a mile before becoming trapped. This way, even if the road was choked with debris, he could always climb over it with the bike on his back. A shot ricocheted off the asphalt no more then a foot from him and he swore and pedaled faster. Ghouls were here as well, though, but spread out enough he was able to pedal around them easily.

He wondered who had shot at him. Did the mysterious shooter think he was one of the dead? So far Carl hadn't seen any of the ghouls do anything but walk and eat living people. If they could ride a bicycle, or shoot a gun, it was news to him.

While he rode through Roxbury, more corpses shambled out into the light, all trying to reach him. He knew he had to keep moving. There would be no salvation in this city. Like Boston, it was now filled with the dead.

He was more then halfway through the ravaged city and nearing the outskirts of it when he saw a small sign on one of the street corners that directed him to the Blue Hills Mountains. That gave him an idea. The Blue Hills was all woods and mountains, a perfect place to go to get away from the ghouls and yet not go so far away that when everything went back to normal he couldn't return easily.

Turning the bike up the next street, he pedaled harder, following the sign toward the Blue Hills Mountains and hopefully, safety. While behind him, the undead mob followed; one small step at a time.

Chapter 14

JUST BEFORE HE reached the city limits and the surrounding buildings began to disappear to be replaced by trees and overgrown shrubbery, he was stopped cold.

He had been so busy concentrating on pedaling the bicycle, he had lost track of his surroundings. Before he realized it, he was becoming surrounded by fresh, walking corpses.

They had silently crept out of nearby buildings and alleyways. Some had seemed to almost hide behind cars until he passed them by, only to pop out and follow his trail. For one brief moment, he wondered if they had actually set a trap for him. He hoped not. Up until now, all the ghouls seemed to act like cattle, simply moving about looking for food, namely him. If they had intelligence, then that would be an entirely new ballgame.

He looked to his left and then to his right, trying to find a hole he could scoot through on the bicycle, but as he watched, the ranks of the undead closed, until he would be caught as soon as he tried to escape them.

Dropping the bike to the street, he decided he'd be better off running, then riding. There was a small gap on his left and he took off at a sprint, hoping to reach it before the ranks of the dead closed it like a vise, trapping him inside.

He barreled past a young, dead child, no more then ten. Small hands flailed out, trying to grab him, and for a moment they succeeded. But Carl's body weight was greater and the tight grip the child had on him only caused the child to fly off its feet, falling to the pavement to smash its face against the asphalt.

The dead child got a serious case of road rash, but ignored it, the tiny hands never letting go of Carl's shirt. Carl kept pulling and in another second and a mighty heave, the last good sleeve he had on his shirt gave way, the threads parting, leaving the prone child with nothing but a piece of material for its trouble. Carl ran like a football player trying to reach the end zone. When a ghoul dived at him, he zigzagged to the left or right when needed, always just staying out of reach of its grasping hands.

His eyes scanned the area, trying to find a place to run, but it was hopeless, he was outnumbered and outclassed. A dead homemaker tried to bite his shoulder and he screamed, jumping away from her, only to fall into another's clutches. Pale hands reached out and wrapped themselves around him and Carl let his body drop to the ground, his form slipping through the torn and shredded arms.

The ghoul stared at the air in-between its arms, not understanding why its prey had disappeared.

Carl stayed low on the street, crawling on hands and knees between the legs of the roving ghouls. This worked for a few more seconds, but then the undead got wise to his game and started looking down by their feet for their slippery prey.

Carl realized his ruse was over and jumped to his feet, dodging more arms. He knew it was only a matter of seconds before he was finally caught and munched on for a midday snack. His eyes spotted an abandoned truck, the words **Hostess** scrawled across the side. The bread truck was half-on, half-off the sidewalk, and the nose of the truck was inside a small boutique.

Knowing it was his only chance, Carl made a dash for it, barely avoiding the teeth and hands that reached out for his body.

Reaching the front of the truck, he scrambled onto the hood and then up onto the roof while the dead tried to follow. With his butt firmly planted on the roof, he used his legs to kick off any of the undead trying to follow him. Bodies flew from the hood to land in the midst of the crowd. The wind shifted and for the first time, Carl noticed the awful fragrance of the crowd. He scanned their clothing, seeing numerous wet spots and brown stains from when bowels and bladders had let go upon that person's particular death. Now the urine and offal only added to the smell of exposed wounds, rotting in the sunlight. He had to wonder, if this was how they smelled after only a week or so, then what would be the fragrance like in another two to three weeks?

Another ghoul, a teenaged girl no more then sixteen, tried to scamper up the windshield and reach him. Carl waited patiently until her head was even with him and he sent the sole of his shoe into her face.

He could feel the teeth and nose giving way and watched the body flail for a moment in midair until gravity took over and pulled her to the sidewalk below her. Her head struck the cement with a meaty thump and the back of her skull ruptured, pink and red brains spilling out onto the sidewalk where they were promptly crushed underneath the shuffling feet of the crowd.

Carl noticed briefly that with the insides of her head painting the sidewalk, she didn't get back up again, though her arms and legs continued to twitch as if they had a mind of their own. Carl filed the information in the back of his head for further contemplation later . . . if he had a later.

Another ghoul tried to crawl up the grille of the bread truck, but then she lost her footing, slipping back to the ground. While Carl watched the dead woman scrambling for a better grip, he thought she reminded him of his mother. He wondered if she was alright. She had a small condo on the edge of East Boston, near the shore. He had always enjoyed the view from her living room window when he would visit her. The Tobin Bridge hovered about a half mile from her building and he had always marveled at the monstrous structure. He would always think about the men who built it all those years ago and if their family members would brag about it to others. How their fathers and grandfathers had helped to build the mighty bridge that connected Boston to the suburbs of northern Massachusetts.

He also had many of his childhood memories wrapped up in East Boston. His grandfather had lived there, as well as his mother, and he had been an eccentric old man that the entire neighborhood had loved. His mother had been Italian and had come over from Naples, Italy when she was sixteen. Her father, though he had loved being in America, could never shake who he once was. So he had taken a burned out open lot two blocks from his house and had made it into a lush garden, filled with tomatoes, grapes, peppers, and cucumbers that he would then distribute among his neighbors every harvest. He had even used wine barrels to catch the rainwater runoff from the shed and so had a free supply of water, just like he had done on his farm in Italy, where what he grew was what he ate. He had used old wooden sheets and planks he'd found in the neighborhood to build a fence around the lot and had then made a small shack where he had raised rabbits. Carl fondly remembered petting one of the rabbits on a Sunday when he would visit his grandfather, only to return the next week and see the same rabbit was now cooked, cleaned and on the dinner table. That was when Carl had learned that in Italy his mother had eaten pigeons. Not the filthy, city pigeons you'd find in all the urban cities, but regular, clean birds that were raised for just this reason. Carl had always wondered if they tasted like chicken. Years later when his grandfather had passed away, it had been like destroying a landmark when the owner of the lot had dictated the garden had to go.

A groan caught his attention and he kicked another ghoul off the windshield, chastising himself for becoming careless. He quickly moved his butt to the left to get a better position on the roof and also to keep away from the sides of the bread truck.

For the moment, he seemed to be at a stalemate. Though he couldn't escape, the undead crowd around him couldn't reach him. As long as he stayed alert and watched the windshield for climbing ghouls, he'd be safe.

But for how long could he keep this up? He was already hungry and thirsty, his stomach rumbling incessantly, and it felt like he could use a weeks worth of sleep. Just how long could he stay on watch until his guard finally dropped and they managed to crawl up the hood of the truck and pull him down into their waiting clutches?

A dead, black man with a torn out jugular stood below the passenger window, eyes vacuous, jaw slack. He was about the same age as Clarence had been before he was killed. In fact, the ghoul reminded Carl so much of his dead friend that Carl felt a twinge of guilt riding up on him again. Had he done everything to help his friend when they had been attacked after leaving the market? Or had he run away like a coward.

No one would ever know but him and he still hadn't come to terms with what had happened just yet. There had been a little too much other stuff to deal with then to wallow in self pity. But now, as he sat trapped in the middle of a city filled with the undead, and the initial terror began to drain away, he found he had nothing to do but think. He wondered once again how long he could live on top of a bread truck without food or water, and as he watched the reaching hands and pale white faces of the dead, moaning and growling for him, he knew he would find out soon enough . . . just not that soon he hoped.

Chapter 15

NIGHT CAME AND went, followed by morning, and no one came to rescue him. On the afternoon of his second day on the bread truck, he was beginning to give up hope. Boston was still in flames, the smoke rising into the distant sky, coloring the horizon black.

His stomach had stopped rumbling, almost as if it had accepted the fact that no food would be entering it today. Despite the fact that he hadn't eaten or taken in any liquids, he felt it was incredibly ironic that he still had to urinate and defecate. Deciding he really didn't have much of a choice on where to go, he had just pulled his pants down and stuck his ass over the edge of the truck, and then sent a smelly loaf down to the asphalt.

A dead man in a policeman's uniform happened to stagger under his butt just as he let go and the dead man got hit right in his upturned face, the runny refuse seeping into his mouth and nose. The dead cop didn't seem to care, only lowered his head so his mouth would become clear and then its face was turned back up to Carl, its hands reaching out and upward, wanting nothing more then to pull Carl from his safe haven.

Pulling up and fastening his pants, Carl turned and looked down at his handiwork, smiling. Talk about poetic justice.

"There ya go, pal, hope it tasted good. I've been eating the shit you and your pals have been throwing at me for two damn years; nice to see the shoe is on the other foot for a change!"

If the zombie cop understood him, he didn't let on. Carl decided he was cracking up. What was he thinking, talking to dead people like they were going to answer him.

He looked out at the surrounding street, sighing. More dead people had arrived in the night, the darkness covering their arrival. Carl had hated the night the worst. It was almost pitch black with all the streetlights and lights from the nearby buildings extinguished. He'd had to fight off the scurrying ghouls with nothing but his feet, using the dim moonlight to see by. The moon was only a half crescent in the sky and with heavy cloud cover, the illumination had been dismal. But he had managed to survive until dawn and then until the afternoon.

He was tired though, the lack of food and water kicking his ass. Not to mention the boredom. All he had to do to keep himself occupied was to watch the ghouls moving about below him. He had made a game of it, trying to see which faces reminded him of people he knew, whether they were real people or just actors on television or in the movies. This had passed the time for hours until he just couldn't do it anymore. So he changed the game. The next one was to see how many ghouls he could kick off the windshield of the bread truck and where they would land after he sent them flying off the truck. Heads or tails, or something in-between were the choices. That had kept him occupied for a short amount of time, but his rumbling stomach had stopped him from focusing too much on anything other then wanting to eat.

Across the street from where he was trapped on the truck, a deli stood, with shattered windows and an open front door. Carl watched as ghouls stumbled into the dwelling only to exit holding chunks of deli meat. His mouth watered while he watched them devour the cold cuts and he had to stop himself from just jumping off the truck and running to the deli. But he knew he wouldn't get ten feet before he was caught and killed.

Late afternoon on the second day, he felt his strength waning. The sun had been strong and had done a number on him and he was almost caught and pulled off the truck when he let his guard down once and nodded off. At the last second, he managed to twist away and kick the ghoul to the sidewalk, where it landed in a heap of arms and legs, its neck snapping with the sound of a dry tree branch. It wasn't dead though. With its head horizontal with its shoulders, it stood back up and resumed the struggle to get him once more. Carl nodded at this. The ghouls may have been carnivorous cannibals, but you had to give them credit for persistence.

After that Carl had stayed focused, though after another hour had passed, he felt his attention slipping once more.

He was just nodding off when he thought he heard the sound of an engine, the throaty roar of a diesel engine to be exact. At first he just figured he was imagining it, but as the minutes passed, he stood up and gazed toward the end of the long street.

At first he didn't understand what he was seeing, only the large yellow plow, similar to what he'd find on a snow plow, appearing. But as the bulldozer grew closer, he started to jump up and down, waving his hands, praying he'd be spotted. A few ghouls tried to sneak behind him now, hoping he wasn't paying attention, but he simply spun around and kicked their heads like they were footballs, shattering jaws and caving in chins with the blows.

The bulldozer slowly came closer, the front plow now lowered and being used for what it was intended for, namely as a plow. Bodies were either forced to the sides or knocked away, or worse, merely driven over when the large, front black tires and the rear treads would flatten and pulverize the twitching corpses to mush.

The squelching sounds of the bodies being crushed made Carl cringe, but he ignored it, knowing if he tried to vomit the dry heaves would kick his ass.

Finally, the bulldozer was almost prepared to pull up alongside him, a woman hanging out the passenger side, waving a white rag.

"Jump on when we get close enough! But be quick, if we stop, they'll just climb on and we'll never get them off!" She yelled to him. Carl nodded, understanding. The only reason the cab of the bulldozer was free of bodies was because the vehicle had kept moving, never giving the ghouls a chance to climb onto the tires.

Carl readied himself, moving to the rear of the bread truck. The second he moved away from the windshield of the truck, ghouls began climbing onto the roof. Five were on top of the roof in the first three seconds of Carl abandoning his post. He was committed now. If something happened and the bulldozer's driver decided to change his mind, it would spell the end of Carl.

But the bulldozer continued forward and though weak from lack of hunger, Carl's adrenalin was pumping.

Escape at last! He thought excitedly.

He timed it just right and when the bulldozer drove even with the bread truck, he jumped, the small gap between the two vehicles seeming like the Grand Canyon. But he was over in a fraction of a second and when he had a firm grip on a stray pipe, the bulldozer's driver gunned the engine, black smoke spewing from the vertical exhaust. The bulldozer bucked and Carl had to reach out and hold on tighter or risk being thrown into the horde of death below him. He felt like he was on a ship in rough waters, the bulldozer bouncing and jumping as it pushed and crushed body after body while it made its way through the crowded street.

A side window opened on the cab and the woman who had called to him smiled. "Just hold on and once we're through the worst of it we'll pull over and let you get inside with us. There's not a lot of room, but you can sit on my lap!" She yelled over the roaring engine.

Carl could only nod in reply while the vehicle bucked and rolled beneath him. Even as he held on for dear life, he couldn't help but notice the woman who had talked to him was quite attractive. Though her face and hair were streaked with dirt and grease from the bulldozer, Carl could see she was about his age and had a nice smile. He knew he shouldn't be thinking about sex at a time like this, but he couldn't help himself. Then the bulldozer bounced over a particularly heavy knot of bodies and he had to hug the frame of the bulldozer or risk tumbling to his death.

Eventually, the street was vacated and the driver continued onward. So far all he could see of the driver was that it was a man, the driver's back always facing him. Carl could only sit and wait for the large machine to stop. He was a passenger and these people had saved his life, the last thing he was going to do is complain because they wouldn't stop. The farther he got from that damn bread truck, the better.

The bulldozer continued down the street, turning at the next intersection. The plow was head height now, the driver still easily able to see in front of him. Every now and then a stumbling corpse would step in front of the bulldozer.

It was a big mistake.

The bulldozer would just barrel along, the plow decapitating the bodies and then continuing on, crushing the bodies under it's already gore covered treads.

Carl looked behind them and was surprised to see the crowd of dead still following them, though the bulldozer was quickly pulling away. The dead parade kind of shuffle-jogged after them, arms out in front of them as if they could just reach out and pull them to their dead chests.

Soon, the city was in the distance and the road opened up. Civilization slowly faded away to be replaced by trees and shrubs. Signs of man were still everywhere, though, gas stations and small restaurants lined the road, enticing travelers to pull over and take a break.

A small rest stop was on the right side of the two-lane blacktop and the bulldozer pulled into it. A low hanging electrical wire drooped across the lot and the bulldozer's plow caught it, ripping the wire from the nearby pole.

But instead of a shower of sparks cascading down around them, nothing happened. The power was off here, as well, and if it hadn't been, it was likely they all would have been fried from the sparking wire.

With a final surge of the engine, the driver shut off the motor and silence descended around them.

Carl's ears were ringing. After listening to the rumbling engine for so long, he wondered if he'd ever be able to hear right again.

The doors of the cab opened and the woman and a man dropped to the ground. Following their lead, he slid off the back of the machine and waited patiently.

He had no reason not to believe these folks were friendly, but with everything that had been happening, you never really knew anymore.

The man reached into his jacket and pulled out a pack of Marlboros, quickly lighting it with practiced ease. He slowly walked toward Carl, and despite himself, Carl gulped.

The man looked to be in his mid to late forties, with deep black hair and a light beard, black as midnight, actually. His eyes were a deep blue and as Carl watched, the man moved up next to him. Carl saw a confidence in those eyes that he wished he could mimic.

"Name's Steven Webb and this here's my daughter Tracey," he said in a low voice. He had the kind of voice that would carry easily if he wanted it to. Carl bet he easily talked over most people at a party or function.

The woman from the cab bounced over to him, holding out her hand politely. "Hi, sorry we couldn't talk earlier, but you know the situation," she smiled.

Carl took her hand and shook it, feeling her soft skin. Underneath the dirt and grime, she was flawless.

"It's all right, I'm just glad to be out of there. The name's Carl Jenkins."

She smiled again and nodded. "Tracey Reynolds. Oh wait, my father just introduced me," she said rolling her eyes, embarrassed. Then she moved back to the cab and started rummaging around inside it.

"All right, enough chit-chat. We need to get moving again. Those bastards will be following us. They're like goddamn bloodhounds once they get your scent."

"But surely we're safe now. They're miles behind us," Carl said, looking back to the lonely road.

Steve shook his head. "Wish that were true, pal, but those damn things can march forever from what I've seen. They know which way we went and there's no other cut-offs around here. You mark my words, they'll be here. Maybe not today or tomorrow, but sooner or later, they'll be here." He pointed to the rear of the bulldozer. "So mount up and we'll get moving. Despite what my daughter said, there's not enough room in the cab for three, so get on the back again."

Doing what he was told, Carl climbed back onto the bulldozer. Tracey jogged over to him and looked up at his face, while she stood on the ground. She tossed him something and he instinctively reached out to catch it before knowing what it was.

It was a half-full bottle of water.

"Thought you might need this," she said.

Carl didn't answer her, but instead undid the cap and drank greedily. He finished the bottle in seconds and with heavy breathing, handed it back.

"Wow, thank you. I forgot how thirsty I was." He looked down at her and frowned. "Look, I hate to ask, but do you have anything to eat? It's been almost two days since I've eaten anything."

She held up her finger to tell him to wait a moment and ran back to the cab. Carl heard muffled talking and then the engine sputtered to life again. Tracey was back a second later and she tossed him a candy bar.

"Here, we raided a gas station earlier. My Dad wants to go now and he told me you're going to ride out here on the back, that there's not enough room in the cab. Is that all right with you, I know what I said earlier about you riding with me?"

Carl ripped open the candy bar and started chewing. It was the best thing he'd ever tasted. "Sure, I'm fine. Hey, does your father know where we're going, exactly?"

Tracey shook her head. "No, not really. He just figures we'll keep going until we're out of gas and then deal with it then." Her face grew serious then, and she gazed up at Carl. "He's a smart man and if anyone can get us someplace safe, it's him."

Carl nodded. "All right, I guess. I don't really have much choice, anyway."

She nodded and her smile widened. She held up her hand and Carl took it. She squeezed it gently, reassuringly, and then she let go, jogging away to climb back up into the cab.

Carl watched her go, already feeling a stirring where his heart was. God, she was pretty. He'd have to get her alone later and try to find out more about her. Then the bulldozer bucked underneath him and Steve pulled back onto the road, slowly chugging up the right side.

* * *

Four hours later the deserted road saw movement.

Slowly, with the falling of dusk, the first stumbling ghoul rounded the bend in the road.

Hundreds followed it, all with the same vacuous look in their eyes and slack-jawed countenances.

One foot fell in front of the other as the parade of the dead marched up the road.

Blood dripped behind them, staining the asphalt maroon, some wounds still leaking. Others merely dragged useless limbs behind them, the need to keep moving driving them onward.

Somewhere deep down in their brains, where they were once human and rational thought remained, they knew this road would take them to more prey.

Slowly, one foot at a time, they marched on.

Chapter 16

WHILE THE BULLDOZER chugged down the road, Carl gazed out at his surroundings. It was beautiful. Tall pine trees dotted the landscape amidst the rolling hills designated the Blue Hills Mountain range. It reminded him a lot of New Hampshire and he felt slightly embarrassed that he had lived his entire life in Boston and had never driven the forty minutes to the mountains. Carl had never been much of an outdoorsman, preferring the comforts of civilization.

The bulldozer slowed and swerved slightly to the right, causing Carl to come out of his ruminations. There was a car on the side of the road, the roof piled high with luggage; as was the trunk.

A man stood in the middle of the road, waving while the bulldozer pulled up next to him.

Steve turned off the engine, the motor much too loud to try and talk over, and climbed down to the street.

"Oh, thank God you came along. We've been out here for hours," the man said. Carl gave him the once over; noticing the man's expensive suit and perfect haircut. If he got a look at his hands, Carl would bet anything the nails would be manicured.

But the man was still talking and so Carl listened, amused.

"I tried calling triple A but they don't answer. There's nothing but a damn busy signal. I tell you, they take your money year after year and when you finally need them . . ."

Steve cut the man off with a rising of his hand, a new cigarette hanging from his mouth. "Are you serious? Triple A? Boston is burning and the dead are walking and your trying to get a tow? I'm afraid you're on your own out here, buddy."

The man shook his head vigorously. "I'm afraid that's out of the question. Look, I'm the head of neurosurgery at Boston General and I need to get there immediately. I have a patient waiting with a tumor in the left hemisphere of her brain. If I don't operate within twenty-four hours, her prognosis is grim."

Steve lounged against the side of the man's BMW, blowing smoke up into the air. "Doc, I got news for ya. If your patient was at Boston General, then she's already dead. The hospitals were the first places to be overrun."

The man seemed to sputter for a moment, not believing what he was hearing. "That's ridiculous; I was just there a week ago. I was on a trip with my wife when I was paged to return back to the hospital, immediately."

For the first time Carl and the others realized there was someone else in the car. A woman with red hair and a tired face leaned forward in the passenger seat and waved slightly. Steve acknowledged her wave with one of his own.

"Mister, did you try calling the hospital?" Tracey asked nicely.

"First of all, young lady, it's Doctor, Doctor Hickman. I didn't go to medical school for almost ten years to be called *mister*." He said the word as if it left a foul taste in his mouth. "And second, yes, I did call the hospital, but the switchboard must be down because all I get is a recorded message."

"There ya go, Doc, the hospitals are overrun. The only people still there are dead people without the damn sense to lie back down and die," Steve added.

"Warren, is that true?" The woman in the car asked.

"Pipe down, Helen, I'm trying to think!" Hickman snapped at her.

Carl caught the look Steve gave Hickman, but if the man noticed, he didn't let on.

"Look, Doc, I don't want to hang around here any longer then I have to. If you want, you and your wife can hitch a ride with us. There's not much room, but I think you can find a spot with Carl back there."

Carl now realized all eyes were on him and he waved at the Doctor. Hickman barely noticed him.

"But what about my luggage, where will you put it? I need everything I've brought with me."

Steve chuckled at that. "Are you serious? Look, Doc, there's enough room for you and your wife and that's it. Take it or leave it." He dropped his cigarette to the ground and stepped on it, stomping out the rest of it without actually consciously thinking about it. Then he climbed back into the cab.

"Can we go with them, Warren, please? I don't think anyone else is going to be coming," Helen said from inside the car.

"Not now, Helen, please, I'm trying to talk here. I can't do that with you constantly interrupting!" He snapped at her again. Steve said nothing, but his hands squeezed the steering wheel a little tighter. Steve had known men like Hickman before. Men who treated their wives like property, women who were to speak when spoken to and no other time.

Steve started the engine again, while Hickman walked around his car.

"Last chance, Doc." Then he turned away from him and looked to Helen. "How about you Miss? You don't have to stay with him, you know."

Carl could see the indecision on Hickman's face as the man tried to decide what to do.

"Oh, did I forget to mention there's about a thousand zombies following us? I don't know how far they are behind us, but I'll bet you anything they're there and coming this way," Steve said.

Hickman's face perked up at that. "Are you serious? But I thought all that business I heard about before I left was just nonsense."

"You mean you really don't know?" Tracey asked him.

Hickman shook his head. "No, I've been camping for the past week, I mean; I heard rumors, but come on, zombies? I'm a man of science, how am I expected to believe such drivel?"

Steve started moving the bulldozer forward a few feet. "Look, Doc, you can believe whatever the hell you want, but if you want to come with us, then let's go, 'cause I'm leaving."

Hickman dry washed his face with his hands, looking at the bulldozer and then at the abandoned road. Finally, he threw his hands down and turned to his wife. "Come on, Helen, we're going with them, I don't know what's happening, but anything has to be better then being stranded in the middle of nowhere."

Helen stepped out of the car and walked over to her husband. Hickman looked up at Steve.

Steve gestured to the rear of the bulldozer. "Go ahead, hop on, and be quick about it."

Hickman gave Steve a curt look, obviously not accustomed to being talked to like a commoner. But he did as he was told, climbing up onto the treads, careful not to get his hands dirty with the gore still attached.

Carl could only watch, mystified, as he totally ignored his wife, only worrying about himself. Carl leaned down and gave Helen his hand, helping her up onto the machine.

"Thank you, young man, that's very nice of you, I'm sure your mother would be proud," Helen said sweetly.

"No problem, happy to help," Carl replied.

With a brief glance over his shoulder to make sure everyone was aboard, Steve started off again, leaving the doctor's disabled car behind.

"So where are we going exactly," Hickman said over the thrumming engine.

Carl just shrugged. "Don't know; guess we'll know when we get there."

* * *

Carl was dozing, the rumbling engine blotting out all other sound. He dreamt of Clarence. In his dream it was he that had become overwhelmed by the ghouls that came out of the alleyway, not Clarence. In his dream, Carl was a ghoul, stumbling around the streets of Boston looking for a free meal.

Then the motor changed pitch and Steve pulled to the side of the road. Carl opened his eyes to see another car hugging the guardrail. Steve pulled up next to the old station wagon, trying to see if it was empty, when a bloody face slammed against the side window. Then another and another after that.

"Holy shit, there's an entire family in there, we need to do something," Carl said, watching the snarling faces inside the car.

Steve shook his head. "Nothing we can do for them. Take a closer look at them. They're not human anymore."

"Well, you can't just leave them like that, you have to do something," Hickman demanded from next to Carl. Steve swung around in his seat, his eyes wide with anger. "And what exactly would you like me to do, Doc? There dead. They're beyond saving."

"Oh my Lord, it's so horrible. How could it have happened way out here?" Helen asked.

Steve shrugged. "Don't know. Maybe one of them was already infected and then turned while they were on the road. Once that happened, the others were fair game," Steve suggested.

Tracey turned away, unable to look anymore. "It's horrible, Dad, even the children?"

Steve hugged her, consoling her. "Death is the great equalizer, honey. Young or old, rich or poor, death cares not."

"That's so poetic, Mr. Webb, you should write a goddamn book. Do something for Christ sake; we can't just leave them like that!" Hickman screamed at Steve.

Steve's jaw set and for a moment Carl thought he was going to get out of the bulldozer and hit Hickman, but a second later he seemed to gain control of himself.

"All right, Doc, you want me to do something, fine, I will." Then Steve revved the engine and backed up the bulldozer, until the plow was behind the station wagon. Inside, the dead family snarled and clawed at the glass, leaving bloody streaks from their smashed nails.

Steve placed the bulldozer in drive and then started to push the station wagon, turning the wheel enough so the car was now pointed in the direction of the guardrail. For a moment it seemed the guardrail would hold, but then the metal gave way, and the car went through to slide down a steep embankment. Even over the bulldozer's engine the sound of crunching metal came to their ears.

When the dust had settled, Steve turned to look at Hickman. "Satisfied, you son-of-a-bitch?"

Hickman was too shocked to answer, but just stared at the gap in the guardrail.

Satisfied with his work, Steve turned the wheel and continued down the road.

A little while later, Carl was sitting near the cab. Steve's head was only two feet away from him and the two had been talking.

"So how did you end up driving a bulldozer around Boston? I've got to tell you, it's not the usual escape vehicle one would think of using."

Steve shrugged, concentrating on driving. "I worked construction until last week. When the Mayor tried to close the city off, I was one of the guys hired to help move Jersey barriers wherever they needed them. I was over near Haymarket, setting up barriers around city hall when a shitload of those fuckers attacked the cops. It was unbelievable. I saw one of those things take ten rounds to the chest and keep coming like it was nothing. The entire squad was slaughtered. I decided then that it was a good time to bug out, so I drove over to the North End and picked up Tracey, and then we got the hell out of Dodge. Figured a bulldozer is about the only machine worth driving with the exception of a tank. Every time the roads were blocked with cars, I just pushed through or drove over them."

Carl nodded, listening. "Wow, that's really a great idea."

Steve smiled at him. "I know; that's why you're still alive right now. Couldn't have reached you in a Toyota."

Carl was hesitant to bring up another subject, but Steve seemed to be in an apparently good mood, so he decided to try.

"So why does Tracey have a different last name then you if she's your daughter?"

Steve looked at him, his jaw growing tight, but then his face softened and he shrugged. "Her mother remarried and took the asshole's name. Gave it to Tracey, too. She was only eight when we divorced."

Carl stayed silent then, happy to get his answer. They drove in silence for a while, neither feeling the need to talk. They were just passing a mile marker on the road when Carl noticed movement in the woods on his left.

"Hey, slow down a little, Steve, I think there's something in the woods," Carl said, his eyes trying to penetrate the forest.

Steve did as he was asked, his foot hovering over the gas pedal. If it was trouble, then he wanted to move quickly.

Carl continued watching the woods and then his peripheral vision caught movement again. His head swiveled in the same direction and a second later a man stumbled out of the tree line to fall over into the dirt. The man was wearing the green uniform of a soldier, minus a helmet.

The moment Carl saw him, he jumped off the bulldozer, cautiously approaching the man. From the way the soldier moved, Carl was fairly certain the man wasn't a ghoul.

Footsteps sounded behind him and he saw Tracey was following him. Steve called after her, telling her to get back inside the bulldozer, but she ignored him.

Catching up to Carl, she moved closer to him.

"Your father only wants what's best for you, you know. That's why he didn't want you following me."

"I know, but he needs to realize I'm not a little girl anymore. I can take care of myself," she answered back.

"Still, just hang back why I check this guy out and be ready to run if I yell."

She nodded, understanding and Carl pulled away from her. Carl slowed when he was only a few feet from the soldier. The man had fallen face first on the ground and he wasn't moving. Carl cautiously moved the remaining few feet and then knelt down next to him.

Feeling the guys neck, Carl breathed a sigh of relief to feel a pulse, slow but strong. Rolling the man over, he could find no discernable marks on him.

"Hey, Tracey, get some water for this guy, I think he's dehydrated," he called to her.

She ran back to the bulldozer and Steve tossed her a bottle of water, hearing what Carl had said. With Tracey running the water back to Carl, Steve turned to look at Doctor Hickman.

"Hey, Doc, why don't you go see if you can help, you're a doctor after all."

Hickman made a disgusted face. "Are you serious? I'm a neurosurgeon, not a common doctor. I don't make house calls, Mr. Webb."

Steve stared at the man, stunned. "You know, Doc, you really are an asshole."

Hickman made a grunt and then turned away from Steve. With her back to her husband, Helen allowed herself a small smile.

Steve had decided the area appeared safe and turned off the engine, hopping down to see if he could help Carl and Tracey.

Jogging across the road, he reached them just as Carl was helping the soldier sit up. The man was drinking greedily from the water bottle and Carl held his head up.

Carl knew how he felt. He had been in the same predicament only a few hours ago.

When the soldier had drunk his fill, he took in a few deep breaths and seemed to finally notice he was with more people then just Carl. His eyes scanned Steve and Tracey, his eyes lingering on Tracey a little long for Carl's tastes. Then, with Carl's help, managed to stand on shaking legs.

"Thank you, thank you so much," the soldier said softly. His voice was raspy from lack of water.

"No problem, soldier, what's your name and where's the rest of your unit?" Steve asked.

Carl looked to Tracey and she smiled. "Dad was in the army. It was a long time ago, though, before I was born."

Carl only nodded, understanding.

With gasps of breath and more sips of water, the soldier answered. "Private Craig Sterns, sir. They're all gone. Slaughtered by those *people*, those dead people. I cut and ran when there was no hope of overcoming them. There was just too many to fight and they ignored our gunfire like they were bee stings."

"Where did this all happen, son?" Steve asked brusquely.

Sterns turned and gestured into the woods. "I don't know how far from here, sir, I've been walking for more than a day, but my platoon set up on Route 93 just outside of Boston. We were supposed to close off the highway. No one in or out. We blocked off both the North and South sides, but then those people came at us. They just marched out of the South Station tunnel and came at us without a care in the world. We figured if we killed a few of the first ones in line, then the others would break and run, but they never even slowed. They just kept coming until they were too close to shoot. I saw everyone in my unit get torn to shreds before I ran. I never considered myself a coward, sir, but what the hell was I supposed to do? If I'd stayed, then I'd be dead now, too."

"Or worse," Carl said softly. "At least you're not walking around when you're supposed to be dead."

"Not now, Carl, lets focus on what's important," Steve told him. He then turned back to Sterns. "You did the right thing, soldier. There are times when retreating isn't a bad thing. Better to retreat and be alive to fight another day, then to die for a lost cause."

"You sound like your talking from experience, Steve." Carl said, fishing for some more information on him.

"More than you'd care to know, Carl, believe me." He looked at Sterns again. "Come on with us, we've still got room on the back of the 'dozer. Can you walk?"

Sterns nodded. "Shit, sir, that's all I've been doing."

Steve gestured to the holster on Stern's hip. "You have a weapon in there?"

Sterns looked down at his side arm and opened it, sliding the .45 pistol out.

"Hell, yeah, I've got a weapon. Low on ammo, though, I've only got about a half clip left. The rest I wasted on those damn creatures."

"Zombies, you mean those damn zombies," Carl said laconically.

Craig just looked at Carl as if he was speaking gibberish.

Steve nodded. "Good, at least we have a weapon now. Listen, Sterns, if you have to shoot one of them, aim for the head. It seems to be the only way to put them down for good."

Carl listened to them and wanted to add that he'd seen some of them hit in the head and they still twitched and moved, but he figured now was not the time for debate on how to kill a zombie. Instead, he started to move back to the bulldozer.

"Daylights fading, we should get going, right Steve?" Carl said. Steve looked at Carl and then up at the sky.

"Yeah, you're right, Carl, we should keep moving. Come on, Sterns, shake a leg and climb aboard." Steve said, walking back to the bulldozer and jumping into the cab. Tracey flashed Sterns a smile and then followed her father.

Carl and Craig moved to the foothold behind the cab and Carl helped him climb up. Hickman merely grunted and complained about there already being no room on the back of the bulldozer.

"Ignore him, he thinks he's better then the rest off us," Carl said to Craig.

"I am better then the rest of you, you're all just too ignorant to realize it," Hickman said to no one in particular.

Sterns looked at the man, not understanding if he was serious. "Private Craig Sterns, sir, nice to meet you," he said politely, holding out his hand to shake.

Hickman stared at it as if it was on fire. "I'm sorry, private, but I don't shake hands. These hands are worth millions, you understand of course," Hickman said brusquely.

"Well actually . . ." Craig said.

Carl patted Craig on the shoulder. "Trust me, man, just leave it alone. Just ignore the guy, he's a jerk."

"I heard that, Carl, I'm right here, you know," Hickman hissed.

Carl smiled back snidely. "Yeah, I know you are and I really don't give a shit."

Hickman huffed and turned around, complaining to his wife. Helen merely nodded, telling him they didn't understand his greatness.

The bulldozer started again and Hickman almost fell off, he was so busy talking to Helen. Carl started laughing, but quickly stopped when Hickman flashed him an evil stare. But as soon as the man turned back around, Carl smiled again.

Helen was able to turn away from her husband, and when she was facing away from him, she flashed Carl a wry smile and nodded.

Carl winked back, knowing what she meant and both shared a silent joke about her husband.

With the bulldozer moving again, and with one more added to their ragtag group of survivors, they continued down the quiet, two lane road, traveling deeper into the mountains, while Hickman grumbled and complained to himself and anyone who would listen about everything and everyone.

Chapter 17

"HEY, STEVE, STOP for a second, will ya?" Carl called from the back of the bulldozer.

With a jolt, the machine stopped, sputtering as the engine idled.

"What's wrong, Dad? Why's it sounding so funny?" Tracey asked from Steve's side.

Frowning, Steve punched the dashboard, cursing. "Shit, I knew this would happen. Frankly, I'm surprised we made it this far."

"What, what's wrong?" Carl asked as he hopped off the back and walked over so he was looking up at Steve.

"The gas tanks about empty. We need diesel and I don't see a gas station around here, do you?"

Carl shook his head, no.

"So what did you want me to stop for?" Steve asked.

Carl ran over to a sign that had fallen over on the side of the road. Picking it up, he held it so that the others could see.

"This," he stated, balancing the sign on his leg. "Though I really just had to take a piss."

Steve squinted as he read the sign. "The Franklin Park Zoo? Shit, that place is still around?"

"Not really, I thought they closed that place last year. I remember reading about something, or catching it on the news, that they were almost out of money. Guess they couldn't find more financing," Tracey said askance of him.

Steve rubbed his chin, thinking. "Come to think of it, I do remember reading something about the zoo going under. It was a tough one finding a home for all the animals. You know what? That might be a good place to hold up for a while. The zoo should have a fence around it to keep out trespassers and ticket dodgers."

"Sure it does, Dad, don't you remember taking me there when I was a kid? It was back when you and Mom were still together," Tracey said.

"No kidding, I took you there? Sorry, honey, I guess the old noggin's gettin' old." He looked back down at Carl. "Come on, Carl, take that piss and then hop on up, let's try and see how much farther we can get before she runs out of fuel."

Carl ran off to the side of the road and after relieving himself, climbed back onto the back of the bulldozer. With a bucking and a sputtering, the machine started again. Steve had a five gallon fuel tank strapped to the back of the machine, but had already emptied the fuel into the tank. If it hadn't been for those extra five gallons, the small group of survivors would have already been walking.

The front tires of the bulldozer drove over the sign as it moved off down the road. The sign had also said that the zoo was two miles away, on the right hand side, and Steve could only cross his fingers as they sputtered down the asphalt. The engine smoothed out for a while and Tracey looked to Steve with a questioning gaze.

"It's probably sucking up the crap in the bottom of the tank. For the moment, the shit has worked its way through the line, but I'm sure that'll change the lower the tank gets."

She nodded, understanding. She turned round in her seat and checked on their passengers. Hickman was hugging a metal protuberance, his wife Helen, next to him. By the look on Hickman's face, he was in a foul mood. She grinned at that. Was the man ever in any other mood? Carl was standing at the rear, holding on to a handhold. He was looking out across the road, admiring the landscape.

When she looked at Craig Sterns she found the man was looking back at her. She quickly looked away, embarrassed. After a second she looked again to find Craig was still watching her.

"What's so interesting?" She called to him over the rumbling engine.

He shrugged. "Nothing really, I was just admiring you. You're a real looker, you know that?"

She blushed with the compliment. "You better be careful, private, this big man here is my father."

In response to his name being spoken, Steve swiveled his head and gave Craig a harsh glare. Craig smiled back, meekly. Then he looked back to Tracey.

"I'm not worried about him, Tracey. He's just a big teddy bear. I'm sure once he gets to know me he'll welcome me into the family with open arms."

"Oh really," she chuckled. "My, you're getting ahead of yourself. We've just met."

Craig shrugged. "Call me overconfident, but I always get what I want." Ending his sentence, he focused his gaze on her more intently, smiling slightly.

She laughed then, loud and full. "Well, Private Sterns, we'll just have to see about that." Then she turned back around, ending the conversation.

Sterns kept the smile on his face and he turned back to look at his fellow passengers. The Hickman's ignored him and as he glanced at Carl, he was greeted by an angry stare.

"What, what's up, bro?" Craig asked Carl.

Carl shook his head. "Nothing, man, nothing's wrong, I just think she's a little out of your league, that's all."

"You think so?" Craig scoffed. "And I suppose she's in your league?"

Carl shrugged. "Maybe, I guess we'll just have to wait and see," he challenged.

Craig nodded, and his grin widened. He reached out and held his hand out for Carl to shake. "May the best man win."

Despite himself, Carl couldn't help but like the young private, even if he was trying to go after Tracey. He took his hand and the two men shook, neither playing the squeezing game.

Carl let go first and nodded, smiling despite himself. "May the best man win, namely me."

Craig started to laugh at Carl's cockiness and a second later Carl joined him. And so began a budding friendship with a woman in the middle.

With the bulldozer coughing and sputtering down the road, the two men started talking about other things of interest, while Dr. Hickman grumbled under his breath.

* * *

Steve turned off the main road, a big white sign directing him to the main parking lot for the zoo. So far the bulldozer was still running, but Steve had all ready prepared everyone for its eventual demise.

The new road was overgrown with tree limbs, making the road feel more like a tunnel. The sun was high in the sky, but as they drove further away from the main road, the sun disappeared, the tops of the trees blotting out the light.

Steve maneuvered down the small, narrow road, barely wide enough for two cars to pass each other.

The road meandered left and right for almost a half mile until it finally opened up to a wide open space. Signs directed visitors to go to the left or right and to remember where they had parked. Steve continued forward, driving over the small copse of grass and bushes that separated the two lanes. The bulldozer crushed the overgrown grass and shrubs and continued onward.

Carl was the first to see the front gate of the zoo and he called out to Steve. Steve followed his hand to where he was pointing and nodded, shifting the bulldozer to go in the right direction.

Everyone watched as the large machine slowly crossed the lot.

Then Steve stopped the bulldozer, Tracey turning to her father. "What's wrong, why'd you stop, we're so close?" She said.

Steve turned off the engine, and with a sputter, it died. He honestly wondered if it would start again, he was driving on fumes now and had been for the past half mile. Evidently, even he didn't know how deep the reserves were on the bulldozer.

Steve climbed out of the cab and jumped to the ground, the others following.

"What's wrong, why'd you stop?" Carl asked, mimicking Tracey.

Steve pointed to the front gate of the zoo, just to the right of the closed main gate and lit another cigarette. He had been able to see more from his cab. The others perched on the back unable to see through all the hanging tree limbs.

"We've got a small problem," Steve told them.

"For crying out loud, what is it, just spit it out!" Dr. Hickman snapped at him.

Steve glared at the man. "Easy doc, you might be some big cheese in Boston, but out here I'll knock you on your ass. You get me?" Steve threatened him.

Hickman swallowed and nodded; understanding perfectly.

Then Craig spoke up, breaking the tension. "So what's up, Steve, what's the problem?"

"Looks like whatever's happening in Boston is spreading. There's at least twenty of those dead people by the front gate."

Carl took a few steps closer to the zoo, his eyes trying to see what Steve had seen. Deciding it was hopeless; he turned and moved back to the group.

"All I see are a few slow moving figures moving around and a couple of cars near the gate. No biggy. Why don't we just move in there and kick their asses?" Carl suggested, sounding braver then he felt.

Craig nodded. "He's right. There's four of us, not including the women. That's like four a piece or so. We can always retreat if it doesn't go our way."

Steve rubbed his chin, thinking. "That's what I thought, I just didn't know if you guys would go along with it and four is still not very good odds." He kicked the side of the bulldozer. It's a shame this damn things out of juice. Otherwise, we could have just run the bastards over and that would have been the end of it."

Craig gestured to an old Pontiac sitting in the parking lot a little to their left. "That's actually not a bad idea, Steve. What about if I can get that car over there started? I can use it like a ram and take out a few that way, then you guys can just come in and clean up the rest."

"You know how to hot wire a car, Craig?" Carl asked, surprised.

Craig grinned from ear to ear. "Hell yes, I'm from Detroit, man, there's a car stolen there every second. An old clunker like that should be a piece of cake as long as the battery's still got a charge."

Steve clapped his hands, settling it. "Okay then, let's get moving. The longer we stay out here in the open, the worse off we are. Private, get that car running, the rest of you find something to use as a weapon."

Craig hesitated for a moment. "Hey guys, I'd appreciate it if you all would just call me, Craig. For the foreseeable future I'm out of the army, if not for good. I am AWOL after all."

Steve nodded. "All right, Craig it is, and that goes for the rest of you, too. Now get going."

Carl, Steve and Craig, along with Tracey, went their separate ways, but Hickman didn't move. Steve noticed this and stopped, returning to Hickman's side. "What's wrong, Doc, why aren't you moving?"

"Because if you think I'm fighting anybody you're even more ignorant then I previously thought you were, that's why," Hickman said with an air of superiority.

"Oh Warren, be nice, he saved us for God's sake." Helen said from his side.

Hickman turned to glare at her. "That's enough out of you, woman. This is man's business." Then he turned back to Steve. "Look, Mr. Webb, these hands are far too valuable for me to just go around swinging clubs with. If I was to damage one of my hands, my practice would be over. I'm sorry, but I just can't help you. If you really need help, my wife will fill in for me."

"But Warren . . ." Helen protested.

"Now, now Helen, be brave. We're living in desperate times, here," Hickman said.

Steve was appalled at the man's pompous attitude.

"Let me get this straight, Doc. You'd send your wife into battle for you so you don't have to get your hands dirty?" Steve asked, amazed.

Hickman seemed to examine his nails and he casually shrugged. "Well, I wouldn't put it quite that way, myself, Mr. Webb."

"Oh really, then how would you put it?" Then Steve held up his hand. "You know what, forget it, I really don't care. Tell you what,

Doc, you just stay here and hide with the women and the rest of us will do the dirty work."

Hickman nodded. "Fine with me, and I wouldn't think to harshly about me, Mr. Webb. If you happen to get a tumor or an aneurysm, you'll be glad you know me, I guarantee it."

Steve only nodded, slowly, amazed at the man's gall. Then he moved away to check on the others, flicking his spent cigarette as he went.

Hickman turned to his wife and smiled. "You see, dear, you just have to know how to talk to the lower class folk."

"Yes, dear, of course," Helen said and then moved away to see if she could help anyone else.

Hickman folded his arms across his chest and sighed. It was so hard being intellectually more intelligent then the common man. They just didn't understand his greatness.

Chapter 18

WITH A ROAR of the six cylinders, the Pontiac surged to life. Craig sat up from lying on the seat and smiled up at Carl and Tracey.

"Told you I could do it, there's not a car made that I can't hotwire."

Carl frowned, not impressed. "Nice to see you've learned a lot of new skills since joining the army."

Craig revved the engine twice, making sure the car wasn't going to stall. "I told you already, I learned this a long time before I joined the army." He looked to Tracey. "You want to ride with me? Should be fun, I mean, how many times in your life do you get to run people over and not have to worry about going to jail for vehicular manslaughter?"

Tracey bit her lip, thinking it over. "Thanks Craig, but I already know what my father will say."

"Aww, come on, honey, you're a big girl now, you can do what you want," he protested.

Tracey shrugged. "Maybe, but I love my father and I do what he asks of me. I'm all he's got right now." She started to walk away from him and back to the bulldozer and her father. "You be careful now," she waved.

Carl looked down at Craig, his right arm leaning on the roof of the car. "Ouch, that must hurt. I've never seen someone crash and burn so hard before."

Craig leaned back in the seat and grinned. "Shit, man, I haven't even gotten started yet, I'm just warming up."

Carl patted the hood of the car. "Whatever man, you just keep thinkin' that. You be careful, okay? It wouldn't be the same if I get Tracey because you're dead. Takes all the fun out of it."

Craig laughed at that, and put the car in drive. "Don't you worry, my man, I'm not going anywhere." Then he stepped on the gas and the Pontiac surged away from Carl, almost running over his foot, if Carl hadn't jumped back at the last second.

Carl watched the Pontiac drive around in circles for a moment, while Craig got used to the car's handling, then he leaned out the window and gave him the thumb's up.

Carl waved back and jogged back to Steve. "Craig's ready. Are you?"

Steve nodded. He held a large tree limb that had fallen from a nearby tree during a storm. The hefty club would serve him well. As for Carl, Steve handed him a tire iron taken from the back of the bulldozer. Carl swung the improvised weapon a few times, getting the feel for its weight; then with a nod, both men moved out for the front gate of the zoo.

Carl glanced back to Hickman as they walked away. "How come the Doc's not coming with us?"

Steve only shrugged. "He's decided to stay and protect the women," he said sarcastically.

Carl waited for more, but Steve was finished talking. Carl turned back again to look at Hickman, but the man was gone, hiding behind the bulldozer. Carl decided he'd talk to Steve about it more later, at the moment, there were more important things to worry about.

The two men moved closer and Carl slowed and pointed to the two cars parked in front of the gate. He could easily see movement inside and as he continued to watch, he could see the faces therein, all animated.

The people inside were banging on the windows, calling for help.

"Holy shit, Steve, there are people in those cars; living people."

Steve nodded, "Yeah, I saw them, too. They're trapped in there with all those dead fucks around the cars just waiting for them to run for it. The second they tried to get out, they'd be lunch."

Carl agreed, "Yeah, but why the hell don't they just drive away?"

Steve shook his head, not knowing the answer, but as they moved even closer it was easily apparent. Both cars were stuck together, their front bumpers entwined. Carl could only guess in their haste to try and leave, they accidentally hit each other, causing the bumpers to become locked. They were trapped with more than a dozen ghouls waiting for them to try and escape the two vehicles.

Then the Pontiac shot by them, Craig doing a beeline for the two stranded cars. He honked the horn repeatedly, grabbing the attention of a few ghouls. They stumbled away from the two cars and started toward the Pontiac. Craig never slowed, but kept the front grille pointed straight at the three oncoming bodies.

The Pontiac struck all three head-on, the two side ghouls flying off to the left and right and the middle one bending over the hood and then rolling over the windshield, cracking it in its passing. Craig swerved for a second and then regained control of the car. With a screeching of tires, he swung the car around and headed back the way he'd just traversed.

Carl and Steve moved in, attacking the fallen corpses. All three were pretty messed up, bones protruding from arms and legs from the fractures and breaks they'd received from the Pontiac; faces rubbed raw from sliding on the pavement. Both club and tire iron rose and fell repeatedly, smashing heads and crushing faces to pulp.

By then Craig had made another pass, knocking four more over that tried to grab him as he approached. Carl watched it all fascinated. Obviously the ghouls didn't have much common sense if they would try to attack a moving car. That just helped reinforce what he'd already seen, that once dead, the people were nothing more than automated automatons, wanting only to kill and eat healthy humans.

With the Pontiac shooting by, Steve and Carl ran at the other prone bodies, making short work of them. Carl's tire iron was covered in blood and gore and he had to keep it pointed down or risk blood dripping down the shaft and onto his hand. His clothes were already spotted with blood, the spray too wide to dodge, though he did manage to keep his face clear.

Steve was in the same position, his tree limb covered with blood, bits and pieces of flesh caught in the bark.

"Okay, that's most of them; you game to finish off the rest?" Steve gasped, holding his club in front of him like a sword.

Carl nodded, wiping sweat from his brow with the back of his hand. "Let's get this done," he said, readying the tire iron.

The Pontiac pulled up behind them and Craig climbed out. "You guys need a hand?" He asked with a grin. In his right hand he had a steering wheel lock, the red steel rod had a hook on each end to wrap around the steering wheel, preventing the wheel from being turned. Carl recognized it from hours of watching late night television. It was called the Club and had been all the rage before some car thief had realized that all you had to do was cut the plastic steering wheel with a hack saw, thereby removing the lock from the steering wheel.

No matter what kind of lock was invented there was always some thief figuring out how to beat it.

Steve slapped him on the back. "Hell yes, but why don't you keep taking them out with the car?"

Craig shook his head. "The steering's shot; I think I threw a tie-rod on that last pass. She doesn't handle too well anymore." He slapped the roof of the car. "Still, she did what was needed. Guess we'll just have to handle the rest the old fashioned way."

Steve and Carl only looked on at the approaching dead people. Carl counted ten more still walking around. For the moment, the ghouls seemed to ignore the two stranded cars, more interested in the three humans moving about.

"Shit, here they come," Steve muttered, preparing himself.

Carl glanced his way, Steve's jaw was set, his mouth a thin line. Carl thought this might be a good time to score a few points with Tracey's Dad, so he puffed up his chest and tried to act tough. "Just relax Steve. I've fought these guys before, just remember, they're slow. Just keep moving and don't let them surround you. It'll be easy."

Craig laughed a little, though not in an amused way. "Yeah, piece of cake," he sneered.

Carl would have liked to send a retort back to Craig, but it was too late for talk, the ghouls only a few feet from them.

"Split up and don't get in each others way. We don't need one of us clubbing one another by accident," Steve said, raising the tree limb over his head.

A city worker with a torn out throat and a slack jaw had decided Steve was his next meal and came charging at him, feet stumbling one in front of the other. Steve brought the tree limb down like he was chopping wood. The dead man's head exploded like a ripe cantaloupe, brains and blood spraying in all directions.

The body continued walking, headless, for a few more feet. Steve merely sidestepped it and charged at the next walking corpse in line.

Carl was holding his own as well. A dead man in a loud Hawaiian shirt and a Polaroid camera hanging from his neck came at him, teeth flashing red in the shade from the overhead tree tops. Carl swung the tire iron in a sideways blow, catching the dead man on the cheek and ripping a wide gash that had the man's tongue hanging out of the open wound like a worm peeking out of its hole in the ground.

Correcting his swing, Carl swiped a backhand blow that caught the man in the nose. Blood poured from his shattered nose, spilling onto the Hawaiian shirt. Carl noticed idly that it was a big improvement on the man's look, then hands were reaching out to grab him and he had to dance back.

Craig popped up next to him, keeping his own attacker at bay. He flashed Carl a smile and said: "Having fun yet?"

Carl frowned. Craig's constant humor could easily become irritating.

"A fucking blast, look, stop playing with them and finish then off. I could use all the help your willing to give over here!"

"Will you two idiots stop talking and fight!" Steve yelled, kicking another dead man in the groin, though it didn't get the desired result, in fact, the dead man seemed unfazed. Spinning around like an Olympian discus-thrower, Steve swung the tree limb as hard as he could, snapping the man's neck, the ghoul falling to the ground where he still twitched slightly.

Carl decided he was done playing with his own attacker, and in an unusual act of courage for him, he spun the tire iron around so the sharp point was facing the ghoul, and with a yell to psych himself up, charged at the corpse, knocking its arms to the sides and jamming the tire iron six inches into the creature's eye. A white—tinged with shades of red—fluid squirted out of the sides of the tire iron as Carl forced the body to the ground. At the visceral sight only a foot in front of him, he felt his stomach heave and he threw up all over the ghoul's face. Bits of candy bar mixed with the blood from the shattered nose slid into the thing's mouth. Not that the corpse cared. It had finally stopped moving, only a few small twitches still remaining in its arms and legs. Carl was about to climb to his feet, when he looked up at another one running straight at him. What was once a middle-aged woman was now barely discernable as once being human. Her nose, mouth and cheeks were ripped off, bits of flesh flapping as she ran at him, only the dress and long hair telling Carl it was once female.

With snapping jaws and hunger in her dead eyes, she came right at him.

He looked around himself, hoping Steve or Craig could help him, but both men were engaged in their own battles.

He knew it was too late to escape her clutches, and though he knew it was hopeless, he desperately tried to release the tire iron from its prison, the tip jammed into the back of the prone corpse's skull, and to try and defend himself.

But he wouldn't be fast enough. All he could do was keep tugging at the tire iron as his eyes locked with the dead woman's own vacuous, yet hungry stare. His own eyes took in every nuance of the jagged and bloody face and he had a feeling he should get a good look, because it was going to be the last thing he ever saw in this lifetime.

Chapter 19

CARL COULDN'T HELP but turn away from the approaching female ghoul as she leaned in for the kill. He closed his eyes, expecting to feel bloody teeth sinking into his skin, but instead he heard a dull thud, as of metal connecting with meat.

He opened his eyes, just as the dead woman fell to his left, her face striking the ground with a sickening thump.

Carl looked up to see Tracey standing over him. In her hand was a large wrench, the end she'd used to strike the dead woman now covered in blood and bits of hair.

She leaned down and helped him up. "Thought you could use some help; the hell with my Dad."

Carl bent over and placed his right foot on the ghoul's head with the tire iron stuck in it. With his foot on the body for leverage, he yanked back, pulling the tire iron free like he was King Arthur freeing Excalibur. With the tire iron back in his hand, he turned to Tracey and gave her the most grateful look he could manage.

"You won't get any argument from me, thanks for saving my ass."

"No problem," she replied. "Feel free to do the same for me some day," then she moved off to help Craig with two particularly feisty attackers.

Carl watched her walk away, admiring the way her ass fit in her jeans. He'd save that ass anytime it needed it, and do a lot more if given the chance, he thought.

Then he had to come back to reality when a small ghoul that had once been an old man in his eighties tried to jump him. Carl ducked low, the old man falling over his back. Carl then spun around and cracked the old guy over the head.

The old man didn't move after that.

He looked around for his next target and was surprised to see there was none.

Steve was off to his right, breathing heavily. Bodies surrounded him, all twitching, but seeming harmless. Carl looked to his left where Craig and Tracey were just finishing up with the last two. He watched Tracey crack a ghoul in the head that had once been a teenager, the boy still carrying an I-pod on his chest, the strap still wrapped around his neck. The boy's temple caved in under the heavy tool, a large, bloody dent appearing on his head. Craig then swung the Club at the boy's head, as well, the second blow rocking the boy's head to the side so hard he tumbled to the ground. Tracey was ready for this and leaned over the boy, bringing the wrench down so hard the tip became buried inside the boy's skull. Carl could hear the crunch the tool made from where he was standing and he felt his stomach spasm inside him again.

He wasn't cut out for this, that was for sure, though he did his best to hide it from the others.

The last ghoul was a young woman in her twenties. She was still beautiful, with long blonde hair and deep blue eyes. Where once the eyes would have been inquisitive and curious, now all that was there was hunger and malice.

The only damage she had on her body was a small wound on her left arm, where something had taken a bite out of her. The wound was still seeping red, though a miniscule amount at that. She was wearing a low cut shirt that showed off her ample cleavage and the low rider jeans showed off the crack of her ass every time she bent over to try and grab Craig.

Carl sighed, watching the scene in front of him. A month earlier when the world still made sense, the scene he watched could have been of a boyfriend and girlfriend playing tag in the parking lot of the zoo. It was only when you moved closer and saw the vacant eyes and drawn expression on the dead woman's face that things showed their true colors.

Especially when Craig dropped to the ground, swept his legs out and tripped the woman to the ground, then jumped up, climbed on top of her and plunged the Club directly into her eyes. The u-shaped prong that was used to hook around the edge of the steering wheel slid right into both her eyes, smashing the eyeballs and continuing forward. The bridge separating her eyes fit perfectly between the two prongs and three inches penetrated until cartilage and bone stopped the weapon. With her brain untouched, she was down but not out of the fight and Craig struggled to keep her pinned while she fought to rise again. Her hands reached out, trying to claw him, and he had to dance back and forth while keeping his weight on her head.

"Someone, please help me, for Christ sake, I can't hold her for long!" Craig called, fighting the dead woman. She was strong and her limbs were still flexible. Craig knew he was only going to be able to hold her for another second. Then a revving engine made him turn around and he saw the Pontiac coming straight for him. With a loud beep of the horn, Steve waved him out of the way.

Craig jumped to the side, rolling on the ground. He quickly came back up; ready for what would come next.

With the dead woman now free of the Club, she quickly stood back up. Now blind, her head darted back and forth and left and right, her ears trying to find where her prey had gone.

Steve hit the horn again and the woman turned in his direction. Steve never slowed, but plowed right into her, the car driving over her, the body rolling under the undercarriage and then spit out the back like a dog's chew toy.

The body rolled for another two feet and then remained still. Carl and the others watched in amazement when the broken and shattered woman tried to pull herself along the ground, only one arm still serviceable. The other arm was lying on her back, only a few bits of gristle still keeping it attached. As for her legs, they were nothing but a shredded mess, ripped and torn in far too many places to list.

She looked like she had gone through a food grinder and lost.

The visceral scene was too much for Carl and he threw up yet again, his stomach dry heaving, the pain excruciating. When he was finished, he wiped his mouth and moved over to the others, now gathering together near the Pontiac.

Steve climbed out and slammed the door. "I see what you mean, Craig, I could barely keep the damn thing straight."

Craig nodded, glad he was right. "See, I told you, the steering's shot."

"What do we do about that?" Tracey asked, pointing to the mangled woman.

"Leave her, I've had enough killing for one day, she's harmless," Steve told them.

"What a waste," Carl said, watching the mass of meat crawling on the pavement; a bloody, red trail left behind her like a snail would make.

Then Steve turned and looked down at his daughter. "What did I tell you? You were supposed to stay with the 'dozer."

Before Tracey could defend herself, Carl spoke up. "Lighten up a little, will ya, Steve? She saved my ass a few minutes ago. I for one am glad she disobeyed you."

Steve looked at Carl and then Tracey. "Is that true?" He asked.

She shrugged. "Guess so, he looked like he was in trouble, so I grabbed a wrench from the tool kit and ran to help, that's all."

Steve sighed. "What am I going to do with you? You're so damn headstrong. Just like your mother."

Tracey smiled wanly and then her voice grew soft. "Dad, what do you think happened to Mom?"

Steve gave her a hug. "Honey, I wish I knew."

Then the moment was broken at the sound of people calling to them.

Craig waved back, and soon the others did, as well.

"Looks like the people in those cars are okay, what do you say we go say hi," Steve suggested, dropping the tree limb to the ground. The limb was covered in gore and if he needed another weapon, he'd prefer to find another limb then to keep using the old one.

The others agreed and started to follow him. Steve slowed and glanced at Carl. "Hey, Carl, go get the Hickman's will you, tell them its safe to come out now and what we're going to do next."

Carl nodded. "Sure, no problem," then he jogged back to the bulldozer. When he got there, the Hickman's were hiding behind the back of the machine. Helen seemed concerned, but fine, but the Doc was scared to death.

When he saw Carl, he stood up, trying to wipe his face clean of the fear that was there only moments ago.

"Is it safe now? Did you get them all?" Dr. Hickman asked.

Carl nodded. "Yeah, Doc, they're all dead. There were people in those cars by the front gate and now, with all the zombies killed, they're free. The others are already going over to introduce themselves and say hi, and I want to, too. You can come if you want."

"Oh Warren, can we? Other people who are okay; that's good news, isn't it?"

Dr. Hickman shook his head. "No, we're good here, you go on ahead. When I know for sure it's safe, we'll be along."

"But Warren . . ." Helen said, but her husband spun around and glared at her.

"I said we're fine here, Helen. Listen to me, goddammit!"

She sighed and looked to Carl. "He's probably right, dear. We'll stay here and keep an eye on the bulldozer. We'll be along later."

Carl smiled at her. He liked Helen, she reminded him of his Mom. How she had ever ended up with an asshole like Dr. Hickman, he'd never know.

He gave Dr. Hickman an icy glare. It seemed the only time the guy was tough was when he had to deal with his wife. He'd known men like him before. A lot of them had been in jail, too.

The chances of Dr. Hickman winding up in jail was slim, especially with the current state of affairs, but Carl made a silent promise to keep an eye on the Doc and deal with him if he got out of control with his wife.

"All right, then, well if you change your mind, you know where we'll be," Carl said, walking away. Helen waved to him and then was quickly stopped by Hickman, the man speaking to her in hushed, angry tones. Carl watched for a second and then turned his back on them.

Starting to jog, the tire iron now weighing heavy in his hand, he moved across the parking lot to meet the people he and his friends had saved.

Chapter 20

CARL ARRIVED JUST as the trapped people from the two cars were finished climbing out. Steve, Tracey and Craig were already busy shaking hands.

The first thing Carl noticed was the stale smell of urine and excrement. With his nose scrunched up, he tried to act like he didn't notice, while he walked up to join the small group of people.

Steve saw him and turned to introduce him. "And this here's, Carl. He was a big help, as well," Steve finished his statement.

Carl was immediately surrounded and between slaps on the back and numerous thank-yous, he tried to extricate himself.

"It's not a problem, really. Glad to have helped," Carl said, his eyes roaming over the new faces. He saw young and old, fat and skinny, and numerous races, all happy to be free of the automobiles. There was only one looker in the bunch, a young Asian woman who hung at the rear of the group.

Backing a few feet away from them, wanting to get away from the urine smell, one man stayed with Carl, hanging near him. Like the others, he smelled of urine and feces. Carl guessed they must have had to go in the car, as they were trapped by the ghouls outside. He didn't even want to think what it must have been like to have been in there with the windows rolled up and six people to a car. And on top of that, they all had to just shit and piss in their pants when the need arose.

"I don't think you understand what you've done for us," the man said next to Carl. Carl looked at him, now really seeing him for the first time. Before he was just one more face in the crowd.

He looked to be forty or so and he had a press pass on his shirt pocket. He had small, wire rimmed glasses, and light brown hair. Carl thought if he was twenty years younger, he would have looked a lot like Jimmy Olsen in the Superman comic books.

"I don't understand?" Carl said. "I mean, I'm sure it was bad for you being trapped in there but . . ."

The man cut him off. "No really. We were in there for almost two days with no food or water. And the smell. You know how people say you usually get used to smells when you have them around you for a while?"

Carl nodded. He'd heard that before. Usually garbage men would say that and even Jasper had mentioned it. He'd said he didn't even notice the smell of the bodies he had to embalm anymore.

The man shook his head back and forth vigorously. "Well, it's a load of bullshit, literally. We had to smell our own and each others shit and piss for two days. You don't know how good it is to be outside in the fresh air again."

Carl smiled, wishing the man would leave him alone. He wanted to get back to Tracey. He could see Craig hovering over her and if he didn't get in there and break it up, Craig would make a move on her.

"Hal Beckett, I'm a reporter for the Boston Globe," the man said holding his hand out.

Carl took it and shook twice, then let go. "Nice to meet you, I'm Carl Jenkins. Look, I'd love to chat, but I really need to get back to my friends. We need to figure out what to do next."

"Oh, okay, sure," Hal said and followed Carl back to the others. Steve was busy talking with the men. There was a heavy set guy with a small poodle on a leash, an older man with a woman who was probably his wife and a young teenager wearing all black. Carl had seen the look before. The boy had black lips and his nails were black, as well. It was Goth, if he was right.

When Carl walked up next to Steve, Craig looked at him from Steve's other side. Craig gave Carl a wink and Carl nodded back. Tracey saw him, too, and smiled.

Carl smiled at her and with the greetings over, Carl nudged Steve.

"So what's next? Do we go into the zoo?"

Steve turned to Carl and sighed. "That's what I was just talking to these guys about. It seems that when they got here the gate was locked tight. That's when the dead people arrived and they all jumped back into the cars. They locked bumpers by accident in their haste to leave and were stuck in there until we got here." Steve finished, looking to the new faces to make sure he had it right.

"That's the gist of it, young man, minus some of the more deplorable things we had to endure," the older man said.

"Yeah, I already heard about it from that guy," Carl said, pointing to Hal. The old man saw where Carl was pointing and nodded, understanding.

"Oh, of course you did. By the way, I'm Paul Thomas and this is my wife, Ethel."

Steve held up his hand. "Save the introductions for later, Paul. Right now we need to get inside the zoo where we should be safe from anymore of those *things*." He said the last word with mild distaste. The word zombie was just too damn hard to say and calling them dead people seemed off, as well. Frankly the entire situation was ridiculous.

How the hell could the dead walk around? They were dead for Christ Sakes!

Carl didn't realize his mind had wandered again and was brought back to the present with Steve clapping his hands for attention. "All right, people listen up! I've got an idea how to get us into the zoo. Now, everyone needs to stay put for a few more minutes and if it works, we'll be golden."

"And who the fuck put you in charge?" Came a voice from the back of the crowd.

The crowd parted to let a black man through, complete with corn rows and pants hanging down below his ass. He strutted more than walked up to Steve and when he was in front of him, he stopped. His face was only a few inches from Steve's, definitely in the man's personal space. If Steve noticed, he didn't let it show.

Hal leaned closer to Carl and whispered into his ear. "That's George. He's a tough guy. Wouldn't listen to anyone. Thinks he knows what's best for everyone."

Carl only nodded, curious about what would happen next.

Steve looked down at the man calmly. "No one put me in charge. But I'm the one with the bulldozer that'll get us inside the zoo. If you don't like my idea, feel free to leave. The dead might be walking around, but it's still a free country, last I checked."

George stared into Steve's face and the crowd held their breath, waiting for what would happen next.

Suddenly a ghoul stumbled out of the tree line, moaning. One arm was completely missing, only a bloody stump still dripping blood while it walked.

The women screamed and some of the men looked around, not knowing what to do. George took one look at the ghoul and then turned back to Steve.

"We'll finish this later, homie," he said in a low voice.

Steve smiled back, but there was no warmth in his smile. "I'll be looking forward to it." Then he had to move out of the way as the ghoul came at him and the others.

The dead guy had so many targets, he didn't know who to go after first, then a woman ran to close to him and he reached out, pulling her close, prepared to rip her throat out. The poodle was barking continuously, nipping at the dead guy's legs, while his victim screamed for help.

She received it a moment later, when the fat guy charged at the ghoul, his arm held out to his side. He clothes-lined the ghoul, knocking it off the ground to fall onto its back. The woman rolled away, crying. Some of the others ran to her side and helped drag her away from the fight.

The ghoul struck the ground hard and if it was still alive, the fall would have knocked the wind out of it, but it was very dead and so quickly rolled onto its side and was about to climb to its feet, when the fat guy ran up to its face and kicked its head like he was going for the extra points in a football game.

The face caved in from the impact of the steel towed boot the man wore, blood shooting out to cover his boot and leg. But the ghoul still moved and so the fat guy pulled his boot back and raised it up into the air, then brought it down with all his bulk behind it.

The head collapsed in on itself, the bone of the skull no match for the man's weight. With a squishy, sucking sound, he removed his boot from the gore puddle and then tried to scrape it on a nearby rock, like he had stepped in shit by accident and wanted to clean it off before entering his home.

Steve came up next to the man, slapping him on the back. "Wow, that was quick thinking, friend," he said, holding out his hand. "I didn't get your name yet."

The heavy set man turned to look at Steve, a wide smile on his face. "The name's Steggman, Matt Steggman. That's with two gg's now." He looked down at the dead corpse. "Those bastards aren't so hard to take down if you just keep your cool, it's just when there's too many of them to fight that things get difficult."

Steve shook his hand. "Amen to that, its good to see at least one more man that's not afraid to get his hands dirty in your group."

Matt looked back at the crowd of people and nodded. "Yeah, I know what you mean, they're either too old or the women are too weak, not like your daughter. I saw her kick some ass earlier."

Steve frowned, remembering. "Yeah, don't remind me."

Matt saw the frown and pressed Steve some more. "Worried about her? You know, you can't protect her forever and she seems pretty capable of taking care of herself."

"Yeah, I know, but it's what a father does, I can't help it."

Matt patted Steve on the shoulder. "Don't apologize, I'm a father myself. Have a boy, he's almost eight." His face grew serious then. "Shit, I hope they're all right. I haven't talked to them in a few days. They're probably wondering about me, too. My wife's not exactly the capable kind, if you know what I mean." He pointed to the poodle. "That's her dog I'm stuck with; I didn't have the heart to leave him when we hid in the car. Man, did the other people with me in the car hate him." He smiled then. "But we made it, all of us, even Scruffy, there."

"Hey, Dad, are we gonna get inside or what? Mr. Thomas says there's probably more dead people around here!" Tracey called. Steve turned to her and started her way, Matt at his side.

"You're right, honey, let's get going before there are too many to deal with," Steve told her. Steve slowed for a moment and looked into Matt's face. "I'm sure your family's fine and they'll be waiting for you when all this shit blows over."

Matt smiled back. "I can only hope, can't I?"

Steve nodded and then moved to the center of the group of people.

He gathered a few of the men around him, and with a smile, laid out his plan.

"All right, guys, here's what we'll do," Steve said.

Carl and the others listened intently, nodding, while the sun hung high in the sky.

* * *

Two miles down the road, the massive parade of the undead marched. Though no horns sounded or drums beat, their feet almost seemed to march in rhythm. They knew the bulldozer had gone this way and they wanted the meat that had ridden on top of the large machine.

Slowly they trudged, walking less then three miles an hour, but that was all right. They weren't in a hurry.

They were patient

They were dead.

They had all the time in the world.

Chapter 21

STEVE'S IDEA WAS simple. He would simply drive the bulldozer to the main gate and then raise the plow on the front of the machine. Once done, it would be child's play for one of the young men, such as Carl or Craig, to climb over the fence and locate the keys to unlock the gate or perhaps find a set of bolt cutters; something to get them inside without irreparably destroying the gate or fence.

"I still don't see why you can't just break through the gate and be done with it," Dr. Hickman said while Steve prepared to climb back onto the bulldozer.

Steve turned and looked at Hickman, sighing. "For the last time, Doc, if I do that then the gate will be smashed and how will we keep out any more walking dead people? No, we need to get in there without damaging the surrounding fence. Once we're inside, we'll be safe until help arrives or the government takes charge and cleans up this mess."

"Warren, let the man do what he thinks is right. He's done well by us and the others so far," Helen told her husband.

Dr. Hickman turned and glared at her. "Dammit, Helen, will you be quiet, I'm trying to talk here," he snapped at her.

Carl had just arrived, leaving the group near the gate, all of them waiting for Steve to drive the bulldozer over. Carl and Steve locked eyes for a brief moment, both thinking the same thing. Hickman was a bully with his wife and sooner or later someone needed to do something about it.

Steve shook his head, no. Whenever that time would be, it wouldn't be now. Now they needed to focus on getting inside the zoo and the protective fence surrounding it.

Carl's stomach rumbled, telling him it wanted to be fed. He tried to ignore it. The rest of the group was hungry, as well, the people who had been trapped in the car having nothing to eat and drink. All were anxiously waiting to get inside the zoo. There had to be something to eat in there. At the moment, Carl would settle for the pellets they fed the deer and rabbits.

"Take it easy, there Doc, we're all on edge," Steve said, trying to get him to lay off Helen without starting anything.

Hickman just looked up at Steve as he climbed onto the bulldozer and then he threw up his hands. "I give up, you're all against me," he spit and walked away.

"Warren, wait, please," Helen called after him.

"Let him go, Helen, he's not going to go far, I guarantee it," Steve said.

Helen looked up at Steve, her hand holding onto one of the rungs used to climb up to the cab.

"You know, he wasn't always this way. It's just the pressure at work. He has so much to worry about and a staff that is incompetent, according to him."

Steve smiled down at her, his beard hiding most of the gesture. "Helen, we're all under a lot of pressure right now and no one else is acting like an asshole. You just watch yourself, all right?"

She nodded. "Of course, and thank you for caring."

"It's what I do, I'm a caring guy; now step back, I'm gonna fire my baby up and get us the hell out of this damn parking lot."

Steve flipped a few switches and turned the key. The bulldozer's engine turned over, not starting. Steve tried to start it a second time with the same results.

"Is it out of gas?" Carl called from his side on the ground.

Steve shrugged. "I hope not, I was hoping there would at least be enough to get me to the gate. Dammit, I shouldn't have stopped it here when we pulled in. I should have kept going right up to the fence." He slapped his hand on the dashboard for emphasis.

Carl shrugged. "Shoulda, woulda, coulda, its all in the wind, man. We'll find another way in." Carl said this, but he didn't truly believe it. He turned to look at the twenty foot high fence. There was nothing they could use like a ladder to help get them over it and the metal fence itself was fashioned so it would be almost impossible to climb. And even if someone had the upper body strength to pull themselves all the way to the top, there were sharp spikes used for decorations, but they were also a deadly deterrent for anyone foolish enough to attempt it.

Steve muttered a few more imprecations and then turned the key one more time. The engine turned over and then started to sputter.

"Come on, baby, just a little more," Steve coaxed the machine, like it would hear him and do as he requested.

Then the engine caught, sputtering, but running. "Hot damn, it started!" Steve yelled. "Get the fuck out of the way; I'm not wasting any time here!" The group quickly dispersed, the sound of the engine filling the area with a rumbling that could be felt through the soles of their shoes.

With a surge of the engine, Steve turned toward the gate, the bulldozer moving forward, the plow already being raised up as he moved across the lot. The body of a few prone corpses were scattered across the parking lot and Steve drove over them, pulverizing the corpses under the churning wheels.

Flies already feasting on the carcasses buzzed away, angry that their meal was being flattened, but once the machine had moved on, they quickly resumed feeding, like nothing amiss had ever occurred.

A severed head of one of the ghouls was knocked across the lot. It rolled like a kickball and came up against a trash barrel. The one eye still remaining intact gazed up at nothing and Carl felt sick again. The bulldozer drove on, red droplets spraying behind it.

Carl watched this and had to turn away, the sight making his stomach roll inside him yet again.

Steve headed straight for the gate, the engine spurting and sputtering the entire time. When he was only fifteen feet away, the engine started to die for good. Steve knew his machine and could tell its death knell when he heard it. He floored the pedal and the machine jumped forward another five feet, but then the engine died completely and the bulldozer shuddered to a halt.

After the roaring of the engine, the parking lot seemed preternaturally quiet.

"Shit, shit, shit!" Steve yelled as he jumped down from the cab. "I was so damn close!"

"What do we do now, Dad?" Tracey asked, walking over to him and looking up at the raised plow only ten feet from the fence.

Some of the group came over as well, watching the bulldozer. "Could someone jump over the fence now?" Hal Beckett asked.

Craig turned to look at the reporter. "Are you crazy? Even if someone could jump that far, how the hell would they land safely?"

"What about if someone jumps all the way to the fence and then grabs the top? And then they climb over it and back down again," Matt suggested from the side.

"That's no good, there's not much to grab on to and even if you could, how do you climb down? It's still the same fence. If you can't climb up it, then how do you go down it?" Paul Thomas asked

"No, man, you guys are all full of shit. Unless you're a friggin' monkey, there's no way anyone's getting' across that gap," George said from the back of the group. "Man, we are truly fucked, right now." He waved his hands in a *see ya* gesture and walked away.

"Will all of you please shut the hell up for a second and let me think?" Steve snapped at them. He walked to the front of the bulldozer and looked straight up. Then he looked across the parking lot. He looked back up again and then back across the lot. Carl watched him and he could almost imagine the gears in Steve's mind formulating a plan. He reached inside his shirt pocket and pulled out his pack of cigarettes, lit one and blew out a cloud of smoke, grinning as he looked at the others.

Then Steve turned and walked back to the group. "All right, I've got another idea. It's not the best, but unless anyone else has a *real* idea, it's the best I can do on short notice."

Carl spoke up. "So, spill it, what's the idea?"

Steve looked at all the faces in front of him and then he grinned like before. "Simple, we make a bridge and crawl over."

Chapter 22

"WHAT ARE YOU talking about?" Asked a voice from the group.

"That's ridiculous," said another.

Steve held out his hands for them to stop talking. "Look, I'm not going to spend the next ten minutes explaining my idea to you, so either come and help or stay out of the way." He turned to look for Carl, Craig and Matt; Tracey already by his side. "You guys gonna help me?"

Craig grinned back. "Hell, yes, just tell us what we need to do."

Carl shot a glance at Craig. He didn't like the man agreeing for him, but the truth was; he was right. Of course he'd help.

Steve nodded and moved away from the group, looking up at the trees surrounding him. "Follow me, guys; I'll talk while we walk." Everyone followed behind him, making their way across the parking lot. Behind them, the rest of the group talked in hushed tones, each giving half-baked ideas that might get them inside the zoo.

Carl looked over his shoulder at them and saw the Goth teenager actually try to scale the fence. He only made it about eight feet before he ran out of hand holds and quickly dropped back to the ground.

ht. If the kid had made it, then all their
Steve was pointing up at the tree limbs,
d to move closer so he could hear him.
enough tree limb that's long enough
it it down and use it to bridge the gap
and the fence."

ed up, his chin high in the air, the stubble showing
y. "But how do we get back down from the top of the fence? It's still a twenty foot drop."

"I'm glad you asked," Steve answered. He pointed to a telephone pole near the entrance to the parking lot. "Right there, all the rope we need. And with the power cut off, it's all safe."

"You hope," Carl added. "For all we know the power's still on around here and I for one don't want to be the idiot who finds out the hard way."

"Relax Carl, I'm in construction. We have to deal with power cables all the time. Even if the line's still hot, I know how to disconnect it from the transformer." He pointed to another telephone pole across the lot. "See that one, with the box on it?"

Carl nodded.

"That's the transformer. We'll be fine," Steve assured him

"Okay, Dad, but how are we going to cut the tree limb from the tree? I didn't see any cutting gear around."

Steve rubbed his beard, scratching his chin. He hated the damn thing and was hoping once inside the zoo he would be able to find some shaving gear to take it off. "That's something I haven't figured out yet. Anyone else have any ideas?"

The four of them all looked up at the tree tops. Carl noticed a couple of squirrels running through the branches and a few small birds sat on the edge of some limbs, chirping happily. Whatever was happening in man's world was no concern of theirs. To the animals, life went on, with nothing changed.

Carl looked around the parking lot, his mind working overtime. There had to be something they could use. His eyes stopped when they landed on the Pontiac.

"What about the car?" He said quietly.

Steve glanced at him. "Huh, what did you say?"

Carl pointed to the Pontiac. "I said the car. What about it. Is there something in the engine that could be used like a saw?"

Before Carl's last word was out of his mouth, Steve's eyes were wide with understanding.

"Holy shit, Carl, that's brilliant. The car, I know exactly what we can do." He turned to Tracey, grabbing her by the shoulders. "Honey, go to the 'dozer and grab the tool kit under the driver's seat," he told her.

"The one in the gray bag?" She asked, already moving across the parking lot.

"Yup, that's the one, and hurry, we're wasting time we probably don't have."

Almost as if on cue to Steve's words of warning, a ghoul stumbled out of the edge of the parking lot, only the forest behind it. The soldier's uniform was apparent, the green fatigues seeming out of place on the dead man once the corpse stumbled onto the hardtop of the parking lot.

All eyes turned to look at it; a few muffled cries came from the group

"Jesus Christ, I think I know that guy," Craig said in a hushed whisper.

"There's only one for now, who wants to deal with it?" Steve asked Carl and Craig.

Carl wasn't about to volunteer if he didn't have to and he was hoping he wasn't going to be put into that position when Craig started walking toward the dead soldier.

"I've got this one. I think he was a friend of mine," he said in a flat tone.

"Okay, but watch your ass. He's not your friend anymore, remember that," Steve called to Craig.

If Craig heard him, he didn't answer, but instead continued walking toward the dead soldier, back straight, shoulders up.

Matt turned to Steve, concern on his face. He had been silent so far, but now felt he needed to voice his objection.

"Are you sure about this, Steve? There are more of us then it, why have only one of us deal with that dead guy?"

Steve shook his head. "I know what you mean, Matt, but I think this is something Craig needs to do himself. If you want, feel free to follow behind him in case he needs help."

Matt grunted. "That's a good idea, I'll do that," then he jogged away after Craig. Carl watched him go, wondering how it must feel to carry all the extra weight the man had on his body. Despite this, Matt seemed to be a mobile person, not afraid to move his muscles. Carl had known a few overweight people who were too tired or lazy to walk ten feet, but had to use the handicapped spots at the grocery store. I mean, what the hell is up with that? Now if you're fat you're considered handicapped? Shaking his head, in remembrance, he watched Craig reach the dead soldier.

Craig slowed when he was a few feet away. The first thing he noticed was the large gash in the front of his friend's throat. The pallor of the dead soldier's skin gave him a jaundiced look; the eyes the color of rotten Tapioca pudding. Blood had seeped out of the wound to drench the front of his uniform, staining the shirt a dull maroon. Craig also noticed the man still carried his issued rifle, the strap still wrapped around his shoulder.

"Oh Jesus, Banner, what the fuck did they do to you?" Craig asked, his voice trembling.

Lucas Banner didn't answer him, only stumbled forward, mouth moving up and down and side to side like he was trying to talk. Craig saw some of his dead friends nails had been ripped clean off, the points of the fingers raw and red.

He and Banner had gone to boot camp together, becoming friends at the end of the two months. They had spent many a weekend partying together and now Lucas Banner was gone, to be replaced by this shambling, empty thing in front of him

Craig wiped his eyes dry and took a step backward, staying out of reach of Banner's hands.

Matt walked up beside him, startling Craig for a moment. "You all right, pal? If you want, I can take him down."

Craig shook his head. "No, he's mine. He's my friend and if he was still alive and could talk to me, I think he'd want me to do it."

Matt shrugged his wide shoulders. "Suit yourself, but let's get it done, okay? We've got a lot of work to do still."

Craig turned on Matt, eyes flashing with anger. "Don't rush me, goddammit! I'll do it when I'm good and fucking ready!"

Matt took a step backward, unaccustomed to the raw rage in Craig's eyes. Holding up his hands, he tried to calm him down, "Whoa there, buddy, okay, fine with me. He's all yours."

Craig stared at Matt for another moment and then turned away. Banner was still approaching him and Craig had to move away again. For the briefest of instances, he thought about what would happen if he just stood still and let his friend reach him. He could imagine the teeth sinking into his throat or face, the skin tearing like taffy. Sure it would hurt, but only for a few seconds. Then death would take him and he could end all this bullshit of running and hiding and running some more.

He stared into Banner's glassy, glazed eyes and wondered if his friend was still in there. Was Banner still inside the dead body, watching what his body was doing, but unable to stop it? Was his soul now gone or was it still inside the rotting husk, trapped for as long as the body moved about.

Matt then grabbed Craig's shirt, pulling him away from the reaching hands. "What the hell, Craig! He almost reached you! Come on, pal, do this thing so we can go back to the others."

Craig shook his head clear and came out of whatever fugue state he had fallen into. "What? Oh shit, Matt, thanks. Okay, stand back. There's gonna be blood spray." Matt did as requested and backed away while Craig pulled his sidearm.

He cocked the weapon and raised the .45 pistol so that it was level with Banner's head.

"Sorry, buddy, but I have to do it," Craig whispered, more for himself then for Banner. Banner only stared, jaw slack, moaning.

Craig squeezed the trigger, a round striking Banner in the forehead. The head snapped back and the corpse dropped to the ground, the rifle clattering as it struck the pavement. The legs twitched for a while, but the man was now definitely dead.

"Jesus Christ," Matt whispered. "You've got a gun with bullets in it? Why the hell didn't you use it earlier when we were trapped in the cars?"

Craig looked over his shoulder, wiping his eyes for the last time. "Because I've only got a few rounds left and when they're gone, they're gone, that's why. Most of these dead fucks can be taken out easily, you know that. So why waste bullets I can't replace?"

Matt nodded. "Good point, sorry, I didn't think." He gestured to Banner's body. "Looks like that guy had a weapon."

Craig looked back down at Banner, realizing again there was a rifle on the corpse's back, now hiding under the body. Though he didn't want to admit it, he was pretty shaken up about having to kill someone he already knew. Bending over the body, careful to make sure his friend was definitely dead, he extricated the rifle from him. Pulling the clip from the rifle, he smiled.

"It's got a full load, guess he never got off a shot."

Matt nodded. "Tough break, you knew him?"

Craig nodded. "Yeah, I knew him." Then he was done talking. Kneeling over the corpse, he quickly stripped it of any useable gear. There was an extra two clips for the .45, the actual sidearm missing, the holster empty. Craig took them all, plus another clip for the rifle. A small canteen hung from the corpse's waist and Craig took this, as well. The last thing Craig took were the man's dog tags, placing them in his pocket for safe keeping.

Then with his new supplies, he stood up and looked at Matt. "Okay, we're done here, let's go."

Matt nodded and the two men crossed the parking lot to join up with the others.

When Craig and Matt had reached the car, Steve was on the ground, under the Pontiac, his legs sticking out the side. A few rocks were under the chassis, and a jack from the trunk was holding the car up. Craig could hear Steve muttering and asking for tools, Tracey quickly handing them to him.

Carl turned to them as they approached. "Hey, all set?"

Craig nodded. "Yeah, we're good. And I got another weapon and some more ammo for my side arm."

"Sweet, that's great man."

Craig gestured with his chin to the car and Steve. "So what's happening here? Is he trying to fix it?"

Carl shook his head. "No man, he's taking the transmission out and then he's going in for the flywheel or something. He really didn't want to tell us everything, said it would be a waste of time."

"Is there anything I can do?" Craig asked.

Carl shook his head. "Nah, we're good. Why don't you take a break? But if you really want to do something, you can make sure the others are doing all right."

Craig grunted, turning away to walk across the lot to the others where they had gathered around the bulldozer. "I'll do that," he said.

Steve grunted from under the car, calling for a different sized socket. Tracey dug in the bag and then quickly bent over and rolled it to him.

"Thanks, honey, that's perfect," Steve said. It was quiet for a second while he fitted the socket and then the sounds of him working floated out once more.

This went on for almost an hour, and finally, when Carl was growing impatient, Steve slid out from under the car and lit a cigarette.

"Almost there, there's just one more bolt to go," he said, stretching his back and arms. "Christ, I hate it under there. Reminds me of my first car. I spent so much time on my back under it, it was a miracle I ever did anything at all."

Tracey walked around the Pontiac and leaned against it, her right hip touching Steve who had rested his back against the car.

"Was that the old Charger you always talk about?" She asked, curious.

Steve nodded. "Yup, my first car. I met your mother in that car. Did I ever tell you that? I loved that car . . . and your mother, once upon a time."

She nodded. She'd heard the story more times then she could count.

"In fact, you were probably conceived in the back of that car."

Tracey scrunched up her face. "Gross, Dad, too much information," she joked.

Deciding that was enough time down memory lane, he pushed off from the car and stood up, stretching one last time.

Looking up at the sky, he frowned slightly.

"It's gonna be dark soon, we better get a move on. Carl, help me under the car, will you? It's a two man job for a few minutes."

Carl did as he was asked, dropping to the ground and rolling under the car. Steve did the same from the opposite side, and with Steve directing him, Carl held the transmission up while Steve loosened the last bolt.

"Now get ready, Carl. It's gonna be heavy," Steve told him. "But I need you to hold it for just a second so I don't get crushed when it falls free. After that, its scrap metal, okay?"

"No problem," Carl replied.

Carl tried to be ready, but as the last bolt slid free, the transmission dropped onto his chest like a ton of bricks. The breath left his lungs and he tried desperately to suck in another lungful of air.

"Holy shit, its heavy, its killing me," he gasped, trying to push it off him. Then Tracey was on the ground and under the car with him, reaching for the transmission. Despite the crushing weight on his chest, he still noticed the smell of her. She was hot and dirty, the smell more musky than sweet, her natural scent. Still, he found himself aroused by it, his animalistic sex drive from a million years ago kicking in to dominate his mind.

Steve rolled closer and slipped his arms under the heavy piece of machinery, and with all three of them working together, Carl was finally able to get it off his chest.

With a loud *clang* the transmission struck the pavement. Carl sucked in air, happy to have the enormous weight off his chest. "Christ that sucked. Tell me that was the worst of it," Carl said.

Steve nodded and slipped back under to grab the flywheel, pushing Carl out of the way as he did so.

After having Tracey hand him another size socket, Steve took off the six bolts securing the flywheel to the engine and then crawled out, smiling widely.

His face was covered in grease and oil and his shirt was filthy from all the times he'd wiped his hands on it. But it hadn't been too clean before he'd started, so it was almost an improvement.

Steve handed the flywheel to Carl. Carl hefted it, surprised by how heavy it was. The flywheel was about twelve inches round with teeth surrounding it. It reminded Carl off what you'd find in an old clock.

"So what the hell am I supposed to do with this?" He asked, holding the flywheel in both his hands.

Steve pointed to a tree across the parking lot, Carl's eyes following the gesture. The maple was at least fifty years old, the roots slowly exploding out of the pavement as time progressed. Its limbs were long and thick, but some of its newer extremities were only a few inches thick.

Find a limb that's not too thick, but thick enough to support us and then use that," he pointed to the flywheel, "like a saw and cut it off."

Carl frowned. "You're not really serious are you?"

Steve's countenance darkened and he glared at Carl. "Goddamn right I'm serious, now move your ass and get started!"

Carl jumped back, not used to the anger in the man's tone. He quickly moved across the parking lot until he was under the tree. The bark was a ripple of waves, easy for him to climb, even with one arm wrapped around the flywheel. He found a limb that would suit their needs when he was only twelve feet into the tree. Straddling the limb, he started to use the flywheel like a saw. It was slow work, but it was working. Sweat beaded on his forehead, threatening to drip into his eyes and the metal cut into his hands until he took off his shirt and used it as protective gear for his hands.

After fifteen minutes had passed, Steve walked over to see how he was doing; Craig, Paul, Matt and now Hal was with him.

"How's it going, Carl?" Steve asked.

Carl stopped sawing and wiped his brow. "Slow, but I'll get there," he said, starting to work at the limb again.

Steve nodded. "Good, keep at it. Craig here will spell you when you want a break. Even Hal said he'd help if we need him."

Hal nodded, smiling. "Sure will, anything to get out of this damn parking lot, not to mention out of these clothes."

Both Craig and Matt vigorously agreed.

Steve looked at them both frowning. "No shit, I didn't want to say anything, but all you guys smell like a port o' potty."

"Well, of course. We've been crapping and pissing in our pants for the past two damn days, what do you expect? My ass is so sore I don't even want to look at it," Matt said, trying to shift position.

Craig made a face. "Now that's a mental picture I could have done without," he joked.

That got the others snickering, and a second later, they we're all chuckling, except Matt, that is. His face was still serious.

"Laugh all you want, but its still sore," he said again.

That just got all of them laughing harder, and while Carl chuckled and sawed, the men all enjoyed a good laugh.

Chapter 23

WITH A CRACK of splitting wood and a crash, the tree limb fell from the tree, Craig beaming widely. "Ha! Finally, now let's get this shit done!"

"No kidding, I'm so hungry I almost started gnawing on the bark of that tree over there," Hal said, bending over to help pick up the limb. The tree limb was over fifteen feet long and almost as thick as an average adult male's leg.

It had taken over an hour of non-stop sawing to finally cut into the moist wood enough for the limb to crack. Then the process began again, now sawing through the rubbery splinters that still connected limb to tree.

"I hear that, I almost thought Matt was a wild boar and shot him," Carl joked, as well. But when he saw Matt's face he quickly stopped laughing.

"That's not funny, Carl. I'm not proud of my weight, it's a thyroid condition. I can't control it."

Carl smiled wanly. "Sorry, man, I didn't mean anything by it, you know, just screwing around."

Matt nodded, his face softening. "That's all right, Carl, as long as you apologized, we're cool."

"So if you two pussies are done with your Oprah moment, can we get this tree to the gate or what?" Craig jibed.

Both Carl and Matt turned to look at Craig, but the wiseass smile he wore said it all.

"Yeah, let's go, already, shit man, I can talk while I work, you know. I know that's a feat for you Army guys, but us civilians are able to multitask," Carl retorted.

Suddenly a voice called from across the parking lot; it was Steve's.

"Will you idiots hurry the hell up, its getting dark and our luck can't hold out forever!"

"Yeah, yeah, we're coming," Carl called back, carrying his share of the tree limb.

While the four men carried the limb across the parking lot, Carl thought about what Steve had said. He'd been right, they had been lucky since arriving at the gates of the zoo. Sure, there had been more than a dozen ghouls about, but they had dispatched them easily.

While they had been sawing at the tree limb, a few other undead had shambled into the lot from the tree line, but they had also been dispatched easily, their bodies still lying where they dropped. But where the others had come from, surely there would be more, and when they finally arrived, the group of survivors needed to be inside the walls of the zoo.

Six minutes later, the four men, now joined by Steve, Tracey and George, struggled to raise the tree limb up to the bulldozer. After a few tries and failures, they finally accomplished it. The tree limb was wedged tight between the spires of the zoo's fence, the other end just sitting on the middle of the plow.

George was on top of the plow and he wiggled the limb, seeing if it was safe.

"Looks pretty good, should I go or what?" He asked, looking down on the others.

"Go for it, the sooner the better," Steve told him.

George nodded and scurried over the limb. He was young and athletic and had no problem. He kept his ass planted firmly and then slid an inch at a time, his legs dangling over the sides. When he reached the fence, he looked down at Steve.

"Okay, now what?" He asked. "I still can't get down; there's no handholds."

"Here, catch," Steve called out.

Steve tossed a roll of telephone wire at him, taken from a nearby utility pole while the others had been sawing the limb from the tree.

"Loop it around the top and then climb down," Steve told him.

George made a face. "What the fuck, man? If you had this wire then why the hell didn't we just use it in the first place?"

Steve pointed at Paul and Ethel Thomas and a few of the women.

"Because these people can't climb up that wire no matter what, so we needed an easier way in, now get down so I can send some others over."

George gave Steve the finger and then did as he was told.

Steve frowned at the gesture, but let it go. There was more to worry about right now then thumping chests at each other.

"Okay, who's next?" Steve asked.

"I'll go, Dad," Tracey said.

Steve nodded. "Okay, honey, but be careful."

She kissed him on the cheek and smiled. "Oh, Dad, I'm not a little girl anymore."

He returned her smile with one of his own. "You always will be to me, now do as I say and be careful."

She climbed up the bulldozer and easily crawled across.

"All right, who's next?" Steve asked.

One at a time, Craig, Hal and a woman Carl hadn't met yet all climbed up the bulldozer and over the makeshift bridge, all of them easily shimmying down the telephone wire.

Carl waited for Steve to go and he passed the time watching the young Asian woman scurrying across.

She was petite with dark black hair that went down to her shoulders. Her skin was a little pale, but still flawless. Carl couldn't help but admire her backside as she crawled across; though she seemed to be having a little more trouble then the others. She kept favoring her left arm and wincing in pain.

Carl moved next to Paul Thomas. "She all right?" He asked him, gesturing to the woman.

Paul shrugged. "Don't ask me. Far as I know, she doesn't speak English. All I know is her name's Kim Lee."

"How'd she wind up here with you guys?" Carl asked.

Ethel leaned forward, giving her opinion. "No one knows, dear. She just came out of the woods like the rest of us. Well, except for Hal and Sherry. Those are their cars over there."

"Who's Sherry?" Carl asked, looking at the few faces he didn't know the names to.

Ethel gestured with her chin. "Over there, near the boy with all the black on. She's a mother, but she doesn't know where her children are. It's a shame really."

"Who's next?" Steve called from above. He was standing on the cab, helping people climb up to the plow.

Paul looked to his wife. "Come on, honey, let's get this over with," he said, starting up the side of the bulldozer and holding out his hand for Ethel to take.

"Good luck," Carl called to her.

"Thank you, dear, I'll need it, I'm not as young as I used to be," she said, climbing up the bulldozer.

Carl looked at the few faces remaining to climb into the zoo. There was a Spanish couple that he hadn't talked to yet, as well as the kid in black. Matt was still waiting too, as well as another woman with a bad dye job. The Hickman's were off near the fence talking together and the woman he now knew was Sherry started to climb up the bulldozer. She flashed Carl a wan smile and he returned it. Carl saw sad eyes looking back at him and worry lines creased into her cheeks.

Then she was up and climbing over the tree limb, going ahead of Paul and Ethel

Carl was starting to relax a little. They were all going to be okay, he thought. They would get inside the zoo and try to contact help or just wait for help to come to them.

He was helping the Spanish couple onto the bulldozer when he heard the sound of many footsteps. It almost sounded like marching, mostly the hard soled shoes and boots some of the wearers had on echoing off the pavement.

He turned to look at the small road/driveway coming off the main road the bulldozer had traveled on to get to the parking lot and what he saw made his blood run cold.

Hundreds of what were once people, but was now a false mockery of life, shambled down the road and into the parking lot, spreading out like water poured from a cup. Ghouls, hundreds of them.

Carl's throat constricted and he couldn't speak, though he desperately wanted to. Then his vocal cords unfroze and he let out a yell that had everyone turning to him and then to where he was pointing.

Helen saw the approaching undead horde and let out a scream, the woman with the bad dye job doing the same.

"Jesus Christ, there must be hundreds of them," Steve said, amazed. From on top of the bulldozer, he had a grand view and would have seen them sooner if he hadn't been preoccupied helping Ethel crawl across the tree limb. Even now, the old woman was struggling to climb down the telephone wire, her arms not up to the task. Steve saw her slip after only sliding down a few feet, but Paul and Hal were there to catch her. She tumbled on top of them, the three of them falling in a heap. Then Steve had bigger problems.

"Everyone, move now, there's no time!" He screamed. The Spanish couple was already prepared to move, only waiting for Ethel to get off the limb. Then the woman and the man quickly moved across, their haste obvious.

The kid in black practically ran up the side of the bulldozer and was over in seconds, his youth an asset.

Only Carl, Steve and the Hickmans still needed to get across. Steve looked down at Carl and he waved him to cross.

"Go, we're right behind you," Carl called, climbing up the bulldozer, Matt right behind him. He looked behind him to see the Hickman's running across the lot to the bulldozer.

Steve climbed across, his biceps flexing as he quickly slid to the fence. After years of construction, his muscles had been toned and shaped so he had the body of a man half his age. His tanned skin, from hours in the sun, only helped to add the allusion of youth.

Carl was on the top of the plow, and as soon as Steve was over the spires and on the fence, his arms holding him easily on the wire, Carl sat on the limb, prepared to move across it.

Looking behind him, he saw the Hickman's making their way onto the bulldozer. Behind them, only ten feet away, were the first ghouls of the undead crowd, arms out in front of them, jaws snapping shut on empty air as they anticipated the flesh only a few feet away.

"Hurry the fuck up, will ya, Doc. They're right behind you!" Carl yelled and started to move across the limb.

"You can do the same, too, okay?" Matt called, ready to move as soon as Carl was at the fence.

"Come on, Helen, I'm not going to die for your lazy ass!" Dr. Hickman screamed.

Carl was at the fence now and just as he was about to climb over and grab the telephone wire; he saw something even worse then the undead crowd attacking them.

Dr. Hickman had decided his wife was too slow and had climbed up the bulldozer, leaving her to trail behind. She was an out of shape woman and the physical labor was too much for her. Dr. Hickman climbed onto the plow easily, and with his wife trailing behind, started to crawl out onto the limb.

Matt was halfway across and he turned to look at Dr. Hickman.

"Jesus, will you wait a second? I'm a big guy, you don't want to be on here with me at the same time; it might crack!"

"Wait, Doc! Help your wife, she's right behind you!" Steve called from the other side of the fence, helpless to help the flailing woman. Hickman ignored them all and started out onto the tree limb.

Carl started to climb down the wire and as he did so, he got a good look at Dr. Hickman's face as he started to shimmy across the tree limb. His face was a mask of terror. The man was petrified. He was looking at nothing; the only thing in his mind was escaping the ghouls below him.

Matt had made it to the spires and with a grunt; he slid his bulk over the side, the telephone wire protesting his weight. But it held and he dropped to the ground in a heap of limbs. Breathing heavily, he stumbled away to catch his breath, limping slightly. Then his eyes went wide and he looked through the fence to see his dog, Scruffy, running around and barking at the ghouls. They tried to grab the animal, but it was too quick, darting in and out of their legs.

"Oh shit, I forgot my dog!" Matt screamed, but he knew it was too late to retrieve him. All he could do was hope the little guy was intelligent enough, and quick enough, to escape the slow moving hands of the dead.

Helen had climbed onto the plow, now, her face red and covered with sweat from the exertion.

"Warren, please, wait, I need your help!" She called, straddling the tree limb.

Behind her, the undead horde surrounded the bulldozer and swarmed under the tree limb, arms outstretched to reach Dr. Hickman's swinging legs. But he was far too high for them to reach him and with a terrified shriek; he reached the fence and swung his legs over the side.

"Doc, you bastard; wait for your wife! She needs your help!" Steve called as he jumped back from the fence to keep away from the probing fingers. Luckily, the same thing that prevented the fence from having foot holds to climb on prevented the undead from reaching through the small gaps and grabbing the survivors. Unfortunately it also prevented Scruffy from squeezing through the bottom of the gate, as well.

Dr. Hickman ignored the cries from Steve and the others to help his wife, only worried about himself. He grabbed the telephone wire and started to climb down just as Helen started her crossing of the tree limb.

Carl was standing next to Steve, Craig on the other side, Tracey behind them. Everyone's eyes were on Helen as she valiantly tried to cross the limb.

"Come on, Helen, you can do it!" Carl cried out to her, trying to giver her some much needed confidence.

If Helen heard him, she didn't show it, her face locked in concentration while she desperately tried to crawl across the limb.

"The old bitch ain't gonna make it," George said from behind them. "Her fuckin' husband left her ass to hang out to dry. Man, that's some cold shit."

Dr. Hickman had landed on the ground and he moved away from the group. He was lost in his own world and didn't meet the gaze of anyone as he stumbled away, his hands hiding his face.

Corpses climbed the bulldozer and balanced on the top of the cab. Some were knocked off by their brethren to fall back into the crowd, crushing others below.

One adventurous ghoul tried to climb out onto the log after Helen only to tumble off with its first step. It slammed into the ground face first, flattening its features into a bloody pulp. A moment later it was back up, though, ready to try again.

Helen was halfway across when she slipped. Her left hand missed the tree limb, her eyes staring at the faces of the undead below her. She let out a shriek that was lost amidst the moaning of the crowd. Her face hit the tree limb hard and her body struck the bark, balancing precariously; her legs dangling below her like worms for the fish of death below.

"Helen, snap out of it, you're almost there," Steve called. Then he cursed and started to climb the telephone wire again, only to be stopped by Tracey.

"Let me go, I need to help her!" Steve demanded, pushing his daughter away from him.

"Too late for that shit, man, the bitch is dead. Look," George said coldly.

All eyes, including Steve's, turned up to stare at Helen in her last moments on earth. She tried valiantly to push herself back to a sitting position and crawl the rest of the way across, but behind her one of the ghouls, either by accident or intent, picked up the tree limb and started to shift it to the right.

Helen screamed and lost her balance, tumbling into the waiting hands below.

"Oh my God, no!" Steve yelled, running to the fence to see if he could find her amidst the walking corpses.

George too, ran to the fence, but he was there for a different reason. "Oh man, this is going to be good."

Steve grabbed him and nearly picked him up, slamming him against the fence. Dead fingers tried to grasp George's clothes, others trying to grab his short curly black hair through the fence.

"You shut the fuck up, do you hear me? That's a living, breathing human being out there!"

George snickered, looking down at Steve. "Not anymore, man, now put me the fuck down or you and me are gonna to go at it."

Carl noticed George's words didn't seem that serious, only mindless talk from a man trying to save face. Steve was almost twice his size and had arms almost as big as George's skinny legs. The fight between the two of them would be a slaughter, favoring Steve.

Steve looked up at the sneering face and then tossed George to the side, "Get the fuck out of my sight before I do something I'll regret."

George fell to the ground, rubbing his chest where Steve had propped him up by his shirt. Then the man raised his hand and mimicked shooting Steve, then he moved away down the fence to see if he could still see Helen.

All this had taken only a few seconds and in that time the ghouls Helen had fallen onto were getting their bearings, realizing they had fresh meat in their ranks.

Helen lay on the ground, dazed and confused and when she opened her eyes, she saw the multiple faces of death hovering above her. She let out a piercing scream that overrode the wailing of the dead, her face locked in a mask of terror.

Then she was lost from sight as a dozen hands and faces dove onto her.

Carl knew he should look away, but like driving by a car crash on the highway, he just couldn't make himself do it.

Helen screamed as teeth and nails dug into her flesh. One hand reached under her left eyelid, pulling back, ripping the flesh away, the eyeball popping out to dangle on her cheek. Another hand plucked the eyeball like a berry and popped it into its mouth, a white fluid squirting from its lips, similar to when a cherry tomato is bitten into.

With muscle and tendons ripped apart by teeth, her limbs were pulled from her body. She was drawn and quartered in front of the gates of the zoo, her screams rising in pitch like a falsetto opera singer. Only her head remained; her one remaining eye wide with shock and fear.

Carl couldn't help but wonder what was going through her mind in those last seconds. Then a face came down on either side of her neck, ripping the flesh and tendons. Another set of hands started to pull on her hair, her head slowly separating from her body. With nothing but her spine still attached, stretched to breaking, her mouth still moved, her scream cutting off in mid-scream when her vocal cords became separated.

Then her head was lost in the crowd. The lucky ghoul who had acquired the head plunged its hand deep into her mouth and pulled out her tongue to chomp on merrily. Her torso was a mess of internal organs and blood, and within minutes, she was almost completely gone, nothing but a few scattered body parts remaining to be fought over by the hundreds of corpses clustering around the site of her death, their feet stomping into the puddle of her blood and tracking it around the parking lot like children playing in the mud.

The smell of blood and decay filled the air, causing Carl to cover his nose. He also knew some of the new smells of blood were from Helen and it made him sick.

Steve stepped away from the fence, his face ash grey, his jaw slack. He'd just watched a woman he'd known, talked to only minutes before, be ripped apart like a pig at a barbecue.

Tracey tried to console him, but he shrugged her off.

"Jesus Christ, I can't believe what just happened," Craig said, his complexion pale. Some of the others had watched, too, and were off to the side, throwing up.

Steve blinked a few times and then started to look around himself.

"What's wrong, Dad?" Tracey asked.

Steve ignored her, still looking around. After ten seconds had passed, his expression changed, becoming more feral. Without another word to the others, he stomped out of the group and into the zoo, the others watching his back as he moved away.

"Dad, where are you going?" Tracey asked, but all she got for her trouble was her father's retreating form.

While outside the fence, the undead howled and wailed, only wanting the meat that was, at the moment, out of their grasp.

Chapter 24

DR. WARREN HICKMAN leaned against the empty ticket booth, breathing heavily. The past few minutes were a blur. All he remembered was seeing a massive crowd of infected people charging at him and his wife.

He remembered grabbing her hand and telling her to run and then he was landing inside the zoo, his wife not around.

He looked up just as Steve ran up to him. He felt himself picked up and thrown across the walkway into a copse of overgrown shrubs. With his arms and legs entangled, he tried to extricate himself only to find himself entangled even more.

Then he felt hands grab his shirt, and with a few ripped buttons, was pulled from the copse and thrown into the ticket booth.

He crashed into the booth, the thin wafer board crumbling under his weight. His head flared in pain as a small splinter pierced his thigh and for a moment, he saw stars.

Then he was being tossed into the air again, this time being held upright.

Through glazed eyes he saw the blur of a fist coming straight at him and then he saw nothing, his jaw rocking from the blow. Semiconscious, he still felt the next blow into his kidneys and he gasped, trying to suck in another gulp of air.

Then he was falling to the cement walkway and the darkening sky was looking down on him, his body now prone on the walkway.

He heard muffled, raised voices around him, but he was too out of it to know who they were from or even why they were screaming. Then blackness descended as he fell into the oblivion of unconsciousness.

Steve fought with the arms holding him back, the weight of his subduers slowing him down. Carl and Craig held on for dear life, and then Matt arrived, adding his considerable bulk to the mix.

When Tracey arrived, she immediately got into her Dad's face, talking to him and trying to calm him down. Behind her, Ethel and one of the other women leaned over the unconscious body of Dr. Hickman, seeing if they could do anything for him.

"God dammit, let me go. I want to kill that son-of-a-bitch!" Steve yelled in anger.

"No way, man, we're holding you until you calm down. So just chill!" Carl yelled into Steve's ear.

George walked up and stood a few feet away, enjoying the tableau. "Aww come on, let him go, I want to see him beat the shit out of the white prick."

"You just get out of here, we don't need your shit right now," Craig snapped at George.

George flipped Craig off, but stopped talking, though he stayed where he was.

"Dad, for God's sake, will you stop this?" Tracey screamed at her father's face.

"No way. That asshole left his wife to die and I'm going to make him pay!" Steve screamed, trying to spring free of Carl, Matt and Craig. But all three squeezed tighter, holding his arms.

"Steve you've got to calm down. We can deal with this shit later. Right now we still don't know if it's safe in here. Do you want us to get attacked again? Maybe get your daughter killed?" Matt said, trying to reason with him.

Steve slowed his struggling, the welfare of his daughter sinking in. Soon he was just standing still, the others now seeming ridiculous holding on to him. Steve turned to look at Carl and then Craig.

"Fine, I'll stop, but its not over. That bastard is going to answer for what he's done," Steve said, pointing at Dr. Hickman.

Hickman was sitting up now, holding his side, Ethel and the other woman still hovering over him.

"Will you guys let me go, please?" Steve asked nicely. "I promise, I'm okay."

Carl could see his eyes were clear, now, the rage gone for the moment.

Nodding, Carl let go. "Okay, guys, let him go, I think he's cool."

Matt and Craig let Steve go, and Steve stepped two feet away, rubbing his arms. All three had squeezed tightly, giving the man some light Indian burns.

Steve looked around himself for the first time since leaving the gate to look for Hickman. The ticket booth was destroyed, and as he looked at the walkway leading into the zoo, seeing all the different paths that led deeper into the zoo, he frowned.

Gesturing for Carl to come to him, he waited while Carl did as requested.

"Look at this place; this isn't a very defensible position. If those things are in here, there's no way to defend ourselves from so many different angles," Steve said while waving his hand around him.

Carl shrugged. "Don't look at me. I'm no tactician; whatever you want to do is cool with me." Carl looked at the overgrown pathways, the tree limbs and shrubbery that lined the walkways so overgrown and encroaching on the paths that you could only fit one person at a time down them. "Look at this place, it looks like shit."

Matt walked up to them, limping slightly. He had landed wrong climbing down off the fence, his weight a problem.

"This place had been closed since last year, Carl. They tried to keep it open, but the funding was gone. You're right about that one, though. No one's been keeping this place up for quite a while. I heard they tried getting some private donations, but it failed miserably, so they shipped all the animals off to other zoos. I think the tigers went to San Diego." He shook his head, sadly. "It's a real shame; this place was a part of history around here. Did you know it's been here since the 1950's?"

Craig walked up to them, followed by Tracey. "So what happens now?" Craig asked, interrupting Matt.

Steve shook his head. "Nothing's changed. We make sure this place is safe and then see about getting help. Maybe its better this way. If the place was closed up tight when the outbreak started, then that means it's probably empty. There's probably no one here but us."

"Oh I wouldn't bet on that," a voice said from a side walkway that had been almost obscured thanks to overgrown shrubs.

Everyone spun around instantly to find an old man in a pair of grey coveralls and a large double barrel shotgun trained on them.

"Now, no one moves and no one gets hurt," the man said. He was in his late fifties or early sixties with white hair and a uni-brow. Despite the shotgun trained on them, Carl thought the man looked kind. If he had met this man in a park, he probably would have taken an instant liking to him, the warm face and warmer voice inviting. But at the moment things could be deceiving.

"And just who are you?" Steve asked, his eyes never wavering from the shotgun.

The shotgun moved slightly. "That should be my question, considering that this is my zoo and you folks are trespassing."

He looked at the ruined ticket kiosk. "Now who's gonna pay for that?"

Craig took a step closer, his hands well away from his sidearm and the rifle across his back. "Now look, Mister, I don't know if you know what's happening out there beyond those fences, but the entire city is falling apart."

The man nodded, the shotgun bobbing with him. "Yes, young man, I know. I have a television here. Don't believe it, though. Must be some kind of a hoax. Some kind of Hollywood stunt for some new horror movie. It's been done before, you know. Remember War of the Worlds?"

Craig looked at Carl and then back to the old man. "What the hell does the Tom Cruise movie have to do with what's happening out there?"

"Tom Cruise? What the hell are you talking about?" The man said, looking befuddled.

Ethel stood up and slid next to the men. "Don't even try, sir, they're too young to know about all that. Look, we're trapped in here with you, so please put that shotgun down. We're no threat to you; we just wanted to get away from *them*. If you don't believe me, then go to the front gate for yourself. Can't you hear them? And what about all that screaming earlier?"

The old man pointed to his left ear. "Sorry, ma'am, I can't hear worth a damn. I've got a couple of hearing aids, but I don't usually put them in. But when I heard some commotion, I came running." He bit his lip for a second, thinking. "Tell you what, you folks stay here and I'm going to the gate. We'll see who's pulling whose leg."

He walked around the path, his eyes watching everyone. No one moved. There was no where to go and it would be easier to let the man see for himself.

He was gone for almost five minutes, and when he returned, his face was as pale as a ghost.

"Now do you believe us?" Carl asked.

The man nodded, lowering the shotgun. "Sweet Mary and Joseph, I wouldn't have believed it if I hadn't seen it with my own two eyes. The parking lot's full of them."

Steve moved closer to the man, but not so close to be threatening. "Can they get in here? Are we safe in here?"

The old man nodded. "Aye, we're safe enough. The fence goes all the way around to the back, where a fifteen foot high stone wall takes over. This place is like a small military camp when you come right down to it." That was when he really got a good look at Ethel and Paul, Matt and some of the others he'd seen at the gate. "You folks look like you could use a good scrubbing. I haven't smelled an odor like that since I had to clean up after the elephants."

Matt stepped forward. "Is there someplace we can get cleaned up? I'd kill for a shower."

The old man frowned. "Sorry, mister, but you're not coming into my place smelling like that. Tell you what, there's a small duck pond in the middle of the zoo. Feel free to use that. Go nuts."

Matt nodded. "I hear that. If anyone needs me, I'll be there," then he started to walk deeper into the zoo, but stopped short, turning back around. "Hey buddy, how about some food, I haven't eaten in two days, and neither have most of the people with me."

"We'll address that after everyone's cleaned up," the old man said.

"Hold up for just one more second, will you Matt? Let's get the others together and we'll all go. That way if there's trouble, we'll all be in one place," Steve told him.

Matt frowned, but he stopped walking. "All right, but hurry up."

Steve turned to Carl.

"Carl, will you go get the others and tell them what's up and to come with you so they can get cleaned up, too."

Carl nodded and ran down the path, nodding as he passed Hal, who had decided to see who the guy with the shotgun was. Returning a few minutes later, Carl had the rest of the group in tow.

"My, there's a lot of you, and you all arrived here together?" He asked.

"Hello, need a bath, can we talk later?" Matt called from the path leading deeper into the zoo.

"He's got a point, mister . . ." Steve left it hanging, wanting the old man to tell him his name.

"Just call me Hector," the man said. "And your friend's right. Let's get everyone cleaned up and then I'll see what I have to feed all of you. Hope you're not expecting anything grand, it's just me in here and I live simply."

Steve shook his head. "That's quite all right, Hector, whatever you've got is fine."

Steve noticed Hickman being helped to his feet and then led to the back of the group and decided to ignore him for now, but his disagreement with the man was far from over.

Then, with Matt limping in the lead, Hector walked the group to the duck pond and a much needed bath, while outside the zoo, the undead rattled the gate and adjoining fence, desperately trying to gain entry, their moans following the group further into the bowels of the deserted zoo.

Chapter 25

WHILE EVERYONE BATHED in the duck pond, the few geese still living there quacking their anger at their home being invaded, Hector disappeared for a while. When he returned, he was carrying a large pitcher of lemonade and a stack of Styrofoam cups.

As each of the group climbed out of the pond, their clothing dripping in their hands, they took a cup, drinking it greedily.

"Now, everyone make sure not to drink too fast. We haven't had anything in our bellies for a while and if you drink too fast you'll just get sick," Hal told everyone.

"Screw you, old man, don't tell me what to do," George scoffed, chugging his lemonade and going back for more.

Hal shrugged, sipping contently, and his grin was a mile wide when ten minutes later, he saw George throwing up in the bushes.

Wiping his face clear of spittle, George flipped Hal off. "Screw you, man, so you was right, big fuckin' deal." Then he walked away, holding his aching stomach.

Matt walked up to Hal, grinning. He was standing in nothing but his underwear, his clothes already spread out on a rock. Hal thought he looked like a Sumo wrestler.

"You really shouldn't agitate him, Hal. I've known guys like him before. That chip on his shoulder will get him or someone else killed one day," Matt told him.

Hal shrugged. "I think we have more things to worry about then just him at the moment, don't you?"

Matt rubbed his two chins. "Yeah, I suppose so." Then he slapped Hal on the shoulder and went back into the water. He had already had two cups of lemonade and his stomach was rumbling. He needed something to take his mind off his hunger.

Carl, Craig, Tracey and Steve splashed at the opposite end of the pond. They weren't that dirty compared to the others and chose to stay out of the immediate area of them. After the others were through washing their foul clothes in the pond, it didn't exactly entice them to want to swim in it. The pond itself was covered in lily pads, the moss floating on the surface easy enough to push out of the way. The floor of the pond was squishy with mud and Carl tried not to think about what he might be stepping in.

While the four of them splashed and enjoyed a few minutes of safety, Carl looked across the pond at some of the women. All were in their bra and panties, a little too old for his taste, but then his eyes fell on the Asian girl. She was still wearing her long sleeve shirt as she washed her pants, which, though odd, didn't ring any bells of danger for Carl. The shirt was plastered against her thin form and Carl couldn't help but admire her beauty, her small nipples easily discernable through the thin cotton shirt. Then Tracey splashed him and he was distracted.

On the edge of the pond, George watched Kim Lee, as well. His eyes roamed up and down her body, as he licked his lips. Man, what he would do to that, he thought. He would tear that up. He liked Asian women and now he had one all alone, trapped inside the zoo with him. Things could be worse, he thought.

Then he moved away to get some more lemonade. His stomach was feeling better now and it wanted food and drink.

Tracey splashed her father again and he wiped his face of water and splashed her back. She laughed, enjoying herself and then decided she'd had enough fun and swam to the edge of the pond and climbed out. Wearing nothing but her bra and panties, she looked like a swimsuit model as she left the water, the liquid sluicing down her back. Both Carl and Craig stopped what they were doing and stared as she walked out.

Then both received a slap to the back of the head by Steve.

"Hey, you two, eyes on me," he said. Both men looked away, longingly, and turned to look at Steve.

"Sorry, man, but you've got to admit, you're daughter is a knockout," Craig said.

Steve glared at him, most of it false. "I don't have to admit anything. You two horn dogs keep your distance, you hear me? We've got enough to worry about without your Three's Company bullshit."

Carl looked at Craig. "What's a Three's Company?"

Steve threw up his hands in frustration and then left the water, as well.

"You two knuckleheads need to stay in a little longer and soak your heads," he joked, climbing out. Then using his shirt for a towel, he tried to wipe himself off. By then Tracey was dressed again and was trying to untangle her hair with her fingers.

"Damn, I wish I had a brush," she said when Steve walked up to her.

"Don't worry about it, honey, you look fine," he placated her. "Now come on, let's get everyone together and see about getting something to eat." Then he rubbed his beard. "And me getting rid of this damn beard."

"Oh, I don't know, Dad, I kind of like it, now that I'm used to it."

Steve smiled at her and then moved away, scratching at his beard. "Maybe so, honey, but it still itches like a bitch and I want it gone."

Tracey shrugged, and with her hair as good as she could get it, followed her father away from the pond.

After Carl and Craig had dried off and redressed, the two men had walked to the other side of the pond where the others were. Most were out of the water now, wearing their clothing again. Though still wet, at least everyone didn't smell like a latrine.

Hector nodded in approval.

"All right then, if you folks want to follow me, I'll take you to my place. There's picnic tables in the back, so you can all use them while I see what I've got to eat."

Filing after the old man, everyone talked amongst themselves.

George slipped in next to Kim Lee, smiling at her innocently. "Hey baby, we never got the chance to be introduced, I'm George," he said slyly.

She only looked at him and answered in Japanese. Despite the bath, she looked tired and fatigued; her skin paler then it should be. George didn't give it much thought. After all, they were all tired and hungry.

"What the fuck's wrong with you, girl, can't you speak English?"

Hal moved next to George and shook his head. "I don't think she knows English, George, Guess you'll just have to use your natural charisma to get her to like you," he joked.

George looked at Hal, his frustration obvious, then his face became more serious. "Man, I don't need her to do anything but moan to get my groove on," he snapped back.

"Good luck with that," Hal answered and then moved away, deciding he was wasting his time. Hal had known many people like George in his career as a reporter for the Globe. Poor black men with no education and a will to prove they weren't useless. Only sometimes that wanting to prove their self worth came out in arrogance. But then again, George could just be an asshole, another low life from the bowels of the city. Deciding it really didn't matter, he slowed his pace, falling back to join up with Matt. He liked the rotund man. He was intelligent and always had something nice to say. While the group moved up the path, the two chatted.

Paul and Ethel walked near the rear, Dr. Hickman trailing behind, last in line.

"Do you think he'll be all right?" Ethel asked her husband.

Paul shrugged. "Honey, whatever he did is between him and God. No one else, Steve needs to learn that. It's a different world at the moment."

"You'd never do that to me, would you?" Ethel asked with concern on her face.

Paul stopped walking and stared at her in shock. "Ethel, how could you even think such a thing? I'd give my life for you, you know that."

She smiled, feeling better and walked on after the others. Paul followed, not realizing his statement would be put to the test soon enough.

* * *

While following Hector, the survivors had passed by the cages where the lions, bears and giraffes had been penned. Hector had given a short tour, pointing out where various animals had been housed. With only empty pens and cages to see, there really wasn't very much interest, but everyone politely listened. The signs with a picture of the animal and brief synopsis of where it lived and what it ate were still present in front of the exhibits. Even George was quiet, focusing most of his attention on Kim Lee. If the young woman noticed, she either didn't care or didn't understand what George wanted from her, but any woman from any country could read what was in his eyes.

Steve walked next to Hector, the two of them chatting.

"So what are you doing here exactly?" Steve asked

Hector spit a wad of phlegm and cleared his throat. "I'm the caretaker for the zoo. Though it's closed, the bank still wanted someone here to keep trespassers away, mostly teenagers looking for a place to drink and screw. I've worked in this zoo for twenty years, ever since it opened. That's probably why I'm still here. Guess someone figured I'd just shrivel up and die without this job."

Steve nodded. "So you live here, in the zoo? Shit, that was pretty convenient, especially with everything that's happened in the city."

Hector grinned. "No kidding, I'm not complaining. I like being alone anyway. Reckon I'd be livin' up in the mountains or somethin' if I wasn't here."

Tracey was behind them, listening intently. "Sorry about crashing your party, Hector," she apologized.

Hector waved his hand in front of him, waving her apology away.

"Think nothin' of it, child. The good book says to do unto others and that's what I'm doing." He slowed as they approached an old one-story brick building. "Ah, we're here. You folks go back there to the picnic tables and I'll be around shortly. Hey, Steve, why don't you give me a hand inside? I could use the help," Hector requested.

Steve agreed and after Tracey asked if she could come, too, Hector had acquiesced.

Steve directed Carl to lead everyone to the rear of the building while he and Tracey helped Hector.

Walking into the building, Steve's nose was immediately assailed by the redolence of the room. The smell of stale cigars and unwashed clothes struck him, reminding him of the locker room at the Gold's Gym he used to attend.

There was an easy chair off in the corner and a television sitting on a makeshift stand. Nothing more than a couple of cinderblocks and a piece of wood stretched across it. He grinned. It reminded him of his college days, he and his buddies had done the same thing. A couple of cinderblocks that cost less then a dollar each and a piece of wood and you had yourself an entertainment center.

Hector immediately went to the small table near the television, quickly scooping up video tapes. The boxes of pornography were spread out on the floor and with a look of embarrassment; he kicked them under the chair.

"Sorry, about that, I wasn't expecting company."

Steve held back his grin and Tracey never noticed, her eyes still looking around, Hector's body blocking the boxes from her view.

Hector gestured to the small kitchen off to the left. "The kitchen's this way," he said, father and daughter following.

It took about fifteen minutes to gather the food. Canned beans and Saltines, plus a couple of loaves of bread were the main staple of the meal. All three of them carried the food out to the tables and hungry hands reached out to help, quickly eating. Bread and water would have seemed like a feast after no food for two days of being inside the cars.

Pitchers of ice cold water were the drinks, Hector now out of instant lemonade. He had told Steve in confidence that he still had a couple of cases of beer, but they were for him, and maybe Steve, too, if he played his cards right. Steve had winked at the man, telling him his secret was safe.

Fifteen minutes later there was nothing left on the two picnic tables—pushed together to make one long one—but empty cans and wrinkled bags. Sitting back, Matt let out a burp that had some of the women frowning and some of the men chuckling.

Steve stood at the end of the table and slapped his hand on the tabletop to get everyone's attention.

"Attention, guys, listen up!" He called.

It took a few seconds for everyone to stop talking, but soon all eyes were on him

"All right, look, we've been so damn busy since we hooked up that I don't even know all your names and who you are. I suppose the same goes for the rest of you, so now that we've washed and ate I say let's do a round of introductions. I'll start. My name is Steven Webb and I'm in construction." He gestured to Tracey. "And this is my daughter, Tracey."

Tracey waved and everyone either waved back or said hello.

Steve pointed to Carl. "You go next and then the person on your left can go until everyone's done."

Carl nodded and stood up. "Uh, hi, I'm Carl, Carl Jenkins. I guess I'm unemployed at the moment." A few chuckles came from that and Carl sat back down.

Craig was next. "Hi guys, I'm Craig Sterns, formally with the Army. Guess I'm AWOL at the moment, though I'm cool with it. Better to be AWOL then dead."

Muttering and acknowledgements floated around the table. Craig sat back down and the torch was passed to Hal.

"Hello there, my name is Hal Beckett and I'm a reporter with the Boston Globe. If I live through this shit then this will probably be the best story of my life." He stopped talking then, realizing he'd depressed himself. He sat back down and Matt patted his shoulder, consoling his friend.

Matt was next and he stood up slightly, his girth not allowing him to come to his full height behind the wooden table.

"Hi guys, my names Matt Steggman. That's with two gg's. I'm a garbage man and damn proud of it. I'm from Revere, but my brother lives in the Back Bay. That's how I wound up on the wrong side of the city and how I got here with you guys. Guess that's it, then." Then he sat down, the wood of the seat actually jumping from his weight, the others all feeling it.

A middle-aged woman stood up then. She looked tired and haggard, not all of it from the past few days. "Umm, hello. I'm Sherry Whitfield and I'm a wife and mother. I live in Waltham and I was on my way home from my mother's house when they closed off the city. I took a detour and then my car broke down. That's how I wound up at the zoo; I pulled in hoping someone could help me. Then we had to live in that car for two days. I thought I was going to die . . ." She paused for a moment, trying to regain her composure, then started again. "I don't know what's happened to my children or husband. My cell phone stopped working. They could be dead for all I know." She sat back down then, a solemn mood falling on the group. With night having fallen, Hector had brought out a few lanterns. Now all their faces were bathed in an eerie yellow glow.

Paul Thomas stood up then. Looking down at Sherry. "Gees, look what I get to follow. How do I top that?" He joked, trying to lighten the mood but failing miserably. Deciding to just get to the point he looked at the surrounding faces. "My name is Paul Thomas and this beautiful woman sitting next to me is my wife, Ethel." Ethel blushed as she looked at the faces looking back. "We've been married for forty-two years this Thursday. We're from New Hampshire actually. We came down to Boston to visit our kids last week when everything fell apart. We tried to get out of town, but they had blocked the main roads. I tried to take some of the back roads and got us lost miserably. That's how we wound up near the zoo. The rest you all know." He sat back down, Ethel taking his hand and squeezing it.

Then he stood back up. "Oh yeah, and this woman next to Ethel is Kim Lee. That's all we know about her 'cause she doesn't speak a word of English."

Hearing her name, Kim Lee perked up a little. She had barely touched her food and her eyes were glassy. Seeing everyone looking at her, she nodded her head politely. That seemed to be enough because then George stood up.

"Uh yeah, I'm George. That's all you people need to know." He sat back down then, crossing his arms on his chest. Hal chuckled at that and when George glared at him, he quickly muffled it.

Next a Spanish man stood up. "Hello. My name is Miguel Esperanza and this is my wife, Rosa," he said with a heavy accent.

"Hello," she said sweetly. Rosa was Latino, her dark features stunning, her eyes radiant. She smiled at the others and her husband continued. "I'm in construction, too. I've been working on the Big Dig, or actually cleaning up what they didn't do right the first time. Then they closed the site when people starting getting sick from the virus or whatever is happening to them. Umm, that's it. I just wanted to say thanks for letting us be with you."

People patted his shoulders and Rosa's, telling him he and his wife were welcome.

Next was a woman with a bad dye job and far too many wrinkles. Her age was hard to define and her face screamed *I'm a crack whore*!

"I'm Tina," she said in a squeaky voice, her hands shaking slightly as if she needed a fix. "I don't work. That's about it really." Then she sat back down.

The next woman at the table stood up and waved. "Hello, I'm Diane Boyd. I'm forty-three and I'm divorced. I won't bore you with my ex-husbands antics, the cheating bastard." With her face filled with anger, she sat back down, signaling there was a long story there if anyone wanted to hear it later.

The second to last person at the table was the teenage boy. Steve looked at him and gestured for him to stand up. "Go on, son, introduce yourself," Steve cajoled him.

The boy hesitantly stood up, brushing his hair from his eyes.

"Uh, what's up? I'm Seth Jacobs. I worked at the top of Newberry Street at the Tower Records until a bunch of crazy fuckers came in and started to attack people. I got the hell out of there and wound up in the woods. I found the zoo by accident and then had to spend two goddamn days in a car while those bastards tried to get at me . . . at us. What the fuck is going on, man? Why's all this shit happening to us?"

Then he sat back down. There was a small tear at the corner of his left eye, but he brushed it away, the gloom hiding it from everyone but Steve who was at the right vantage point to see it. Steve leaned down close to him.

"Don't you worry, son, we'll figure out what to do, I promise."

"Don't make promises you can't keep, motherfucker, because from the way I sees it, we're all pretty fucked," George called from across the table.

Steve looked up, looking for George in the gloom. He was out of the light of the nearest lamp and his dark skin blended into the night.

"That's enough out of you, George. We need to stay positive right now. If we lose hope, then we're already dead."

George climbed out of his seat and stretched. "You can hope all you want, homie, but that ain't gonna bring the cops to save our asses. We gonna die here, man." Then he started to walk away. "I'm tired of talking to all you crackers. I'm gonna go grab some shuteye somewhere."

Steve was about to call after him and tell him they weren't finished talking, when Tracey touched his arm. "Let him go, Dad, he's just scared and angry. He's no different from the rest of us; he just doesn't want to admit it."

Steve sighed, touching her hand. "Okay, honey." Then he looked at the last man to introduce himself.

"Go ahead, Doc, why don't you introduce yourself. Oh, and don't forget to introduce your wife to us, too. Oh wait, you can't, because you left her to be ripped apart by those *things* outside the fence!" His voice had slowly gone up in pitch until he was screaming. All voices stopped, everyone watching the scene in front of them. All had seen what had happened to Helen, though not everyone knew all the details.

"What is he talking about?" Miguel asked the people around him. "Did she not fall as she climbed over the gate?"

A few people shrugged, saying they didn't know the details. Hector had sat quietly while everyone introduced themselves, now he stood up and walked over to Steve.

"What are you taking about? What did this man do?"

Steve's eyes were wide with anger. "He ran like a child and left his wife behind! All he had to do was slow down and reach out for her, but instead he ran like a coward. She wasn't strong enough and she fell. End of story. If I had my way, I'd throw this miserable piece of shit over the fence and be done with it!"

Hickman kept his head down, not saying anything. Whether he was scared or felt guilty, no one knew.

Steve stared at the man and then finally threw his hands up in surrender. "Fuck it," he said. "I'm going for a walk. If I stay here I don't know what I might do." He pointed at Hickman. "But mark my words, Doc; you'll pay for what you did, one way or the other." Then he stood up and left the circle of light.

"Dad?" Tracey called to him.

"I'll be fine, honey, I just need to cool off, don't worry." He glanced at Carl and Craig. "You guys look after her."

Carl waved and Craig nodded, then Steve was swallowed up by the darkness.

Hector stood at the end of the table where Steve had sat. "Well folks, if you've had enough entertainment for the night, what do you say about getting some rest?"

Murmurs of agreement covered the table, everyone exhausted. Hector pointed to a few of the surrounding cages. "You can use any of the cages for shelter and the bear cage with its pretend caves is around the bend when we walked up here. Feel free to use any of it. The restrooms are at the far end of the lion exhibit, right next to the Aviary. There's signs that tell you what is where on the paths. So far the plumbing works; can't say the same about the electricity, though. I've got myself a generator, but I'm afraid the rest of you are on your own."

No one seemed to mind, and after Hector gave out a few extra sheets and blankets, everyone went their separate ways, a few glancing at Hickman as they left. Some paired up with others, while some stayed alone.

Soon the picnic area was empty, only Carl, Craig and Tracey waiting for Steve to return. Hector bid them goodnight and walked away.

"When Steve gets back, tell him to come see me. We've got a lot to talk about," Hector told them.

Carl nodded and told him they would and then the three of them were alone

Tracey smiled at the two of them.

"You guys don't have to protect me, I can handle myself."

Carl nodded. "Don't I know it, but your Dad said to wait until he comes back and that's what we'll do. Right Craig?"

Craig nodded. "Damn straight." Then Craig produced a deck of cards from one of his voluminous pockets. "Anyone for a game of strip poker?" He leered at Tracey as he said this.

Tracey frowned, crossing her arms and shaking her head no.

Carl said: "Sure, I'll play but I think it should just be regular poker." He tried to yawn but failed. "I don't know about you guys, but at the moment, I'm so pumped up I don't think I could sleep anyway."

"Yeah, I feel about the same," Craig answered and Tracey agreed.

With the crickets chirping in the nearby grass and the moans of the surrounding dead floating on the wind, the three friends played cards under the protective halo of the flickering lanterns.

Chapter 26

STEVE KNOCKED ON Hector's open door and poked his head inside. "Hello, anyone here? My daughter said you wanted to talk with me."

He could hear the distinctive sounds of voices and he wondered who Hector was talking to.

"Come on in, Steve, I'm in here," Hector called.

Steve stepped inside, seeing Hector now sitting in his easy chair. The voices Steve heard were on the television. There was a news broadcast on, the anchorman reading from a sheaf of papers. Stepping closer, Steve sat down on a wooden chair. Hector offered him a beer and he took it, nodding his head in thanks, then he pulled a cigarette from the pack in his shirt pocket, lighting it quickly with a disposable lighter. Then he thought maybe Hector wouldn't allow it, so he gave the old man a subtle look.

"Do you mind if I smoke?" Steve asked Hector.

Hector grunted and waved him to go ahead.

"This is my next to last one. I don't know what I'm gonna do when I'm out, I guess I'll try to quit," Steve told Hector, blowing a smoke cloud toward the ceiling.

Hector nodded, sympathetically, but his attention was on the television.

Steve followed Hector's gaze and watched the television, as well. The first thing he noticed was the anchorman's normally immaculate hair and wardrobe was replaced by a disheveled look and nothing but a shirt and tie, the tie was loosened around his neck and the top button of the newsman's shirt was unfastened. The anchorman's face looked harried and worried, and Steve could see sweat beading on the man's forehead.

Hector gestured to the television with the hand holding the beer. "I've been waiting for this broadcast. In the past few days the news has been sporadic. Sometimes there's nothin' but that Emergency Broadcast Logo and that damn dial tone. Then they played a message across the screen that they would be broadcasting at eight tonight, sharp. Figured you'd want to see it. Good timing by the way."

Steve sipped his beer and shrugged. "Got lucky, I guess."

Then he stopped talking and focused on the anchorman. On the bottom of the screen, rescue stations scrolled by, some of them now saying they were closed and to go to alternative stations. It was all a mess, hard to make sense of any of it, as if the person who was punching the messages in was barely receiving time to check their work before running it on the screen.

Behind the man—instead of a plain backdrop or a simulated picture—numerous people were running by and the usually quiet stage was filled with other voices, some of them raised in panic.

Steve looked to Hector and the man just blinked back, not knowing what to make of the chaotic news station.

The anchorman cleared his throat and called for the people around him to be quiet, talking to unknown personnel out of sight of the camera, normally something an anchorman would never do while on a live broadcast. The chaos quieted a little, but voices could still be heard. What was weird was there were no sounds of telephones ringing, which was odd for a news station.

Then the man started to talk, beginning his report.

"Umm, good evening and thank you for tuning in, that is, those of you that are lucky enough to still have power. Despite the chaos on the streets of Boston, this is what we know. Most citizens in Boston and the surrounding suburbs, all the way to New Hampshire and Rhode Island, are being faced with the collapse of the Police and Fire Departments. Many citizens have begun taking the law into their own hands, despite the pleading of local law officials to do no such thing.

All residents are urged to leave their homes, no matter how safe or fortified they believe them to be and to report to the nearest rescue station."

The man looked around himself, pausing as two men walked behind him arguing about rescue stations not being active anymore.

"Almost all civil and social services have been discontinued until further notice and most areas are without both cell phones and land lines. After an unidentified explosion at the Edison plant in South Boston, many are without power. Also, gas service had been cut off, as ruptures in the city's main pipelines have caused all gas to be turned off until further notice."

The anchorman shuffled a few papers and then looked up and around him and then back down. Clearing his throat yet again, he continued.

"The scientific community is focusing their research on the outbreak, especially the homicidal and cannibalistic tendencies of the infected populace. They have been considering whether it's a behavioral disorder or if it's from some sort of viral outbreak or a new strain of an old one. The government has been looking into all state and private run facilities to see if there have been any breaches in security reported. As of now we haven't gotten word.

Other cities are reporting isolated outbreaks, as well, and are now trying to control it before it can spread further. As far away as Florida and Texas have reported attacks, though not all reports have been substantiated at this time.

But what could have caused such a widespread pandemic as the one that has descended on our city? We've heard speculation from everything from a biological outbreak, as the by product of terrorism, to voodoo, to aliens from another world." He said the last sentence with a bit of a smile, believing what he's reading to be ridiculous. He shuffles a few more papers and then continues.

"A biologist from Berkley California has released a report stating that the infected are in fact dead and that once infected by a carrier, any person will then die and return to life to attack the living. They appear to be driven by some unknown force to seek out and attack all who are not infected. From a few captured test subjects it appears that the only way to stop one of these infected people is to destroy the brain. When all brain functions cease, the host body will cease to function and die. It's the brain that somehow keeps these people moving."

He sneers as he reads the final words, shaking his head at the ridiculous assumption that the brain keeps people living after death. Then he continues, looking down at the papers in his hands and not worrying too much about making eye contact with the camera.

"Doctors at the Center for Disease control, the CDC for those of you more familiar with the term. The CDC in Atlanta rejects the brain theory, calling it 'ridiculous and impossible'. They believe from the in-depth research they have done so far, that it must be some kind of virus or infection that has some form of mind altering effect on the host body. Though it does not, I repeat, does not appear to be airborne. An infected person must bite you. It appears there is something in the saliva that is carrying the actual virus." The man looked around the room again and then back to the screen. He wasn't reading from the papers anymore.

"But what kind of virus could strike down so many, so fast, and yet leave others unaffected is still a mystery. In religious circles, some are saying this is the Rapture finally coming to pass and others, that this is Judgment day. I for one think it's all a bunch of crap. We'll keep broadcasting for as long as our generators remain functioning." He looked to his right and listened to someone talking, then nodded back.

"Next up is a professor from Northeastern with some tips for survival in these trying times."

Hector picked up the remote control for the television and turned it off.

"Well, what do you think of that?" He asked Steve.

Steve sat stock still, his face a mask of shock as he stared at the blank screen.

"Jesus Christ, I can't believe it's gotten so bad, so fast. We're stranded here. There's no one coming for us, is there."

Hector slowly nodded his head. "Seems that way. Listen, we need to talk about some other stuff, too. I don't mind you people staying here with me, but I don't have enough food for everyone. Even if I had stockpiles, eventually I'd run out and then where would I be? If there's gonna be more then fifteen of us we need to figure out a way to get food. So far the water's still flowing, but what if it stops? Have you seen that duck pond? I don't want to have to drink from that."

Steve leaned back in his chair. "That's not a problem, actually. All we need to do is boil the water and strain it. A T-shirt would do the job. As for food . . . ." Steve rubbed his face with his hands, the exhaustion of the day washing over him.

It was hard to believe everything that had happened since that morning and his mind was wasted. All he wanted to do was sleep.

". . . As for food, can we deal with it in the morning when I'm rested up? I can't even see straight anymore."

"Okay, fine with me. You go get some sleep and we'll talk more in the morning, but remember, this problem isn't going to go away," Hector told him.

Steve sat up, a wave of dizziness washing over him for a moment. Then he moved over to Hector and shook the man's hand. "Thanks again for everything, really. You've been a life saver."

Hector grinned back, his few remaining teeth resembling stalactites and stalagmites in a hollow cave. "Happy to help, as I said before, the good Lord wants us to look out for each other and I follow the Lord."

Steve frowned impatiently. "If your Lord's so damn great, then why is all this shit happening?"

Hector leaned back in his chair and closed his eyes for a moment, thinking. With his eyes still closed he began speaking.

"It's not up to me to try to figure out the Lord's grand design. If he wants a plague to descend on mankind, then so be it. Call this the flood, only it's the twentieth century's version."

"Okay, if you say so, goodnight," Steve said leaving. The last thing he wanted to do was get into a debate about God and religion with the old man.

Still, as he walked out of the building and down the small path to the picnic area, where Carl, Craig and Tracey were still waiting for him, he shook his head. He hated religion. Man made his own destiny and luck. Falling down on your knees and praying for something to happen, or not to happen, will just get you sore knees in the end. Religion was only there so man could feel superior to the animals he shared the world with. No man or woman wants to think they are no better then a simple ant or mosquito. That when a person dies, the consciousness of that person is snuffed out like a light being turned off in a room, leaving nothing but darkness. Man was just another creature, who just happens to be able to reason and think. *If I am aware of myself, does not that make me alive?* Someone once spoke something similar and the answer was yes, you are alive, but still just an animal. The soul was a crock of shit, put there to brainwash millions into thinking there was more after this lifetime. Steve believed there wasn't. Once he died that was it, no more, game over. There was only one chance to play this game and whether you won or lost was irrelevant. Everyone lost in the end, the trick was to make your mark before the game was truly over. His mark was his daughter, Tracey. When he was dead and gone, she would be there, still alive, hopefully remembering him. But then again, when he looked up at death in the end and *knew* he was going to die, he sure as hell hoped he was proved wrong and he would go someplace else, his fictional soul finding happiness. Wishful thinking was human nature, he didn't deny that.

Stepping into the small clearing, he smiled when he saw Tracey. She was laughing while she played cards with the two young men. He liked them both. Carl and Craig were each good guys, though he would never admit that to them. He knew both had eyes out for his daughter and he was a protective father. But in the end, if she chose one of them as a boyfriend, he would endorse the union.

"Hey guys, how 'bout we go to bed, I'm wasted," Steve said, slowing as he reached their table.

Carl turned to him and smiled. "Sounds good, we were just talking about that, but the card shark here wanted to wait for you to get back."

Tracey shrugged. "What can I say, I learned from the best. Plus, both of these guys have tells. I always knew when either of you had a good hand or a bad one."

Both Carl and Craig frowned, thinking they were crafty players.

Steve chuckled. "Don't even try to argue with her, trust me. She's like her mother in that regard, too. She knows how to play the cards she's been dealt."

Tracey stood up and walked over and hugged Steve.

"You better believe it. So are we going to bed or what?"

Craig stood up, the deck of cards disappearing into a pocket and then he checked his weapons to make sure all was secure.

With a wide yawn, he nodded. "Sounds good to me. Truth is, I can't even see straight anymore," Craig said.

The others started yawning, now, the gesture contagious.

"Dammit, man, don't do that, it's catchy," Carl said, stifling a yawn as he stood up to join the others. He picked up the lantern so they had light to walk by, the dark paths of the zoo engulfing all available light.

The four of them left the picnic area, walking down the path. There were a couple of blankets left in the pile from Hector and they picked them up, walking with them under their arms. While they walked, the dim illumination from fires could be seen winking inside some of the exhibits, the rest of the group bedding down for the night

"So where are we gonna sleep tonight?" Craig asked, looking around at the dark cages and pits that had once housed the animals.

Steve pointed down a side path. "Lets go to the bear caves, I don't think anyone else is there," Steve suggested.

"Like a camping trip, huh? Sure beats the hell out of last night on that damn bread truck," Carl joked.

"Or in the middle of the woods," Craig added.

The four friends chatted softly, every now and then a voice rising in pitch in a soft laugh as they made their way to their berths, while inside the zoo, the other survivors slept, not needing to have nightmares, because their nightmares were already with them, clustering around the zoo, just waiting to invade their waking life; their moans drifting through the empty cages to permeate the walls.

At least in sleep, they could pretend things were normal and safe. When the world made sense and when people died, they stayed dead.

Chapter 27

IT WAS WELL past midnight when George awoke from a restless slumber. Reaching down under the wool blanket he was curled up in, he felt his hard-on. Man, he was so horny he would fuck just about anything right about now.

Tossing off the blanket, he sat up. An idea came to him and he grinned in the dark. He was alone in a small structure that had been used as a concession stand when the zoo had been running. Now it was nothing but an empty shell, everything of value stripped clean from inside.

Standing up, he walked to the partially open door. The lock had been busted, so he had decided to just screw it and leave the door open. Besides, if someone had been stupid enough to mess with him, he would have fucked them up bad.

George stretched, shaking the sleep from his limbs. Across the path from where he stood was another building. He wasn't sure, but he thought it was for the birds or something. Most of it was glass and the ceiling was see-thru, the few stars shining in the sky easy to see from inside the structure.

From where he stood, he could see the halo of the burning buildings of the Boston skyline. The smoke rising into the air was invisible, blending into the dark horizon.

Let it burn, he thought. The damn city and everyone he knew in it was disposable. He had tried to get a temp job in one of the mailrooms at one of the lawyer firms on State Street. A buddy of his had recommended him and George had done everything right. He had dressed up in a suit, borrowed from his father, of course, and had shaved and gotten a haircut. But when he arrived, the interviewer had taken one look at him and said: "*Next.*"

That had been the only time George had tried to go straight and do the right thing like his Pops had always told him, and what did he get for his trouble?

Humiliation and embarrassment, that's what.

He had gone home that day and tossed the suit back at his father and had gone back to the corner where he sold crack. At least he was in charge on the corners. Nobody messed with him, that is, until some of his customers went plum crazy and started attacking and eating his friends. He had gotten the hell out of there and had run for most of the day; finding that no matter where he went, it was the same, people had gone apeshit. Eventually he had ended up in the Blue Hills Mountains. It had been dumb luck that had brought him to the zoo and all the spoiled white folk that were trying to gain access to it. Then the dead people had arrived and everyone had huddled into the two cars. Frowning, he thought back to how it had been inside that car for two goddamn days. He had almost wanted to just get out and let the damn dead people eat him then sit in that car, smelling other people's shit and listening to them whine and scream every time a dead hand banged on the car, which was almost every second.

The only ray of light in the terrible ordeal was Kim Lee. She had sat behind him inside the car. He had snuck looks at her whenever he had the chance. If she noticed, she didn't let on. He had always liked Asian women and as he sat there, squeezed between Matt and Sherry, he had daydreamed of tapping that ass again and again.

Now, as he looked out at where she was sleeping, he decided it was time. He knew she was in there alone, no one else pairing up with her. It was probably because she didn't know English. After all, what kind of conversation could you have with someone that couldn't understand what the fuck you were saying? But that was fine with him. What he wanted, she didn't need to do anything but spread her legs wide.

Stepping out onto the path, he strolled across the walkway until he was at the entrance to the bird sanctuary. His heart was beating with the anticipation of what was to come. He was confidant she would want to screw him and even if she didn't, he was still going to have his way with her, no matter what she wanted.

Stepping into the sanctuary, he tried to peer into the gloom. A few wilted trees surrounded an empty pond and dead grass covered the ground.

Moving warily through the open room, he slowed when he saw a huddled form near one of the denuded trees.

There she was.

He rubbed his chin, almost hesitating for a second, but then his sexual desire took over and he continued walking. He stopped when he was standing over her, his body casting another shadow onto her sleeping form.

Kneeling down, he carefully pulled back the blanket. In the wan light from the overhead skylights, he could see her petite body easily. Her head was lying to the side, her chest still. She must be taking shallow breathes, he thought, as he slid down on the ground next to her. His hand went under her shirt, caressing her small breasts. She stirred slightly and he halted his movements. Then, showing no signs of waking up, he continued his ministrations. While he caressed her breasts, he quickly undid his pants, sliding them off over his shoes. He was so hard he thought he could cut diamonds with his pecker if given the chance and his heart was pumping fast with the expectation of what was to come.

With his pants off, he reached down and undid her pants, surprised by how cold she was. She was like ice, but still soft, so he ignored the strange sensation.

Lost in his own excitement, he didn't ponder why she hadn't woken up from his petting and prodding, only having eyes for the small sweet form next to him.

With her pants down at her ankles, he reached between her legs. Though moist, it was cold there, as well. That was fine with him, he thought. He would warm her up soon enough.

Sliding on top of her, he gently slid inside of her, slowly pumping while he got his groove just right. He had made many a woman squeal from his lovemaking and he was sure Kim Lee would be no exception.

While he penetrated her again and again, he was almost disappointed that she didn't wake up. It was almost no fun if they didn't fight even a little.

Then she stirred under him and her arm rolled to the side. Too busy to notice, George didn't see the weeping bite mark on her flesh, long blue lines that trailed under her skin to be lost near her shoulder, like varicose veins gone amuck.

The moon peeked out from behind a few clouds, bathing the sanctuary in yellow moonlight. George looked down at the sweet face below him and realized she seemed paler then usual, even with the moonlight distorting her countenance.

Still, he was enjoying himself to much and decided to ignore this strange occurrence. He was pumping faster now, on his way to an orgasm. Then she opened her eyes and her head turned to look up at him.

Moving up and down, George smiled. "Hey there baby, lay back and enjoy it, you know I'm giving you what you want."

She didn't say anything, her eyes looking back and forth as if she had woken up and didn't understand where she was.

George leaned over her then, nuzzling his lips against her cool neck.

"Oh yeah, baby, I'm going to cum!" He screamed.

Then he really did scream when Kim Lee's mouth tore out the side of his throat. Orgasming at the exact moment, he went into shock immediately as his carotid artery shot his life's blood into the air and to the side.

In the gloom, from a distance, it would have looked like he was still pumping into her, but if an observer moved closer they would see that George was twitching in his death throes.

Kim Lee chewed what was in her mouth and then sank her teeth in for more, ripping another chunk of flesh and tendons from George's neck. Blood poured into her mouth and she drank it greedily, her eyes flaring with enjoyment.

Before getting into the car days ago, she had been bitten on the arm by an attacking ghoul. Not understanding what was happening, she had hid her wound from everyone, cleaning it herself when the rest were sleeping. With nothing but her own saliva, she had spit on it and then wiped it with the bottom of her shirt. With almost everyone covered in blood or gore somewhere on their clothing, no one had noticed. That was why she had kept her shirt on while bathing, not wanting to call attention to herself. She had slowly started feeling ill, until she didn't even want to eat food at dinner that night.

Not realizing she was infected and dying, she had gone to sleep in the sanctuary, immediately passing out to never wake up again.

That is, until George came in to have his way with her.

He had no way of understanding that while he was raping her she was breathing her last breathes and it was just bad luck that she had died and returned while George was still having his fun.

George stopped twitching and lay silent, his eyes still open, but unseeing. She tossed him off of her trapped body, her frail form stronger in death. George's penis was still hard, the blood trapped inside his member on the moment of his death. It slid out of her and then she stood up, her pants down at her ankles. She knelt over George, then, feeding, her teeth ripping into his thigh and removing a pork chop size piece of tissue. Once finished, she tore off his penis and testicles from between his legs and began chomping happily. Meat was meat to her, and the rules of society did not apply to her any longer.

She finally stopped eating him when he started moving, his eyes coming into focus once again and he looked around himself, his head barely moving thanks to all the torn muscles. George reached out, stealing the half eaten penis from her hands, and started chomping on the meat himself. Not realizing the irony of the situation.

Standing up, naked from the waist down, blood dripping down his legs, he looked at her. Kim Lee looked back, but if there was recognition in her dead eyes then she once again chose not to show it.

As a couple, the two half-naked, walking corpses shuffled out of the sanctuary to find more prey with George in the lead.

While she walked forward, her pants eventually fell off, her bare feet working their way through the folds of clothing. Turning down the path, Kim Lee followed George deeper into the zoo, her hunger already growing once more with each step she took.

Chapter 28

THE UNSUB TOSSED and turned in the makeshift bedroll. It had been days since he/she had killed anyone and the need was growing to the point of utter frustration.

It had been hard sitting next to people, trapped inside that car for two days, wanting to reach out and slit a throat, but knowing to do so would be utterly foolish.

Now he/she was inside the zoo and safe.

The Unsub knew the other survivors were spread out across the zoo. Unfortunately, who was with who was an unknown item. The Unsub didn't want to be in the middle of a slaughter only to be caught in the act. In fact, now would be the most extreme time for discretion.

Since the collapse of the city, the Unsub had been having a field day. No longer did he/she have to skulk around in the shadows. Now the Unsub could kill with wild abandon and make all who wronged him/her suffer.

Man or woman for a victim was irrelevant. Only a nuance, a subtle similarity with the person he/she secretly wanted to kill, but didn't have the courage to, would set him/her off.

And the Unsub knew who needed to die tonight.

Deciding it was time, and that the need could no longer be ignored, the Unsub stood up and fixed the disheveled clothes on his/her body. Across the cage floor, spread out in a loose circle were some of the other survivors of the day. They had all picked the lion's cage, the cage connected to a wide open pit ten feet deep so the lions could move around freely. At one time there would have been a small pool for them to drink and bathe in and there were numerous rocks for them to sun themselves on. Now it was nothing but ghosts of animals far removed.

Walking up the path, the Unsub kept to the shadows, the moonlight bathing the walkway with a wan light. Not enough to see by clearly, but more than adequate to navigate by.

Upon reaching the home of Hector, the Unsub reached out to the door, surprised to find it unlocked. But then again, the old man did live in a fenced in zoo with no one but him as the sole occupant. At least until the Unsub and the others arrived.

Opening the door, the Unsub crept inside, the room all shadows and shapes, making sure to close the door behind him/her. Not paying attention, though, the Unsub left the door slightly ajar.

Snoring caught his/her ear and the Unsub turned and entered the small room with a television and an easy chair. The old man was fast asleep in the chair, mouth hanging open, snoring with each outtake of breath.

A shotgun was propped against the wall, out of reach even if the man woke up.

Pulling the knives from under his/her shirt, one for each part of the anatomy, the Unsub stepped closer and grinned.

All alone with no one around and hours until morning.

This was going to be fun.

* * *

Paul and Ethel Thomas walked down a side path near the bird sanctuary.

Because most of the others they had bunked down with had decided to turn in, the couple had decided to go for a walk. Neither slept much these days, the need for less sleep now just part of getting older.

But they had each other and would usually keep each other company.

It was a beautiful night, the air cool, and both walked side by side, holding hands like young lovers.

Ethel glanced at Paul, who was gazing up at the night sky.

"Penny for your thoughts," she said.

"Huh? Oh, sorry, honey, I was just thinking about how insignificant we really are in the scheme of the grand cosmos. I mean, here we are trying to stay alive on our small blue world while thousands of light years, maybe hundreds of thousands even, there could be other civilizations going about their business, bringing their children to school and paying their mortgages. Just makes me feel kind of small."

She chuckled when he finished. "Wow, Paul, sorry I asked. Why don't you just focus on the here and now and let the rest handle itself." She squeezed his hand tighter. "You were always one to take on more than you could handle, I guess now's no exception."

He stopped walking and turned to look at her. "You know, it's been more than forty years and I love you more everyday." He waved his hand around him, gesturing to the world outside. "All this would have been a lot harder to take if you weren't here with me, you know that, right?"

She nodded. "Same here, handsome, now come on, I'm getting a cramp, let's keep walking."

They started walking again, and had passed the bird sanctuary and were rounding a corner to head to the bear caves when Paul heard a shuffling noise coming from behind them. He stopped and turned around, trying to pierce the darkness. The moans of the dead coming from the nearby parking lot floated to him, but he tried his best to filter out the ambient noise.

"What's wrong, Paul?" Ethel asked, but he shushed her so he could hear better.

Then he saw two shapes coming towards them down the path, moving slowly.

"Hello, who's there? Please identify yourselves," Paul called.

"Who is it, Paul, why don't they answer?" Ethel asked.

He gave her a small shove up the path. "I don't know, do me a favor, honey, and keep moving until we know who's there. It's probably just some of the guys or maybe Hector. The man did say he couldn't hear well."

"No, I'm not going anywhere without you. You come, too, there's no reason why we need to know who's down there, it's probably just some of the others sneaking around."

Paul shook his head. "No, I need to know who it is. If its trouble, then the others need to know about it, now go," he said, trying to raise his voice, though still whispering.

She stood and looked at him, her jaw set, her eyes creased. Paul knew that look. She had made up her mind and if there was one thing he knew about his wife, was that when her mind was made up, then that was it, argument over.

Reaching out, he took her hand, and together, they moved back down the path.

The shrouded figures had continued toward them and now only a few yards separated them.

The bodies were still impossible to see, only the outlines of the forms visible.

"Come on, who's there, why don't you answer?" Paul asked, squinting into the shadows and starting to get a little nervous. Ethel squeezed his hand so tight he almost let out a yelp of pain.

When the two figures were only a few feet away, a sliver of light crossed the pathway between the trees. Paul and Ethel looked down at the figure's feet, the first parts of the bodies to be illuminated, and both were surprised to see one person barefoot and the other with shoes on, but no pants. As the two shambling figures continued forward, the sliver of light slowly rose up their bodies, illuminating first their legs, then their torsos, and finally their faces.

Paul's jaw went slack with surprise, a bubble of fear in his throat, when the sliver of light landed on the hideous, mangled groin area of George. It was seeing the two ghoul's faces that, of course, sealed the deal.

Even in the pale moonlight, he could see their equally pale complexions and vacuous eyes.

Ethel let out a squeak, her interpretation of a scream, and took a step backward. Paul already knew they both needed to get away, but before he could overcome his awe at the two amalgamations of animated dead flesh, George lunged at Paul, while Kim Lee simultaneously did the same to Ethel.

In a tangle of arms and legs, all four people fell to the pavement. Paul's head struck the pathway hard and he saw stars for a brief moment.

Though Kim Lee's petite body was a third the size of Ethel, the older woman was having a tough time keeping the smaller woman at bay.

Kim Lee kept trying to snap at her throat or exposed cheeks, pleased to sink her bloody teeth into whatever was available. Paul was having an even more difficult time. George was like an animal, slavering mouth drooling over his face and hair, his teeth already bloody from feeding on himself.

Paul managed a weak punch at George's face, the blow pushing his jaw to the side. George's teeth clamped down on empty air, but he ignored the blow and after recovering far too quickly for Paul's tastes, dove back in again.

Ethel uttered a muffled scream, Kim Lee desperately trying to bite her, but missing thanks to Ethel's outstretched hands. Paul shoved George away from him, more of a roll off, really, and then reached over and pulled Kim Lee off his wife.

"Go, Ethel, run, now! Find Steve; tell him what's going on!" He ordered her.

Crawling away on her hands and legs like a crab, Ethel looked over her shoulder at her husband.

"But what about you? You can't fight them both, come with me, please," she begged.

Paul was holding Kim Lee by the waist, the dead woman trying to turn around so she could sink her teeth into Paul's arms.

"No, if I let go, she'll go after you! Go, I'll be right behind you, I promise!"

Ethel climbed to her feet, wiping her hands on her pants instinctively. She looked at her husband and then back up the pathway. She knew he was right. Steve and the others needed to know what was happening or else these things that were once people would find and kill them all. She felt a small spasm in her chest but ignored it, too much going on for a diagnostic of her body.

With one more glance to her husband, she turned and ran up the path, yelling for help, praying to God that Paul would be all right.

Paul watched her run away for the briefest instant, then he had to force Kim Lee's face away from his own when she tried to bite off his nose. Mouth open wide, a snarl like an animal slipping from her throat, he fought with the dead woman, amazed at her strength. He was so preoccupied with the ghoul in his arms, he had momentarily forgotten about George.

George rolled to his feet and charged directly into Paul and Kim Lee, all of them becoming entangled once again. Paul was trying to extricate himself and escape now that his wife was safely away, when he felt a sharp pain in his side, then a warmness spreading into his shirt.

Letting out a bark of pain, he barely had time to register that he was bleeding, when another flash of pain shot up from his ankle. Looking down, he saw Kim Lee gnawing on his left ankle like it was a turkey leg. He kicked her away, the bottom of his shoe flattening her nose, and tried to pull away from his two dead attackers.

Crawling like a dog, he managed three feet before he felt a weight on his back. He heard the sound of heavy breathing as George sucked out air that he didn't need anymore, his lungs working on automatic, and then he uttered a groan of success.

Paul felt bright white, exquisite pain then, like he had never felt before as George went in for the killing bite, leaning over Paul's throat and ripping out a four-inch piece, tendons and muscle stretching like vermilion elastics.

Paul let out a silent scream that soon was nothing but bubbles as his throat and mouth filled with his own blood. His eyes opened and closed a few times, his cheeks twitching in pain, then he dropped to the path, his nose breaking on impact, thanks to the added weight of George on top of him.

Kim Lee and George climbed onto his prone body, ripping and pulling his clothes off as they tore more flesh from his corpse.

This went on for almost ten minutes, until Paul started to twitch again and a moment later rolled over and sat up. Both George and Kim Lee, backed away, then, not interested anymore. Both wandered away in search of more living meat, Paul now forgotten.

Paul slowly pulled himself to a standing position, swaying from side to side. His bloodshot eyes looked around him, unsure of where to go. His shirt was covered in gore, leftovers from George's feeding frenzy. He picked a small red gobbet from off his chest and popped it into his mouth, chewing happily. Half his neck and a good portion of his right shoulder were gone, now inside George's stomach, and his head had a bad habit of listing to the right while he walked, like an off kilter table. Then he heard the echoing groans carried on the air from outside the zoo and he turned, moving toward them like the groans were a siren, calling him home.

As he stumbled along, his left foot dragged behind him like a lead weight. Kim Lee had devoured too much muscle for the leg to be of any use. Still, he persevered, trudging down the path, now with only one purpose.

To find living humans and feed.

Chapter 29

CARL WAS DEEP asleep as he lay on the ground inside the bear caves. Next to him were Craig, Steve and Tracey, also fast asleep.

They had talked for awhile after setting up camp and had then turned in, the long day taking its toll on both their minds and bodies.

Carl slept fitfully, tossing and turning on the hard ground.

He fell into a nightmare, though he didn't realize it. To him, the landscape he now found himself in was as real as the day he had spent struggling to stay alive.

He found himself walking down one of the small pathways in the zoo, the empty cages and pits now full of animals. It was how he remembered the zoo as a child, when his father had taken him on a Sunday afternoon when he had been ten.

He remembered sitting on his shoulders, feeling like the tallest person in the world, his father's head bobbing below him while they walked from exhibit to exhibit.

But now the zoo seemed more oppressive, and though he didn't know what it was, he knew this wasn't the same zoo he had visited as a child.

There was death in the air now.

The redolence floated to him on the wind and he winced at the sickly-sweet smell. Covering his nose with his arm, he continued walking; now wanting only to find the exit and leave this cursed place.

He stopped walking at the sound of a growl coming from behind him. Not wanting to turn around, but realizing he had no choice, he slowly spun his top half to the side; his feet remaining planted on the cement.

What he saw froze his insides to the core. A large male lion was standing no more then fifteen yards from him, its mouth open wide, its eyes menacing.

Normally seeing a lion no more then a few feet from him would have had him filling his pants with shit, but that wasn't what turned his insides to mush.

The lion was dead, but yet was still mobile.

A large section of its ribcage was missing; the bones protruding at odd angles like something out of an Alien movie had tried to escape from its body. Its once majestic mane was now flattened to its head, encrusted with maroon, and black ichor.

One of its eyes was hanging out of its socket, dangling near its mouth.

The lion roared its displeasure at Carl and the swinging eye ended up inside the cavity of teeth. The lion chopped down hard, severing the few bits of red gristle holding the eye and chewed merrily. Carl felt a spasm in his stomach and swallowed hard, tasting bile; trying to keep it down.

The lion took a halting step forward, one of its legs dragging behind it. The rear foreleg looked like a car or a truck had driven over it, flattening the limb to the point of uselessness.

The three legged lion took another step and Carl tasted the fear inside him as he stared at those dead, milky eyes.

A small voice in his head told him to run and he did, turning forward and taking off at a sprint. With a growl from deep in its throat, the lion took off after him, only the lack of one of its limbs slowing it down.

Carl ran up the path, arms pumping, legs moving like a sprinter. He rounded a corner and came up fast, seeing another animal blocking his path. An elephant stood stock still, its trunk hanging low. Its gray skin was covered in sores and lesions, and it had large chunks of its tough hide missing from around its legs.

Carl heard the lion behind him and he knew he had no choice but to go for it. Running as fast as he could, he charged the elephant, diving to the ground and rolling under its massive body. As he rolled, he saw a large slice in its abdomen, intestines hanging down like vines in a jungle.

He rolled through the tree-like legs and came out on the other side. Picking himself up, he prepared to keep running just as the lion reached the elephant.

The elephant roared at the lion and without hesitation, the lion jumped at the elephant's head, talons raking its eyes as it struggled to overcome the insurmountable odds.

Carl watched for a second, fascinated as the two zombie animals battled to the . . . what . . . death? That didn't seem right, as the animals were already dead. Then he realized he didn't want to be around to see who the victor was. No matter the winner, he was doomed if he stayed.

He turned and ran, the sounds of the battle disappearing behind him.

When he was no more then fifty feet away, he was thrown off the path by a charging giraffe. Falling into the shrubs lining the path, he looked up into the neck and head of something that should have been long dead. The long neck was riddled with sores and bite marks, some of them so deep the animal's spine glistened in the sun. The mouth dripped bloody drool and its eyes flashed malevolently at him.

He knew he needed to escape and he tried to climb out of the shrubs only to find his leg trapped between two twisted branches. Pulling on his leg, he desperately tried to free himself, his heart trip-hammering inside his chest.

Desperately trying to release his trapped leg, he looked up in time to see the sun blocked by the rapidly descending head of the giraffe. Its mouth was opened wide and its brown teeth flashed in the light of the sun.

He let out a scream that filled his head and he closed his eyes, knowing he was about to die and there wasn't a damn thing he could do about it.

His screams seemed to go on forever.

* * *

Steve tossed in his sleep, as well. He was reliving Helen's murder. That's what she was to him, a murder victim; killed by her own damn coward of a husband.

Since Steve had beaten Hickman up, the doctor had done his best to stay out of Steve's way. That was smart for the man; Steve wanted nothing more than to crush the life from the pathetic excuse for a human being.

He thought back to Helen's face as she was ripped limb from limb and a single tear rolled down his face.

Steve had always been a problem solver. A man who wasn't afraid to make a decision and then accept the consequences if the decision had been wrong.

He'd still stand by it, though, because at the time, he had made the best educated decision with the information at his disposal.

Hindsight was twenty-twenty, the saying went. It was always so easy to criticize once the problem had resolved itself for good or bad.

When Steve had found the others on the road and then the group trapped inside the cars, he had taken them on as his responsibility. He was a natural leader and only wanted what was best for all of them, namely, to stay alive and not starve to death.

Everyone in the group had seemed to sense this, too, and no one had contested him as leader, with the exception of George and he was just blowing steam. That was good. That gave them all more time to focus on what was important, instead of having to deal with petty rivalries.

Yelling and voices penetrated his mind and he woke with a shock. Carl was lying near him, waving his arms in the air, screaming. Craig was up nearby and was already moving to Carl's side to see what was wrong with his friend.

Steve sat up, Tracey now awake, as well.

"What's wrong with him?" She asked her father.

Steve climbed to his feet, shakily. He hadn't had nearly enough rest and his body protested.

Craig had been shaking Carl with no result and so finally, he slapped Carl across the face. The screams stopped in mid-yelp and Carl looked up at his friend, eyes wide as they focused. In the shadows of the cave, it appeared he had a red spot on the side of his cheek.

Rubbing his face, Carl frowned, pushing Craig away from him.

"Ouch, that hurts, what the hell did you do that for?" He asked, rubbing his cheek.

"You were having a damn nightmare, that's why. You woke us all up." Craig said, leaning back and sitting on his butt. Then he let his body fall back down onto the cave floor, stretching out with his knees in the air and his feet flat on the floor.

"Christ, can I have another ten hours of sleep, please?" Craig asked, looking at his wristwatch.

"What time is it?" Tracey inquired, rubbing her eyes and yawning.

"It's about twelve. We've only been asleep for a few hours," Craig said, crawling back to his makeshift bedroll and burying his head under the small blanket he was using to keep warm.

Tracey was about to say something else, when Steve held up his hand for her to be silent. She was about to talk anyway, when he glared at her.

"Quiet, dammit, do you hear that? It's someone yelling."

All four of them cocked their ears to the entrance of the cave. Now, with no one talking or moving about, the distinctive sounds of frantic yelling could be heard.

Steve immediately started pulling his boots on, looking at Craig as he did so.

"Craig, I need a weapon, you don't need two of them. If there's yelling then there's something wrong out there, I don't want to go walking around in the dark unarmed."

Craig handed him his pistol, lying next to him on the rocks. "Here, do you know how to use this?"

Steve took the pistol and then checked the safety and released the clip. Then he popped it back in, cocking the weapon.

"Yeah, I think I'll manage." He turned and looked at Craig. "You come with me." Then he looked to Carl. "Carl, you stay with Tracey. If something comes to the opening of the cave and doesn't identify itself as me or Craig then get out the back way and meet us at the picnic site near Hector's place."

Tracey frowned, almost pouting. "But I want to go, too, you might need me."

Steve turned to her and looked down at his daughter. Though she was just past twenty, he would always think of her as being five years old with a lollipop in her mouth and her dolly in her hand.

"No honey, not this time. I can't deal with whatever's happening outside if I'm always worrying about your safety. Please, for once in your life, just do as I ask."

Tracey frowned but nodded, yes.

Steve leaned over and kissed her on the cheek, smiling. Then he brushed an errant hair away from her face. "You really are the spitting image of your mother, you know that?"

"Dad," she said embarrassed. "Stop it, please. Now go if you're going, before I change my mind."

He nodded and looked to Craig. "You ready, soldier?"

Craig answered by sliding a bullet into the chamber of his rifle. "Fuckin' A, let's do this."

Steve stepped toward the entrance to the cave then, and with Craig by his side, they both slipped out into the cool night air.

No sooner had Steve and Craig walked the few yards to the main pathway bisecting the zoo's east and west sides then others appeared from the shadows.

Hal Beckett and Matt were both looking about curiously, their eyes still half open from sleep.

"What the hell's all the racket out here? I just got to sleep, for Christ Sake!" Matt yelled groggily at anyone who would listen.

"Is something wrong?" Hal asked. "Have the dead people gotten into the zoo? Oh shit, we're screwed now, where the hell do we go from here?" Hal finished, looking around nervously as if he expected monsters to jump out of the shadows and try to eat him.

"Now both of you, just relax, I don't know what's going on, me and Craig just got here, too," Steve told them, Craig nodding at his side.

From behind them, the sound of bare feet slapping on cement floated to them and both Steve and Craig spun around, weapons ready.

In the deep shadows, all that could be seen was that the two approaching figures were one male and one female.

Swallowing hard, Steve prepared to blast whatever was there to hell as soon as he could see their faces.

The two figures moved forward, jogging more than walking and a second later their faces became clear to the others, the trees thinner on the path, letting some moonlight seep through.

Steve and Craig's fingers tensed on triggers as the forms became close enough to almost reach out and touch. Then their faces were illuminated and Rosa and Miguel's worried countenances were seen clearly, their faces lined with worry and concern.

Steve and Craig lowered their weapons, sharing a silent understanding. Both had been a hair's breath away from killing the young Spanish couple.

"Jesus Christ, Miguel, we almost killed you, why didn't you say something to tell us it was you?" Steve asked.

Miguel grinned slightly and looked at his wife next to him. "Oh yeah, that would be smart. I didn't know who you were, either, but I'm going to yell out so that whoever's around will know where I am. Didn't you hear the screaming? Someone's in trouble."

Craig grunted, repositioning his rifle in front of him. "That's why we're out here. Anyone know who's yelling?"

Everyone shrugged. The calls for help were as yet unidentified and the echoes bounced off the empty cages and other structures like inside a canyon. Direction was hard to pinpoint.

Movement from behind had everyone spinning around, prepared for anything. What they got was the young kid, Seth, looking like he was about to crap his pants as he looked down the barrels of the two loaded weapons.

"Whoa, dudes, I surrender, don't shoot," he said, his eyes never leaving the barrel of the guns.

Steve and Craig lowered their weapons once more, frustrated.

"What the hell is going on around here?" Steve asked the faces around him.

The sounds of more bare feet came to them and Steve turned to see another two people coming up the path. The shadows were ominous, seeming to suck any ambient light in the vicinity.

Steve looked casually at the two newcomers and then looked away.

"We've got two more coming, at this rate every damn one of us will be on this walkway," Steve summarized.

"At least it'll be easier to know who's missing if everyone gets together down here," Craig said with a wan smile.

"So what's next? Personally, without a weapon, I don't like the idea of running around this deserted place," Hal said, looking around himself.

A few more grunts of agreement floated back to Steve and he waved his hands in the air, quieting everybody down.

"All right, hold on now. Why don't we all stick together and we'll investigate as a team, that way no one will get hurt or shot by accident, okay?"

Mutters of agreement came to him and he nodded. "All right, then, lets go back to Hector's and from there we'll see if we can find the disturbance that woke us all up."

With Steve and Craig in the lead, the group began moving again. Everyone shuffled forward, Rosa and Miguel coming second to last.

Neither of the two people noticed the two others behind them, as nothing more then shadows; just two others of the group following Steve and Craig.

It was only when one of the faces appeared in a spot of light on the path that the Esperanzas' realized they were in big trouble.

"Dios Mio," Rosa whispered, making the sign of the cross as the bodies of George and Kim Lee emerged into the dim light.

"Oh my sweet Jesus," Miguel muttered, his voice gone from fright.

Both ghouls growled deep in their throats, red drool leaking out of their maroon covered mouths. Before either of the two humans could do more then stagger backwards, the dead couple attacked, falling onto the Esperanzas' with teeth and nails.

Miguel cried out as soon as he felt teeth sink into his shoulder and Rosa let out a piercing scream when Kim Lee ripped half her cheek off her face like a starving man ripping the crispy skin of a cooked chicken.

Both victims fell to the walkway, muffled screams still coming from their mouths.

Steve and Craig both heard the screams at the same time, and with a shared look at one another, both turned around and pushed past the others.

Running back down the path, they stopped when they saw the dim forms of both attackers and victims.

Craig never hesitated, but aimed the rifle at the right body and squeezed the trigger. George was knocked from Miguel like a giant fist had swatted him away.

He rolled on the path, but a second later was sitting up, slowly he went to all fours and then rose to his feet again.

Steve shot at Kim Lee, his bullet hitting her in the top of the head while she fed on Rosa. He was just lucky; actually aiming for whatever body part was exposed in his haste to save the beleaguered woman.

The bullet entered the top of Kim Lee's skull and then exited out her mouth, the body dropping limp on top of Rosa. Rosa was screaming louder now, her blood filling her mouth to add to the gurgling sound of her pleas.

Craig ran to her and pulled Kim Lee off her, pushing the body to the path.

Steve was now next to Craig and both stared in shock as one of their own, namely George, staggered towards them, arms out in front of him like he was auditioning for the Frankenstein monster in the school play. He now had a ragged hole in his chest to add to the other ghastly wounds on his body.

"Holy shit, look at him? How the fuck is he still walking around?" Craig gasped.

"Simple, he's one of them now. Somehow he got bit," Steve said, glancing at the prone body of Miguel.

Miguel was on the path, unconscious, his blood pooling under his body and spreading on the path, a dark pool as black as night shimmering across the cement.

George waved his arms in front of him as he approached Steve and Craig. It was like he was unhappy because they weren't paying enough attention to him.

Steve nudged Craig and raised his gun. Craig did the same.

Steve fired the first shot, plus one more, not wanting to waste ammo, Craig mimicking him. But Craig had a full clip and extra mags to boot and didn't hold back. Bullets from the rifle pounded into George's body, making him dance the jig. Flesh and bone sprayed out behind him, covering the path in a red mist. Craig had started his gunfire at George's waist and he slowly walked his line of fire up his chest, working with the rise of the shotgun's muzzle. Bullet after bullet struck home. Then a bullet struck George's face, his nose disappearing in a spray of blood. The next one put him down, plowing into his forehead and exiting out the back, taking a fist size chunk of skull. George toppled over like a fallen tree, his head striking the ground with a meaty smack. Brain matter oozed out of the large hole in the back of his head and Craig lowered his weapon.

Steve turned to look at the others and waved them over.

"Its safe, now, come over here and give us a hand with these two," he said gesturing to the Esperanzas'. "They're hurt bad, we need to get them medical attention fast."

Matt, Hal and Seth all ran to help, each picking up a body, Craig helping Hal.

With the two bodies lying unconscious between them, the group headed up the path towards Hector's place.

"What about those two?" Craig asked, looking back at the corpses of Kim Lee and George.

"They're not going anywhere, and we have more important things to worry about. Namely, how the hell did they get like that?"

By the time they reached Hector's place, everyone but Steve was huffing and puffing.

"Go to the tables and put them down there, I'll get some towels and water from Hector's. Plus, the old man's deaf. He probably hasn't heard shit despite the fact it sounded like there was a war going on in his own backyard."

While the others moved off to the rear of the building, Steve headed for the door that led to Hector's small living quarters.

He stopped at the door, prepared to start banging on it.

It was ajar, which seemed unusual.

Steve opened the door enough so he could stick his head inside.

"Hello, Hector, its Steve! We need some help out here!"

No answer.

Opening the door a little more, he moved into the room, his gun hanging by his side. Why wouldn't it? There should be no cause for alarm.

The room was all dark, only a few gloomy slivers of light coming in from behind him, the door having opened further once Steve had let it go.

Steve reached out for a switch to turn on the lights and wasn't surprised when the light stayed off. Hector probably turned off his small generator when he went to bed. Reaching around by feel, Steve tried to call up the mental picture he had of the room, where the trash had been on the floor and where the couch was.

Suddenly, out of the darkness, a shadow ran at him, knocking him off balance and causing him to tumble over a small end table and fall to the floor with a sloppy crash of limbs and legs.

Before he could get off a yell of surprise, the shadow was at the door and running into the night.

Steve rolled over on the floor, cursing, his hand searching for the pistol he'd dropped in the fall. A moment later, his hand wrapped around the grip and he pulled it to him, still on his knees.

Breathing hard, he looked around himself, but whoever had been in the room with him was gone, running like a thief in the night.

Steve stood up; rubbing his elbow where he'd smacked it on the floor on his way down, and with a muffled curse about getting caught unawares, moved deeper into the room. His hands searched around and after a minute or so had passed, he found a candle sitting on top of the television. Flicking his lighter a few times, he lit the candle and looked around the small circle of light it cast around him.

Turning around the room, he stopped when he came to Hector's easy chair.

The old man was still in his chair, but most of his blood was leaking out of him and into the cushions. His neck was slashed and it looked like he had at least one more wound on his chest. It was hard to tell, the blood had soaked into everything, dying his clothes and the chair cushions a dull red.

Steve stepped closer, the smell of urine and feces mingling with the sickly smell of the blood, overwhelming him in the small room.

Steve reached out and closed Hector's eyes, still open and staring at the ceiling.

A call for towels and water floated in from the picnic area and Steve knew Hector would have to wait.

Finding the few items that would help the group, he quickly left the room, his arms now full of supplies. But as he left, he knew one thing. Hector had died from a blade, not from teeth marks. A ghoul hadn't killed Hector in a murderous attack to consume his flesh.

No, Hector was murdered by a human being with a knife.

As he ran around the building and towards the others, his jaw set tight, his mind whirled with what he had discovered; now knowing something awful.

Whoever had run from him and knocked him over was one of their little group. And that person had slaughtered and killed Hector mercilessly.

If the ghouls weren't bad enough, now he had to contend with a murderer. A murderer whose identity he had no way of knowing.

Chapter 30

STEVE RETURNED TO the picnic area with towels and miscellaneous supplies, whatever he thought would help the wounded couple. Hal looked up as he rounded the building and ran over to him, grabbing the towels and a bottle of water from his arms.

"Jesus Christ, man, what the hell were you doing in there? They need help out here." Hal said in a frustrated tone, turning and rushing back to the two bodies lying side by side on one of the picnic tables. He quickly tossed Matt a towel and then used one for himself, pressing down on Rosa's wound. Matt did the same, leaning on Miguel with as much force as he thought the man could take.

Others were arriving now, woken from all the gunfire and yelling. Each one stumbled into the picnic area, eyes wide when they saw the Esperanzas'.

"Oh my Lord, what's happened to them? What was all that shooting about? Are those *people* inside here with us?" Sherry asked with a frightened voice as she stood to the side.

Steve shook his head, and looked into her eyes. "No, we're fine, but George and the Asian woman are dead, I forgot her name, sorry."

"It was Kim Lee," Hal said. "That's all we ever got from her. And now she's dead. Christ, I didn't even know her last name or how old she was."

"Her last name was probably Lee, Hal," Matt said.

Hal looked up. "You think? Maybe it was part of her first name. Shit, Matt, its not like we can ask her now, can we?"

Diane walked into the clearing, stalling the conversation and all eyes turned to her. She smiled wanly and walked over to be next to Sherry, sensing she was interrupting something. Sherry nodded curtly in a greeting and then looked back to Steve.

"But what about George and Kim? How did they die?" Sherry asked with eyes wide with panic.

Craig walked over to her and shrugged. "Don't know, somehow they were infected, like all the people outside. Don't know how it happened, though."

"Look," Steve said, getting the others attention, "it doesn't matter how this or that happened, but there are a few things you guys need to know about. Before we went to bed last night, I saw a news report on the television." Steve tried to tell more, but everyone started asking him questions.

"Enough, please!" Steve yelled, holding his hands out for them to stop badgering him. "Look, I'm sorry. I didn't say anything about the report because there wasn't much that was positive about it. I figured all it would do is make everyone even more worried and upset than they already were."

Then he went through what he'd seen and heard, including what happens to a victim if bitten by an infected person.

"And there's one other thing. Hector's dead. But it wasn't from a zombie or whatever you want to call them. His throat was slashed with something sharp." He looked at each face and then said: "He was murdered in cold blood; probably while we were all sleeping."

Everyone started talking at once, each giving ideas on what they should do next.

Steve let them talk. It was good to talk about things, even if it was for no reason other than to vent.

He moved over to Hal and looked down at Rosa.

"How's she doing? Will she live?" Steve asked, though he already knew the answer.

Hal looked into Steve's face, a few drops of blood on his forehead. "That's a damn good question. She's lost a lot of blood and there's no way to get more into her." He shrugged. "Look, I'm not a doctor, so I can't say."

Craig turned around the clearing, looking for something, or someone.

"Hey, that's right, where the hell is Doctor Hickman? He's the only one not here other then Carl and Tracey."

"No, we're missing a couple more. The lady with the crazy hair. What was her name, Tammy, Tula?" Seth said, thinking.

"It was Tina," Diane said from the side. "I didn't see them on my way up here."

Steve frowned. "Hmmm. We've got a dead body and a missing doctor. Craig, go see if you can find him on your way to get Carl and my daughter and watch your back. Who else is missing?"

Matt looked up and knew immediately. "Where's Paul and Ethel? They should have been here by now." He was still holding the towel over Miguel's torn shoulder, but he wasn't feeling positive about it.

Steve saw his face and moved closer. "How's he doing?"

Matt shook his head. "He's lost a shitload of blood and he's unconscious. He's been that way since we carried him here. Maybe it's for the best. Here look," Matt said, pulling the towel back so Steve could see.

Steve cringed slightly, feeling the wounded man's pain. His shoulder was missing inches of flesh, muscles glistening red around the deep pivot. Even if he was an expert at stitching wounds there wasn't any flesh to stitch. Plus, the man had been bitten by an infected person. There was only one place this would all end.

"Do your best, Matt; just try to make him as comfortable as possible."

Matt nodded, actually doing nothing different. The truth was; there was really nothing more he could do even if he wanted to.

Steve moved to the end of the table so the Esperanzas' feet were in front of him. Then he hopped up on the adjacent picnic table and sat down, not moving, just watching the Esperanzas', his pistol in his lap.

Diane moved over to him, her face creased in worry. "So what now? What do we do now?"

Steve leaned back on his left hand and glanced at her. "We do nothing. You and the others might as well go back to bed. I know that sounds callous, but there's really nothing else any of you can do. A few of us are going to find the others and then deal with poor Hector, then we'll go back to bed and try to grab a few hours of sleep before sunrise."

"What? I can't sleep with everything that's happened," Diane retorted.

"Fine, then stay up, but stay out of the way, will you, please?"

Sherry walked over to Steve. "But what about them?" She asked, pointing to the Esperanzas'. "We need to do something for them. Get medical help, something."

Steve shook his head, not believing how naive some people could be. "There's nothing we can do for them, now. All we can do is wait and then deal with what comes next."

"And what's that, man?" Seth asked.

Steve looked him square in the face. "We wait for them to come back."

* * *

Carl and Tracey had just left the caves, deciding they had waited long enough. Once they began to hear gunfire and screams and shouts, that had cinched the deal. They had stayed another ten minutes and had then decided to go to the rendezvous like Steve had told them.

"You know, if your Dad's pissed at us for leaving the cave, you better protect me," Carl said nervously.

"Oh relax; my Dad's just a big teddy bear when you get to know him."

"Yeah," Carl answered back under his breath, "a teddy bear with claws and big muscles."

The two moved through the winding pathways, the shadows encroaching on them. They were only a few yards away from the picnic area and could already hear voices floating on the air, when Paul jumped out of the nearby bushes and attacked Tracey.

She fell to the pavement, rolling and wriggling out from under Paul. He lay on his back, hissing, and then he rolled to his feet, ready to attack again.

"Paul? Mr. Thomas? What's wrong with you?" Carl asked, pulling Tracey behind him. Breathing hard, she let herself be pulled, too scared to worry about the man protecting the woman thing. Feminism had its place, but right now all the help she could get was welcomed with open arms.

Paul growled again, drool leaking from a corner of his mouth.

He took a halting step forward, hands grasping empty air. It was now that both Carl and Tracey saw the condition of Paul. He was missing a huge side of his throat, the blood only seeping out of the glistening wound and his stomach was torn open, intestines peeking out like a nest of scared snakes afraid of the dark. He limped heavily, favoring his wounded left ankle, hobbling like he was in a three-legged race.

"Oh my God, he's one of them, he's dead. But how?" Tracey gasped, holding down her seizing insides.

Carl didn't care how Paul had become one of them, all that mattered was that he was one of them now and he wanted Carl and Tracey to be his next meal. He told her as much.

The entire time they talked, they were moving backwards, keeping away from the shambling ghoul.

"If he's died and come back again, then where's his wife? Is she dead, too?" Tracey asked, fending of a clawed hand. She wanted to run, but was worried Paul would jump on them from behind. The old man was pretty quick for a dead guy.

"Don't know, frankly I'm worried about my own ass right now!" Carl said kicking Paul away as he tried to lunge at him.

"Shit, this could go on all day, we need to find something to kill him with," Tracey snarled, looking around the ground. There was nothing. The zoo was spotless, all loose debris cleaned up before the place had been closed.

A voice sounded from further up the path, lost in the shadows. "*Get down and stay down!*" The voice called.

Carl and Tracey dropped, obeying the command. Paul saw his prey drop and seemed to grin, thinking he'd won. Carl looked up into those soulless eyes and wondered if by obeying the command to drop, he'd just signed his own death warrant.

Just as Paul lunged at Carl's prone body, his head rocked back and a large portion of his face disintegrated. Paul stumbled to the side, hands clawing air. Then another rifle shot cracked through the night and the rest of Paul's head exploded in a glorious spray of red mist and brain matter.

Tracey and Carl rolled away from the spreading spray, coming up against a pair of legs. Carl looked up at the face of Craig, the rifle still aimed at Paul.

"Hey, buddy, what took you so long?" Carl joked.

Paul's body dropped to the ground, bouncing slightly. Then remained still, the exposed neck stump seeping ichor onto the path.

Craig helped Tracey up and let Carl climb to his feet himself. "Your Dad wants you back at the picnic area and he sent me to fetch you." He said to Tracey and then looked at Carl "And you too, Carl," Craig said flashing him a smile.

"Not a problem, man, thanks for the love." Carl quipped.

Craig grinned some more. "Happy to help. Damn, did you see that head explode? I had larger caliber ammo, so I thought I'd try some out." He thought about the hit once more. "Damn, that was intense. Well, come on, let's go. Oh yeah, we're looking for a few people, too. I guess we found Paul," he said, looking back at the body. "But we need to find his wife; and the Doc and that little woman with the crazy hair, Tina. Tina is still missing, too."

"Well then, let's go?" Tracey said, scratching her arm.

Carl saw this and stopped her. "Hey, wait a sec'. Let me see that, did you get hurt?" He asked, taking her arm in his hand.

Craig stopped walking and returned to them. "What's wrong?"

"Nothing really, it's just a scratch; must have happened when Paul jumped on me."

Carl and Craig stared at the scratch closer. The distinct impression of a bite mark was on her skin; though only one tooth had apparently broken the skin.

"Shit, Tracey, you've been bit," Craig gasped.

"So, it's no big deal. A little iodine and I'll be fine."

Craig shook his head. "No, you don't understand." He looked up and down the path, as if he was debating something in his head. "Fuck this shit, come on, we need to get you back to your Dad right now, he need's to see this."

"But why? It's just a small scratch," she said again.

Craig looked into her eyes, his face as serious as it had ever been since meeting her.

"Because your Dad told us about some newscast he saw on TV last night about what happens if you get bit by one of them. You're infected now. If you get bit by one of them, then you turn into one of them, now no more talk, times wasting; we need to see your Dad."

Then the three of them took off at a ground eating run, trying to beat the clock on Tracey's bite.

Chapter 31

STEVE SAT QUIETLY on the edge of the picnic table, watching the body of Miguel, while all around him the others moved about and talked. Some threw out ideas that they should leave the zoo, others thought they should stay.

Steve ignored them all. In the end, they could do whatever the hell they wanted. As long as they didn't endanger him or his daughter, he didn't care.

All he could do was try to steer them in the right direction and hope they followed his lead.

Hal and Sherry were arguing in a corner of the picnic area and off to his left, Seth and Matt were discussing how the dead could be running around instead of lying on the ground, well, like dead people.

Steve's hearing caught the sound of gunshots, his head turning toward the sound; the echo sounding like Craig's rifle. Then all was silent once again, only a few night birds in the trees to break the deafening silence.

When Steve looked back at Miguel's body, he could have sworn he saw Miguel's hand twitch. At first he thought it might have been a trick of the shadows, perhaps from an overhead cloud blocking the moonlight. But then the arm moved slowly and a moment later, Miguel sat up.

Steve could see his eyes reflecting the wan light in the clearing and even from six feet away he could tell there was something off about the man. The way his jaw hung open, and the eyes searched around, but yet seemed to focus on nothing.

No one else noticed Miguel, all lost in their own arguments and opinions.

Calmly, but with a knot of fear in his chest as he watched something that should be scientifically impossible, Steve raised the pistol. He had four shots left, the ten round clip nearly depleted.

Miguel's head turned to look at him and his mouth opened wider, like a snake attempting to swallow something large. A soft moan drifted out of his mouth, sounding almost sad and far away. Steve squeezed the trigger, a neat hole appearing in Miguel's forehead, a larger one appearing like magic on the back of his skull. Miguel's head snapped back and the body fell back to the picnic table with a gentleness that belayed its death.

Everyone in the clearing stopped talking, Sherry and Hal actually dropping to the ground thinking there was danger.

Steve slid off the table and stood up, looking at the faces around him. Casually, he walked over to Rosa and looked down at the supine woman, admiring the strong lines of her face; even though her complexion was far paler then she ever was when healthy.

Matt walked over to him and looked down at the pale woman, as well.

"Are you sure she's going to die?" Steve asked quietly, the others watching him closely.

Matt nodded. "Yeah, I'm afraid so. Even if she was able to survive the wound and blood loss . . . I mean, look at the size of that bite . . . she's still infected; big time."

Steve nodded. "I just wanted to make sure, that's all." Then he placed the barrel of the pistol against Rosa's right ear and shot her in the head.

The left side of her head exploded, parts of her brain and bits of bone covering Miguel's still form.

Matt jumped back so fast he almost tripped over his two feet.

"Jesus Christ! What the fuck did you do that for?" Matt cried, staring at Rosa's head, and checking to see if he had any pieces of her on him.

Steve shoved the pistol inside the front waistband of his pants and then sighed. "Because I had to, that's why. Look, we all knew she was coming back and frankly, I didn't feel like waiting around for it to happen. Listen and believe this when I say this. I'm not two-faced. If I'm bit and unconscious you have my permission to blow me away." He smiled slightly then. "Just make sure I'm really gonna die, okay?"

Matt nodded slowly, still looking at the sight of Rosa's shattered head.

Steve gestured to the two bodies. "Someone grab something to cover them up. We can deal with them later. Not to mention the bodies of George and Kim Lee. Right now, we need to still figure out what happened to Hector and find the others."

He looked back to the opening that led around to the path and the front of Hector's building, wondering where Craig was with the others. After hearing those gunshots, he could only hope Craig, Carl and Tracey were all right. But mostly he was concerned about Tracey. Then he pushed it from his mind. Craig was a soldier in the Army, for God's sake. If he couldn't take care of himself, then what hope do the others have as warriors? And that's what they all needed to be. Whether they liked it or not, they had all become holy warriors where death wasn't the end, but was in fact, only the beginning. Craig would find Tracey and Carl and bring them back to him safe and sound.

He was pulled from his reverie when Craig, Carl and Tracey came into the picnic area. Steve saw Carl's face and immediately knew something was amiss.

Tracey ran up to him, her face a mask of what she was truly feeling: terror.

"What's wrong? Where are the others? Why are you back so quickly?"

Craig grabbed Tracey's arm and shoved it into Steve's face. "This is why, she's been bit. Paul was one of them; he jumped out onto the path and attacked her. We got him off her, but not before . . ."

Steve's face showed at least five emotions in the same amount of seconds, but then his face hardened.

"What are we going to do? She's not going to turn into one of them, is she?" Carl asked, looking at Tracey and then Steve.

Steve shook his head, an idea floating in the back of his mind.

"No, dammit, I won't let them have her." He turned and waved Hal over to him, the others keeping their distance, not knowing what was happening, but knowing to stay out of it. Hal jogged over, expectation on his face.

"Whatever you need, buddy, just name it," he said.

Steve gestured to Hector's place. "Go inside Hector's and see if you can find me some oil, like for cooking. Olive oil is better."

Hal obeyed, not wasting time asking questions. Steve turned back to Craig and Carl.

"How long ago was she bit?" Steve asked them.

Carl shrugged, and looked to Craig for confirmation. "Shit, I don't know, maybe two or three minutes ago. We ran all the way here when we found out. Why, what does that matter?"

"Because it's possible the infection isn't fully in her bloodstream yet." He waved to Tracey. "Honey, come over here and sit down," Steve told her.

Tracey did as she was told, her countenance one of nervousness.

"Oh my God, am I going to become one of them?" She asked Steve.

"No!" He yelled, slapping his fist on the table. "No, Tracey, you'll be fine, I won't let them take you from me."

Hal returned then, breathing heavily. In his hand was a can of Olive oil.

"Here, Steve, I found this in the back of one of the cupboards. Is this what you want?"

Steve took it and nodded. "I need a knife, the sharper the better, anyone got one?"

Craig stepped forward and handed him a small pocket knife. Steve could read a small inscription on its side; Craig's name by the looks of it.

Craig saw this and frowned. "It was from my father on my twelfth birthday. Now it's the only thing I have left of him or my family."

Steve flipped open the knife and grunted. "I'm sorry, Craig . . . for all of us."

Then he took Tracey's arm and held it on the table. "Okay, honey, you remember that time Uncle Tommy got bit by a snake and I told you how I saved him?"

She nodded, her face growing pale.

"All right, then just stay still and it'll be over in a second." Steve then picked up the Olive oil and took a swig, swishing it around in his mouth. When he was sure he had coated the inside of his mouth as best he could, he spit it out onto the grass at his feet.

Then he picked up the knife and held it over the bite.

"You might want to turn away for a second, honey," he told her softly and then deftly sliced her arm; a one-inch incision just over the small bite mark. As soon as the blood started flowing, he leaned in and started sucking the wound, treating it like a snake bite. Suck, spit, suck, and spit. He did this for almost five minutes, only stopping when he rinsed with more Olive oil. Tracey watched fascinated, while her father sucked at her arm like a vampire. In the shadows of the night, and blood coating his mouth and chin, he resembled one of the undead.

Tracey tried to blot out the similarity and look away. Out of nowhere she started feeling woozy, whether from the shock of the bite or from loss of blood. She didn't want to think how much blood her father had drained from her with nothing more then his mouth.

Steve stopped and looked up at Hal and Matt. "Either of you guys have something I can bandage her arm with?"

Matt held up a finger and then moved to one of the picnic tables, the sound of ripping coming to him. He returned a second later holding a piece of cloth. Steve noticed the rag was the same color as Miguel's shirt, but didn't comment on it. The cloth was free of blood, so it was good enough for him at the moment.

Wrapping her arm, he looked into her eyes. "You'll be fine, honey, I'm sure I got it in time."

"But what if you didn't?" A voice said from the path that led to the rest of the zoo.

All eyes, including Steve's, looked up at the voice.

Warren Hickman stood at the entrance to the picnic area, with Tina next to him.

"You. Where the fuck have you been, Doc? We've been looking for you. Didn't you hear all the gunshots?" Craig asked, moving closer to the man.

Hickman stepped closer, as well. "Yes, I heard the commotion and because I didn't know what was happening, I decided to stay hidden. When nothing happened and no dead people arrived, I decided it must be safe."

Carl spoke up then, gesturing to Tina. The small woman was hanging onto Hickman like they were an item. "Already found you someone new, 'ay Doc?"

Hickman waved the question away. "What if I did? Since when do my private affairs matter to any of you?"

He stepped closer and pointed to Tracey. "I'll ask you again, Mr. Webb. What if you didn't get the infection in time? What if her bite isn't similar to a snakebite? She'll become one of them. And then she'll try to eat the rest of us."

Steve stood up and walked over to Hickman. Though Hickman flinched slightly, he held his ground.

"I'll worry about my daughter, Doc, and you worry about your wife. Oh wait, you can't, because you left her to die!" His voice slowly went up in volume until he was yelling.

Hickman tried to stand straighter, though he was still a few inches shorter than Steve.

"Don't try to derail the conversation, Mr. Webb. I'll ask you one more time, in front of all these people. What will you do if your daughter turns into one of them? These people should know the answer, because it could be one of them she goes after."

Steve pulled the pistol from his waistband and placed it in front of Hickman's nose.

"If she turns, then I'll kill her myself. Happy?"

Hickman shrugged. "Not really, but I'll tell you this, until we know one way or the other, I'll be staying at the opposite end of the zoo. Goodnight to you and to you others." Then he took Tina's hand and walked away.

"Hickman, you get your ass back here, right now! There's still some unanswered questions you need to answer to!" Steve took a step after Hickman, squeezing the grip on the gun in his hand until his knuckles turned white. "Hickman, you little prick, get back here!"

Carl and Craig both moved next to Steve. "Let it go, man, its not like he's leaving the zoo. We'll find him when we need to," Craig said softly. "Right now just worry about your daughter."

Steve's face softened then and he turned to see Tracey with her head down on the picnic table, either sleeping or unconscious. Walking over to her, he picked her up and carried her down the path. His destination: Hector's place.

"Hal and Matt, will you guys come with me? There's something I need you to see," Steve said.

As the two men did as asked, Carl called out to Steve and asked the obvious question. "What about me and Craig?"

"You guys stay here and hold down the fort, I'll be back in a few minutes." Then he was lost in the shadows of the path, Matt and Hal with him.

Carl and Craig sat down on the picnic table where Tracey had been, careful to avoid the blood that had pooled on the ground under the table and for now just ignoring the covered bodies of the Esperanzas' on the other table. Carl looked at the others around him, Sherry, Diane and Seth all waiting for what was to come next. They had lost so many of their group in one night. To say it was hard to digest would have been an understatement.

Craig reached into one of his pockets and pulled out his trusty deck of cards; then he made eye contact with each of the others and asked with a grin: "So, anyone up for a game of strip poker?"

Chapter 32

PUSHING THROUGH THE door, Steve carried Tracey into a small room in the back of Hector's place. Inside were a small cot and a milk crate for a nightstand. Steve set her down and covered her up with a light sheet. Then he brushed her hair from off her forehead and walked away to let her rest.

Deep in the back of his mind, he was thinking of what he'd said to Hickman. Would he kill her if she turned? He honestly didn't know if he had the strength to pull the trigger.

Stepping back into the main room, he saw both Hal and Matt inspecting Hector's corpse.

Hal looked up when he entered and pointed at the body. "I know these wounds, I've seen them before," he said, anxiously.

"Before? What the hell do you mean by that?" Steve asked, while moving next to the two men. Matt had found a few candles and had lit them, the room now flickering as the flames moved about from subtle air currents caused by the passage of the men.

Hal leaned in and pointed to the slash on Hector's neck and the one on his chest.

"See these? Well, I've been following the story of the Three-bladed Killer. You've heard of him, right?"

Matt and Steve both shrugged. "Sure, who hasn't, it's been in the papers and on the news," Matt said.

"Exactly," Hal nodded. "The papers were told by the cops to keep it quiet, you know, not sensationalize it, but it's really a lot worse then you think."

Hal opened Hector's shirt and let out a pleased grunt. "And there it is, the third knife wound. If you look real hard, you'll see that each wound was done with a different sized blade, hence the name of the killer."

Matt took a step back. "Holy shit, you're telling us there's a serial killer inside the zoo with us?"

Hal held his hands up to calm Matt down. "Whoa, there, slow down. It's possible the killer's already dead. How many people have died tonight?"

"Too damn many, that's for sure," Steve said, glaring at Hector's body. "He didn't deserve this, none of them did. We need to find out if the killer is dead or is still one of us."

"But how the hell are we going to do that?" Matt asked, his eyes now darting back and forth warily, as if he expected the killer to jump out at him at any moment.

Hal grinned. "I think I might have an idea how to catch our killer if he's still with us, but I don't think you'll like it."

"What is it, because truth be told, I got nothin'," Steve told him.

Hal gestured to Tracey sleeping in the back room. "It involves your daughter. She's the bait."

Steve's eyes went wide and then he lowered them, his forehead creasing as he weighed the options. Finally he nodded.

"Fine, we'll do it. We need to know one way or another or we'll never be able to rest easy here again. Only Ethel is missing and once we find her, and know whether she's okay or not, we should be safe again. We'll lay your trap tomorrow night, after everything's calmed down. Hopefully after that we'll be okay here, at least until the food runs out."

"Well, there is a bright side to losing so many people so quickly," Matt said as he moved across the room.

"Oh yeah, and what's that, my rotund friend?" Hal asked.

Matt smiled wanly, almost embarrassed to tell them. "Well, with less people it means there's more food for the rest of us."

Hal made a face and he was about to chastise the man for being so selfish, when Steve stopped him with a hand on his shoulder.

"Hold up, Hal, he's right. Its terrible so many died tonight, but it takes the burden off the rest of us. The law of survival, only the strong survive."

Hal nodded, still not pleased with the idea of others dying so he could eat, but he acknowledged Matt.

"Fine, fine, I guess you've got a point, though it's pretty morbid for my tastes," Hal answered.

Steve turned back to Hector's corpse, waving the other two men to his side. "Come on, let's get him outside with Rosa and Miguel and then we'll see about burying them properly," Steve directed the men. "Oh, and grab his shotgun out of the corner there, we might need it."

With the three of them it was easy to carry the old man outside, in fact, Steve was sure he could have done it himself, the old man was so light.

Once Hector was placed outside with the others, the shotgun balancing on his chest as he was carried, Steve sent Craig back into the building.

"Keep an eye on Tracey, will you? And when I'm done with the burials I'll take your place," Steve told Craig.

"Not a problem, take as long as you like," Craig told him and disappeared down the walkway. Steve checked his wristwatch, pleased to see it was only a few more hours until dawn. It seemed like the day before and now the night was talking forever to end.

Steve turned to Carl. "Hey, go see if you can find some kind of tool shed or something. We need a couple of shovels to dig some graves," he told him. Carl waved okay and took off down the rear path.

"Hey, watch out for Ethel, she's out there somewhere!" Steve called after Carl!

Carl waved back and trotted off.

Steve pointed to Seth and the two women, Sherry and Diane. "You two guys go and get George and Kim Lee. They're not too far down the main path. You can't miss them; they're all over the walkway." He looked to Matt and nodded toward the shotgun. You go with them and watch their backs, we don't need anymore people dying tonight, that shit stops right now."

Matt nodded, picking the shotgun off Hector's corpse. Cracking the weapon in half, he was pleased to see two shells, one in each side, ready to go if needed. Snapping the weapon shut, he nodded to Steve and then the girls.

"Ladies, and gentleman, after you."

Sherry made a face, not wanting to go. "Why should I have to do this? I don't want to touch dead people, let someone else do it," she whined.

Steve stopped what he was doing and looked at the woman. Normally, he would have been patient with the woman and explained to her how they all had to do things they didn't like to survive, but his patience had worn thin after everything that had happened that night, plus he was out of smokes, and needed one bad, that added a whole other edge to his temperament. So instead he glared at her, his face a mask of anger.

"You'll do it because I goddamn tell you to, lady, that's why! If you don't want to help, then you can just get the fuck out of here! We need people that'll pull their weight. If you're useless, then you're excess baggage!"

Sherry's face was one of surprise and shock. Tears started to roll down her cheeks and she started to cry. Steve saw this and his anger fled, guilt taking its place.

"Look, I'm sorry I yelled at you. It's just . . . well, with my daughter and everything. We need everyone to pitch in, so just go and do what you can, all right?"

Sherry nodded, moving past him and down the path, tears covering her cheeks. Diane followed, her eyes flashing disproval at him.

"Real tough guy, yelling at women. What do you do for an encore, beat up little children?" Diane said in a wiseass voice, "You remind me of my ex-husband." Then she was past him, moving out of the picnic area.

Seth said nothing, just walked by him, following the women. Matt slowed when he reached Steve, setting his hand on his shoulder.

"Hang in there, pal, it's got to get better from here, right?"

Steve patted the man's hand, returning the sentiment. "I sure as hell hope so, Matt, because if it doesn't, then we're all dead . . . or worse. We become one of them and get to wander around forever."

* * *

Carl walked for the next ten minutes while searching for some kind of tool shed or landscape box where maintenance might have kept some of the gear used in maintaining the zoo.

He was near the rear wall of the zoo, now, and he slowed as he walked, listening to the sounds of the undead.

There was a large oak tree near the wall, so he decided to scale it, leaning out over one of the limbs that reached to the rear wall.

Looking down into the gloom of the woods, he saw countless bodies moving about. Breaking off a tree limb that was less then an inch thick, he tossed it over the wall to see what would happen.

The moment the stick landed on the leaves, making only the slightest noise, groans and moans began sounding as bodies converged where the stick had landed. Carl frowned as he watched the ghouls investigate the stick and then disperse, wandering around again. One ghoul seemed to hang around a little longer. This one actually looked up and stared at Carl. He swallowed, not knowing how the thing had seen him. He studied this one for a moment. The ghoul had once been an old black woman, a heart shaped pendant still hanging on her chest. She was wearing a nightgown, like she was just getting ready for sleep, and that was probably when she must have been attacked. From where Carl was perched in the tree, he was able to see the terrible wound on the old woman's arm. A large piece of flesh was missing; the wound now dried and crusted over, black lines shooting off it up her arm to disappear under her nightgown. Evidently the bite was how she had become infected.

The old woman looked up at him with mournful eyes and her mouth opened, only a dry moan issuing.

Carl felt his heart jump into his throat. It was like this one was trying to talk to him. The feeling was so uncomfortable he decided it was time to get down and finish his task. Steve and the others would be waiting and wondering if he was all right.

He shook his head slowly as he watched the woman and the others shuffling about. There was no escape from the zoo. What was their haven was also their prison. The dead were everywhere; completely surrounding it.

Climbing back down, careful not to slip and break something, he started walking again, and stopped abruptly when he saw something lying on the path a few yards in front of him. Picking up a nearby rock, he tossed it as hard as he could at the still form. The rock landed true and with a soft thump, struck the form and rolled off.

Carl was hesitant, but feeling better by the second.

Picking up a larger rock, he slowly moved closer to the lump, arms back and ready to throw the rock and run at the first sign of danger.

He wished he had a gun, but there were only so many to go around at the moment and truth be told, he'd never fired a weapon in his life and would probably just blow his own foot off by accident.

Better to let the heroes of his ragtag bunch of survivors handle the guns. He'd stick to tire irons and clubs, thank you.

He'd reached the still form now and it was pretty obvious it was a body.

He moved closer until he was right on top of the figure and his eyes immediately recognized the dress that Ethel was wearing earlier in the day.

Rolling her over, careful in case she wasn't dead, yet still kicking; he looked down on her still face.

Her eyes were wide open and her mouth hung slack. There appeared to be no signs of foul play and Carl was stumped to know what had happened to her.

Maybe she had an aneurism or a heart attack while she was out here, he thought. If that was true, talk about total irony. The woman manages to reach the safety of the zoo, surviving when countless others have died, only to kick it from a heart attack.

Making the sign of the cross, he leaned down and closed her eyes, then he moved on. He needed to find some shovels or other digging apparatus, now having yet another body to bury.

A few minutes later, he came upon an old shed that abutted the rear wall of the zoo. The shed was a plain box with peeling paint, no windows and only the one door. There were no cages or attractions back here, only some old farm supplies and other miscellaneous items used to run the zoo at one time or another. He would need to come back in the daytime to see everything more clearly.

He found a couple of shovels leaning against the side of the shed and grabbed them, tossing both over his shoulder and balancing them like a lumberjack. His eyes caught something else near the half open door of the shed and he pulled it open and peeked inside, careful not to disturb any wildlife that had decided to make the shed their new home.

The moonlight slid into the opening and illuminated the right side of the small structure. Carl's eyes immediately spotted one item that stood out amongst the others. There was a chainsaw sitting quietly on the middle shelf; its chain a little rusty, but still looking serviceable. Reaching in, he plucked it from the shelf, feeling its weight. It wasn't too heavy, and a guy like him could easily wield it.

There was a small, one gallon gas can on the ground and he picked it up, shaking it. A small amount of liquid sloshed around and he decided to take that, as well.

Now he had the gas can under his arm, the chain saw in his other hand and the shovels balanced precariously on his shoulder, the gas can arm now also pulling double duty balancing the shovels. His eyes spotted one more item of notice. A metal, five gallon can with the words: **DIESEL** written across it in chalk, the partially missing **D** all but obscured with time.

He kicked the can with his foot, feeling the weight of the container and made a happy sound to himself. He had found fuel for the bulldozer. Now all they needed was a way to get to it, then fight off the hungry hordes of the dead and then refuel the machine while the dead tried to attack and kill them.

He chuckled to himself thinking about it. If he was right, then Steve would just shrug and then come up with some crazy plan to do just that.

With everything in his arms, he headed back to the picnic area, detouring around the corpse of Ethel. As he passed her, he half expected her to jump up, eyes flashing red, teeth drooling at him, wanting nothing more then to rip him to pieces. But she stayed where she was; dead for good.

Happy with his collection of assorted items, Carl picked up his pace, wanting to return to the others, the shadows surrounding him giving him the chills, like they were pressing down on him, ready to envelop him in their dark embrace until there was nothing left of him to take.

While outside the zoo's walls, the symphony of the dead continued as they called out to the abyss in their hunger.

Chapter 33

BY THE TIME all the bodies were buried, the sun was just beginning to peek over the horizon. It had been hot, sweaty work. Everyone's faces were covered with dirt, the dust mixing with their perspiring bodies. Carl's muscles ached like he had been working out with weights for the past week, and with the last shovel full of dirt finally placed on its mound; he tossed the shovel to the ground.

Steve wiped the sweat from his brow and turned to look at Carl, Craig and Matt.

"Does anyone want to say anything?" He asked them, looking down at the seven unmarked graves.

Matt stepped forward, his face dirty from digging. "I'll say something, suppose someone should." He cleared his throat and lowered his head, the others doing the same. "Dear Lord, take the souls of these seven people into your loving embrace and look over them. Do not judge them too harshly, for they were human, with all the imperfections that you gave them, and the rest of us, when you created man. Know that they were taken far before their time, but at least now they know peace. No more will they suffer from hunger, jealousy, hate or fear. Now they are one with you. Amen."

"Amen," said the others.

They all moved away from the graves, carrying the shovels with them. They had found a clearing surrounded by fencing not too far from the picnic area. It had once been used as a petting zoo, now the area devoid of life.

The only inhabitants now, were the seven graves of their lost friends.

"I don't know about you guys, but I'm ready to go back to bed and get some rest," Craig said while they wearily walked down the path.

"I hear that. Look, I'm gonna grab whatever there is to eat and I'm gonna do just that," Carl added.

"Sounds like a plan, boys," Matt agreed. "What about you, Steve? Gonna go back and get some shut eye?"

Steve shook his head. "No, once I'm cleaned up, I'm gonna check on my daughter. Plus, I'm sure Hal wants a break."

Carl made a raspberry sound and looked at the others. "Don't see why. He got to baby-sit Tracey while we had to dig graves. Guess I can add another job to my resume now: gravedigger."

"Hey, it's an honest job, kid, someone's got to do it, might as well be you," Matt joked.

Carl nodded. "Yeah, guess so, maybe."

Steve and Matt chuckled at him and the four men walked the rest of the way in silence. They were all exhausted. It had been hard work retrieving all the bodies scattered around the zoo. Using a wheel barrel they'd procured from behind an exhibit, they'd transported each corpse to the burial site and had then set to digging.

Now, with the sun rising on a new day, they were all beat, just wanting to lie down and sleep. Steve had told both Sherry and Diane to get some rest and had decided Seth wasn't needed for the grisly work of burying the dead and had sent him away, as well.

Hal was watching over Tracey, the shotgun now with him for protection. As for Hickman and the weird girl, Tina; no one had seen them since last night.

That was fine with Steve. The less he saw of Hickman the better.

While they had dug the graves, Steve had filled the rest of them in on Hector's murder. While everyone was a suspect, no one could come up with any real idea on who the killer might be.

Steve's money was on Hickman, but he wouldn't do anything until he was sure. Both Matt and Hal had said as much. Though they were all alone in the zoo, they wouldn't allow Steve to become judge, jury and executioner, especially going on nothing more then a hunch.

So it had been decided to just wait, and hopefully the killer would tip his hand. Steve had also suggested that no one go anywhere alone anymore. If there were always two people together, it would be harder for someone else to become the next victim. That of course, was assuming Hal was correct in his assumption that Hector was killed by a serial killer and not someone who just had it in for the old coot.

Steve's head hurt with all the thinking and planning. If it wasn't bad enough that a massive army of undead people were surrounding the zoo, wanting nothing more then to kill and eat Steve and the others, now he had to deal with a killer inside his own camp. What the hell could happen next?

That was a question he didn't want answered.

Carl and Craig ran ahead when they neared the picnic area, wanting to grab some grub. Matt followed them and with a nod, Steve headed off into Hector's home which had inadvertently become his.

If the others minded, no one said anything.

Walking inside, he called out to Hal. He didn't want to startle the man and end up getting shot.

"I'm in here, Steve. I'm with Tracey," he called from the back room.

Steve walked through the small living space, glancing at the easy chair with the blood stains on it and then he reached Tracey.

"Hey there, honey, how you feeling?" Steve asked her, moving to her side.

She was pale, but not ridiculously so. A cup of water sat next to her, as well as a few uneaten crackers.

"I'm okay, Dad, Hal filled me in. Exactly how much blood did you suck out of me, anyway?"

Steve shrugged, taking her hand. It was cold and it gave him a tingle up his back. She was so cold, like she was already dead.

"I don't really know, honey, I just kept sucking. Hopefully, I got the infection out of you in time."

Hal leaned back in the chair he was in and smiled. "That was good thinkin' on your part, Steve. Who would have even thought about treating her wound like a snakebite?"

Steve waved the compliment away. "I just took a chance, hopefully we got lucky."

"Yeah, about that, Dad. Look, if it doesn't work and I get sick . . ."

Steve cut her off. "Don't even say that, honey. You're gonna be fine, just think good thoughts. That's all we can do." He stood up, leaned over her and kissed her on the forehead. Her skin felt warm here; perhaps she was running a fever.

"You rest now and Hal and I will be right outside the front door, okay?"

She nodded, and closed her eyes, obviously still exhausted.

The two men walked outside into the morning sun.

"What do you think, Hal? You've been with her all night."

"I don't know what to tell you, Steve. First she's hot, then she's cold. She's definitely fighting off something. Plus, she's lost a lot of blood. I've had her drinking as much as I can, but she's too tired to really take it all in. Wish we had an IV, that would do the job better," Hal said.

Steve only nodded, taking it all in. His eyes seemed to take on a far away look and he rubbed his face with his hands.

"You know, this reminds me of something that happened to her when she was a child. We went to Italy for a vacation and Tracey ended up getting sick. The doctors said it was some mutated form of meningitis. She almost died from it, but then her immune system kicked in and fought if off. It was a miracle. It feels like I'm right back there in that hospital all over again."

Hal said nothing, believing Steve was just thinking out loud, then Steve turned and placed his hand on Hal's shoulder.

"Well, thanks for looking out for her. I'm sorry you're here with me, but at the same time I'm glad. I feel I can trust you, you know?" Before Hal could answer Steve straightened his back and became more serious. "Listen, I just want to get cleaned up and then I'll spell you, all right?"

"Sure, take your time," Hal said.

Steve started to move away when Hal called to him.

"Hey, Steve, how'd the burials go?"

Steve flashed him a cold stare, void of emotion. "About what you'd expect when you bury seven people at the same time. It sucks. I'll see you in a few minutes."

Hal waved and then disappeared back inside. Steve went back to the picnic area where the small amount of food had been set up by the women before they had gone off to rest.

With Carl, Craig and Matt still there, the four chatted for awhile, with everybody eating. A few cans of fruit and a stale loaf of bread consisted of their meager breakfast.

Then Carl and Craig left, first going to the duck pond to wash up and then heading back to the bear caves, where their blankets were still set up from the previous night. Matt said he'd wait for Hal to be relieved, the two of them returning to their place of sleep together once he was finished watching Tracey.

Steve then relieved Hal and took up watch over his daughter in a chair near her bed, his bare feet propped up on the edge. He watched her sleeping for a few minutes, praying in his heart she would be alright, then his eyes started to droop and he gave in to the call of slumber. He was deep asleep in no time, his soft snoring filling the room.

Tracey opened her eyes once, saw her father sleeping and smiled. Then she closed her eyes again and drifted off.

Chapter 34

IT WAS ALMOST noon before Craig and Carl roused themselves and returned to the picnic area.

Entering the path that led to the area, Carl saw they weren't alone. Both Sherry and Diane were present, both busily doing inventory on the meager supplies they had left, plus trying to straighten up a bit. Sherry had a bucket of water and was in the process of cleaning the picnic table that had held the bodies of the Esperanza's only a few hours ago.

Carl said good morning and the two men sat down and ate a small meal. Craig had inquired about the others, but neither Sherry nor Diane knew where they might be.

Everyone just assumed they were all still sleeping, because of the late hour everyone had finally returned to bed.

Finishing their meal, Carl suggested he and Craig investigate the tool shed he'd found the night before. With Craig agreeing, the two men had set off down the path to the rear of the zoo.

Carl slowed at the spot where he had found Ethel Thomas.

"That's where I found her," he told Craig.

"And she was just lying there? No bite marks or anything?"

Carl nodded. "Yeah, it's like she just dropped dead."

Craig repositioned the rifle on his back. "Maybe she did. You know, just because people are getting eaten and turning into zombies, doesn't mean that people still don't die of natural causes."

Carl mulled that over as they walked side by side.

"That's a good point, I guess. I didn't really think of it."

"Don't blame yourself. It seems like the only way to die anymore is to be attacked by one of them," he said, gesturing to the wall on their left, the sounds of the undead calling out and floating over the wall to them like a living thing.

"Jesus, do you think they ever sleep?" Carl asked, glancing at the wall.

Craig shrugged. "Don't know and frankly, man, I don't want to. All I want is for them to drop over and stay dead. That would make me a very happy guy."

They reached the shed and the two men started to explore. Carl picked up the diesel fuel and placed it onto the path and then went back in for more useful items. Craig was all the way in the back of the shed, searching through a pile of wood.

Suddenly, Craig let out a scream and Carl ran over to him. Picking up a set of bolt cutters lying on a nearby shelf, he raised them over his head, prepared to bash in the head of whatever had frightened his friend.

Craig turned around, his eyes wide when he saw Carl coming at him, and he put out both his hands to stop him.

"Whoa, slow down there, I just saw a rat; it's gone now."

Carl lowered the bolt cutters, his breathing coming fast and quick. "Holy shit, man, you scared the crap out of me. Don't do that."

Craig smiled wanly. "Sorry, I just hate rats. They really creep me out, what with their skinny tales and beady eyes."

The two continued searching, dust filling the air of the tool shed each time they disturbed the contents on the shelves. Finally they gave up and stepped back out into the light of the afternoon.

"Well, I've had enough, how 'bout you?" Carl asked his friend.

Craig nodded. "Yeah, we've got some good stuff, let's get it back so the others can see and then grab something to eat."

"We just ate a little while ago," Carl stated.

"Yeah, but after digging around in that shit hole I've gotten hungry again."

The two men gathered their supplies and headed back to the picnic area.

Carl carried the diesel fuel and the bolt cutters, liking the feel of them. They would work well as a club.

Craig carried a set of hedge clippers and a large extension cord. He figured they would come in handy as a rope if the need arose. Chatting up about music and women, the two men made their way back up the walkway crisscrossing the zoo.

Carl was at ease, the shadows from the night before banished by the sun.

Now the path was filled with light, the overgrown trees and shrubbery bursting with color, though green was the predominant one.

Though he was trapped inside a zoo with dead people howling for his blood, he had to admit he hadn't felt as good as he did right now in a long time.

By the time they reached the picnic area, Steve was up and about, Hal with him. Carl saw Seth sitting alone in a corner and when he looked to his right, he saw the bright hair of Tina.

She looked at him, the two making eye contact, then she picked up a few things of food and disappeared down a side path. As for Dr. Hickman, there was no sign.

"Hey guys, you eat yet?" Steve asked, munching on a can of beans.

Carl was about to answer, but Craig spoke up first.

"No, not yet, and I'm starving." Then just to make sure he wouldn't get caught in a lie, he looked around for Sherry and Diane.

"Where are the ladies?" He asked casually.

Steve shrugged. "Don't know where they went. They left a little while ago. Why do you ask?" The suspicion was obvious in his voice.

Craig brushed the question away. "No reason, I just like older women, that's all."

Steve looked at him, disbelief on his face, but let it go.

Hal left the table, giving Steve a pat on the back and went to join Seth, trying to get to know the boy a little better.

Carl walked over with the items in his hands and dropped them next to the chainsaw and gas can from the night before.

"Hey Steve, I found some diesel fuel. Maybe we could get the bulldozer running again," Carl said.

"And go where? Not to mention we'd have to fight through hundreds of those dead bastards just to get to the 'dozer. Nice idea, but no thanks," Steve told him.

Craig grabbed some more chow, eating fruit out of a can, and joined Steve. Hector had stocked up well, adding to his supplies before the city had collapsed. Now that same food was helping the group survive.

Carl sat down next to Steve and grabbed a bottle of water. There were half a dozen cases in the back of Hector's place and so far they had plenty.

"Not hungry, Carl?" Steve asked around a mouthful of beans.

Carl shot Craig a dirty look and then shook his head no. "No, I'm good. How's Tracey doing?"

Steve set the can down and shifted position on his seat. "I just don't know. She's still sleeping. Hal thinks it's from loss of blood and she just needs to get her strength back but . . ."

He trailed off, leaving the unspoken question in the air.

"You don't think . . ." Craig said.

Steve shrugged. "Honestly guys, I just don't know."

They sat quietly for a while, Hal and Seth talking quietly at the corner table.

Carl decided to change the subject. "So what are we going to do about what's happened to Hector? I mean, shit, someone killed him, right?"

Steve nodded. "Yeah, but I'm pretty sure it's safe in the day. If the person who killed Hector is one of us, they only seem to want to attack at night. When I found Hector, there was someone in the room with him, now he could have surprised me and tried to kill me, too, but instead he ran away. That means that whoever it is, he's a coward. Besides, he might already be dead; it could have been one of the people we buried last night."

Craig chuckled. "More like this morning."

Steve looked at him impatiently. "Morning, night, whatever. Listen guys, both of you know how to handle yourselves, so just stay sharp and don't go anywhere alone and you'll be fine."

Craig patted his rifle lying next to him on his seat. "And if someone's stupid enough to fuck with us, they'll get a bullet in the brainpan."

* * *

After finishing eating yet again, Craig asked Carl if he wanted to go down to the main gate and check out all the dead people in the parking lot. With nothing else to do to pass the time, Carl had agreed. They said goodbye to Steve and the others and walked down the winding pathways. Carl had decided to take the hedge clippers with him, just in case there was trouble. Though a little rusty, the clippers were still sharp enough to cut a finger sized tree limb. The clippers were made more for pruning, the angle of the blade more like snipers then cutters.

Carl carried them on his shoulder, balancing them casually. Craig had shouldered his rifle and the two walked in silence for a while.

Craig then stopped abruptly and held up his hand for Carl to stop, as well.

"What's wrong? You hear something?" Carl asked him.

Craig pointed to the right, where a wide open, grassy area with a four foot high chain-link fence surrounding it was located. At one time, deer or other tame animals had wondered around inside, allowing the zoo's visitors to be able to pet them. Now the open area was nothing but dead grass and mud.

But that wasn't what Craig had found so interesting. Across the landscape on the other side of the plain, the path circling around in a rough circle, was Tina, carrying a bucket of water, probably from the duck pond which was nearby.

The two men watched her, wondering where she was going. It was only when Hickman stepped out of a nearby building that both men's eyes went wide.

"So there's the Doc, huh? Looks like he's shacking up with the little crack whore," Craig said softly, though even if he spoke normally there would be no way he'd be heard.

Carl frowned. "She's not so bad; you don't know that for sure. If you look closely, she's got a cute little body under her clothing, its just that her hair is so . . ."

"Fucked up?" Craig finished.

Carl nodded. "Yeah, I guess so."

"When we get back, we'll let Steve know where he is. He's been wanting to know, but Tracey's been taking up all his time," Craig said.

The two started walking again, enjoying the day.

"Do you think she'll be all right?" Carl asked him.

Craig shrugged. "I don't know, man. I sure hope so. She's really nice, isn't she?"

Carl agreed. "Oh yeah, and she's really hot. If things work out, I'm pretty sure me and her are gonna hook up."

Craig turned and looked at his friend with surprise in his eyes.

"You do, huh? Well, I'm sorry to disappoint you, but it's me she's gonna be with. Haven't you seen the way she looks at me?"

Carl laughed out loud. "Oh yeah, she's looking. Because she can't believe how homely you are."

Craig punched him in the side jokingly and Carl bent over slightly from the blow, laughing harder. Craig joined in and the two friends enjoyed a laugh together, hoping Tracey would pull through.

Carl knew when they were near the gate long before it was in sight.

The sound of the dead came to his ears, a haunting melody that made his bowels cringe and twist inside of him. When he had been further inside the zoo, the wails of the undead army had seemed distant, more like background noise. But now, as he approached the front gate, the moans and groans became more predominate.

Not to mention the smell. The redolence of the walking copses struck him when he was still more then a hundred feet away, the odor almost overpowering him.

With his arm over his nose, he turned and reached out for Craig's arm, stopping him from moving forward.

"Maybe we should just go back with the others, I mean, Christ, what a stench."

Craig made a face and actually *sniffed* the air.

"Oh, stop being such a baby. It's not that bad. You should try sleeping in a barracks with fifty men who don't want to shower on a regular basis, then you can talk to me about what's smelly."

Then he twisted out of Carl's grasp and moved on. Carl watched his back for a few seconds and let out a sigh. Then he continued after his friend, deciding to stay with him, at least for now.

A few minutes later they arrived at the front gate of the zoo. The large swinging gate was set in two so that it would open like a set of giant French doors. At the moment, the gate flexed in and out each time some of the undead pushed on it. Luckily, there was a large chain with a sturdy padlock preventing the gate from opening.

Craig whistled and stopped walking, staring at all the walking corpses.

"Wow, will you look at all of them. Where the fuck did they all come from?"

Carl stared as well. "The city and suburbs I guess. A lot of Boston is on fire now, so they probably abandoned it. Guess this is one of the places they wound up."

Craig raised his rifle and tried to line up a shot, but Carl placed his hand on the rifle and lowered it.

"What the hell are you doing? You can't shoot one from here; the bullet will probably just hit one of the bars and ricochet back at us."

Craig made a face, not liking being told what to do, but saw the wisdom of Carl's thoughts.

"Shit, you're right," he said, looking around the gate and fence that went from left to right. Finally he found what he wanted and then, with a gesture to Carl to follow him, moved off to the side of the gate.

There were a few old signs that were used when certain attractions were available, leaning off to the side of the gate in a cluttered heap. Craig went straight for them, picking them up and moving them away from the fence. Turning, he pointed to the hedge clippers in Carl's hand.

"Hey, make yourself useful with those things and poke a few holes in these signs so I can use them like a ladder. I want to get on top of the fence so I'll have a clear shot at those fuckers."

Carl frowned. "Is all this really necessary? Why don't we go back to the picnic area and play some more cards." Carl said, trying once again to change Craig's mind. This was all starting to seem like a bad idea.

"Man, I'm sick of playing cards, besides, you didn't see what those bastards did to my platoon the other day. Now's my chance to get a little payback."

Carl sighed, seeing the determination in his friend's eyes. With a look through the gate at the snarling, moaning faces, he got to work punching holes in the signs.

It was actually very easy, the sharp tip of the hedge clippers punching through the signs like they were made of cardboard. Once finished, Craig inspected Carl's handiwork and then with a wide smile, leaned the signs against the fence and climbed up them.

Once on top, he swung his right leg over the side and tried to get comfortable, his ass on a few of the spires. Below him, hands clawed upward trying to reach the tasty leg, only to fall short again and again. Craig ignored them, confident in his elevation.

Carl looked up watching him. "Doesn't that hurt?"

Craig winced as one of the points pinched his ass, but he shook his head no, then changed his mind. "Well, a little, maybe, I think my balls are about to become a shish-cabob if I'm not careful, but I'm good."

He turned and raised his rifle to his shoulder, lining up his shot with the small sight on the end of the rifle. Locking his legs tight on the top of the fence, he casually shot a ghoul twenty feet away. The head seemed to implode for a second and then the body dropped to the ground to be lost amidst the others surrounding it.

Craig frowned. "I got him, but was a little off-center, guess I'm rusty." He looked down at Carl. "Got anyone you want me to put out of their misery?"

Despite himself, Carl found himself getting into it. Climbing up the sign, he held onto the metal rungs of the fence and looked out across the sea of weaving heads.

Then he spotted one in a police uniform and he couldn't resist.

"Over there, on your right; the cop, get the cop. Send him back to hell where he belongs," Carl said gleefully.

"Do I sense some unresolved rage against authority figures?" Craig joked.

Carl frowned. "Just shut up and shoot the bastard, will ya?"

Craig looked where he was pointing and lined up the shot. A second later the ghoul cop was gone, lost under the shuffling legs of the others surrounding it. If the ghouls cared that they were being slaughtered like cattle, they gave no notice. Only the ones near Craig even paid them any attention at all, the others only shuffling around without a purpose.

Carl cheered as he saw the cop go down, and Craig sent out a whoop of delight.

"Oh yeah, another one bites the dust." He looked down at Carl's smiling face. "Who's next?"

Carl looked out at the sea of bodies, trying to decide who to take out next when he got an idea.

"Hey, Craig, how about the Pontiac? Think you could hit the gas tank from here?"

Craig looked across the large parking lot at the Pontiac off in the distance.

"I don't know, that's pretty far, plus, there's all the bodies moving around it."

"So you can't hit it then, right? That's okay, a man should know his limitations," Carl said with a slight smile, taunting him.

Craig made a face. A challenge was something he never ignored. "All right, I'll do it, but I want a wager first."

"Go on," Carl said.

"If I get the shot, you have to lay off Tracey and let me have her."

"And if you don't get the shot?" Carl asked curiously.

Craig frowned, realizing he'd just been put into a corner.

"If I lose and miss then I'll do the same and step aside and let love take its natural course. Of course, that's assuming she becomes blind and loses her sense of smell and somehow becomes attracted to you, anyway."

Carl shot him a look that said to *go jump in a lake*, but then he raised his hand for Craig to shake.

"Fine, shake on it, dead-eye."

"Not a problem, chump." Craig snipped back with a grin.

Craig reached down carefully and the two shook, Carl wondering if he'd just been hustled. Then Craig sat back up, carefully, and prepared to make the shot.

"All right, my boy, prepared to be amazed by my expert marksmanship."

"Just shut up and shoot," Carl snapped back, aggravated by Craig's confidence.

Carl leaned on the sign just below Craig, his hands wrapped around the fence near the top as he watched the Pontiac sitting unawares of its coming fate. The car was useless anyway. The steering was shot and the transmission had been ripped out of her like a bad appendix to get at the flywheel. No, she was going to a better place, now, with a Viking funeral.

Craig fired a round that seemed to do little but agitate the ghouls below him.

"Hah, you missed, I win!" Carl said happily.

"Nu-huh, we didn't agree on how many shots. I get at least another two. Should have read the fine print, pal."

Carl pursed his lips, but had to give in on that one. He should have agreed on how many shots.

"Fine, I'll give you that one, but two more shots and its over."

"Deal," Craig said, leaning over a little more, his upper body hanging over the ghouls more then he would have liked. But there was a tree limb in the way and he needed to get below it to line up the shot properly.

Craig fired again, the Pontiac still sitting immobile.

"Shit, I know I hit it that time. I just need to adjust for the tank better," he mumbled to himself.

Below him, Carl was humming happily, already prepared to win the bet.

"What the hell is going on here?" Matt called from down the walkway. He had heard the shots and had come to investigate.

"Hey Matt, nothing much, we're just having a little fun, is all. Craig's about to lose a little wager, you're just in time to watch."

Matt looked up at Craig perched on the fence like a crow. "Jesus, Craig, you be careful up there, one slip and you're toast."

Craig waved his warning away. "I'm cool; I'm like a gymnast, always agile and sure-footed. Like Carl said, you're just in time to see me beat his ass in a wager."

"Oh, what's the wager for?" Matt inquired.

Both men knew Matt and Steve were becoming close, so decided to leave the part about Tracey out of it.

"Doesn't matter, but what does matter is I'm about to blow up the Pontiac with this shot, so watch and be amazed."

Matt waved for him to proceed, frowning a little. But he understood. Both Craig and Carl were young and needed to blow off some steam. This was as good as anything else.

Craig raised the rifle and lined up the rear of the Pontiac in his sights once again. He leaned over the fence some more, the ghouls below him becoming seriously agitated. Craig ignored their sounds and concentrated on making the shot like his drill instructor had taught him in basic training.

His right leg was trembling as it held him in place, but he ignored it, wanting to make this last shot count. Slowly, he let out his breath, then squeezed the trigger.

This time his shot was right on target and the Pontiac went up in a blazing fireball that consumed all the walking bodies surrounding it.

Carl cursed as he watched the Pontiac jump into the air and then crash back down, flaming parts flying off in all directions.

Above him, Craig whooped it up, waving his hands in the air and cheering, proud of his marksmanship.

But then he lost his balance and started to fall over the fence, his body hovering over the reaching hands and open mouths below him. He let out a yell and tried to reach back and grab the top of the fence, but his body was too far out. He had over extended himself when he tried to get under the tree limb that had blocked his shot.

For Craig, everything happened in slow motion, his arms waving in the air like he was trying to fly and then he was falling towards the waiting dead faces of the undead below him.

Just before he would have reached the first head, his other leg that had been wrapped around the fence caught on one of the sharp spires, spearing his leg, but stopping his downward descent. He let out a sharp yell of pain as the spire punctured his leg and his arms fell straight down, like he was hanging unconscious.

"Holy shit, Craig! Hold on, I'm coming!" Carl yelled, climbing the sign and trying to save his friend.

Craig was woozy from the leg wound and blood rushed to his head. He heard Carl calling his name, but it sounded like it was far away. What wasn't far away were the hungry corpses directly below him. Before he realized what was happening, an ambidextrous ghoul climbed up on the shoulders of another one and reached up and grabbed Craig's right arm, pulling him down. Though his pinned leg stopped him from falling, he was still pulled down another few inches; more then enough for the ghoul's rotten teeth to sink into his wrist and rip a two-inch chunk of flesh from his arm.

Craig screamed to the heavens, his blood shooting out and raining on the other undead creatures below him. They immediately became agitated, moaning louder as they tried their best to reach the fresh meat dangling above them tauntingly.

Craig's vision grew dim and he tried to breathe through the pain. In his flailing, he managed to push the ghoul on his wrist away from him, the creature falling back into the dead masses below.

Then he felt himself being pulled upward, and just before he passed out from shock, he saw Carl's face hovering over him and heard Matt's voice coming from somewhere far away.

Then he was lost in a sea of darkness as he mercifully fell unconscious from pain and shock.

Chapter 35

"GET HIM UP, get him up!" Screamed Matt; bouncing around on the ground while Carl tried to heave Craig's unconscious form over the fence with no results.

"I'm trying, goddammit, but he's a little heavy. You could help, you know!" Carl screamed back, struggling to balance himself while pulling Craig up and over the top of the spires.

"I can't, I'm too big. If I try to come up, the signs will probably collapse!" Matt called from below, dancing around like he had to use the bathroom.

"Great, so my friend dies because you like Twinkies too much!" Carl snapped at him.

Carl was halfway over the fence with Craig's limp body and he could see the sharp spire poking out of his leg like a dagger. With a shout of exertion, he lifted Craig as high as he could and managed to half-pull, half-swing his body over the spire, only the leg was still pinned to the fence. But at least now he was on the inside of the fence hanging down, instead of the outside. But it didn't come without a price. Carl hadn't been gentle, Craig's body matching his own weight and the gash in his leg had doubled in size, bleeding across his leg and dripping down his clothes.

"How the fuck am I supposed to lift him off this damn fence? I'm not Superman for Christ's sake!" Carl hollered while he tried to support Craig's still form.

"Should I go get Steve?" Matt asked with a face covered in worry and panic.

Carl shook his head from side to side, spraying droplets of sweat from his forehead. "No, there's no time for you to go all the way back there and then return. We need to deal with this now. Okay, I've rested for a second, so listen up. I'm gonna push straight up, and when his legs free, I'm gonna drop him. Do you think you can catch him without letting his head split open on the ground?"

Matt nodded. "Yeah, I can do that, just hurry up; he's losing a lot of blood!"

Carl could see that, but decided not to answer. Craig was lucky he had passed out from the pain, because it had to be absolute agony.

His rifle was still miraculously attached to his body, the strap catching on his shoulder. Carl ignored it and, pushing his head and shoulders under Craig's back, he started to climb the sign-ladder, slowly pushing the wounded leg off the spire.

With his back screaming in protest and his neck at a crazy angle to the point he couldn't see anything; he pushed Craig off the spire. Then, balancing for a moment, he leaned back and let him go; praying Matt was there on the ground waiting to catch him.

Breathing heavily, he turned around, almost expecting to see his friend lying on the pavement with a broken neck, but Matt had been true to his word and had managed a sloppy catch. Matt was even now setting Craig down on the ground, checking his leg to see how bad it was.

Carl jumped down and knelt next to Craig, pushing Matt away.

"Forget about his leg right now. We need to take care of that bite or he's fucked."

"What do we do?" Matt screamed. "This isn't like with Tracey. That's no damn snakebite on his arm. Christ, half his wrist is gone!"

Carl agreed, but knew something had to be done or his friend was dead. He'd been infected. Even if they got the bleeding under control, none of it would matter because the virus or whatever the hell it was, was now inside him.

Then his eyes spotted the hedge clippers and he got a crazy idea.

He ran over and grabbed the clippers and ran back, falling next to Craig in his haste.

"What are you going to do with those?" Matt asked with suspicion in his voice and a little bit of terror thrown in for good measure.

"What I have to do to save him, now do what I say and don't give me any shit!" Carl snapped at him.

Matt nodded, letting Carl take the lead.

Carl opened the hedge clippers and placed Craig's wrist just a few inches past the bite between the blades, then he called Matt over to his side.

"What do you need me for? You do it," Matt said, seeing what he was doing and trying hard not to throw up.

"I can't, I'm not strong enough. I need all your weight to push down on his arm and cut through the bone, now come on and get over here, he's running out of time!"

Matt did as he was told, sliding across Craig until he was next to Carl. Carl placed Matt's hands on the clippers and looked him straight in the face.

"Okay, when you close them, put as much force as you can on them; the cleaner the cut, the better. Once you do it, get away from him so I can tie off the wound or he's gonna bleed to death."

"And this is going to save him?" Matt asked nervously.

"I don't really know for sure, I'm making this shit up as I go! Now get ready, on the count of three."

Matt positioned himself over the clippers, ready to snap them like he was cutting a thick tree branch.

Carl swallowed and wiped his forehead, holding Craig's arm near the elbow.

"Okay, one . . . two . . . may God forgive me if I'm wrong . . . Three!"

Matt leaned forward with all his formidable weight, the hedge clippers slicing closed like a paper cutter. The blade hung up on the wrist bone for a fraction of a second, but Matt's weight was the winner, the hand separating at the wrist and lying there on the ground, blood spurting from the stump like a water fountain.

Matt saw the fingers twitching despite the fact the hand wasn't attached and that was it for him. Leaning over to the side, he threw up his breakfast, the vomit splashing all over his hands.

Carl ignored him; the man's work finished, and quickly tied the wrist off with a makeshift tourniquet torn from a piece of his own shirt.

That was when Craig woke up, screaming at the top of his lungs. Carl started to panic, not finished tying the tourniquet. Blood was spraying everywhere, the stump like a scarlet fire hose.

Carl's mind froze and for a few heartbeats he just watched Craig screaming on the ground, staring at his missing hand. The reality slammed back home and Carl reached over and picked the rifle up, slamming the butt stock against Craig's forehead. The wounded soldier dropped back to the ground, unconscious, a big red bruise on his forehead where the stock had struck him.

"Sorry, buddy," Carl said. "You'll thank me later . . . I hope."

After making sure the tourniquet was secured, he went to work on the leg, doing the same thing as the wrist. He had no idea what to do and could only hope if the tourniquets stopped the bleeding then they could get him back to Steve who might have a better idea what to do. Tying off the leg, the blood stopping for the moment, Carl fell back on his butt and let out a large breath he'd been holding. His hands and clothes were covered in blood and for a second he wondered if he'd somehow been hurt, but after a quick check of himself he found he was unharmed.

Moans called his attention to the fence and he stared at the dead faces of the dead. They were even more excited now, a few of them actually tasting blood today. Carl spit in their direction and climbed to his feet.

"Come on, Matt, we need to get him to Steve. Maybe he can help."

Matt nodded, and heaved his considerable bulk to a standing position, wiping his chin of a few stray pieces of his upchucked breakfast.

Matt grabbed Craig under the shoulders and Carl got his legs, careful of the wound, and the two of them started back up the path, the rifle now on Carl's back.

"Do you really think you stopped the infection by cutting off the bite?" Matt asked as they walked side by side, turned slightly to carry Craig between them.

Carl shook his head. "I don't know, but it seemed like a good idea at the time. If I didn't do it, we know what the result would be, so what did I have to lose?"

"Good point, I guess," Matt said and then they concentrated on moving as fast as they could.

Five minutes later they had reached the side path that led to the picnic area. Carl called out as they passed Hector's door, the door ajar. Steve popped his head out and his jaw dropped.

"What the hell happened to him? Are they inside the zoo?" He asked while running towards them and helping to carry Craig the rest of the way by reaching under his waist.

Carl shook his head no, too tired to talk. "We're fine, something else happened. Doesn't matter now," he stammered.

"Here, place him over here, on the table," Hal said as he ran up to see what he could do.

"We need the Doc, we saw him over by the duck pond, he's in a small building over there with Tina," Carl said, stepping away from Craig's body.

Steve turned to Hal and said: "Go find the Doc. Tell him I said to get his ass over here, right now. Tell him I said he really doesn't want me coming for him. Tell him what happened here."

Hal nodded and took off at a run.

Steve turned back to Matt and Carl, seeing the blood all over Carl.

"What about you, are you hurt, too?" He asked Carl.

Carl shook his head. "No, I'm fine, all this is from him," Carl said, pointing to Craig.

"What the fuck do we do, Steve?" Matt asked.

Steve stared at Craig, his eyes settling on the missing hand; seeing it gone for the first time.

"Where the fuck is his hand, Carl?" Steve asked, shocked, but his voice almost normal. He hadn't noticed in all the confusion that it was missing.

"He got bit and I remembered what you did with Tracey. The bite was too big to do what you did so I kicked it up a notch."

"You kicked it up a . . ." He didn't finish his sentence, too shocked and appalled.

"Jesus Christ, you cut his fucking hand off, are you crazy?"

Carl stepped closer to Steve, his eyes wide with pain for his friend and shock at what he'd just done.

"Yeah, maybe I am, just a little. You weren't there, Steve, so don't fucking judge me! I did what I thought was right at the time and I stand by it, now what the hell are we going to do now?"

Just then Hal returned with Hickman following. Tina crept behind the others, trying to stay inconspicuous.

"You have a man hurt and you want me to do something about it?" Hickman asked, his voice filled with irritation. "I told you before I'm a neurologist; I don't do general practitioner's work."

Steve ran over to Hickman and grabbed him by the front of the shirt. "Now you listen to me, you stuck up prick. Though I hate to admit it, you're the best qualified to help Craig, so by God you're going to do it or I'm going to beat the living shit out of you. Do I make myself clear?"

Hickman stepped back, pulling himself away from Steve. "Yes, I'm afraid you do. Fine, let's see what you've got. The sooner I do what you want, the sooner I can remove myself from the sight of you."

Steve waved his arm so Hickman would go to Craig.

Hickman walked over and looked down at Craig's still form, his breathing shallow. He checked the tourniquets and then inspected both wounds.

"This man is going to die unless we get him to a hospital immediately."

"Are you fucking serious, Doc? There's no hospital. You need to do something here and now. Please help him," Carl pleaded.

Hickman looked into Carl's eyes and it seemed his countenance actually softened for a second.

"Fine, son, I'll see what I can do, but there are no guarantees. I need a needle and thread, something to sterilize the wounds with and a sharp blade to excise the ripped tissue; the sooner the better."

Steve ran off into Hector's to see what he could find while the others got towels and water prepared. Carl pulled out Craig's own blade from his pocket and got to work sterilizing it.

When Steve returned with all the supplies, Hickman washed his hands and sat down on the bench connected to the table.

"All right, boys and girls, get ready because you are about to see a master at work. This is going to take awhile, so get comfortable."

Hickman started working, cleaning the wounds and suturing them as best he could. It took more then two hours and by the time he was done, the rest of their shrinking group had arrived, all watching Hickman work.

When the doctor was finally done, he leaned back on the bench and let out a breath.

"All right, that's all I can do. If you have anything to kill the pain with, I most definitely recommend it. Morphine would be best, but even an Advil will help. Just no aspirin, it thins the blood and this man needs to clot as soon as possible."

He leaned forward, inspected the bandages one last time, then continued talking.

"Change the bandages every two hours or so and keep an eye out for any excess leakage."

"Why can't you do all that stuff, Doc?" Carl asked from his side.

Hickman turned and looked up at the standing young man. "Why? Because I've done what I can. You people can handle the rest. Besides, if it wasn't for that gorilla over there," he gestured to Steve, "I wouldn't have bothered doing this at all. Without the sterile conditions of an operating room your friend's chances are slim, especially without antibiotics. Plus, you said he was bitten, right?"

Carl nodded.

"Well, then he's infected and will die anyway. I'm sorry, but it's true," Hickman stated in an unctuous tone.

Steve moved up next to Hickman and looked down on the sitting man.

"We'll see about that. It's possible that Carl could have cut off the wound before it had a chance to spread into his blood. From what he told us, it was less then two minutes before he cut off the infected bite."

Hickman stood up and moved away from the picnic table while wiping his hands on a towel.

"Look, Mr. Webb, I'm not going to argue medicine with a *construction worker*." He said the last words with utter contempt. "Now I've done what you want, let me leave in peace."

Steve stepped back, but his eyes said a different story. "Fine, Doc, you can go. But don't go far."

Hickman lowered his eyes at Steve, his mouth turning into a sneer.

"My dear, Mr. Webb, I'm stuck inside a deserted zoo with the living dead surrounding it on all sides. Where exactly am I supposed to go?"

Steve just grunted and turned away from him. Tina grabbed a few more things from the table that contained food and bottled water on it and then scurried after Hickman like a dog.

Steve watched this and wanted to puke. The Doc had found yet another woman to kowtow to his every whim, only he had liked Helen. Tina was a little crack whore who he wanted to beat senseless. She was probably only with the Doc because he'd lied to her and told her he could get her another fix when everything was better.

Only the chances of that seemed slimmer as every hour went by. Since the other night, the television had been silent, only a test pattern on the screen. And even that had stopped sending a few hours ago. He had decided to keep the news of the television blackout to himself, not wanting to worry the others anymore then they already were.

He wondered if that was the right thing to do, but as before, he wasn't afraid to make a decision whether it was the right or wrong one.

"Come on, let's get him inside Hector's place, we can set up something next to Tracey so we can keep an eye on both of them at once."

Carl nodded, moving to Craig's side.

"How is Tracey?" he asked quietly, almost dreading the answer.

Steve shrugged. "Don't know. She's pale and sleeps a lot. Either she's just sick from the shock or she's dying. I try not to think on it too much. She's all I have left in this world."

Carl stayed silent, Hal and Matt doing the same.

After a few seconds had passed, Steve shook off his melancholy and reached under Craig's prone body.

Hal and Matt did the same, telling Carl to rest.

They carried him into Hector's and, after a few minutes of fussing around, set up a cot on the floor using an old door and the cinderblocks that had held the television, the TV now sitting on the floor, unplugged.

Once Craig was made as comfortable as possible, they left him alone, only taking a moment to check on Tracey.

She was still fast asleep, her breathing shallow. Steve kissed her forehead and then left with the others.

"Well, that's all we can do for now. You did good Carl. That was some quick thinking, I'm proud of you," Steve told him.

Carl beamed with pride. He didn't know why, but he was pleased that Steve thought so highly of him.

"Thanks, Steve; that means a lot. So listen, if the drama of the day is over, I think I'll go down to the pond and get cleaned up."

"Okay, sure," Steve said and then looked to Matt. "Matt, why don't you go, too, you could use a good scrubbing, as well," he told him, the smell of vomit filling the area around the man.

Matt chuckled. "Yeah, with everything's that's happened, I hardly noticed. Okay, come on, squirt. Let's get going."

Carl nodded and the two left the picnic area. Sherry and Diane were cleaning up from the operation, Seth hanging out to the side. Carl thought to ask the kid if he wanted to come, but changed his mind. He was exhausted and he wasn't in the mood to try and make any new friends at the moment.

So together, Matt and Carl headed for the pond for a much needed bath.

Chapter 36

LUCKILY FOR EVERYONE, the rest of the day was quiet; each person going about their business trying to keep busy and take their minds off their predicament.

Carl stayed with Craig almost the entire day, trying to keep him company on the few occasions he would regain consciousness. Steve had found a bottle of Jack Daniels in one of Hector's cupboards, and with his help; Craig had almost finished the bottle by the time the sun was setting on the day; the alcohol helping with the pain.

Tracey woke up a few times, as well, Carl filling her in on what had happened. She had gone even paler than she already was and had then slipped back into a light doze.

Carl had let her, knowing she needed her rest.

A few hours after dark, Steve and Hal had come in and told him they would take over.

Carl had reluctantly consented, telling them he would be back in the morning. He had picked up the deck of cards he'd taken from Craig and left.

As he walked out of Hector's place, he noticed a bulletin board on the wall near the door. On it was a schedule of activities and a work schedule for non-existent employees. Carl looked back into the main room with its small kitchenette and realized this building must have been used for the employees; perhaps a break room or staging room before each shift. Then he left the building and walked down the path, the rifle bumping his shoulder.

Though it was late and the day's activities weighed heavily on him, he was restless and he continued walking, no particular place in mind. Eventually he found himself near the front gate again and he turned and walked up to it.

In the light of the moon, the dark stain on the pavement was a black color, remnants from Craig's amputation. A few ghouls noticed him and started making noise. Carl ignored them.

Turning his head to the side and searching the shadows, he noticed the stray hand still on the ground, the bloody hedge clippers nearby where Matt had dropped them. Walking over to the severed hand, he picked it up, holding it in his own hand. Then he tossed it over the fence to the waiting dead.

A flurry of activity filled the night as the ghouls closest to the hand fought over it. Carl watched them quietly, not moving.

After a few minutes of watching them, he stepped as close to the fence as he could. Fingers tried to grab him, but came up short. Carl stared into the dead eyes of a ghoul directly opposite him. From the looks of it, the thing had once been a woman, the hair still in curlers and a dirty mini skirt covering her lower half. Her upper half wore a torn and ripped blouse, the middle hanging open; her filthy breasts open for all to see. Evidently ghouls didn't know modesty.

While Carl looked at the hideous thing, he wondered about what kind of life the dead woman had enjoyed before being turned into a walking dead creature that defied the laws of nature. Had she been a mother? Or maybe she was single and had a boyfriend. Did she have parents and brothers and sisters?

Carl bent over and picked up a sharp stick that had fallen from a nearby tree. Taking the stick like a spear, he casually stuck it into the right eye of the dead woman. The ghoul flinched, and backed away, but a second later was back at the fence trying to grab him again. Carl took the stick and jammed it into her left eye, blinding her.

The dead woman wailed then, now blind, and stumbled away from the fence.

Carl watched her disappear into the crowd, but soon focused his attention on the next dead face to take her place. Carl did the same thing to this one, and the one after that. Poke, poke, poke, like a child fascinated with a bug. He only stopped when he was tired of his sick game.

But he had also learned something. Whatever the ghouls were, whatever they had become, they were not intelligent. How else could he explain each one lining up so he could blind it?

Tossing the stick to the ground, he decided he'd had enough for the night.

Walking away from the gate, he headed off in the direction of the bear caves and his bedroll.

Once inside the cave, the shadows surrounding him like a giant blanket, he had tried to settle down for the night. But it felt weird, the cave now empty except for him. When he finally stretched out and tried to get comfortable, closing his eyes and hoping for sleep, he found he couldn't relax, his mind filled with images from the day.

With a heavy sigh, he sat up and looked around himself, realizing he wouldn't be sleeping just yet.

Reaching into a pocket, he took out Craig's deck of cards, and by the light of the full moon, played a few games of solitaire. He could almost imagine Craig sitting across from him, telling him where to put the cards. He smiled then, a wistful smirk that touched his eyes. He had grown fond of Craig in the few days since they had met and he could only pray that he'd succeeded in saving the man's life by cutting off the infected bite and playing with the cards helped him feel a little closer to his friend.

After his third game of cards, he put them back into his pants pocket, feeling the reassuring bulge. Crag's rifle was leaning against the stone wall of the cave and he stared at it for a while. He had inherited it for now, but he vowed he would return it to Craig just as soon as the man was better.

With the night birds calling out to each other in the tree tops of the zoo, and mixing with the calls of the undead outside the walls, he closed his eyes and drifted off to sleep.

* * *

Steve stared down at the sleeping form of his daughter and at the adjacent one of Craig. Satisfied all was as well as it could be, Steve went back into the small main room. Hal was playing with the television, but was only finding static.

"Anything?" Steve asked, sitting in a small chair near the corner.

Hal shook his head. "No, not a damn thing. Not even that annoying test signal or emergency broadcast logo."

"Well, this might be the last time for a while, Hal. The generator is getting low and I don't know where Hector kept any extra fuel, so when it's gone, it's gone," Steve told him.

Hal fell back and leaned against the wall. "Just as well, I suppose. You know Steve, we can't stay here forever. Sure, this was a good place to fall back to, but sooner or later we're all gonna have to leave. There's sure to be an outpost or rescue station still up and running."

Steve nodded, agreeing. "The trick is how to get there without being eaten."

"Exactly," Hal replied and shifted position on the floor, stretching his legs out from under him. "So are you ready for tonight?"

Steve looked over his shoulder into the back room, just seeing the legs of both Tracey and Craig; then turned back to look at Hal.

"Yeah, I'm ready. The trick is to let the killer think both Tracey and Craig are alone. I can't believe he won't take the bait."

"You know the police have been trying to catch this guy for weeks with no luck, what makes you think you'll be better at it then them?"

"Because the pickings are slimmer now. Look," Steve said, leaning closer to Hal, "if the killer could stop what he's doing, then he sure as hell wouldn't have killed Hector. No, this is one sick son-of-a-bitch and I bet you he can't stop killing. He's one of those, *please stop me before I kill again, I can't help myself* kind of psychos."

"That could be true, but how are you going to get him in here?"

"That's easy, I had Matt go around and visit with everyone, talk a little and make sure he told them that Tracey, and now Craig, will be left alone for a while tonight. I told him to make up whatever he thought would work to make each of them believe him."

Hal rubbed his chin, thinking. "Yeah, but what if Matt is the killer, what then?"

Steve shook his head. "No way, Hal. The guy who ran past me last night was thin, no way was it Matt."

Hal nodded. "So what are you going to do if you find out who the killer is?"

Steve's face grew hard as stone and his voice grew low. "I'm going to send the sick bastard to hell where he belongs."

* * *

Hickman stretched out on the wool blanket he was presently lying on. He was naked from the waist down and he rolled over and watched while Tina got dressed.

"What's the matter, doll, not happy?"

Tina looked down on his face. "Happy? No, I'm not happy. You promised me if I took care of you, you'd get me a fix. I need it, man. It's been days and I'm so tired I could sleep for a year. I need my fix."

Hickman nodded and kept talking in a soothing voice. "And I told you just as soon as we get rescued, I'd get you some. What do you want me to do?"

"I don't know, dammit, but I know what I need!" She moved across the room and leaned against the wall, her hair covering her face, "Don't you even care that they all hate you?"

Hickman sat up, unashamed of his nudity. "Ashamed? Of course not, they're all just jealous of me. I've done something with my life and what have they done? Nothing. That's what was wrong with my wife. She had no vision. All she did was drag me down. I'm glad she's gone. One less anchor trying to pull me under the depths of ineptitude."

Tina stared at him, her eyes wide. "You really are a ruthless bastard, aren't you?"

Hickman smiled then, laying back down and placing his hands under his head. "In my business, darlin', its either sink or swim and

I'm a damn good swimmer." He leered at her then and spread his legs wide. "Now why don't you come over here and give me a blow job."

Tina made a disgusted face and stepped toward the exit. "Fuck you, *Doctor* Hickman. I don't need you. I think you've been bullshitting me from the start and I've had it. I'm gonna try and make nice with Steve and get in with the others before it's too late." Then she left, leaving Hickman with a semi-hard penis and no one to play with.

"You'll be back, bitch, and when you do, be prepared to work hard for my forgiveness!"

"Screw you, asshole!" Floated back through the door.

Unfazed, Hickman lay back and stroked himself. "She'll be back and when she does . . ." he closed his eyes, dreaming of the ways he would make her beg. Her back door looked more and more promising now. With a smile on his face, he started masturbating, forgetting about his troubles for the time being.

Tina was full of rage as she moved down the darkened walkway on her way to Hector's place and Steve. Hickman was an asshole, but he wasn't so different from the other men she'd known in her life. Ever since she had become a drug addict she'd had to do depraving things to get her fix. No, she wasn't proud of herself, but she would be the first to admit she had no willpower.

And now Hickman was playing her like so many men had before him. But the laugh was on him. Her Hepatitis was in full bloom and the great and powerful doctor hadn't even noticed. She smiled as she walked; a swing to her buttocks.

Oh, but he'd be finding out soon enough, just a little payback for him screwing her over and lying to her so he could get into her pants.

As she walked up the deserted path, she didn't see the shadow on her left step out of the other, deeper shadows and become incarnate. Without warning, she felt an arm slide around her neck and before she could even let out a scream of surprise she felt a sting to her throat. She tried to talk, to ask what was going on, but her throat filled with blood and nothing but red, froth-like bubbles appeared.

She was spun around, then, and she stared into the familiar face of one of the group. The Unsub saw recognition there, but it was too late for Tina to do anything but gasp. The Unsub took the second blade from a pocket and thrust it into Tina's chest, pulling up and sliding the blade out. Tina exhaled sharply, the pain mind-numbing.

Tina was already weak on her feet, her hands trying to staunch the blood spilling from her severed throat and covering her shirt. All thoughts of fighting back were gone, only thoughts of keeping her own fluids inside her where they belonged ran through her mind.

She barely felt the third blade when it was forced into her abdomen.

The Unsub twisted it sharply, and upon pulling it free, Tina's intestines spilled out of her like a gutted fish.

Her knees grew weak and she fell to the dark path, her lungs desperately trying to suck in one more precious ounce of oxygen.

"Why?" She managed through blood bubbles, her hands trying to shove her bloody intestines back inside her.

The Unsub looked down at her and smiled sadly. "Because I have to." Then the shadow disappeared into the darkness, the killer's footsteps soon dwindling away to be lost in the background noise of the undead outside the zoo walls.

Tina watched the figure leave, gagging on her own blood. A small voice inside her head told her she was dying and that there was no way around it. Inside her mind, she smiled slightly. She had always figured she would just die of an overdose one of these days, not lying in a pool of her own blood in the middle of a deserted zoo.

Her bloody hand reached out in front of her and she tried to drag herself along the path, but it was hopeless. She was too weak from loss of blood. Her vision was already fading and with the last ounce of her strength, she stretched out a blood soaked finger, and drew the first letter of her killer's name on the path in scarlet.

She actually felt her heart stop beating and her eyes seemed to lose focus, but just as her mind shut down, her lips curved up into a smile, one that would remain frozen on her bloody face even in death.

Her death mask.

When they found her body, they'd know who killed her and she would get her revenge . . . even if she wouldn't be around to savor it.

Chapter 37

STEVE SAT QUIETLY in the corner of the main room just outside Tracey and Craig's sickroom. His legs were bent and close to his body and he really wanted to stretch.

The room was deathly silent, nothing could be heard but the sound of Craig's ragged breath as the man breathed in and out.

Tracey had showed signs of improvement as the day had passed into night; Craig on the other hand had been growing weaker. At the moment, both patients were sleeping soundly.

Matt had done his job well, informing the others in the group that Tracey and Craig would be unattended this night. Now all Steve had to do is wait and hope to catch the killer in a trap, but as the hours passed, he was beginning to think the night was a bust.

Deciding he would chance making a noise, he stretched out his legs, his knees popping in the darkness. Wincing from the sound, he stayed motionless, waiting to see if he had been discovered by any unwelcome intruders.

The front door of Hector's had been left unlocked, hopefully seeming a simple oversight by anyone who investigated.

The pistol lay on the floor next to him and, as he sat in the darkness, all he could do was think. He thought back to Tracey when she was a child and how happy the three of them had been. That was before her mother had decided she wasn't happy with him anymore and had asked for a divorce.

Now, years later, Tracey was a young woman herself, and he saw more and more of his ex-wife in her everyday.

Odds were, Tracey's mother was dead, either killed or worse, she had become infected and now walked the city as one of the undead. Though Steve tried to picture that image, he honestly didn't feel good about that becoming her fate. Despite everything she'd done to him, he still loved the woman, though he had feigned indifference to save face.

Every time he looked at Tracey he saw her mother, and was reminded of what might have been.

Tracey sighed in her sleep, causing Steve to come back to the here and now. She mumbled something in her sleep and then grew quiet once again.

Steve checked his watch, the small hands glowing in the dark. It was almost dawn and still no killer. He was contemplating how much longer he should wait when the door opened slowly and a figure stepped inside.

Steve reached down and picked up the pistol, the weapon already prepared to be fired, his finger hovering over the trigger when a soft voice called out to him.

"Hey, Steve, its Hal, don't shoot me," he whispered.

"Hal? Jesus Christ, I thought you were our killer. You almost got yourself shot," Steve said while standing up.

"Oh yeah? Well, me and Matt have had enough out there. We want to go get some sleep, it's almost dawn and we're both cold and hungry."

Both Matt and Hal had hidden in the overgrown bushes across from Hector's front door. The goal was to catch the killer in a vice and then squeeze it shut.

Yawning, Steve had to agree the night was most definitely a bust.

"Shit, I can't believe that was all for nothing," he said, while working out a crick in his neck.

"Well, maybe we should just get everyone together and try to figure it out from there, I mean, we don't even know if the killer is still alive. It could have been one of the seven people we buried yesterday. My money's on George, or maybe Paul. He was still pretty spry for an old guy."

Steve shook his head. "No, I told you before, no one is just going to say, *yeah it was me, you found me out*, no, we need to catch them in the act, it's the only way. But you already know who I think it is, don't you?"

Hal frowned. "You're not going to say Dr. Hickman are you? Man, what is your beef with that guy, I know he's an ass, but wow, Steve, your taking it to the next level."

"Are you and me talking about the same guy? The man I'm talking about left his wife to get torn apart by those dead fucks out there. He didn't even try to help her. I don't know about you, but that's not the person I want watching my back when the shit hits the fan."

Hal was about to reply when Matt stuck his head inside the doorway. "Hey, if you hens are done cackling, I'm going to bed. Are you coming Hal or should I just go alone?" Matt called.

Hal turned to Matt and held up his hand, his index finger up in the air in a wait a second gesture. "One sec', Matt, I promise."

Matt frowned and then his head disappeared, the man waiting outside once again.

Hal turned back to Steve. "Look, Steve, I like you, you know that, and I think you're a good leader, that's why everyone's deferred to you, but this thing with Hickman . . . he saved Craig's life for God's sake, the man isn't that bad, he's just human."

"More like inhuman, you mean," Steve retorted.

Hal threw his hands in the air. "You're impossible; I'm going to bed for a few hours, I'll see you later." He turned and left then, closing the front door behind him. Steve stood there in the gloom, watching the door.

They were all fools, he thought. Hickman was a danger to them all; the man just hadn't shown his true colors to the rest of them. Deciding the night was most definitely over and he was exhausted, he quickly checked on Tracey and Craig, not happy with the way Craig looked. His face was pale and his forehead was cold, his breath shallow.

Deciding he'd address any other issues after a few hours of sleep, he plopped down in the easy chair Hector had died in, now minus the cushions, the blood saturating them to the point they were useless, and was asleep in a matter of minutes.

He awoke in what seemed like minutes, but was in fact hours later, when the front door started to shake, someone pounding on it heavily. Though groggy from sleep, he picked up the pistol from the small table next to the chair and stumbled, like one of the ghouls outside the zoo, towards the door.

Upon opening it, he was blasted by daylight and he couldn't see a thing while his eyes tried to adjust.

But he could still hear and all he heard were the frantic ravings of Sherry and Seth. Sherry, missing her two children, had taken Seth under her wing, the two becoming friends.

Now both of them stood in front of Steve, rambling about a body and blood and murder.

Steve's vision finally cleared and he held up his hands for them to stop talking,

"For the love of God, will you two please shut up!" He screamed over them, both of them quieting down for the moment.

Steve first saw that Sherry had tears in her eyes and Seth looked more uncomfortable then he'd normally seen the kid, with the exception of that first day at the picnic area when everyone had introduced themselves. Seth seemed to be adjusting to the dead walking like it was no big thing, just another part of the day. In less than a day, he was already adapting to his new world.

"Now what's wrong? And please, one at a time."

Sherry started, Seth deferring to her.

"Its Tina, she's dead. Someone killed her!" Sherry said.

"What? When, how did it happen, where is she?" Steve asked all at once.

Seth pointed back down the path, toward the duck pond.

"She's down there, man, near the pond. Shit, you should see her, it's like someone was carving a turkey; she's all fucked up."

"Goddammit, the fucker not only didn't take the bait, but went out and found someone else while the rest of us were occupied!" Steve said angrily.

"What? What are you talking about?" Sherry asked, confused.

Steve realized he'd spoken out loud, and waved her question away. "Nothing, Sherry, its nothing." He changed the subject quickly. "Take me to her, will you? I need to see this for myself."

Seth nodded. "Sure, dude, we didn't touch nothin', just like in those crime shows. I watch CSI every night and they say never touch the body or you'll destroy evidence."

Steve almost grinned at that. He highly doubted any forensic units would be inspecting the scene of Tina's murder anytime soon.

"That's good work, Seth, now let's go." Steve closed and locked the door to Hector's, the keys in his front pocket. He had seemed to have inherited the building from Hector, though he felt he was only there because Tracey and Craig needed a real bed and a warm place to recover. Once they were well, he'd relinquish the building to whoever wanted it, or they could share it as a communal building.

The three of them moved down the pathway, Seth all but running. Steve took his time, his eyes trying to see into every bush and shrub that lined the walkway. He wondered if he should get Carl, but decided not to, he wanted to inspect the body immediately, both his curiosity and his rage for his failed attempt at catching the killer eating at him.

They headed off, passing Dr. Hickman as they went. Steve slowed for a second and stopped the man.

"Hey, Doc, you're up pretty early, where're you going?" Steve asked him.

"If you must know, I'm getting some breakfast," Hickman answered back unctuously. "Not that's it's any of your business, now if you'll kindly step out of the way, I'll be moving on."

Steve did so, stopping Sherry and Seth from saying anything to the Doctor. He wanted to keep things quiet for now, not giving the killer the upper hand.

Stepping aside, Hickman moved along the path and Steve and the others continued to the pond.

Seven minutes later the duck pond came into view and Steve saw a prone body lying on the path. All three ran now, racing for no apparent reason. The woman was dead; she was in no hurry to be found.

When Steve reached Tina, both Sherry and Seth hung back a little, seeming to be wary of the corpse.

Steve had to admit he was, as well. If Tina had been attacked by a ghoul somehow, then she could wake up at any moment, hungry for blood.

Steve moved slowly, crossing the few remaining feet to the dead woman and his eyes tried to take in everything at once. He saw the neck wound first, the slice looking like a second mouth. The intestines were seen next, the red loops glistening in the sun. With all the blood on her shirt, the chest wound went unnoticed, but after what Hal had told him, he was almost positive this was the same killer. Steve still remembered Hector's wounds clearly and these were as close as you could get.

Lowering his pistol, he turned to both Sherry and Seth.

"Don't worry, she's dead for real, she's not coming back."

"Oh, thank God for small favors," Sherry said, holding Seth's hands.

Seth stepped a foot closer and pointed to Tina's right hand. "Steve, look over there by her hand, it's like she was trying to write something in her blood."

Steve looked where the boy pointed and sure enough, there was a letter scrawled on the pavement.

"Holy shit, you're right. Good job, son. It look's like . . ." he tried to read it.

"You think she saw who killed her and tried to leave us a clue?" Seth asked, excited.

"Yeah, I think you're right. It looks like a **D**, what do you think, Seth?"

Seth leaned closer, now, enjoying the mystery, despite the dead woman lying in the sun at his feet.

"Fuck yeah, that's a **D**, no doubt about it."

"A **D**? If it's a **D** then it could only be two people, couldn't it?" Sherry asked.

Seth nodded. "Fuckin' A. It's either Diane or . . ."

Steve finished the sentence for him.

"Or it stands for *Doctor,* as in *Doctor* Hickman. I knew it; I knew that fucker was guilty!"

Steve jumped up and took off across the cement walkway, running at full tilt.

"Oh shit, Sherry, I think he's going after Doc Hickman!" Seth said, watching Steve running away.

"Oh my lord, he'll kill him, did you see his face? We need to get the others. You go get Carl and I'll get Matt and Hal. And hurry, there's no time to lose!"

Seth nodded and took off at a run, he knew where Carl was and he'd be there in a few minutes. Running as fast as his legs would let him, he could only hope he was in time.

Chapter 38

STEVE RAN AS fast as he could, his powerful leg muscles pushing him foreword. His face was a mask of anger, his eyes almost glowing with hate.

He had known all along who the killer was, but no one would believe him. Hickman was a murderer, it all made sense. The killer used blades and Hickman was a doctor, he used knives and scalpels everyday. And the way he had treated his wife. He was a man who had no sympathy for anyone but himself.

A classic sign of a sociopath.

But Steve would end this once and for all. No one else would die under the man's hand.

Steve hurdled a pair of saplings, the landscaping having been ignored for more than a year. He cut across some shaded, grassy area, once used for deer, and jumped back onto the walkway.

Hector's building was in sight and he surged forward, the adrenalin filling his veins, giving him the energy he needed to run even faster. Within three minutes, he was back at the picnic area.

Running into the back, Hickman looked up from a table, where he was eating some peanut butter and crackers. Steve never slowed, but charged at the man, hurdling over the picnic table and knocking

Hickman to the ground. If it had been hard cement instead of denuded, compacted dirt with spots of grass, Hickman would have cracked his head, but instead his skull struck the dirt and the man was only dazed.

Steve rolled over the man and came up in a crouch.

"You bastard. You killed Tina didn't you? What happened, did she find out about you and you had to shut her up?" Steve snarled at him.

Hickman raised himself onto his elbows and stared in shock at Steve.

"Are you mad? What is the meaning of this? What the hell is wrong with you? What about Tina, is she all right?" He asked, spitting bits of cracker across his lap.

"Don't act like you don't know. I'm through playing with you, Doc. I'm gonna end your miserable life once and for all, right here and now!"

Hickman rolled to his side and raised his hands to try and stop Steve. "Now just wait a damn minute here, Mr. Webb. I don't know what you're going on about, but you've had it in for me ever since we got inside this cursed place. And I won't stand for it any longer!"

Steve climbed to his feet, glaring at Hickman. He tossed his gun onto the ground, wanting to squeeze the life out of Hickman with his bare hands; he wasn't going to give him the mercy of a quick death.

"Oh, don't worry Doc, when I get through with you, you won't be standing ever again . . . because I'm going to break your legs and toss you to those dead bastards outside the walls!" Steve roared at him, and then charged, his arms out to wrap around Hickman and pick him up in a bear hug.

Hickman felt his feet leave the earth and a moment later his chest felt like it was in a vise. He looked down at the face of Steve, and saw nothing but a feral rage: and he had no idea what it was for.

Hickman panicked, kicking his feet as he tried to extricate himself from Steve's grasp. He got lucky and one of his knees connected with Steve's groin, crushing the larger man's testicles. Steve went ash-grey and dropped Hickman to the ground; following the doctor an instant later as he fell to his knees with a wheeze of pain.

Hickman lay where he dropped, trying to breathe through a crushed chest. He honestly thought he might have cracked a few ribs.

Then he was being picked up again and thrown across the picnic area, his head colliding with a few loose trashcans.

Steve stomped slowly toward him as Hickman lay on the ground amidst the month's old trash.

"That was dirty pool, Doc, kicking me in the nuts. I guess you ain't as upper class as you try to act."

Hickman raised his hands over his head like he could somehow shield himself from Steve's blows. He was in no way a fighter and was in absolute terror.

"Please, Mr. Webb, Steve, what did I do to you to deserve this?" He pleaded.

Steve leaned over and picked him up again, grabbing two fistfuls of his shirt and saying: "Don't act like you don't know, you murdering bastard. But I'll tell you this much; you won't be getting your hands on my daughter. This is your wake and funeral, Doc, and I'm the undertaker!"

Steve picked him up and threw him across the picnic area again, Hickman landing on a nearby table and rolling off it. He saw stars and his breath left his lungs like he'd been punched in the gut, which wasn't far from the truth. His right arm screamed in pain and if he was right, and he was a doctor after all, he had just dislocated his shoulder.

Steve didn't wait for him to revive, but instead climbed on top of him and started to rain blows on his face. Hickman's head rocked back and forth as Steve struck him again and again.

Hickman's jaw became dislocated, his nose was shattered to the point only absolute and extensive cosmetic surgery would ever have it back to the way it was. His right eye swelled up into a massive black eye, fluids making it look like a big black and blue balloon. But Steve's next blow punctured the welts, pus and blood oozing over his face to settle in his one good eye. Teeth were fractured and broken, a few sliding down his throat, threatening to choke him.

In a brief flash of lucidity, he knew he was about to die, bludgeoned to death by a mad man. He lost all focus on reality, slipping into a state of madness and pain, not of his own volition.

Then Steve's blows abruptly stopped and the weight on his body lifted.

Looking up with his one good eye, he saw Carl on top of Steve, both of them rolling on the ground together next to him.

Hickman rolled to his knees, only his pain and adrenalin the reason he was up at all. Swaying back and forth like a drunk, he watched the two men fighting before him, too dazed to even comprehend what had happened to him, but a sense of utter humiliation was growing inside him like a time bomb and it would soon explode outward, taking everyone within its blast radius with it.

Carl had run as fast as he could to the picnic area after being roused by Seth and when he had arrived and saw Steve literally beating the shit out of Doctor Hickman, he had tackled Steve, his rifle flying off into the grass near the edge of the picnic area. Seth was behind him, but Carl told him to stay out of the way, Seth was small and Steve was liable to kill him by accident.

Steve fought him, as if he didn't know who he was. He was in one of those berserker rages he'd heard Viking warriors would get into in the past on the battlefield.

But Carl had spent some time in prison and had never been raped or made to do anything he didn't like. There was a reason for that. He knew how to handle himself in a fight.

He managed to block almost all of Steve's punches, the ones that got through making his ears ring. He didn't want to hurt his friend, but he was quickly realizing if he wanted to stop him, he would have to start fighting back. But then Hal and Matt charged up the path and Matt jumped on top of Steve, as well, just behind Carl who was on his chest, his bulk pushing the wind from Steve in an instant. Steve struggled valiantly, but with Matt's massive bulk on him he was trapped. Hal had come around them and was trying to hold Steve's arms, but Hal was no athlete and was losing despite the fact Steve was trapped under both Carl and Matt.

"Jesus Christ, Steve, will you cut the shit?" Carl yelled at him, trying to get his friend to stop. Steve kept squirming, but Matt's weight just forced him tighter to the ground and Carl could see Steve was starting to turn red.

"I can do this all day, Steve. Shit, I'll take a nap if you want, now cut the shit!" Matt told him, looking to his side at Steve's face.

Slowly, Steve slowed his struggling and finally his arms fell to the ground above his head. Hal held them down, but there was no need. Steve had given in, and as Carl watched, he saw sanity come back into his friends eyes.

"For Christ's sake, let me up? You're killing me, you fat bastard," Steve snapped at Matt.

Grinning widely, Matt rolled off him. "Okay, but one wrong move and I'll sit on your head, I mean it," Matt said.

Steve nodded his head up in surrender. "All right, I give, that's enough."

Hal let go of Steve's hands and Carl rolled away from him, warily.

"What the hell is going on here, Steve? Why are you trying to kill the Doc?" Carl asked, trying to gain his breath back.

Steve pointed to Hickman, his knuckles bruised and bloody from pounding Hickman's face.

"Ask him. Ask the killer what I'm doing!" Steve said; screaming with spittle flying from his mouth. Whatever small piece of sanity he had regained was already slipping away again.

Carl looked at Hickman and his mouth fell open. The doctor's face was a mass of meat with an opening for a mouth and one bloodshot eye peeking out.

"Holy shit, what the fuck did you do to him?" Carl asked, Matt and Hal staring, as well.

Hickman tried to raise his hand and say something, but all that came out of his mouth were some gurgles and a few broken teeth. Red drool slid out of the side of his mouth to drip on the ground and his head was bent at an odd angle.

"Oh my Lord, you flattened his face, there's nothing left of him," Hal said.

Steve started laughing, staring at Hickman. "Ha, physician, heal thyself, you fuck!"

Then he laughed some more, almost hysterical.

"Jesus Christ, Carl. I think he's lost it," Matt said, as he watched Steve rolling around on the ground.

Carl nodded, agreeing with him. "Hal, get that extension cord over there and tie Steve's hands behind his back. He's gone crazy. Until we figure all this shit out, I want him secured. He's too big and mean to let loose again."

Hal hesitated, looking down at his friend.

"Dammit, Hal, do it, I don't like it either, but it's safer for everyone," Carl told him.

"He's right, buddy, get the cord," Matt said, next to Carl.

Hal sighed and retrieved the cord, quickly binding Steve with one end. Steve barely noticed, laughing on the ground.

Once Steve was secured, lying quietly on the ground, a few muffled laughs still coming from him, Sherry arrived.

"Oh thank God you stopped him," Sherry gasped, seeing Steve tied up on the trampled grass.

"Stopped him? Do you know what the hell is going on here?" Carl asked the newcomers.

"Steve thinks Tina was killed by Doctor Hickman," Seth said matter-of-factly, moving closer now that it was safe.

Carl did a double take, as well as both Matt and Hal.

"What did you say? Tina's dead?" Carl asked.

"Tina's the one with the crazy hair, right? Skinny chick?" Matt asked from behind him.

Sherry nodded, "Yes, we found her dead on the walkway near the duck pond. We got Steve and he came with us. There was the letter **D** written in blood by her hand, Tina must have done it before she died. Steve saw it and said it meant **D** for Doctor. The he ran off like lightning. We didn't know what to do, so me and Seth went to get you guys."

Seth nodded, agreeing with everything she said.

Matt and Hal listened intently. All any of them had been told when Sherry had come and woken them up was that Steve needed help at the picnic area. Both men had taken off at a run, Matt with the shotgun in his hand. Neither man had expected what they found.

Before anyone could say another word, there was a massive explosion to the west. The ground shook, making everyone feel like there was an earthquake taking place.

Carl fell to his knees, looking around in terror. "What the hells happening?" He asked anyone who would listen.

Hal pointed over the tree tops at the huge smoke cloud rising into the sky. "Oh my God, that's where the gas tanks are over in Quincy. They just exploded," he said in awe.

"Oh shit, something even worse has happened, if that's even possible," Matt said, staring at the massive smoke cloud.

The gas tanks were massive, six-story tall tanks that were filled with refined gas. Tankers from all over Massachusetts and New England would deliver to the yard and offload their payload. From there, the gas would be sent off to gas stations and other facilities that handled fuel. The yard was more than a half-mile wide and if one tank went up and there was no one to fight the fire, then in no time there would be nothing but a massive conflagration miles long, depending on the blowing wind.

Sherry leaned against a picnic table, trying to stay standing. "Oh my lord, it's so big, look at that cloud. Are we safe here?"

Hal shrugged. "We should be, there's miles between us and the tanks, but if the fire is as massive as I think and the winds are high and blow the flames and embers in our direction, then we could be in trouble in a few days, if it heads our way."

Carl picked himself up. "We'll worry about that later; right now we've got shit to deal with in the here and now." He turned to look for Hickman, but the man was gone.

"Hey, where's the Doc?" Carl asked.

"He was here a second ago," Hal added, turning in a circle.

"He must have walked off during the quake," Matt said.

"Forget about him, right now we need to get Steve calmed down and right in the head." He turned to Matt. "Go check on Tracey and Craig, make sure they're all right, then come back here, we're gonna need your help."

Matt nodded, picking up the shotgun from where he'd dropped it upon arriving and headed off to the front door. He returned less then a minute later saying the door was locked.

Hal told him to wait a second and found the keys in Steve's pocket, taking a wild guess. He tossed them to Matt and the man went off again.

Carl leaned against a picnic table, exhausted.

"Man, what a wake up call," he said.

"You think you got it bad? Me and Matt were hiding in the bushes all night, waiting for our killer to show up. We only got a few hours sleep," Hal told him.

"And did the killer show up?" Carl asked.

Hal answered by shaking his head. "No, guess the killer decided to get Tina instead. Maybe Steve's right and it was the Doc, make's sense, I guess. If it's not him, then who else could it be?"

Everyone shrugged, not knowing the answer.

While the four of them talked it over and Steve muttered to himself incoherently, none of them noticed the set of bolt cutters that were missing from the items Carl and Craig had retrieved from the tool shed the day before.

Chapter 39

DR. WARREN HICKMAN was literally blind with pain. With his one remaining eye, he slowly staggered down one of the winding walkways of the zoo, trying to peer through the fog that had become his vision. The bolt cutters bounced on the pavement behind him as he dragged them along, his one good hand holding them despite the coating of blood slathered on his palm.

He was furious, humiliated, embarrassed and a dozen other emotions all at the same time, all swirling around inside him like a maelstrom.

Webb had to pay, they all did, but how could he get his revenge on them? He thought to himself. There were more of them then there was of him and Webb was twice his size, with muscles that could pulverize him in minutes.

He reached up with his hand then, touching his face. His shoulder screamed in protest, but he ignored it. There was so much pain and agony in his body right now; the shoulder was like a pinprick.

His hand ran over the contours of his face, coming away bloody. He hadn't seen himself yet, there were no reflective surfaces to be found, but he was fairly certain he would be horrified when he did.

While the others had been wrestling Steve to the ground, he had moved across the picnic area, looking for something to defend himself with when Webb came at him again. He knew the man would.

He had grabbed the first available weapon he saw, the bolt cutters, but then the world had rocked him to his knees and he had fallen into the foliage surrounding the picnic area.

With everyone looking to the west, he had used the distraction to crawl deeper into the foliage, soon coming out on one of the dozens of walkways that intertwined the zoo. With no other thoughts but of escape, he had shuffled off; resembling one of the ghouls outside the zoo more then his former distinguished self.

He slowed his shambling gate when he approached a pile of trash near a dented trashcan. A few stray rats scurried away, chattering at being disturbed, but Hickman ignored them. One of the items buried in the refuse was a hubcap, found by one of the custodial staff in the parking lot twelve months earlier. The janitor had brought the hubcap into the zoo and had left it near the trashcan to be retrieved later, but then the zoo had began shutting down and the man had never returned to clean up his pile of trash.

Hickman saw the hubcap and leaned over, back and ribs protesting, and picked it up. Though tarnished with age, the reflective surface still provided use as a meager mirror. Hickman held it up and looked at his once handsome face for the first time since Steve had pummeled him.

The instant his one good eye made contact with the eye looking back at him, he dropped the hubcap and fell to the ground. He started sobbing, but all that came out were a few gurgles and bloody drool slipped out of the side of his mouth.

He was a monster, now. A freak!

As a surgeon, he knew how truly bad his face actually was. In a perfect world, he could glimpse in his mind's eye the amount of surgery and recovery and then surgery again to even try to get his face to look half as good as it had been before the beating.

He wailed at the sky, his grasp on sanity slipping a little more each second.

Five minutes passed while he cried and wailed, and then slowly, he began to regain a small modicum of his old self.

Webb had done this to him. It was Webb's fault. He needed to pay for this; revenge was all he had left. If he had possession of a firearm, he could simply walk back to the picnic area and blow Steve's damn head off, but he had none and the few inside the zoo were well guarded by their owners.

The hatred he felt for Webb, and a lesser extent the others, continued to grow. He needed to get the man, to see him killed. He needed to vindicate himself, but how?

Then he heard the song of the undead, a soulless moaning that would rise and fall in pitch.

The zombies! That's it! He thought, stumbling to his feet and moving toward the front of the zoo and the massive gate that blocked the entrance.

It was true he was only one man. There was no way he could overcome the others and get his revenge, but he didn't need to.

Just outside the walls of the zoo was an army of the dead that would be happy to be the architects of his vengeance.

Wincing in pain from his cracked ribs, he slowly shuffled to the gate and its large chain that secured the gate. The bolt cutters would do the job nicely.

And then they would all pay.

The Unsub crept deeper into the foliage that surrounded the picnic area, trying to hear the conversations within.

She couldn't believe her luck, Steve and the others seemed to believe Doctor Hickman was the serial killer.

She grinned widely, pleased with the results of last nights activities. Slowly and carefully, she backed away from the shrubs and circled around the front of Hector's house. Though she was pleased that she had eluded detection, she knew the urge to kill was still strong in her and the next time she would be found out, as there were no more suspects to defer blame.

Deciding she needed to kill at least one more person, and then she would take her leave of the zoo, she moved toward Hector's front door. Once she had accomplished her task, she would find a spot along the back wall somewhere and then, up and over, and through the zombies that waited outside. From experience, she knew they were slow and stupid creatures. All she would need is an area where they were spaced out and she could easily get around them and into the woods, where she would then play the damsel in distress until she found some other group of survivors to take her in. And then the cycle would start all over again.

The plan was beautiful in its simplicity.

She tried not to analyze why she needed to kill people that reminded her of her husband and his lovers, but she did. It wasn't that he cheated on her, hell, most men do at one time or another; it was how he had cheated on her.

Her husband had been bi-sexual and when it had gotten out that he had cheated on her with other men, well, that was a humiliation she couldn't handle.

She had gone a little crazy then, the betrayal and humiliation overwhelming her. She had stayed in her home for almost two months, not wanting to leave the apartment, fearing that every person she met was somehow laughing at her, enjoying her shame.

But then a few months ago, just before the first body was found, she had received a knock on her apartment door. When she had opened it, she was shocked to find it was one of her husband's mistress'. The woman had wanted to apologize for any pain she had caused and had asked to come in.

Diane had let the temptress enter her apartment and the two had talked, but somewhere in the conversation, the wrong thing had been said and the two of them had become combative, now using words to slice and cause pain.

Diane had excused herself, then, going into the kitchen to pour herself another cup of coffee, but in fact, she just wanted to cry out of sight of the woman.

She had already been through so much humiliation; she didn't want this *woman*, this *bitch* to see her crying. Then the *other* woman, as they are so fondly called, called out to her, making a jibe that cut her to the quick.

Diane held back her tears and instead picked up a carving knife she had set on the counter after using the tip to pry open a coffee can lid. Those damn old can openers never seemed to go all the way around.

Staring down at the knife in her hands and listening to the woman in the other room cackling about her husband, Diane lost a little bit of her sanity and the humiliation she'd felt turned into something darker, something more feral.

She had walked out into the living room again, her face carved in stone. The woman had looked up into Diane's face, seeing the change in her countenance and was about to ask what was the problem, when Diane pulled the knife from behind her back, where she was hiding it, and sliced the woman across the throat, severing her carotid artery in one even slice. She had been surprised how easy the blade had sliced through her throat and severed the artery beneath, like a hot knife through butter.

The woman had gasped, and had tried to shout out in surprise, but nothing but a large dollop of blood spilled from her mouth. Her mouth opened and closed like a fish as scarlet spray shot out to strike Diane in the chest.

She ignored it, watching the woman expire, the life's glow in her eyes slowly becoming extinguished. The woman's hands twitched, the spasms slowing until her hands were motionless, her eyes glazing over in death.

When the woman was finally dead, Diane couldn't believe how good she felt. She felt empowered and strong, no longer a victim of her husband's depravities.

She had taken her life back and the power was now in her hands.

She had disposed of the corpse—a simple body dump, actually—in an alley near the edge of Boston's city limits, just on the border for Cambridge. She had simply slowed down and then reached over and opened the passenger door, then pushed the corpse out to fall into the street, then she had driven on, like there was no hurry. She had felt like a Mafioso as she drove away.

After that, she had needed to keep killing, each time imagining it was her husband or one of his sluts.

And all those events had now had brought her to the front door of Hector's place and her target within. Her target, lying unconscious inside, was Craig. The young man lent an uncanny resemblance to her husband and all Diane wanted to do was slit the man's throat. But he had always been with the others of the group so she had settled for one of the other survivors that had been out alone at night. And the old man, of course; Hector had just been for the fun of it, the opportunity being available.

But now the others were all talking in the picnic area, discussing what to do with Steve and the Doctor and the ever growing fire on the horizon. It was the perfect time to strike. She would sneak in there and would be gone in less then three minutes, more then enough time to slit his throat and watch him bleed out.

As she opened the door and slipped inside, she was already mulling it over if she should just kill Tracey, as well.

Yes, she thought, why not. The woman did bear a resemblance to the first woman she'd killed in her apartment all those months ago. And when she looked back on it, she had always regretted simply slicing her throat. The bitch really hadn't suffered that much.

Well that was okay, now she could make up for lost chances and slice this one up good, making her feel every sting of the blades, then, just maybe, Diane could find some peace.

Chapter 40

TRACEY TOSSED AND turned in her bed while frightful dreams of dead things clawing for her from the darkness of her mind flitted across her subconscious.

She had been in a bad state for the past two days, her body fighting off the miniscule amount of infection that had remained in her system. But whether it was because of luck or some strange immunity her body possessed, she was starting to recover.

Her father had saved her life.

In the gloom of the room, she had heard the muffled explosion of the gas tanks, but had been too tired to get up and investigate. Matt had been in the front room and had run outside when the building had started to shake.

Deciding that if the explosion was important enough for her to be warned and that someone would come in and tell her if the need arose, she lay back down and rested.

Her stomach was starting to rumble and she was pretty sure she'd want to actually eat in a little while, but for now, she was content to just lay there in the room and relax. Next to her, Craig stirred fitfully, his head was all but buried in the covers of his blanket and she couldn't see him very well. He had moaned a few times in his sleep, but otherwise had been quiet.

Her heart went out to him. She had been so lucky compared to him, only receiving a small bite on her arm; he on the other hand had been unfortunate enough to have both his hand and wrist severed from his body.

She couldn't even imagine the pain he must be in.

A wave of weariness came over her and she decided she'd go back to sleep. Soon, though, she'd be better and then she could help look after Craig.

* * *

The door to the front room creaked open and a figure entered, the bright sun of the day all but hiding the face of the intruder.

Diane slowly moved into the depths of Hector's home, her eyes trying to take in the corners of the place for any signs of a surprise. She was almost certain the abode was empty, with the exception of its two bed-ridden patients, but she wasn't about to become careless now. Not after doing everything right for so long.

With her blade leading the way, she stepped into the main room, her eyes spotting the beds and the feet of Craig and Tracey in the next room. She glanced at the easy chair in the corner of the main room, minus its cushions, and she smiled to herself. She had enjoyed slaughtering the old man. Thinking back, he had barely put up a fight, but it had still been a pleasant experience for her; not so much for the old man. Slowly, so as to not disturb Tracey and Craig, she tip-toed to the doorway. There they were, both sleeping soundly, like pigs waiting for the slaughter.

She thought back to the day she'd had to give a disposition for her divorce. Her husband had been there and his lawyer had asked her why she thought her husband had strayed so far from their bed.

She had answered that he was a pig, like all men were, and it was no fault of her own.

Her husband had laughed then and had said to everyone in the room that she was a lousy lover and he'd had no choice but to expand his horizons or else wallow in the muck that had been their sex life. Everyone had chuckled at his statement, all eyes staring at her, though some tried to be at least a little discreet about it, but Diane knew they were laughing inside where she couldn't hear them.

The anger and humiliation she'd felt that day surged up and threatened to consume her. She felt a burning inside her that could only be extinguished with blood, but at the time was far too afraid to do anything more than dream about it.

Not now though, now she had made her dreams come true.

Stepping into the room and looking down at Craig, she reached out to pull the blanket off his sleeping form, the blade already up and ready to plunge into his body. The only thing left to decide was if she was going to first slice his throat or plunge the knife into his heart.

* * *

Dr. Warren Hickman finally reached the front gate to the zoo. Behind him was a trail of blood, his face bleeding profusely. His vision continued to fade in and out and he believed he had a punctured lung, thanks to one of the many broken ribs he had received from Steve.

He started choking, blood shooting out of his mouth like a geyser, and he nodded to himself.

Oh yeah, he was pretty well screwed.

Of all the ways he thought he would die someday, he had to admit the one in front of him would have been his last. He fell against the steel gate, and it rattled slightly from his weight. On the other side of it, the dead moved about excitedly, seeing Hickman before them. They wanted him, badly, he could tell.

With a heave, he brought up the bolt cutters and placed them against the chain. He was having trouble with depth perception and it took him more then a minute to actually get the chain between the teeth of the cutters.

He tried to smile, then, but the amount of agony it cost him wasn't worth it. So he smiled inside, where it was painless.

Using all his waning strength, he tried to close the bolt cutters, but he couldn't do it. He barked out a laugh, finding it all so ironic. To make it all the way to the gate only to find he didn't have the strength to finish the job. He was pathetic, he chastised himself.

The ghouls tried to force their fingers through the small holes in the fence, shaking it back and forth, using the few inches of play allowed.

Hickman sucked in a breath that caused him sharp pain and then, pulling up the last reservoirs of energy still left in his beaten body, he squeezed the bolt cutters with all his might.

A scream left his mouth as his dislocated shoulder protested and he found his vision failing him, the pain overwhelming his senses. But just as he blacked out, the cutters did their job, slicing through one of the meaty links and breaking the chain securing the gate.

Hickman fell to the pavement, unconscious, his breath wheezing in and out as red drool dripped from the side of his mouth.

On the other side of the metal gate, the massive crowd of ghouls pushed against it, rattling it, wanting nothing more then to reach his body and consume it, but the heavy chain was still interwoven through the two gates.

The gate was still secured, the zoo safe, while Dr. Warren Hickman lay dead to the world at the feet of an army of the undead.

* * *

Diane pulled the blanket from Craig's still form and without hesitation, plunged the knife into his heart, deciding that would be the preferred position to start from, but she was already reaching around her back to pull another blade and use that one to slice across his throat, all within one heartbeat of Craig's eviscerated heart.

She watched the blade slice through his clothes and into his chest, more then three inches disappearing in a flash.

But what she expected to happen didn't.

What she expected to happen was for Craig's eyes to open wide in shock when he felt the blade slice through his heart. He would turn and look up at her, amazed, his eyes already losing focus. Then before he was dead, she would slash his throat for good measure, imagining it was her husband she was slaying.

That's what was supposed to happen, what had happened countless times when she had slaughtered innocents on the streets of Boston.

But things had changed in the past few weeks and the impossible had become a reality.

Craig did gaze up at her, but his eyes were already dead, and had been dead since she had walked into the room. Carl had tried to save his friend, but it had been too little, too late. He had been infected, despite the amputated hand, and had died and had then returned like thousands of others; the knife in his heart meant nothing to him.

Before Diane could do anything but utter a surprised squeak, Craig's hand shot out from under the blanket and wrapped itself around her dangling wrist.

Diane was scared, but she still had the upper hand, using the other knife in her hand to slash his throat. A small amount of blood seeped from the wound, but with his heart destroyed there was nothing to pump, either alive or dead.

Craig yanked her to him and she stumbled forward, her face falling onto his chest, the hilt of the blade bouncing off her forehead, her eye missing the hilt of the knife in Craig's heart by an inch.

Craig leaned forward, Diane's throat only a few inches from his mouth and sank his teeth into the side of her neck, ripping a massive piece of flesh from her throat.

She screamed then, the pain exquisite and Craig dove in for another bite, her blood squirting out and covering his face and neck like he was being baptized.

Tracey stirred then, roused from her slumber. She opened her eyes and couldn't believe what she was seeing.

Tossing the covers from her, she staggered out of bed and around Diane's kicking legs. Craig ignored her, feasting on Diane like she was a giant turkey leg.

Diane's screams had already slowed to a muffled gurgle and Tracey ran into the main room of the small structure and towards the already open front door.

Just as she was about to run out into the light, a shadow blocked the sun and stopped her, grabbing her by the arms, trapping her. Tracey let out one more scream, fearing she was doomed and then passed out, the exertion to much for her still healing body.

Behind her, the sounds of Craig's feast floated out into the sunlit day.

* * *

Doctor Hickman came awake not knowing where he was. For a brief moment, he thought he was back in the gift shop he had made his new home with Tina.

But then pain flooded through his body and he smelled the stench of death and heard the moans and wails of the dead. That was when reality came crashing back with a vengeance.

He didn't know how long he'd lay unconscious on the ground, but as he tried to move, he was filled with absolute mind-numbing pain.

But that was all right. He had only one more thing to do before he could rest forever.

Reaching up with one bloody hand, he wrapped shaking fingers around the chain holding the gates secured. With a loud clanking sound, the chain slid through the slots in the metal, the broken link hanging up for a second and then submitting to the doctor's ministrations.

The dead surged forward and Hickman found himself being pushed across the ground, as the weight of hundreds of bodies forced the gate open, sweeping him to the side like a paper bag.

But he wasn't ignored for long. Just as the walking corpses poured into the open gates of the zoo, a few turned and leaned over him, their bodies blocking out the sun.

Dr. Warren Hickman started to laugh then, though it sounded more like gurgles. His plan was not going exactly as he would have preferred.

Sure, he wanted the undead to kill his enemies, but in his blind need for revenge he had forgotten that once inside the zoo, the dead would eat him, as well. His screams rose into the sky while teeth and hands ripped into him, dissecting him like a lab experiment.

At first the pain was unbearable, but then he realized it wasn't any more terrible then how he had already been feeling. His vision started to fade and he saw his life's blood shooting up into the air to fall back like rain onto his shattered face.

Then there was only darkness and he didn't feel pain anymore.

Chapter 41

EVERYONE WAS STILL gathered in the picnic area, trying to decide what to do when Tracey's screams floated out to them.

Steve's glazed over expression was gone instantly and he looked up into Hal's eyes, pleading to be released.

Matt was already on the move, running back to the front door and a moment later, just as he was about to enter, Tracey came rushing out and fell into his arms. She screamed again and then passed out, Matt picking her up and carrying her back to the others.

"Oh my God, is she all right?" Steve asked, struggling with his bindings. "For the love of God, let me loose, she's my daughter," he pleaded.

Carl glanced at him, but he was more worried about Tracey. Matt carried her to them and set her down on one of the picnic tables, the same one that had held the Esperanzas' just a day before.

Sherry came over and picked up Tracey's arm, feeling for a pulse on her wrist; then she felt her forehead.

"Is she all right?" Carl asked. "What's wrong with her?"

Sherry shook her head. "I don't know, I'm no doctor, she's seems fine. Heartbeat is steady and her forehead's cool. If I had to guess, I'd say she's just passed out."

Carl turned to look at Steve, who was staring at Tracey with a worried look on his face.

"Relax, Steve, she's okay, she's just passed out." Carl looked up at Matt who was hovering nearby. "Matt, go see how Craig's doing, will ya? Then get back here. We need to figure out what the hell to do next and Diane is missing, too. Not to mention the Doc. He's beat up pretty bad and he's gonna need help."

Matt nodded, and with shotgun in hand, moved back to the building.

"Carl, come on, please, she's my daughter. I'm fine now. Screw Hickman, all I care about is Tracey, now. Cut me loose, please," Steve begged.

Carl looked over to Hal who was standing quietly with his arms crossed over his chest.

"What do you think?" Carl asked him.

Hal looked at Steve, who returned his gaze and then back to Carl.

"I think he's okay, now. Whatever made him freak-out, it's gone now. All he wants is to be with his daughter. Besides, I have his pistol; he'll be a good boy, right Steve?"

Carl looked at Steve again, the man nodding profusely. "Its fine, I'm fine, just let me go to her."

"And you're not going to try to get even with us for tying you up?" Carl asked.

Steve shook his head back and forth vigorously. "No way, I don't blame you; I was pretty gone there for a while. I guess I lost it. Its just Hickman . . . you know? He does something to me."

Carl smiled then. "Yeah, I know, more then you might believe. We all have someone like that," he sighed. "Go ahead, Hal, let him loose, besides, we need him with us, not against us."

Hal did as he was told and a second later, Steve was free, rubbing his wrists and moving to Tracey, touching her face and brushing her hair off her forehead, while he whispered platitudes to her.

Carl relaxed a little, maybe things would calm down a little, he thought.

That's when the sound of the double barrel shotgun firing from inside Hector's came to his ears and he knew everything was far from calming down.

Matt stepped through the front door moving quickly. He had no reason to expect danger. Tracey was outside and Craig was bedridden.

So when he had made his way to the back room to find Craig sitting up, face and chest covered in blood and gore with the half eaten corpse of Diane lying on his chest, he was more than a little surprised.

Craig looked up from eating Diane and his eyes grew wide, his teeth flaring back like a wild animal. A low growl issued from his throat, and he grabbed Diane's shirt collar and pulled her body off of him. She fell in a tangled heap of shredded meat.

Craig swung his legs off the bed and stood up, his left hand already clawing for Matt's throat, the right hand now missing and just a knob where Hickman had sutured the flesh closed.

"Oh shit, not you, too, Craig," Matt said, not wanting to believe what he was seeing.

Craig moaned loudly and charged at him, Matt having no choice but to level the shotgun and fire, point blank, at Craig.

The first barrage caught Craig in the left side of the head, blowing off his ear and some hair, destroying his left eye and blinding him in one orb. He staggered back for a second, seeming to be dazed, but then the remaining eye refocused and he charged at Matt again.

Matt swallowed hard, trying not to panic and repositioned the shotgun. He fired again with the other barrel and this time the shot blew Craig's head off at the shoulders, the neck disappearing from the barrage of firepower.

Craig's body continued forward, plowing into Matt. Matt screamed and pushed the headless corpse from him, the body falling to the floor, the left hand still trying to grab him. Craig's head had fallen across the floor and had landed right side up. The remaining eye still looked up at him and his mouth chewed empty air. If he was trying to talk, he didn't have the vocal cords to so much as utter a moan.

Matt made the sign of the cross on his chest and then turned at the sound of footsteps behind him.

Raising his hands to show it was all right, he waved Carl over to him.

"I'm afraid there's something you need to see," Matt said.

Carl moved closer, the rifle in his hands. When he saw Craig's headless body lying on the floor, the arms still twitching slightly; he cursed to himself.

"Oh shit, not him, too," he said softly, his eyes never leaving Craig's decapitated body.

Matt nodded. "Afraid so, his head's over there, still alive actually."

Carl looked where he was pointing and Craig's head winked at him with the one remaining eye.

"Oh shit, what the fuck?" He said, walking across the floor and looking down at his friend's severed head. Carl reached down and grabbed Craig's head by the hair, staring at the one good eye. Craig tried to bite him, impossible unless Carl was stupid enough to get in that close.

"Oh shit, man, I'm so fuckin' sorry. I tried to save you, I really did."

Craig's head snapped shut, teeth clicking.

Matt walked over and looked at the head. "So what do we do with it . . . I mean, him?"

That was when Carl spotted Diane's corpse and moved closer to investigate.

"Did you see her in here?" Carl asked Matt.

Matt shook his head. "No, I was still dealing with Craig. Shit, is that Diane?"

"Look's like her; what's left of her, anyway. Christ, Craig did a number on her."

Matt pointed to a set of knives lying on the floor.

"Those weren't here when I checked on Tracey and Craig earlier; she must have brought them with her."

Carl nodded, kicking one with his foot. "Yeah, and what would she be doing in here when we were all outside?"

A light went on in Matt's head. "Oh shit, you don't think she was . . ."

"The killer you guys have been chasing?" Carl finished. "Yeah I think so, Christ, wait till Steve finds out. And what he did to the Doc. It was all for nothing."

Then Diane's body began to twitch and her head swiveled around and stared at Carl. She hissed, her face already bloody from Craig's feeding and she rolled over and started to crawl toward him.

"Oh God, she's not dead!" Carl screamed, tossing Craig's head onto Tracey's bed and bringing up his rifle. Craig's head bounced like a bowling ball and ended up gazing at the wall.

"Actually, Carl, yeah she is, shoot her before she gets us!" Matt screamed, loudly as he tried to use the shotgun, but it only clicked on an empty chamber. "I'm out, I need to reload," Matt yelled, dancing away from Diane's grasping hands.

Carl flicked off the safety to the rifle, leveled it at Diane, and fired three shots into her, each one striking her torso. Still she came, only shuddering for a moment as each round struck her body.

"Oh shit, the fucking head, I forgot," Carl spit, realigning the rifle and shooting Diane point blank in the head. The back of her skull, mixed with her hair, flew across the room to paint the wall scarlet. She dropped to the floor, unmoving; this time she wouldn't be getting up. The smell of burnt hair came to Carl, mixing with the redolence of the room.

Carl leaned against the nearest wall, his heart beating too fast to manage. At least he had managed to fire the rifle correctly and hadn't ended up killing him or Matt by accident. Craig would have been proud of him.

Craig's teeth clacking on the bed caught his attention and he walked over and picked it up, then he pulled a garbage bag from a small box on a nearby table and shoved the head into the bag, tying it shut and then turning to stare at Matt.

"I'll figure out what to do with Craig later, for now, let's get back outside. I bet Hal and the others are shitting bricks wondering what's been happening in here."

Matt nodded and the two men left Hector's house, the smell of cordite and blood suffusing the room behind them.

* * *

Down by the main gate of the zoo, the undead swarmed through the opening, Hickman's body nothing but a red stain on the walkway. Almost every piece of him had been consumed by the hungry corpses, only a few tattered bits of clothes and his shoes to mark his existence on the earth. The dead staggered and shambled into the zoo, still carrying gristle covered bones that once belonged to Hickman, not quite knowing where to go. They wandered around aimlessly for a while, the zoo just another place to inhabit until food came along.

Then the sounds of gunshots floated across the deserted zoo, and all dead faces turned as one, ears trying to pinpoint where the gunshots had come from.

At first the location couldn't be found and they just hovered in place, like some kind of bizarre holding pattern. But then a rifle cracked three times, then once more, and as one group, they turned up the main path and started forward.

They had pinpointed the gunshots and were on the move.

Chapter 42

TRACEY'S EYES SNAPPED open and she sat up, her face filled with terror.

Steve was standing near her and the moment she sat up, he was next to her, holding her.

"Dad? Oh God, it's you," she cried. Then she looked around her, concern on her face. "Craig, he was . . ."

"Shhh, it's all right, honey, your safe now," Steve told her, hugging her.

Carl was on her other side, having returned from the house and he moved close so she could see him.

"I'm sorry, Tracey, Craig is dead. He turned into one of them." Carl said sadly.

For a moment she just stared at Carl, as if he must be wrong, but she knew he was telling the truth, she had seen what he had done to Diane. She started crying then, her head buried in her father's chest.

Carl tossed the plastic bag with Craig's head in it off to the side of the picnic area and then quickly filled Steve in on finding Diane's body and the knives on the floor. He told him about Diane reanimating and what he'd done to put her back down. He left out the part about Craig's head, though.

Steve held Tracey, rubbing her back while he looked at Carl, shaking his head.

"Christ, I can't believe it was Diane. That was one person I never would have thought of."

Carl nodded. "No shit. And that's why Tina drew a **D**. It was for Diane, not for Doctor. Poor Doctor Hickman took a beating for nothing," Carl stated.

Steve grunted at that. "Yeah, I guess I owe the jerk a big apology, Christ, how could I have jumped the gun so fast?"

"Doesn't matter, now, all that matters is making sure we're all safe and you've done that to the best of your ability, Steve." Hal said from Steve's side. "It was an honest mistake, if a bit rash, but understandable given the circumstances."

Sherry shifted position on the next picnic table and hugged herself protectively, her eyes wide in shock.

"Oh my Lord, I slept next to her. She could have killed me at anytime."

Hal moved next to her, patting her shoulder. "I doubt that Sherry, if she had, we would have been on to her in a red hot minute. No, Diane needed to kill outside her area, so to speak. Christ, you know I'd get my own byline for a story like this one, it's too bad there isn't a Boston Globe anymore to print it."

"There's always the internet," Carl joked.

Seth watched the adults talking and joking, bored with the whole thing. He was restless and wanted to leave, not that there was anything to do. No TV, no videogames. He missed the porn he used to look up on the internet. Shit, he missed girls. Out of all the people he found himself with, Sherry seemed the only one to have taken a liking to him and she was old enough to be his mom.

Tracey seemed to be with either Craig or Carl. Probably just Carl now that Craig had bitten the big one.

"I'm going for a walk, now that everything's okay," Seth said.

"Don't go far, Seth, we need to talk about everything that's happened and what to do if that fire at the gas yard keeps spreading," Sherry called to him.

Seth waved his hand at her, pretty much blowing her off and headed back out to the main path that led around the zoo.

He had only walked a few hundred feet when he saw some people walking down the path. At first he was elated, finally help had arrived to save them, but as he moved closer to the walkers, he realized they weren't acting normal. He had seen that slow gait before and he quickly realized what it meant.

The dead had made it into the zoo.

Turning around, he high-tailed it back to the picnic area, having actually only been gone for a little over ten minutes.

At first, no one noticed him as he ran full tilt into the picnic area, but when he stopped, leaning over, hands on his knees, taking in great gulps of air, he let out a yell that had all eyes on him.

"They're in the zoo! Holy shit, man, they're walking around in here with us!"

"What are you talking about?" Steve asked. He was back to his old self, whatever had pushed him near the edge was forgotten, his concern for his daughter more important.

"The zombies, man, they're in the fucking zoo! Oh, Jesus Christ, I don't want to die, oh God!" He said, waving his hands like they were on fire. Sherry ran to him and hugged him. Seth was too scared to argue with her, like he normally would, not thinking it was cool, but was just glad to be held by someone.

"It'll be okay, honey, don't you worry, Steve and the others will think of something," she told him, trying to calm him down.

Steve turned to face Hal. "Unless you know how to use that gun, I suggest you give it back, right now," Steve told him.

Hal pulled the pistol from his waistband, staring at it like it was a toy. Then he passed it to Steve. "Here, take it, I'm a lousy shot anyway."

Steve turned to Matt. "Matt, go see how many there are and how far away they are," he told the larger man.

Matt nodded and took off at a run that made the man jiggle like a bowl of jell-o.

Steve started looking around himself. "We need to get out of here or they'll trap us like rats," he said, his eyes falling on the diesel can.

"There, that fuel can. Carl, we have to make a run for the bulldozer, it's our only chance. If we can refuel it with what's in that can, we can drive out of here."

"But where will we go?" Sherry asked.

"I have no fuckin' idea, but at the moment, I think anywhere's gonna be better then here. Now let's get everything that's worth taking together and we'll have to make a run for it. Find anything you can use as a weapon, and I mean anything."

Carl moved in close to Steve, stopping him for a second. "Look, I was watching some of those things yesterday and they're slow and dumb. The trick is not to let them surround you. If we keep moving, there's no reason why we can't get by them," Carl said, trying to sound positive.

Steve turned and looked at him, disdain on his face. "No shit, Carl, but all that doesn't matter when there's hundreds of them on your ass."

Matt returned then, his face covered in sweat. "They're here all right, and there's a boatload of them. I lost count after more than fifty."

"Okay, fine; at least now we know for sure what we're up against. Matt, get inside Hector's and grab anything worth taking, then get back out here. We're gonna make a run for the bulldozer and try to refuel it. It's a long shot, but it's all we've got," Steve told the large man.

Matt nodded and took off back to Hector's. He already knew he needed to retrieve all the shells for the shotgun and those knives on the floor would be useful, too.

Carl ran across the picnic area to the table that had the few items retrieved from the tool shed. Looking at the items made him think of Craig. He looked across the picnic area to the plastic bag lying on the ground. He hadn't told any of the others that Craig's head was in there, nor did any of them ask what was in the bag. Matt seemed not to care and so hadn't said anything.

Carl picked up the chainsaw, holding it in his hand. Picking up the small one-gallon gas can, he started to fill the chainsaw's small fuel tank, quickly topping off the small reservoir. He was lucky; the chainsaw was a new model that didn't need an oil to gas mixture. If it had, it would have been useless to him.

He pulled the cord a few times until the chainsaw roared to life; he revved the small engine once or twice to get the fluids going and then turned it off.

"Hot damn, I feel like Ash fighting the Deadites," he joked.

Seth looked at him, not understanding what he was talking about.

"Forget it, kid, it'll take too long to explain." Carl told him. He then quickly fastened a makeshift strap out of some pieces of the electrical cord used to tie Steve up and slung the chainsaw over his shoulder.

Matt returned a second later with a large sheet hanging over his shoulder like a sack, miscellaneous items inside jangling around as he ran. His pockets were bulging with the shells he found for the shotgun. As he approached the others, he grinned jovially.

"Ho, ho, ho, Merry Christmas," he joked, "shall we get the hell out of here?"

Steve slammed a fresh clip into his pistol and grinned back. "That, my large friend, is a great idea." He picked up the diesel can and moved back to Tracey. She was up and around now, her complexion looking better.

"You ready, honey?" He asked her.

She nodded. "Yeah, Dad, I guess so. I'm not afraid to say I'm scared, though."

Steve pushed back an errant hair from her face. "We all are, honey, believe me. Only a damn fool wouldn't be."

"What about Dr. Hickman? We don't know where he went to," Hal said, holding a metal garbage can lid like the shield of a gladiator.

"Fuck Hickman, he can rot for all I care!" Steve snapped back, then regained control of himself. "Sorry, that was uncalled for. Look, you can go looking for him if you want, but I'm going for my bulldozer."

Hal frowned slightly, shaking his head. "No, I'm fine; I'm sticking with you guys."

"All right then, if everyone's ready, let's move out. Now, those of you without guns stay behind the rest of us and we'll clear a path. But once we're out of ammo its full speed ahead," Steve told them all with a grim look of determination on his face. They would make it through this, they would survive.

They had to.

Everyone nodded, agreeing with him, while Carl walked over to the edge of the picnic area and picked up the plastic bag. He tied the top to his belt, ignoring the looks from the others.

"What? It's my lunch," he told them. Whatever it was, no one argued, having more important things on their minds.

With Steve in the lead, Tracey right behind him, the small group moved out; Carl and Matt directly behind them both. Once they had reached the main walkway that cut through the zoo, the first signs of the dead could be seen.

"Pick your shots carefully; don't waste ammo," Steve told Carl and Matt. "We want to escape, not try to kill them all."

Both men nodded and followed his lead.

As they approached the first few ghouls staggering down the walkway, Carl gestured that he would deal with them. Aiming the rifle at the first one in line, he fired from less then twelve feet away, he fired the rifle in single-shot, following Steve's advice.

The first shot struck the ghoul in the neck, but the second struck it right in the middle of the face, blood and gore exploding out of the back of its skull and peppering the ones behind it like shrapnel from a grenade.

Before the first ghoul had fallen to the ground, Carl had swung and taken out the next one in line. Three more times he shot his rifle and three more times bodies collapsed to the ground.

Carl turned and looked at Steve, a wide smile on his face, proud of himself.

Steve grunted in approval and they continued on.

On Steve's right, a ghoul lunged from the bushes, but Steve held back from shooting it at the last moment and reached out and grabbed it by its filthy shirt. Tossing it to the walkway, he lifted his right construction boot high and stomped down on the ghoul's head, crushing it to mush.

He never slowed, only waved the others to move on now that the coast was clear. But there were dozens more and it would be a hard fight to reach the front gate and the bulldozer.

One of the advantages the survivors had was that the undead horde had immediately split up upon entering the zoo, going off in all different directions. Only about half had followed the sounds of gunshots, following the echoes like a dinner bell. By doing this, the individual pathways that intertwined the zoo were full of walking corpses, but they weren't packed.

They were more than halfway to the front gate when they suffered their first casualty.

After putting down six ghouls in their path, the group had hurried along, stepping over the dead bodies. But one hadn't been completely dead yet, only stunned from the impact of the gunshot it had received to its chest. Sherry had stepped over it just as it had leaned up and sunk its teeth into her calf. She called out in pain and surprise, falling partway to the walkway as her legs became tangled in the ghoul's arms, but she had been last in line, and by the time Hal had turned around to try and help her, the ghoul had already succeeded in crawling up her flailing body and pulling her to the ground; ripping out her throat in an instant. Sherry stared up into Hal's face, her mouth opening and closing as she asked him for help.

Steve had seen this, turned on his heels and had sprinted back to Sherry and Hal, coming up next to Hal so fast he actually startled the man for a moment.

He looked down at Sherry and his face went slack.

"Jesus Christ, I'm sorry about this, Sherry, but this is for your own good," Steve said and aimed the barrel of the pistol at the top of her head and fired, the bullet penetrating the top of her skull and exiting out her chin. The attacking ghoul he kicked in the chin, the head snapping back to crack on the pavement.

"There, that's all we can do for her. At least this way she stays dead," Steve said, flatly.

Hal nodded. "I know, it's just . . ."

"Yeah, man, I know. Come on, we've got to keep moving or they'll surround us."

Hal and Steve caught up to the others, but before they turned a bend in the path, Steve shot a quick glance over his shoulder at Sherry's body. Already other ghouls had reached her and were tearing into her corpse, feeding on her. They hadn't eaten fresh meat in so long they were willing to settle for recently dead, though live meat was always preferred.

The group continued on, passing the duck pond and coming up to the bear caves. In this section of the zoo, the path widened, like a large cul-de-sac that opened to five different paths that led to all corners of the zoo.

Now it was filled with undead bodies, shambling about, looking for a meal.

The second Carl and Matt came up to the top of the cul-de-sac, all dead eyes turned to look at them

"Aww shit, I think they saw us," Carl said, staring at the crowd of dead people now starting toward them. The chainsaw had been rebounding off his back, causing him to wince every time his body bounced while he ran, but he knew he might need it, so he dealt with the pain.

Bringing up his rifle, he sprayed half a clip at the approaching horde, careful to keep his shots at head height. Almost every bullet found its mark, a dozen bodies falling to the flagstones that made up the cul-de-sac.

Steve looked on with a stern face, his jaw set in a tight grimace.

"Dammit, we're gonna have to make a run for it," Steve told Carl. "It's our only chance. Just plow through them and knock them over. Once we're through, they'll be too slow to catch up to us."

"Let me go first, I can knock these lightweights out of the way like candlepins," Matt said, moving closer to Steve and holding the shotgun in front of him like a club. While the weapon was powerful, he had to time his two shots carefully, or else risk having to reload in a bad spot.

"Okay Matt, go for it," Steve told him.

Tracey was behind Steve, Seth next to her. The boy was in rough shape after seeing Sherry killed. Evidently, he had been more attached to her then he'd let on.

Steve gave her a wink, trying to reassure her. "Don't worry, honey, we'll get through this, I promise," he told her.

She smiled back wanly. "And I'm going to keep you to that promise, Dad."

Matt let out a yell and charged into the cul-de-sac, swinging his shotgun like a baseball bat.

"Okay, guys, that's our cue, let's go, and watch your backs," Steve said, the others only looking more nervous with each passing second.

Carl and Steve took the lead; Hal came next, followed by Tracey and Seth. Matt was a few yards in front of them, his arms punching and his meaty legs kicking. He was like a Sumo wrestler on crack, Carl thought, watching the large man barrel through the ghouls like they were made of paper. One ghoul was almost as large as Matt and the man decided it was time to use one of his precious shells in the shotgun. Swinging the gun in his hand like a gunslinger from the Wild West, he sent a barrage into the ghoul's chest that ripped it open and sent the creature staggering backward to fall in the overgrown shrubbery lining the cul-de-sac.

"Watch out for that one, it ain't dead yet!" He called over his shoulder to the others. One at a time, they hastily moved around it, careful to avoid its reaching hands as it tried to crawl out of the bushes.

One ghoul, an old lady of at least seventy-five years, came at Hal, dentures clicking on air and hands curled like claws to slash his face. Hal slammed the garbage can lid into her face, the metallic sound reverberating across the cul-de-sac. The old lady fell backward to land hard on the ground, cracking one of her hips and other bones from her landing.

Carl saw this and called back to Hal. "Hey, she's fallen and she can't get up!"

Then he had to focus on the job at hand when two small children, their throats ripped to shreds, came charging at him. He swung the rifle around and slammed the butt into each small head, the tiny tots falling away from him. Tracey was behind him and she kicked the girl tot in the head, breaking her jaw and actually making the corpse roll away a foot or so.

Carl nodded at her in thanks and she smiled back, then they were both too busy for amenities.

A shriek came from behind Tracey and she turned to see Seth covered by three ghouls. He screamed to her, his hand with its black-painted fingernails reaching out as if she could somehow grasp his hand from four feet away and save him from a terrible death.

The ghouls swarmed over him, pressing their bodies onto his, and then setting to his flesh with a vengeance. His stomach was torn open; intestines dragged out and away, some of the ghouls fighting over them. His Mohawk was ripped from his scalp as one determined ghoul tried to gain access to his brain. Tracey caught a flash of Seth's mutilated face when a ghoul moved to the side to get into a better position and what she saw made her turn away in horror, her stomach becoming one giant spastic organ inside her.

She jumped when she felt a hand grasp her arm, but it was only her father.

"Forget, him, honey, its too late," Steve said, "we need to keep moving. We'll mourn the dead tomorrow, if we're still alive."

She let Steve pull her onward and they crossed the cul-de-sac and down the main path that would bring them to the front gate.

"We lost Seth!" Steve called out to the others while they ran down the path, either shooting guns or knocking bodies away from them to clear a path for the others. "What? Oh shit, not the kid, too," Carl said, shoving his rifle barrel under the chin of a naked man in bedroom slippers and a sagging condom on his penis. He blew the top of the naked ghoul's head clean off, like it was a jack-in-the-box.

"Doesn't matter, right now all that matter's is getting to that 'dozer," Steve called out, ramming his elbow into an already mutilated face, the ghoul falling back to the pavement.

Matt was still moving forward, his arms swinging back and forth like a scythe. Whenever a ghoul came too close, Matt's shotgun would crack into a head or chop at its neck. The others had to step over his conquests as they slowly fought battles of their own.

Hal cried out then, a ghoul taking a bite out of his left arm. Hal punched it in the nose and then slammed the garbage can lid on its head, dislodging the face from his arm. Steve turned to look for him, to see if he was all right, and both of their eyes made contact.

"Go, I'm all right!" Hal yelled to Steve. Steve nodded, not knowing why the man had cried out, but he seemed to be all right.

Minutes later, the front gate came into sight. Matt was like a raging bull, plowing into ghouls head first, lifting them off their feet to send them tumbling away. Some landed hard, limbs breaking and necks cracking, but others simply rolled back to their feet and tried to attack the others following Matt's trail.

Carl would dive in, then, cracking a head with the stock of the rifle or shooting it point blank in the head or face.

He had no idea how many rounds were left in the rifle's magazine and he only had one extra magazine left in his pants pocket. All he could do was shoot, punch, kick and repeat, again and again, as he made his way through the undead crowd.

Tracey screamed just as two ghouls lunged at her. She kicked one in the face, but the other wrapped its arms around her, trying to drag her down. She pushed at its face, trying to keep its jaws away from her body, and her hand slid into its flesh like it was warm pudding. Her stomach heaved when the flesh surrounded her fingers, the feeling indescribable. The tips of her fingers could feel the contours of the ghoul's skull, her index finger sliding into the hole where its nose once was.

Then Steve pulled the creature off her, tossing it into the nearby shrubs, where it took two more down as it went.

Breathing heavily from the exertions of the moment, Steve looked down at Tracey with concern.

"You all right?" He asked her quickly, the words spilling out of his mouth.

"I'm fine. Thanks, Dad, let's go," she told him, taking his hand so he could help her up off the ground; then they quickly moved on. There was no time for any more conversation, the zoo path looking more like the gateway to hell, full of demons wanting nothing more then to rip them apart, and perhaps, consume their souls, as well.

Matt had made it to the front entrance of the zoo, and he charged out into the parking lot, too caught up in his private battle to realize the others were still too far behind him to give him support if he needed it.

Yelling at the top of his lungs, his entire body covered in blood and gore, Matt charged out into the parking lot, waving his shotgun like a mace.

Every dead ghoul in the parking lot turned as one, seeing Matt yelling at them like he was ringing the dinner bell.

"Matt, stop, wait for us!" Steve called to him, but the large man was lost in his own world.

Every ghoul in the parking lot came at him and Matt roared with excitement as the first ones in line were near enough to grab. Picking up a small ghoul by the shirt, he knocked it down and then picked it up again, this time by its feet. He started spinning in a circle, the dead body flying out as it struck ghoul after ghoul. Matt continued spinning round and round until the ghoul in his arms was nothing but a bloody stump, the head and shoulders worn away from countless strikes against other attacking ghouls.

When he realized his meat weapon was broken, he let it go, the torso and legs crashing into two ghouls that were on his left, all three bodies falling to the ground in a heap.

Others merely climbed over the pile, seeking Matt.

Matt kept punching and slashing, now using one of the knives he'd found left in Hector's place when Diane had been killed, but it was evident even to him, he was being overwhelmed. He looked over the heads of his attackers and saw he was halfway across the parking lot, the bulldozer lost in a sea of heads.

He had continued moving while he battled the undead, like he had been floating on the ocean and slowly moving with the current. He was now cut off from the others and further help.

"Matt, come back here, you're too far!" Carl yelled to him, the others still working their way to the bulldozer.

"No, shit!" Matt called back, wondering if Carl had even heard him. Then it happened, just as he knew it would. He felt a sharp pain on his leg, just below his knee. He looked down to see a dead face sinking its teeth into his leg and he kicked out, sending the ghoul falling back to the ground, but another was there to replace it and though he fought valiantly, there were just too many to hold off for very long. He aimed his shotgun at a ghoul that was only inches from his face, so close he could smell its rotting breath, and fired his last loaded round from the shotgun at point blank range. The ghoul's head disappeared in a spray of blood and bone and Matt found himself closing his eyes or risk being blinded by the shrapnel from the destroyed head.

His face was covered in blood, the scarlet drips giving him the look of some kind of demon himself, come to the earth to rid the world of the undead menace, but he wasn't. He was only a man; a man vastly outnumbered.

He felt skeletal arms wrap around his neck and when he tried to remove them, another ghoul dove in and bit into his side, ripping the material, as well as a small hunk of his skin. He roared again, ripping the ghoul from him, but he already knew he was fighting a losing battle. He had lost his head and had left the others behind him, now he was all alone in a sea of the dead.

Like piranhas, the undead kept nipping at him, diving in only to be knocked aside. Matt had more than a dozen wounds on him with more being added to his large frame every second.

He felt a sharp pain on his ankle, right on his Achilles heel and his leg buckled, not being able to withstand his weight. He went to one knee, wincing with the pain, the smell of death and blood filling his nostrils until he thought that was all that existed in the world.

A ghoul lunged at his face, and before he could pull away, powerful teeth clamped down on his nose, ripping cartilage and skin away to leave the exposed red canal.

He shrieked in pain, white light flashing before his eyes and at that moment, the surrounding ghouls took their opening and swarmed over him, teeth tearing and hands clawing. With so much fat on his body, it took longer for him to die then an ordinary sized-man, and his shrieks of pain carried across the parking lot to the others, who had reached the bulldozer and were desperately trying to fight off the undead horde and refuel the machine.

Slowly, Matt's cries faded and were replaced by the sounds of dozens of mouths chewing and ripping his body apart. Some moved away, holding chunks of fat, like whale blubber, chomping on it merrily. Others had gone deeper, pulling his entrails from his body like buried treasure.

If there was one thing that Matt's demise signified, it's that the ghouls would be fed well this day.

Chapter 43

CARL WATCHED MATT fall under the ghouls, consumed alive by the undead, and he let out a shout one last time, calling to Matt. But even as he yelled, he knew it was too late for the man.

He was dead, like so many before him. And Carl knew if he didn't focus on the here and now, he'd be joining him in a few seconds.

Carl, Hal, Steve and Tracey had managed to reach the bulldozer, and were even now trying to clear it of any ghouls that posed a threat.

"Tracey, get up in the cab and be ready to prime the engine as soon as I give you the word," Steve told her, almost barking the order. She did what she was told, obeying without hesitation. Now was the time for action, to hesitate could spell certain death for them all.

"Carl, get up on the 'dozer and protect Tracey," Steve told him, Carl obeying and climbing up, flashing Tracey a smile. She returned it slightly, her fear still showing on her face. He couldn't blame her, he was scared shitless.

Steve swung around after cracking a ghoul in the face and called to Hal.

"Hal, take this can and fuel up my baby, the gas cap is right by your arm!" Steve told him. Hal looked where he was pointing and spotted the gas cap, running the few feet to Steve and grabbing the diesel can from his hand, then returning to the gas cap and popping it open.

Carl balanced on top of the bulldozer near Tracey, his rifle ready. Whenever a ghoul stumbled too close, Carl took it down. So far things were going smooth and he was feeling optimistic about their progress, despite the death of Matt and the others.

While Hal poured the fuel into the bulldozer's fuel tank, more then half the can spilling across the side of the machine in Hal's haste to empty it, Steve hovered near him, protecting his back. Steve muttered a curse when he saw the diesel missing the fuel opening, but he was far too busy to yell at Hal and tell the man to slow down and make sure every drop went into the bulldozer's tank instead of onto the ground.

Steve was like an animal, venting all his pent up rage on the ghouls as they came at them. He punched one in the face so hard his hand sank up to his wrist in gore. For a brief moment the head stayed stuck to his fist, the suction preventing him from freeing himself. The ghoul hung limp by his side, like a purse, while he used his remaining fist and legs to kick out and destroy any ghoul foolish enough to come at him and Hal. When he had a free second, he stepped on one of the legs of the ghoul around his hand, pinning it to the ground, and then yanked back, brain and snot flying in all directions. Flicking his hand to get off most of the scarlet goop, he shot the next two ghouls in the face, both dropping to the ground like wet, leather bags.

A small dog ran up to Steve and he almost shot it, but then realized it was Scruffy, Matt's dog. Picking the dog up, he tossed it onto the bulldozer. If the dog was smart enough to stay on the machine, great, if it didn't, then it could be zombie chow for all he cared. Scruffy ran up the side of the bulldozer and found a spot in the cab just behind Tracey's seat. If she saw the animal, she didn't do anything about it.

"Okay, I'm finished," Hal screamed, throwing the can at an oncoming ghoul. The can merely bounced off its chest and rolled across the ground, forgotten.

"Start 'er up, Tracey!" Steve yelled to her, slamming his elbow into a ghoul that came at him from his side. The elbow shattered its nose and it fell away, only to start climbing to its feet a moment later.

Tracey turned the key on the dashboard, making sure to warm up the glowplugs first. When she saw the light go out on the dash, she turned the engine over, the motor coughing and spitting. Not wanting to burn out the starter or plugs, she stopped.

"That's okay, honey, just give it a sec' and try again." Steve called to her calmly, not wanting her to get nervous and make a mistake, like it was just the two of them on a Sunday morning back when he had brought her to one of his construction sites and taught her how to drive the large machine.

Tracey waited, counting in her head, while Carl shot ghoul after ghoul. She wondered how much ammunition he had left, knowing in her heart he had to be almost out.

Hoping she had waited long enough, she turned the engine over again. This time it slowly gained momentum, and with a roar and a belching of smoke from the exhaust, the bulldozer surged to life.

"Oh yeah, hoo-hah!" Steve yelled. "That's my girl." He turned to Hal. "Come on, Hal, the bus is leaving, its time to get the hell out of here. Get on the 'dozer!"

Hal did as he was told, Steve already climbing up onto the rear of the machine. Hal turned to start climbing and was halfway up just as Tracey started to move the bulldozer toward the parking lot exit. Hal wasn't prepared for the bulldozer to start moving and he slipped from his perch, his legs dangling for one precious instant. Steve saw this and reached out his hand to Hal, Hal grabbing Steve's hand with a tight grip of his own. But in that brief instant, his legs had dangled below, into the bodies surrounding the bulldozer; the surrounding dead flooding in, sinking teeth into cloth and flesh while grabbing his legs with vise-like grips.

With Steve holding him, Hal jerked back down a few inches, like a victim in a Jaws movie. His face was one of concern, not quite understanding what was happening to him. His eyes seemed to penetrate into Steve's head, as if they were saying. *No, this can't be happening, not to me!*

Steve tried to squeeze harder, holding onto Hal's hand, but his palm was covered in blood, making the connection tenuous at best.

"Hold on, Hal, you can do it!" Steve yelled; riding the bucking bulldozer as Tracey drove over bodies that were becoming churned up meat under the massive machine's treads.

"Don't let me go, Steve, for the love of God, don't let me go!" Hal screamed, but he was pulled, inch by inch, deeper into the undead crowd surrounding the bulldozer.

"Don't worry, buddy, I got you!" Steve yelled, just as their hands split apart. "No!" Steve yelled at the top of his lungs, but Hal was already lost from sight, the bulldozer still moving forward.

Carl fired his last shot, now using the rifle as a club to keep any ambitious ghouls from climbing onto the bulldozer to the entrance of the parking lot and the main road beyond.

Steve stared at the spot where Hal had disappeared from, his hand still stretched outward. Though filled with grief at the loss of Hal, Steve pushed the feelings down inside himself. Now there was only survival, there was no time to mourn the dead yet.

Shaking his head to clear it, Steve tried to shift position, wanting to get closer to Tracey. As he did, his foot slipped on the slick metal, his boots covered in gore. When his foot slipped down on the side, teeth flashed in the sun and sank deep into his ankle. He roared from the pain, and kicked the ghoul away from him. He looked down at his wound, blood pooling up to soak into his sock and boot and knew he was fucked.

There would be no sucking the wound clean on the large bite he'd received, even if they had the time to try.

Standing tall, Steve ignored the bite and tried to get to the cab and Tracey. A ghoul lunged at Tracey from the opposite side, her right side exposed, Carl missing it as he focused his attention on his left, using up the last of his ammunition on a crowd of ghouls trying to climb onto the bulldozer. A bloody hand wrapped around Tracey's arm and she screamed, throwing the bulldozer to the right as she tried to shake the appendage off her.

Steve lost his balance, not expecting the machine to buck under him and he slid off the bulldozer, his hands reaching out for something to stop his downward descent.

Tracey managed to remove the rotting fingers off her arm, bending and breaking each one back with a sickening snap until only the pinky remained around her arm. It wasn't enough to hold her arm in its grip and the ghoul's shattered hand slid from view, her arm now free again.

She looked behind her to see where her Dad was and she let out a scream that had Carl looking around him.

"Oh shit, Steve!" Carl called out to him. Steve was fighting for his life once again, punching and kicking every ghoul that came near him, but Carl could see there was no way he could last for long.

"Dad!" Tracey called out to him.

"Keep going, don't stop or they'll get on the 'dozer, don't worry, I'll catch up!" Steve called to her in-between pummeling bodies with his ham-sized fists.

"Carl, what do we do, I can't leave my Dad behind, they'll kill him," Tracey pleaded with him.

Carl saw the angst in her face and he did something he would never believe he was capable of in his life before the undead outbreak, though in the past few days, he had slowly been growing more courageous and confident in himself then at anytime before in his life.

Courage, real unadulterated courage, mixed in with a little heroism filled him as he watched Steve fighting for his life.

Carl dropped the empty rifle to the ground, conking a ghoul on the head. He reached around his body and pulled the chainsaw from his back, priming the small engine and pulling the cord. It started on the second pull, the small engine whining loudly and filling the air with its song of death.

He turned and looked at Tracey. "I'll be back with your Dad, just keep this bad boy moving!" Then he jumped into the fray, swinging the chainsaw like a bad horror movie icon.

Arms and hands were sliced off like they were made of paper and glue and he started working his way toward Steve. Steve heard the sound of the chainsaw and turned to see Carl advancing on him, sweeping the chainsaw back and forth like he was cutting wheat.

"What the fuck are you doing? Go back to the 'dozer and protect my daughter!" He yelled at him.

Carl kept coming. "She's fine, she needs her Dad, so shut up and let me rescue you!" Carl barked at him.

Steve had his pistol out and he shot a ghoul through the mouth, then pistol whipped another across the eyes.

"No, Carl, you don't understand, I've been bit, I'm dead anyway, you need to go back to her!"

Carl had reached Steve and he placed his back against him, both men keeping the dead at bay, but only barely. Steve popped out the clip on the pistol and pulled the last clip from his pocket, sliding it in with an almost practiced ease during a small two second lull from the undead around him, then he began firing into undead faces once again. The bodies had begun to pile up in front of him, slowing the others down, but only barely.

Carl looked over his shoulder, the bulldozer moving away.

"If she doesn't keep moving, they'll get on with her!" Carl yelled to Steve.

"Tracey, keep moving, dammit, we're right behind you!" Steve screamed at the top of his lungs. He saw his daughter's worried face and the hesitant nod she tossed his way, then the engine surged louder as she moved into the long, street-like driveway that led to the main road.

Carl saw her face and for a brief moment, he could see she was crying. But then she was out of sight and moving further away with every second that ticked by.

"Shit, Steve, this isn't working out as I planned it. I was supposed to swoop down here and save your ass and you were supposed to give me your daughter's hand in gratitude!" Carl said, cutting off the head of two ghouls, the blood and gore spraying everywhere. Carl wiped his forehead with his sleeve, trying to keep the blood and sweat out of his eyes.

Steve barked out a laugh at that. "You did, did you? Well then you should be glad you're gonna die here today, because I would have killed you if you touched my daughter!"

Carl turned to see Steve's face and he could see the big man smiling. That made Carl feel good, at least he wasn't serious.

Steve fired the pistol again and again, until one ghoul got under his guard and wrapped its body around his gun hand. The ghoul pulled Steve's arm to the ground with it, and Steve couldn't fire the weapon. His pistol was useless, and with his other hand, he reached out and grabbed the shirt of the closest ghoul, a woman in a beehive hairdo with half her face missing, and tried to use her as a shield while he desperately tried to free his gun.

A ghoul on the ground, crawling on all fours, snuck up under Steve's guard and took a large bite out of his calf, just below his knee. Steve screamed in pain, dropping the ghoul and pistol so he could pull his hand free and reach down to knock away what was attacking him in the vicinity of where the pain had come from. But then the ghoul he had dropped lunged at his thigh and sank its teeth deep into his leg. Lashing out, his hand wrapped around bloody, greasy hair and he pulled the ghoul off him, its teeth still clamped in the flesh of his thigh. Steve's leg shot blood like a geyser, unknown to him, his femoral artery had been torn. Though he continued fighting, he didn't understand why he was growing weaker and groggy. Slowly, he started to collapse to the ground.

"Steve? What's wrong man, get up. I need you!" Carl yelled at him, but it was no use, Steve's eyes were closed, lack of blood already painting his face white under the blood and gore.

Then the ghouls fell on top of Steve and he was lost from sight. Even over the motor of the chainsaw, Carl could hear the ghouls feeding on his friend.

"Shit, shit, shit," Carl screamed, swiping at the creatures of horror as they came for him. The chainsaw was covered in gore, as was Carl. From a glance, he looked as bad as any of the ghouls surrounding him. He backed up a step and kicked something hard with his foot. Glancing down and expecting to see a head or something equally gruesome, he spotted Steve's pistol.

Swinging the chainsaw in a wide arc around him, he cleared the way for him to bend over and pick it up. Shoving it in his waistband, he continued swinging, limbs and heads piling up around him like cordwood. Then the chainsaw started to sputter and he knew he was running out of gas.

"Oh shit, oh no, don't do this to me!" He pleaded to the chainsaw, but still it sputtered and coughed.

Stepping on top of a torso, he looked over the heads of the dead surrounding him. There had to be at least a hundred, the rest having entered the zoo. Then he spotted the two cars that had locked bumpers near the front gate. With no other safe haven in sight, the bulldozer long gone, he started chewing his way towards the cars. The chainsaw continued sputtering, but still remained active and Carl moved through the ghouls around him like he was pushing through a corn field. Whenever one tried to grab him from behind, he would put his arms over his head and let the chainsaw strike what it would. He would feel the splatter of blood on his back and hair and then would pull the chainsaw back around to destroy what was in front of him.

His vision was impaired by all the blood on his face and he had to continually wipe his forehead and eyes, his shirt sleeve so full of meat and blood it was all but useful.

Just as the chainsaw was about to sputter its last breath, Carl reached the cars. When the chainsaw stopped, he used it like a sledgehammer and smashed it over a ghoul that tried to come straight at him. The housing crushed its skull and he let both weapon and corpse drop away from him.

Jumping over the hood to escape grasping hands, he landed on his feet and ran to the passenger side door, praying one of the others who had been trapped in the car previously hadn't locked the door when exiting it out of some bizarre force of habit.

It was unlocked!

He threw open the door and dove inside, slamming the door closed behind him.

Locking all the doors, he sat there, breathing heavily, heart pounding in his chest, ignoring the smell of urine and feces already in the car. Just breathing in and out, his mind still in fight or flight mode, adrenaline still pumping, coursing through his veins, still not sure he was actually safe.

Hands beat on the windows and windshield, but he was pretty sure if the car had held up to the ghouls before, it would hold up to their onslaught now.

Slowly, his breathing slowed and he watched the faces of the dead as they rubbed back and forth on the windows. Macabre and gruesome shades of humanity stared at him and he tried to keep his eyes down.

He felt a stirring by his thigh and he looked down to find in surprise that Craig's head was still secured to his belt, the plastic bag ripped in a few places, but still strong. Pulling the bag from his belt, he reached inside, carefully, and pulled Craig's severed head out and set it on the seat next to him.

The head rolled its right eye and the mouth moved like it was trying to talk or eat something. Carl just sat there and stared at it, the minutes ticking by.

He pulled the pistol from his waistband and after checking how many rounds it had left, he set it carefully on the dash. It had only one bullet left in the chamber, the clip empty. It was almost worthless. There were more then a hundred of those things outside the car and he had one bullet. If he didn't realize how dire his situation was, he might have laughed at that one.

Taking off his shirt, he turned it inside out and did his best to wipe the blood and gore from his face and arms, then tossed the shirt in the back with the other debris.

After an hour passed, Carl was starting to relax, knowing that for the present moment, at least, he was safe. Reaching into his pocket, he pulled out the deck of cards that had belonged to Craig. He looked down at the severed head and waved the cards in front of its pale face.

"How 'bout a game?" he asked the head. Craig's head only rolled its remaining eye and tried to hiss at him. Carl played a game of solitaire, then tried poker with Craig's head. It didn't really work; Craig's head was not the same gambler it had been when it was attached to his body.

Time went by and Carl started to get hungry. He soon realized there was nothing to eat or drink, and though he had saved himself by hiding in the car, he was still just as dead, only now it would be slower and more painful. He'd heard what it was like to starve to death from reading books and what he'd seen on television and he knew he wouldn't be able to take it.

He looked at the door locks, thinking he could just open one of the doors and let the ghouls inside. But he definitely knew he didn't want that. How painful was it to be ripped apart and eaten alive? It can't be better then starving to death.

The banging on the car seemed to disappear as he focused his mind inward. Carl was all alone in perpetual quiet as he contemplated his own death. He had never really done that before. Through everything that had happened to him in the past few weeks, he had never actually thought he would die, despite the fact that others were dropping like flies around him. No way, man, not him. He was *Carl the Invincible* and death couldn't touch him.

Then his eyes locked on the pistol on the dashboard. Slowly he picked it up, weighing the option of using it. He actually raised it to his temple and closed his eyes.

Just squeeze the trigger, he thought, and *boom*, nothing but darkness.

His finger tensed on the trigger, and at the last second he stopped, taking it away and setting it back on the dashboard.

"No, not yet, man, I'm not ready yet," he said to Craig's head. "Come on, buddy, one more game of cards and then we'll see what happens. We'll try Gin Rummy this time. I've got the time to teach you."

With Craig's head rolling its eye at Carl, he started to deal the first hand. And maybe after that hand he'd deal another and then another after that.

And then? Well, who knows?

Epilogue

TRACEY HAD BEEN walking for hours on the lonely road deep in the Blue Hills, the bulldozer far behind her, out of fuel once again. On the horizon, the smoke from the gas yards filled the sky, but luckily it seemed the flames were going in the opposite direction, sparing the mountains its brute force.

By her feet was Scruffy. She was amazed that no matter how far they walked, the little poodle seemed to have so much energy that he never stopped running. He would run ahead of her and then turn and bark for her to hurry up, she ignored the dog, moving at her own pace. She had been surprised to find the little poodle in the back of the bulldozer's cab, but was pleased, as well. At least now she had someone to talk to.

Her cheeks were still wet from the last time she'd cried, still thinking about her father and Carl and the rest.

Her father had to be dead, there was no way he could have survived after being surrounded like he was, and Carl, too, was probably either dead or one of them by now. She knew Steve had told her to keep going so she would live, even though he knew he was sending away his only chance of salvation.

When she had reached the main road, she had hesitated for a minute, almost turning back to see if her Dad was still there, but she quickly realized the folly of those actions and continued onward up the road, deeper into the Blue Hills.

The least she could do was honor his last order and keep moving. Besides, it seemed in the new world she found herself in; death had become as common as the sun coming up every morning.

It was well past dusk when she heard the sound of a motor approaching her from further down the road. There was a sharp bend in the road so she wouldn't be able to see who it was until they were right on top of her. Moving to the side, near the shoulder, she held a large wrench by her side, just in case the oncoming vehicle was hostile. She realized she'd be helpless if they had firearms, but one problem at a time.

She let out a small sigh of relief when she saw it was a military jeep. Two soldiers rode in the two front seats and another soldier rode in the back with a large machine-gun mounted on a tripod.

She waited patiently, her knuckles turning white on the wrench as the jeep pulled up near her. The three soldiers looked her up and down and the driver pushed his helmet off his eyes so he could see her better.

"Hey there, Miss, you shouldn't be out here all alone. There's a large group of infected around here and if they find you, you're screwed," the soldier said, his eyes scanning the road behind her.

"Yeah, I've seen them, they're about four or five miles behind me, give or take," Tracey said, her eyes scanning the faces of the men. She was a woman all alone on a deserted road and no one around to aid her. If they got any funny ideas about her, they would learn quickly that they would pay dearly for a roll in the hay with her.

But the soldiers were decent and honorable and none looked at her with anything but respect.

"Look, Miss, we have an army camp set up on the edge of Franklin, we're slowly gathering survivors and staging there for an upcoming assault on Boston. There's even a rumor that the President is going to authorize a full tactical strike on all major cities that have been overrun. Boston's gonna be the first one in line. Why don't you let us take you back there? There's a doctor if you're hurt and we've got food and running water for a shower."

"If you call a barrel with holes in it and a round curtain a shower, then yeah, we've got a shower," the soldier by the machine-gun joked.

The soldier talking to Tracey flashed his buddy a look of annoyance and then turned back to Tracey.

Tracey looked at them one last time and decided she really had nothing to lose by going with them.

"Can I bring my dog?" She asked.

The soldier shrugged, not really caring. "Sure, it's cool; there are a few dogs in the camp already and even a few cats. Bring him along."

Tracey climbed into the back with the gunner and Scruffy jumped up onto her lap.

"So, are you all alone out here, are there any other survivors with you? Maybe they're down the road and they need us to go pick them up?" The soldier on the machine gun asked.

The driver turned the jeep around and headed back up the road, the wind drying the sweat on Tracey's forehead.

Tracey looked up at the solder's face, her own growing hard, her jaw setting tight in a grimace.

She'd never looked more like her father then at that moment in time, at that precise instance, riding in a jeep in the middle of a deserted highway.

"No, soldier," she said, shaking her head. "There's no one else, I'm the only one left."

Grunting, the soldier nodded, the three men riding in silence, which was fine with Tracey.

The jeep continued down the lonely road, its taillights fading into the night until they were just two red dots, like demon's eyes glaring out at the world through a rift in space.

Then they winked out and were gone; swallowed up in the darkness as if they had never existed in the first place.